Jilly the Hitter

Corry Novosel

A Yinzer love letter

The 212 Press

ISBN (Paperback): 979-8-9883376-0-7
ISBN (eBook): 979-8-9883376-1-4

Interior Design by Aaxel Author Services
Cover Design by Aaxel Author Services and Lily Shen
Cover Illustrations by Lily Shen

Printed in the United States of America

Dedicated to Fred and Jonas, the Great Roberto and all my other 'Burgh heroes from Sophie to Squiggy to Batman and King Cool. You have made me proud to be a Pittsburgher all my life.

Prologue

Archangel Uriel had requested a meeting with Jesus. In fact, he had made the trip back upstairs for this specific reason. It was time to fulfill his destiny. He was wearing his very best robe, the white one with the black embroidery around the edges, neckline, and cuffs. The woman who had made it for him refused any kind of payment, saying it was an honor to make something for an archangel. Uri held her in the highest regard but couldn't actually remember her name, if pressed. He sat in Jesus' waiting room, back straight, eyes front. Today this was all business, and he was ready.

There were several others in the waiting room, and Uri absently took stock of them. A small man with a Fu Manchu moustache wearing what appeared to be a robe made from burlap and horseshit. Nice. Uri assumed his goat was tethered somewhere outside. Probably from Pittsburgh he assumed. There was a woman in a wool business suit, maybe circa 1950. Next to her was a man who had some kind of Gandhi thing going—brown skin, toga, skinny, bald, totally pious looking. Wait, was it Gandhi? He looked closer. Yep, Gandhi. Maybe. No, totally him. Interesting. The man met Uri's eyes and Uri looked away, but not quickly enough.

"Uriel?" Gandhi said.

Uri looked at the man and smiled thinly. "Yes, have we met?"

"Well, no, sir," Gandhi said. "I am Mohandas, but most would know me as just 'Gandhi.'"

Uri stared at the man and affected deep thought. "No," he said, drawing out the vowel, "the name doesn't ring a bell. Sorry, I just can never keep up with all the amazing folks up here. Gandhi, you say. Roman?" Uri gestured to Gandhi's white linen wrap.

"Oh heavens, no, sir," Gandhi said, chuckling. "But it does not matter. What a pleasure to meet such a historically important figure, the great Uriel the Archangel. One meets the most interesting people in the afterlife."

"Well," Uri said, preening a little, unable to help himself, "so kind of you to say. I try."

"We all try," Gandhi said. "You succeed."

"Thank you," Uri replied. Gandhi reached into his robes and removed a Sharpie and grabbed the pad of "Office of Jesus Christ" stationary that was sitting on the waiting room table. Jesus knew people regularly and shamelessly stole these notepads as souvenirs. But that was okay. Jesus actually kept decks of playing cards with his seal on them—an intertwined J and C in very ornate scrollwork—in his office for special guests.

"If you don't mind," Gandhi said, "can I get an autograph? It's not for me, you understand, but for my nephew." He smiled sheepishly.

"Your nephew?" Uri asked, raising an eyebrow.

"Oh yes, definitely," Gandhi replied. "Hand to God." He raised his right hand palm forward as though taking an oath.

"Well, okay," Uri said, taking the pen and pad and scratching out a message:

Smite 'em!
Best Wishes,
Uriel
HOF A.D. 384

"I better not see that on eBay!" Uriel said, pointing a finger like a gun at Gandhi.

"Certainly not!" said the Mahatma. "I will treasure it—I mean, *he* will treasure it, always. Thank you, sir."

Uri sighed. Fans.

One of the double doors of Jesus' office opened, and a severe-looking woman came out and said to Uri, "He will see you now."

"Must run," Uri said to Gandhi. "Pleasure meeting you, Randy. Bye now." Then he headed in to see the Son of Man.

As it was Casual Friday, Jesus was wearing a Notre Dame football jersey, and as Uri approached his desk, he realized he was probably overdressed in his best robe. Uncool. He made a note to give Oliver a good tongue lashing for not reminding him they'd adopted Casual Fridays up here about five years ago. Jesus' idea. Of course it was.

"Hey, buddy!" Jesus said, getting up from his desk chair and coming around to give Uri a big bro hug, patting him on the shoulder. "How ya been, pal? Everything good?"

This was classic Jesus. Uri, though a hardened cynic, had to admit that deep down he was flattered. Jesus just made you feel like you were the most important person in the world.

"I'm good, I'm good," Uri said. "And you?"

"Good," Jesus replied. "You know, busy. Of course."

"Of course," Uri echoed.

"Lot of suffering going on down there, ya know?" Jesus said, shaking his head, his facial expression suddenly pained. Then he brightened. "Hey, job security, right? Am I right?!" He burst out in genuine laughter and Uri couldn't help but join in. "Sit down, sit down, buddy," Jesus continued. "You want a soft drink?"

"No thank you, Lord. I'm good."

"Something stronger?" Jesus made a tipping motion with his thumb to his lips and pinky finger raised while raising his eyebrows Groucho Marx style.

"No thank you, but kind of you to offer, Lord," Uri said.

Once seated, Jesus leaned back in his chair and laced his hands behind his head. Uri had noticed that the name on the back of his jersey was "#1 Son." Absently, he wondered who had given it to him. Probably Archangel Michael. What a suck-up.

"So, how's it going down there in Pittsburgh?" Jesus asked. "How's that bartender?"

Uri had to pause a second to process what Jesus had just said. "The bartender," he repeated dumbly. He realized he sounded like a tool, but he was desperately trying to regain his footing. This was not the way he had planned this.

"Yes, the bartender. He's the key to this whole thing. You know that, right?"

"Yes. Of course. Yes," Uri said automatically, now scrambling.

Although Uri did not know this, the reality of the situation was that Jesus hadn't exactly been closely watching the reports Uri had been sending up. Okay, he really hadn't read them at all. But his father had said watch the bartender. And let's face it, Dad was never wrong. So, bartender it was. Jesus had no idea who the bartender was, nor frankly exactly what a bartender was, as he wasn't a big drinker. He assumed a bartender was some kind of wine merchant. He remembered wine merchants from Galilee, but that was a *very* long time ago.

"The thing is, Lord," Uri began, trying to get this back on track. "We have been assembling information. Our team has infiltrated the Dark Forces, and we feel certain the Antichrist is walking the planet right now."

Jesus looked at Uri, eyes widening. "No shit?" Jesus said, then covered his mouth and grimaced, looking around as if a nun was about to come over and slap his hand with a ruler. "Sorry," Jesus said, then continued, "The real Antichrist. Like, the Guy?"

"Yes, Lord," Uriel said. "The Guy."

"Wow." Jesus swiveled his chair to his right and stared out at the clouds. "Well, we always knew it was going to happen. The Book says so. Was always just a question of when."

Uri's mind still swirled. Jesus' acceptance and lack of skepticism had been too easy, and he awaited the next thing Jesus might say as a man in the middle of a minefield, not sure where to place his foot next.

"Of course," Jesus began, "we'd want to be absolutely certain." He swiveled and faced Uri again, his gaze suddenly more intense. He leaned forward, his elbows on his desk, hands interlocked under his chin. "We'd *need* to be absolutely certain."

Uri looked at Jesus, not sure what to say, so he didn't say

anything at all.

Jesus raised his eyebrows. "Are we certain, Uri?"

Chapter One

Leonard had had enough. Shit, truth be told he'd had enough about six beers ago. But he didn't really care. Leonard didn't care about much these days. The order on Leonard's caring went: 1) Steelers, 2) Beer, and 3) Steelers. From February to August, you could slot the Pittsburgh Penguins and Pittsburgh Pirates in there, but he hadn't cared for the Pirates that much since the days of Clemente and Pops Stargell, and hockey was for sissies. When your idea of fighting was grabbing another man's shirt and dancing around on ice skates... Well, no offense to Mario Lemieux, but he'd take Johnny Blood McNally with no facemask any fuckin' day.

Leonard got up off his barstool, lurched sideways (not too much), corrected (way too much), crashed into the guy on the next barstool, called the guy a douchebag, looked at the guy, and realized that was a mistake. All of this happened in about eight seconds.

Now, Leonard was not completely stupid. He'd briefly boxed Golden Gloves back in the day, been married to and dated, slept with and generally commiserated with women mean as snakes and twice as ugly, and he had learned one thing about fights, which were as frequent as jagoffs going slow in the passing lane: when your back was to the wall, you double down. Go all Crazy Eyes and twice the volume. Sound, Fury, grab your nuts and wail. Worked most of the time. Hell, if it didn't, it usually wasted enough time so that the bouncer would come around and stop the other guy from kicking your ass. Leonard, consulting his options and influenced in no small part by nine Miller Lite draft beers, decided this was the way to go tonight, Option A.

Leonard turned and said to the bar, "This fuckstick doesn't know who he's messing with."

Now, the fact of the matter was, if the Fuckstick didn't know who he was messing with, the bar patrons sure did. Regulars at J's Bar were as familiar with Leonard as they were with mosquitoes, acid indigestion, New England Patriots fans, and that rash you get in places that rub when it's hot outside. In short, the patrons of J's, Southside, Pittsburgh, Penn-Syl-Vain-I-Ay knew annoying, and Leonard was annoying as hell. Leonard had, in fact, annoyed most everyone in the bar at one time or another, and from their point of view, watching Leonard get his ass kicked would be a nice distraction from watching an autopsy special on the Last Hours of Liberace on the bar TV.

The Fuckstick Leonard had run into calmly put his beer down, got off his stool, and punched Leonard in the solar plexus. Leonard had just been about to suggest the guy's mother was of low moral character (not in those exact words) but only got out what sounded like "Your muuuuu" before the wind was removed from his lungs, and he doubled over and fell down.

Trying to breathe in deeply while you're face down on the floor of an old barroom does not rank up there with your first feel or the Superbowl, Leonard thought. He felt his five-foot-four, 140-pound body lifted by the back of his denim jacket (Styx, Grand Illusion Tour, '77) as easily as a suitcase and carried out the front door. There's a point, and this had happened to Leonard before, when you realize you are about to get your ass whooped, and as long as you are pretty oiled, you always go down swinging, at least verbally.

"Listen, Princess," Leonard croaked as he was unceremoniously dropped face down on the pavement, "I don't know if this is how your regular boyfriend takes care of you out in the street, but I like a little romance first, maybe buy me a drink..." Then he stopped. It was at this point he realized the guy who had dumped him in the street was not the Fuckstick. This guy was bigger. And quiet. Quiet like a ton of bricks about ready to fall on your goddamn stupid, shouldn't-have-had-that-ninth-beer, fucking ankle-monitoring-bracelet head.

"Hey, shit. Jilly. How are ya, man?" Leonard asked casually as though he wasn't lying in the street half in a puddle of rainwater. There was no response from the ton of bricks. Leonard opted to continue to fill the silence. "You see that guy go after me? Jagoff. I was gonna kick his ass, but, you know, I didn't want to do that in your place. You know, create a disturbance. Fucking Flyers fans. He said something about Sidney Crosby and I—" It occurred to Leonard he was babbling, and Jilly, the proprietor of J's, had turned and was headed back inside. "All right, Chief, I'll see you around. You be cool," Leonard continued before picking himself up and heading home. Fuckin' Flyers fans. Shit.

—

J's Bar was a remnant of the days when the Southside of Pittsburgh was almost exclusively the home of steelmill workers at the enormous furnaces that Jones & Laughlin had built hard by the Monongahela River. The standard bar setup from places originally built from around 1930 to 1950 was as follows: walk in the front door, to your left was a wall running the length of the building. To your right was the main bar, probably thirty feet or so with about fifteen stools. Back bar was home to various hard liquor bottles and the beer taps, neon beer signs, some framed photos of various local celebs who may have been in the place over the years and a front corner TV mounted near the ceiling. Past the bar were some tables and four booths. Past that, the kitchen and bathrooms.

After Jilly had removed Leonard from the establishment he had named after his very own first initial, he headed back behind the long bar. It had been said of Jilly, and he had heard it although never acknowledged it, that he had the face of one of those cigar store Indian statues from the old days. Carved from a solid log. With a hatchet. An old friend had suggested he looked "like Shrek after being smacked in the face with a cast iron skillet."

Well, that was just mean-spirited, wasn't it? At six foot three and 240(ish) pounds depending on the time of year, Jilly wasn't really fat and he wasn't really fit. He was just...solid. Solid in a way that made bouncers take note, big-boned women who never liked the George Clooney-type Nancy boys take a breath, and drunk jagoffs in J's on a Saturday night—whose balls were bigger than their brains—think twice. He knew it, and it made him calm.

"You smack Leonard a good one?" said the olive-skinned man at the end of the bar. "Jack him up? C'mon, man, I have a bet to settle. A single punch, one shot. That's all I need."

Jilly looked at him flatly, then turned his attention to placing some glasses in the dishwasher behind the bar.

The man smiled and continued. "Yeah. Didn't think so. You are a man of extremes, Julian. All violence or no violence. A riddle wrapped in an enigma, rolled into a burrito, or however the fuck that saying goes. With me, it's much simpler. Black, white, dead, alive, no grey matters, no confusion."

"Angelo," Jilly said, his attention still focused on his glassware, "if there is one thing we can agree on, it's that grey matter is definitely the difference between us."

Angelo pretended to itch his right eye with his right middle finger. Jilly's back was to him, since even Angelo "Angie Twice" Fanzi Jr. wouldn't fly the bird at Jilly to his face. But Jilly saw it in the bar mirror, and Angelo saw him see it, then quickly scratched his eye again with his index finger. Even wise guys are careful poking bears. Jilly shook his head slightly and smiled to himself.

Angelo said, "You sure you don't want some work, Jilly? The guys ask about you all the time. We got work."

"I'm a simple saloon keeper, Angelo," Jilly said, "just like you are in the import export business. I got all the work I need right here. Another Crown?"

Chapter Two

Illegal business is illegal business and has been around in one form or another ever since mankind first traded a saber-toothed tiger pelt for a basket of coconuts. Back in 1991 when a then twenty-year-old Jilly was still full of youth and vigor, the illegal business in Pittsburgh had been video poker, the union game, and the cash cow: bookmaking. Prostitution had gone the way of the horse and buggy with the advent of serious drugs. The narcotics business had become so volatile that anyone who had something to live for didn't bother with it anymore.

When you run an illegal business, one that requires ironclad management, you don't suffer fools or idiots, and when there is competition, you get rid of it. Andrew Carnegie did the very same thing, no? The American Dream was about making the most of your circumstances, and Marino Fanzi—"Mia" to his familia, but "Don Fanzi" to many in Pittsburgh—was no exception.

"O'Connor, the bookie, is a problem for us, Angie," the Don said to his brother Angelo during their daily morning business discussion. "We let this go and it could become a larger problem." As always, the Don spoke quietly, but his eyes communicated his intense focus.

"The guy is an idiot, se pazzo!" Angie said. "I've talked to him, he doesn't listen. Deaf maybe."

"Talk to him one more time," the Don said. "If he still won't listen, maybe more direct action is needed…"

His brother instantly knew what that meant. "Jilly?" Ang offered.

"Jilly, yes," Don Fanzi said. "We need to be careful with this one."

The bookie and Fanzi problem Michael O'Connor wasn't all that different in his upbringing from Jilly's own; his parents had been more memory than Mom and Pop, nobody loved him, he hit the streets running. He had been raised with an 87 percent probability he'd become a card-carrying Loser, and he had met expectations fabulously. O'Connor was known to his associates (he had no true friends) as, in no particular order, O, Irish, Paddy, Red, Big Red, and the one he enjoyed the most, Mick.

In the absence of any defining personality trait, intelligence, or defining characteristic, Michael O'Connor had decided to embrace his Irishness with a religious fervor. He wore tartan cabby hats. Although born and raised in Carnegie, PA, he adopted the occasional lilting Irish accent, greeting people with "Top 'o the mornin' to ya." He pretended to care about the Catholic religion, going so far as to regularly be seen kneeling in the pews at St. Mary's, deep in apparent prayer for his lost sainted mother, although the careful observer might note he never stayed more than a minute or two and never actually paid for the memorial candles he carefully lit. In short, he wore his Irishness like a sweater. And all the time.

What Mick was, was big. His size intimidated most, and the rest were intimidated by his bravado. Somewhere around the seventh grade, he had learned if you're big, and you push hard, it's very likely nobody will push back. When they don't push back, you win. It is in this fashion that dullards become big kings of small kingdoms. The method had served him well as he grew into adulthood. Theft turned into bigger theft, bullying turned into extortion, the occasional loan turned into putting money on the street.

Eventually, as the river runs to the sea, he ended up bookmaking. In itself, that would have been fine. In point of fact, Paddy Mick Red O'Connor had a talent for the business. Regularly telling customers he was related to the Steeler-owning and Northsidedwelling Rooney family (a lie), he had developed a solid customer base of sports bettors. But there was no Irish mafia in the 'Burgh by the 1990s. If you wanted to book in the 'Dahntahn, 'Norside or 'Sahsside, you had to go through the Fanzi organization. And so had Mr. O'Connor. Until lately. Organized crime was not so organized anymore, and Red felt, as an Irishman, he shouldn't have to pay fealty to the Italians. He had mentioned this. To many people. Repeatedly. One can only ignore this kind of blasphemy for so long. He had also stopped making his regular payments on his book. This was simply not done.

And thus were the circumstances under which Angie Sr.—in suit and tie, as always—had met with Paddy at the Black Irish. By 1991, Allegheny City had long ago been annexed by the city of Pittsburgh across the river and become commonly known as the Northside to Jilly's Southside. The downtown Pittsburgh area was a triangle, bounded on two sides by the Allegheny and Monongahela rivers, which met at an angle to form the Ohio. Across the Allegheny to the north was the Northside. Across the Mon to the south was the Southside. East Ohio street on the Northside, once home to stately German homes and businesses had, by the late 1970s, settled into payday loan check-cashing emporiums and wig shops and was now an often uneasy mix of Irish-American and African-American cultures. As Mick O'Connor sat in the Black Irish pub, if he understood the irony of the bar's name, you wouldn't have known it.

Angelo Fanzi Sr. sat in front of a club soda. Today was business. "This is a nice place. I remember seeing George Benson here. He was a kid when it was called Teddy Brick's."

"Was Benson Irish?" O'Connor asked. Angie looked at him for a long moment, at first thinking the big Irishman was putting him on, then realizing he was serious.

"Maybe," Angelo said. "I think somewhere in the family there were Irish involved."

"Thought so," said O'Connor.

"Mick," Angie said, adopting a grave look, "we haven't been getting your payments. I'm sure you've been busy and this is just an oversight. The Don is concerned that—"

"Fuck the Don," O'Connor interrupted, stopping the conversation as with a sledgehammer. "There is no Italian mafia in Pittsburgh. You guys are living a Francis Ford Cappelini movie and I'm tired of it. Nobody fears you anymore. Bunch of fat guys eating pasta, rolling bocci balls, no edge, no toughness." The bookie finished this declaration and sat back smugly, his head slightly tilted, chin thrust out.

"Coppola," Angie corrected after a pause, his eyes fixed on his club soda.

"Don't give me any of that Italian profanity, Angie," O'Connor said. "Coppola to you too. Twice. And on your family." Then O'Connor brushed his hand under his chin, palm facing in and sat back, smiling. "That's right, I said it. You think I don't understand Italian?"

Angelo just looked at him flatly. It took a few seconds to process what he had just heard, a few more to make sure he had heard it correctly. Then he looked down at his trousers, picked some imaginary lint off his knee. He smiled mildly into the distance and said, "You need to make your payments, Michael." Any warmth had disappeared from his voice. "I'd like to tell the Don we have come to an understanding."

O'Connor smiled and leaned toward the older man. "You tell Donnie, Angelo, he ain't putting any food on my table, and if he thinks he can make me swim with the carp in the Mon, he's welcome to come look this Irishman up. You tell him that. Coppola to him. You got that, paesano?" His hand moved slightly and rested on his waist where Ang assumed he had a pistol tucked.

Angelo sighed and nodded slowly. "Okay, Mick. I'll tell him." He then got up and left with a nod to the bartender.

Chapter Three

The next day, Angelo Fanzi Sr. headed over to the Southside area of Pittsburgh and walked the four blocks off Carson Street to a small row house, repeatedly stopping to say hello to people he knew. His destination—2112 Judy—was an aluminum-sided row house like many and was unremarkable. Clean, orderly, but nothing to write home about.

Angie smiled at the flimsy lawn chair in front of 2112 protecting the always-valuable parking spot. You protected two things on the Southside: your sister's virginity and your parking space. Ang smiled because he suspected that although the lawn chair was generally sacrosanct, the occasional blasphemy was not unheard of. Fights, assaults, and cops being called were not uncommon when parking spot etiquette was violated, but he was fairly certain nobody was crazy enough to move the sixteen-ounce weight of the aluminum Hills Discount Store lawn chair resting regally in front of 2112. He sure as hell would have thought twice. He headed up the two steps and knocked on the screen door.

"How you been, Jilly?" Angelo asked the young man carrying the red paperback book, just up off the couch where he had been reading.

"Fine, Mr. Fanzi, fine."

"What's the book? You reading about beautiful young maidens that want their Prince Charming to come and save them?"

"Well, sure, something like that," replied Jilly, smiling.

"What's *Catcher in The Rye,* Jils? Sports book? Baseball?"

As he looked down at the cover of his book in his hand and understood Angelo Fanzi was referring to the J.D. Salinger novel, Jilly said, "Baseball. Yes, baseball. Yes, Mr. Fanzi. That's it." He moved aside to let the older man into his home. "What can I do for you, sir? Anne really appreciated the groceries you had sent over and the sewer being fixed. Please tell the Don we appreciate everything; we know he's busy."

"My brother is not too busy for family, Jilly. And you and your sister are family to us. You know that. Now, to business. Let's go out back."

They headed through the narrow row house and out to the back porch. Jilly's faced eight backsides of other row houses—completely public but completely private. Everyone was paying attention, but nobody was paying attention.

Once settled, the dignified, middle-aged man became serious, leaning forward, his palms face down on his thighs. "This thing on the Northside, this guy O'Connor. He doesn't listen. He's collecting but not paying, and he's proud of it, shows off. This is not the way things are done. There has to be some order. The Don, he's a kind man, a generous man. He sees the good in everyone. You know this. But you and I, we...we are different. We were born to maintain order. Everyone has their role in a family, no?"

As always, Jilly listened, listened very closely, nodding, but said nothing.

"The Don likes you because you are loyal, Julian. Not crazy, not ambitious, just loyal. One can live a very good life being loyal. I've been happy to see you grow into a fine young man. He thinks of you as he would a son. And so do I." Angelo Fanzi got up to leave, straightening his suit jacket with dignity. He was as close to an uncle as Jilly would ever know.

"This thing, this O'Connor, it's a problem that troubles the Padrino. Can you take care of this thing?"

"Of course, Mr. Fanzi. Please don't think about it again. Please tell the Don I'll handle this myself and not to worry about it," said a young Jilly, not yet known as "the Hitter."

A few weeks later, Jilly, in his own cabbie hat (for he was no dummy), sat at the Black Irish bar and minded his own business. This was his fourth time in the place over the past two weeks, but always at differing times, with different bartenders. He preferred to appear as just another millworker drinking his beer and reading about the Pirates. He'd watched O'Connor each time he was there, studying his habits and movements. His third time in, he had noticed O'Connor usually made the bar his last stop before heading home. So another two weeks later, he was sitting at the bar at 1 a.m. when O'Connor got up off his stool and left the bar. Jilly waited about thirty seconds before following him. At that hour, the streets were empty, and Jilly quickly spotted his man walking slowly down East Ohio Street.

"Paddy, my boy, been too long!" Jilly said, loud enough to be heard but not shouting.

O'Connor turned around to look and saw a man with his arms outstretched, swaying, apparently drunk. "Son, you should show a little respect," O'Connor said.

"Respect! For certain, Laddy! For certain!" Jilly said, approaching and swaying more. As he reached O'Connor, he brought his pistol out from his jacket and shot him in the face. The shot echoed, but there was no one around to hear it. O'Connor fell to the ground without a sound, but his body jerked and twitched where it lay on the sidewalk. Jilly leaned over and shot him again in the head, and O'Connor stopped moving. Jilly waited a few seconds to see if there would be any more movement, then walked away briskly but without running.

On the way home, he dropped the gun in the Monongahela River, and by the time he undressed and went to bed, he was thinking about Holden Caulfield, Michael O'Connor a distant memory. The acts of the evening had been conducted with cold purpose. Jilly gave them no more thought than he would have changing the oil in his car. He'd had a plan, he'd executed it, and he had done good work for his employers, whom he thought of as family.

Chapter Four

So how did Jilly become a hitman? Contract killer, hired gun, or in underworld vernacular: "hitter." When did he decide he was capable, for a fee, of taking from a person their most important possession without remorse? In this particular instance, similar to the birth of a pearl and starting with a single grain of sand lodged in an oyster, it took a while.

Julian and his sister Anne had about as much chance of succeeding as two of those little sea turtles who hatch and struggle out of the nest with fifty-seven of their siblings and start to crawl to the sea because they don't know anything else. Twenty get eaten by seagulls before they've gone fifty feet. Like D-Day, the remaining thirty-seven just keep trying to move forward while watching their brethren get blown up all around them. Jilly and his sister watched the world around them happen as bystanders, as innocent as children can be and as far removed from having any impact on it as a leaf has on determining where it will hit the ground. At a certain point, you blow with the prevailing wind.

Jilly killed his stepfather when he was fourteen. Jilly's mother had eventually re-married an often-unemployed plumber and general loser to try and improve her children's life after explaining to them the father they had never known had died in a mill accident when both were very young. Then Jilly's mother had died in a car accident.

Official Pittsburgh City police reports from 1984 indicate the death of Jilly's stepfather was an accident. The details are not important, but somewhere along his path to fourteen years old, Jilly had decided there are things that you stand and things you do not stand. His heroes—and at fourteen, he did not understand they were his heroes—were characters he had read about in books.

Late at night, sometimes in the dark and often, although he didn't understand it at the time, to stop thinking about things that bothered him, he had formulated a Code. It made him feel better. It did not make sense. As an intelligent child, he knew that on some level it wasn't real, but he didn't care. It let him sleep. Made things orderly. Would Tom Joad allow this to happen without addressing it? How could he? Could you sleep, knowing you had let it happen? Jilly didn't think so. In the absence of any kind of parental involvement, he had made fictional parents from a variety of characters.

When his Code intersected with his stepfather, there needed to be a decision. His world might collapse if he stopped believing in his construct. He couldn't allow that to happen. The survival skills of a fourteen-year-old. The decision to act, once the stakes were clear to him, was not something he probably ever even thought about. It involved his sister. He cared about Anne. Anne did not necessarily care about him in the way that older sisters seem not to care about younger brothers, but none of that mattered to young Julian. He was not built to think about nuances or split hairs; he acted. It did not bother him to act. When it was done, he arranged things to relieve him of culpability, told his sister he was going to bed, and then he did.

This handling of his circumstances via murder, circumstances he did not feel were fair to him or his sister and certainly not their fault, was the first step in Jilly's journey to what became, for a time, his profession. Later, as his relationship with his grade school friend Angelo Fanzi Jr. and Angelo's extended family had deepened, he had shown a willingness and an aptitude to handle assignments for his adopted family. He wanted to demonstrate his ever-growing gratitude for that family, ensuring he and his sister were taken care of.

Fourteen years later, in 2005, Jilly was a seasoned professional and had traveled to San Antonio, Texas to hit a man the Mexican Cartel felt was out of control. Although Jilly was an unofficial employee of the Fanzi family, he had an understanding with the Don that he could do freelance work where there was no conflict of interest. In fact, most of his freelance work came through Fanzi contacts. Jilly was a competent professional, had no moral issues with killing criminals, and had established himself as a reliable hitter. It had made him financially comfortable over the years and allowed him to take care of his sister. If she knew what his line of work was, it was never directly discussed.

Having followed his mark for two days and learned his habits, Jilly had decided to make his move the next morning when the man headed out to the same diner he always went to for breakfast. With his plan set and the rest of the day free, he decided to check out the Alamo. Having expected to see a Disney-type tourist attraction, Jilly was surprised that the Alamo was more like a church than Space Mountain.

As he read the history of the building, saw the wreaths of flowers still placed along the walls for the men who had knowingly gone to their deaths there so long ago for the sake of an ideal, he had something of an epiphany. It had been late in the day, and he was alone, and in the silence some kind of new understanding of life came to him. He had never looked at a life as something you might decide to give up or not give up. He was a survivor and, as such, assumed everyone always did everything they could to stay alive.

These guys had known they were going to die and didn't surrender. They gave up their lives. In a way he didn't completely understand at the time, this had a profound impact on Jilly. It made life something sacred, something more valuable than anything else. Until then, life to Jilly was random. People lived, people died. There was no particular connection; things just happened. When it occurred to him he might be interfering with a larger universe, it made him question his right to take someone else's life.

He had seen himself as just a weapon used by others for a fee. He had no interest in, or beef with, those he had killed. He didn't give it much thought. He knew they were all criminals of one type or another and many pretty despicable, but they had known the risks, had known someone like him might eventually come calling. It was part of the Life. But something had changed in his thought process. Did he wax the Mexican target? Yes. But for the first time he could ever remember, he cringed a little when he pulled the trigger, now fully realizing he was ending a man's life.

Did he become filled with self-loathing or end up spending countless hours in church pews trying to redeem his mortal soul? No. But he had decided hit number forty-six, by his unofficial count, would be his last. Jilly the Hitter was retiring.

And he had. He had sit downs with Angie Sr. and eventually the Don and explained to them he was done. He did not explain why, and they did not ask. In the Fanzis' world, no man tries to convince another man to commit murder. It was an unspoken rule. It shifted accountability for the action from the actor to the convincer, and nobody wanted that responsibility. The decision was business, but the action itself was reserved for a certain kind of person comfortable with that action. Jilly was no longer comfortable. And that was fine. The Fanzis had no concerns about Jilly's allegiance, and frankly he was part of the family, had been almost raised along with Angie Jr. as another son. Jilly let them know he intended to go into the bar business, and the Don had promised to help in any way he could. And thus, like Jordan, Jilly had retired at the top of his game.

Chapter Five

By 2017, Jilly had owned his bar for twelve years. As long as he was constantly present, it was profitable. "Bartenders will rob you fucking blind," his pal Angie Twice had told him. "You gotta stay on top of that."

Jilly suspected that since his reputation was fairly well known on the Southside, it would be unlikely a bartender would try and rob the Hitter blind, but nonetheless, he was a constant presence, usually behind the bar although often not actually serving patrons. He had bar staff for that. He usually sat on his stool, half-moon reading glasses on, reading either the *Post-Gazette* or one of the constantly present books. A silent gargoyle perhaps, but always a presence.

A man or woman's best friend can sometimes be his or her bartender. Jilly was no different. Generally stoic by nature, he had evolved into a very attentive listener.

"Here's another fucking thing, Jilly, here's another fucking goddamn thing. I don't mean to be an asshole"—this, Jilly thought, was sort of the universal signal someone was about to be an asshole—"but she never loved me. Never for one goddamn minute." The man who called himself Donny D continued, "Goddamn cheating sonuva... for Christ's sake, she took photos of the lawn guy, the Hispanic dude, when he had his shirt off. I saw her do it. I knew. Hell, I just wanted one go a week, one roll in the hay. All that money, the implants, fuck, I didn't deserve that?"

Jilly slid another Tito's and soda toward Donny. "Women will be women," he said. He liked Donny. Bartenders learn to watch the stages of drunkenness as scientists watch Petri dishes. It's as predictable as night follows day. Stage 1: Good Guy, just having a cocktail. Stage 2: Still a Good Guy, getting louder, getting friendlier. At a point, and this always escaped Jilly, the Good Guy started to need everyone to agree with him and needed to be louder. Stage 3: Melancholy sets in. "I loved her, I'm so upset, life is not worth living." Stage 4: "Are you looking at me? I will totally fuck you up." Jilly had seen Donny D—Double D to his friends—in all the stages.

"Donny," Jilly said, hoping he might settle the check and move a fairly intoxicated Double D on his way.

"Jilly, my man," Donald DeSimon, son of intelligent and overindulgent parents, said as though just noticing Jilly was there. "Jilly the Hitter. How are you, my boy?"

Well then, Jilly thought. Well, well, well. Donny had called him Jilly the Hitter. No shit. This was a name Jilly did not tolerate. Whether he was in fact, or at least had been, in that profession in another lifetime was not relevant. He did not permit it. The big man's expression changed as though cold water had been thrown upon his person. "Fifty-seven dollars. I'll need a credit card." No nicknames now.

It occurred to Double D he had made a mistake.

Chapter Six

s Double D considered taking a little time off from his favorite watering hole to allow that same establishment's feared proprietor a little cooling off period, and in a place many would call "Heaven" but whose actual residents did not, the Archangel Uriel considered his next move.

Throughout the ages, since time began, there had been a set of Rules. Although they existed in no book, and there was no written form, the Rules had always been there. Some knew the Rules, most did not. You either did or you didn't. They were not taught, never directly spoken out loud, only referenced obliquely as a smaller part of a larger conversation.

But they most definitely existed. And they governed Existence. They were His rules, and He simply decided a certain number of his creations would understand them but most would not. While nobody handed you a golden ticket at birth, in Uriel's case, he had been born in what was now the Middle East to a goatherder in 271 AD, once you were given the gift of understanding the rules, you were going to be a Player on the universal stage. It was just a question of whether the Player was good or bad. Uriel believed, as every soul given the gift of Knowing did, that the choice was ultimately yours. There were pros and cons to both paths. Sort of like being drunk at the party—you could go Good and head home or go Bad and have a lot more fun but wake up feeling a little dirty and unsure of exactly what you did last night.

The selection of being good or evil was never actually that specific decision. It was more a series of decisions, and you ended up hanging with the Bad kids and nobody trusted each other and you had to watch your back, or you ended up with the Good kids and you slept very well and never doubted your ultimate destination but late at night you wondered sometimes if the Bad kids had a lot more fun. In Uriel's case, he had gone Good, but it was a close thing, and he'd always felt he wasn't exactly cut from the same cloth as his peers. He had eventually decided his migration to Good was the correct move, and if he sometimes had doubts, he made up for them by doubling his fervor, tripling his effort.

In this manner, and over hundreds and thousands of years since his official "death," he had risen to archangel. Given his birth, one could go no higher. In the current Pantheon of Souls, which numbered in the billions, he was a One Hundredth Percenter. He was different than the masses of those who had gone Good without Understanding. In the cosmic order He had created (Uriel sometimes suspected mostly to amuse Himself), archangels had swing. They were the fighter pilots of the aircraft carrier, the A-List actors on the film. They could be late because they knew nothing started until they arrived.

Uriel paid little attention to the Souls. He considered them more or less flowers on his walk. Window dressing that made the view nicer but nothing to consider to any great depth. This was the common view among archangels, that Souls were like pretty flowers—you took care of them, made sure they thrived, but who has a meaningful conversation with a lilac? Seriously.

"Where in the hell is Pittsburgh?" Uriel asked. "Near Gaza?"

"Well, not exactly," said Oliver, Uriel's well-meaning but usually slightly terrified assistant. "It's in Pennsylvania."

"Where Dracula is from?"

"No, that's Transylvania," said Oliver, "which sort of doesn't exist anymore, and Dracula is really more of a myth than—"

"Oliver, if you don't tell me where Pittsburgh is in thirty seconds,

I'll have you doing 2 a.m.'s for the next five hundred years."

Oliver had no interest in doing 2 a.m.'s. No sane member of the Holy Host did. But at one time or another, nearly all of them had. If you had one of those bell curves, or maybe a spreadsheet, that plotted when the most prayers were sent up the Holy Highway, 2 a.m. was far and away the Michael Jackson or Garth Brooks of the Triple Platinum bestsellers. Who prays more than the 2 a.m. crowd?

Sort of like a much larger Jerry Lewis telethon, prayers to Him didn't exactly go straight to the Man himself. Operators were standing by. The small stuff was filtered, based on a very complex algorithm. Some prayers were answered, some were ignored. Lets' face it, on a planet of billions, one can't expect their petition for assistance to go right to the CEO himself. More urgent matters went to supervisors, and above that, shift supervisors.

Eventually, the most serious matters went to The Show as the Holy Host tended to refer to it. Matters that were determined to potentially Alter Existence (AE) were sent up for review once a week. Short of AE, the Kahuna didn't see it. Sorry all you petitioning sons of bitches, you ended up beseeching a guy named Lao who emptied spit buckets for the Ming Dynasty in a former life. On the bright side, he probably had no idea what you meant about "covering the spread" or "hoping the rabbit don't die" so he didn't judge you.

Oliver said, "Pennsylvania is in the United States of America, eastern third of that country, western part of the state. Cold in the winter but not really cold, hot in the summer but not really hot. Not rich, not poor, kinda middle. The system says they are 'generally hardworking and reliable, loyal, stout, and follow their core beliefs as night follows the day.'"

"So they are oxen," said Uriel. "Fabulous."

Oliver didn't reply. It had taken him a long time to become assistant to an archangel. About 732 years, actually. He had learned to take his Master with a grain of salt. And he liked oxen.

—

At that moment, from a small but tasteful apartment south of Pittsburgh, a man headed out into the night. He walked with a calm assurance; he was in no hurry. He was thirty-six years old, attractive, fit, intelligent, and worth at that moment about three million dollars. He was the kind of man you deferred to without really thinking about it because something inside you told you to. His name was Dave. He wore very good shoes, liked bespoke cocktails, got laid (a lot), and Uriel was fairly certain he was the Antichrist.

—

Leonard was getting damn tired of working with potheads. A lot like six-year-olds, they were easy to get to follow your orders—hell, they'd pretty much throw themselves in front of a bus for twenty bucks—but were generally dirty, fucked everything up, and had the attention span of an Alzheimer's patient. "Ernie, where is your neck brace?" Leonard asked.

"My neck brace?" Ernie repeated.

"No, my neck brace. Yes, your neck brace, jackass! The neck brace I gave you yesterday and told you to bring today. *That* neck brace."

"Well, I don't think you gave me no neck brace," Ernie said. "I don't have no neck brace and my neck is fine, just fine. Yep. Hey, you got my, you know, my stuff?"

Leonard looked at Ernie. Ernie had a vacant, mildly confused expression on his grimy face. He changed that look to thoughtful consternation as he stared at Leonard.

"I got your stuff, but you aren't getting it, you cheesedick. I told you, wear the neck brace, meet me here, and we'd do some work. *Then* I'd give you some stuff.

"Where am I gonna get a neck brace?" Ernie asked, now genuinely confused.

"I gave you a fuckin' neck brace yesterday you stupid, brain-dead, toothless douchebag!"

Ernie looked up at the sky, as if lost in thought. Then he returned his gaze to Leonard. "Did you ever notice the clouds look like spaghetti on Tuesdays and Thursdays?"

"Oh, for fuck's sake," Leonard said before walking away, shaking his head.

Chapter Seven

Anne finished doing the dishes, wiped her apron, and then took it off, carefully laying it over the kitchen table chair back. Anne noticed that, as usual, Julian had left his dirty shoes in the kitchen, not in the mudroom where they belonged. She frowned. Her younger brother never did pay attention to details, important details. Men. Men were always messing up your tidy life, tracking mud on things you tried to keep clean. Men made life difficult. Ruined things. Lied to you and—Anne stopped. Looked through the window of the row house at nothing at all.

For a moment, she had seen a child playing in the street, the most beautiful child. Some part of her collapsed upon itself, some part of her knew that child wasn't there. Some part of her tripped the warning bell saying, "Let's let this go, for this way lies madness." She shook her head, as a dog does who has a fly buzzing in his ear. Things cleared. No child in the street.

Her attention wandered to the Mary Magdalene portrait on the wall over the kitchen table. "I'm sorry," she said.

She'd have no recollection of saying this later while at Wednesday evening mass, only a feeling of peace and contentment that she was in a safe, protected place.

Chapter Eight

"Go fuck yourself, you fucking fuck!" screamed Leonard, currently being held by his neck up against the men's room door by a man over twice his size. Leonard's t-shirt (Joan Jett and the Blackhearts Tour 1992) had slid up above his bony ribs. "I will kick your fucking a—" Leonard said before the knee that had connected with his testicles interrupted the synapse of thought and voice. Leonard crumpled to the floor.

"Leonard," Angie Twice said from the other end of the bar. "Leonard, you are pissing me off."

Leonard wasn't exactly listening to Angie. The Dickhead who smote his scrotum had gone back to his barstool. Leonard muttered a few thoughts, rolled to his side, got a knee under himself, and then got up on both legs. Wobbly as a four-month-old baby stork, he paused, his hand against the Touchtunes. "I'll be back in five, and then you and I are going to go round and round, you horsefaced sacksucking knobbobber," Leonard said, but the Dickhead was not paying attention.

Having watched this entertainment from the other end of the bar, Angelo Jr. said to Jilly, "How many times has Leonard been banned from this place?"

"I stopped counting around the first Mötley Crüe reunion tour,"

Jilly said. "You remember when I had that guy in here that did the balloon animals? He charged me two hundred a night and kinda creeped everyone out. Then I went with the caricature guy. Same deal. Nobody wanted to make eye contact, and he was saying things to the women that were going to get his nuts removed. Eventually I figured Leonard was more entertaining than both of those guys and way less creepy. Cost me nothing, and you just know any given night he's going to do something that beats the shit out of a balloon version of a wiener dog."

"Jilly, I got a thing," Angie Jr. said, changing the subject. "I respect your retirement, but business is business. We have a serious problem. Sensitive. Needs a true professional. I got ten guys who wanna be Biggie Smalls or Tupac or whatever the fuck, got guns in their waistbands, driving around in a 2007 Lexus because they're dealing weed to Point Park College kids and watching rap videos."

Jilly looked at his friend but without any discernable reaction. He felt like he knew where this was headed.

Angie continued "Most of them live in their parents' basement. What we do, the thing that the family relies on, is getting threatened. We got Russians, guys whose mothers beat them with a pine log to get them the fuck out of bed at six a.m. so they could go wash in the river and then pull a plow all goddamn day, who decided going to work in the US of fucking A for Konstantine the Destroyer is a way better deal. When you can't go back and you can only go forward, it's a hell of a motivator. These people aren't fucking around. Uncle Martin wants to talk to you. The Don wants to talk to you."

"Sure, Angie, sure." Jilly said. "I'll talk to the Don and Martin anytime they want. You know that. But understand I'm through with all the...wet work. Done with it." Jilly's face hardened and Angie found himself tightening up, pulling back. Jilly was a man that could be truly frightening to men who were not frightened easily.

"Understood," Angelo Jr. said. "Absolutely. They'd just like you to hear them out."

Chapter Nine

Don Fanzi's house on Cedar Avenue looked a lot like all the other big old houses on the Northside—brick, three stories, massive, old. That is, until you looked closer. It wasn't cut up into six apartments. Didn't have air conditioners hanging out of the windows or a half-assed pine deck built off the second floor or plastic stack chairs on the front porch. No, none of that. If you took a second look, and nobody did, you might have noticed the brickwork had been repointed, the windows were new. The peeling paint in the eves, so typical of the Northside, had been banished like the memory of Sid Bream. The porch was free of plastic, and wicker ran the show.

Jilly walked up to the front porch. The casual observer might have ignored the older African-American gentleman sitting comfortably in a wicker rocker. Jilly did not.

"Still cold for April, isn't it, Jimmy?" Jilly asked.

"Cold doesn't bother me, Julian. Never has. How's Anne?"

"Anne is Anne. When that trumpet blows, and you and I say 'Well, now it hits the fan,' she'll be dancing like Mazeroski's home run just cleared the wall."

Jimmy smiled at the old joke. Jimmy Hallendorf was a third-generation resident of Allegheny City, aka Northside Pittsburgh, son of an African-American mother who taught school and a divorced German brewmaster. Jimmy and Jilly had history. The kind you didn't really talk about. Professional history. They had understood that the coin of the realm was commitment, and in their time and place, you paid for your education with loyalty.

"I'm going to have to search you," Jimmy said.

"Certainly," Jilly said. "I have a rocket launcher down my shorts and a phone in my shoe."

"You got no rocket launcher in your pants from what I hear coming over from the Southside, and as far as a shoe phone, by the time you reached over your belly to talk to your faithful sidekick Leonard, we'd have you on a barge to Vanport." Jimmy straightened Jilly's Kaufmann's sportscoat and patted his shoulder. "The Don is looking forward to seeing you, J. You've been a stranger."

One expects a Don's home to have several overstuffed chairs, heavy drapery, maybe some religious icons, lamps with beaded shades, etc. Don Fanzi's Northside home had none of those things. It had a Don all right, a real one. One of the last true Italian patriarchs. But if you were looking for some kind of Corleone-Prizzi funeral home atmosphere, you'd be better off heading up to your Nonna's house in Bloomfield where they still had restaurants with checked tablecloths and photos of Frank, the Pope, and Canonsburg's own Perry Como on the walls.

No, upon entering Don Marino Fanzi's home, you were simply struck by it's...elegance. The Cedar Avenue home was large and stately but not enormous. Over the fifty-plus years Mia had lived there, and as the Northside had moved through its down period, he had quietly purchased surrounding properties next door and out back across the alley until he owned the block. So what appeared to be a row of old and well-maintained individual homes was actually a sort of corporate headquarters of Fanzi, USA.

For while the Don had been buying the block, he had also been buying Apple, Nike, Broadcast.com, and later Google and Amazon along with oil, gas, fast food restaurants, and beer distributors. The house next door was actually offices of the Don's in-house law firm. Next to that were accounting, payroll, security, and what passed for a sort of Human Resources department. The back alley had been closed off and become an interior driveway as a favor from then-Mayor Richard Caliguiri in 1986. The resulting compound covered an entire city block, had ample parking, small greenspaces, and allowed the Don's beloved Labrador retrievers to wander freely around the premises.

Jilly was shown to a waiting room outside two very large mahogany doors just off the main hallway. "Shouldn't be long," said Jimmy. "He's on the phone with London. You ever think about going back to work, Jilly? Always thought you had a little skill there. A real craftsman. Not Michelangelo, more Mike the Plumber, but a competent craftsman, good with his tools."

"Jimmy," Jilly said, "eventually a plumber gets tired of cleaning the clogged toilets others leave behind. I like going to bed at night without that sewer smell on me."

"To each his own," said Jimmy. "We all clean up after someone."

Jilly looked around, amazed as always by the feeling of calm he always felt in this place. Beautiful inlaid Brazilian hardwood floors, the wrought-iron banister leading up to the second floor that he figured had to have cost north of $50,000. The light coming in from the oversized front windows overlooking Cedar Avenue made the entire two-story entryway bright and highlighted the modern artwork hung on the walls by Warhol, Lichtenstein, and Burton Morris. Jilly sat in a butter-colored leather chair he could have fallen asleep in after about ten seconds if he wasn't careful. The Don knew good furniture. They had an espresso machine exclusively for the Don at Perlora near Jilly's home on the Southside, and another at WeissHouse over in Squirrel Hill. Jilly estimated nothing within his range of vision cost less than $10,000.

"Julian. What a pleasure to see you. It's been a while," the large but oddly dainty man said, descending the staircase from the second floor. The fact that the man was wearing a suit complete with waistcoat that had been born on Jermyn Street in London and likely cost about half of what Jilly's 1966 restored Lincoln Continental (with the suicide doors) was worth was not lost on Jilly.

"Martin. You look good. How ya been?" Jilly said.

"I look old, fat, and faded like a newspaper left in the sun. But I can't complain. Beats the hell out of digging ditches. Jilly, you look the same. Big, handsome, and frightening in that way that makes the ladies swoon. I remember when you were about as tall as my ass and thought nobody noticed you stole entire handfuls of the Don's candy from that bowl right over there," Martin said, pointing to what was the very same enormous seashell candy dish from which Jilly had in fact stolen pocketfuls of the caramel candies the Don always kept for visitors. A lifetime ago. "Give me a hug, killer," said Martin.

And Jilly did. While his mother was never going to be much more than an abstract concept to him, on some level this big, fragrant, seventy-year-old man had always made him feel more comfortable than he had ever felt in his life. Jilly had a clear recollection of Martin teaching him to tie a necktie, taking him to Kaufmann's and getting him his first suit and first pair of good shoes. And then there were the household dogs. The dogs loved Martin, and he them. They were the kids he'd never have. Jilly didn't spend a lot of time contemplating the mysteries of life, but he was certain that had anyone ever so much as made this man uncomfortable, he would have made them sorry for having done that. Very quickly.

"The Don will see you in minute, Julian. He's on the phone with—"

"Yes, London. Jimmy told me," said Jilly. "I was on the phone with London today too. London, Ohio."

"How's the bar?" asked Martin.

"Oh, it's like Darwin's waiting room. Sometimes I feel like I can actually see the de-evolution of man between seven p.m. and midnight through the miracle of alcohol."

Martin laughed hard. "Keep an eye on your little Petri dish over there, Jilly, but keep a .45 under the bar." And then Martin opened the massive doors to the study.

Chapter Ten

Expecting to see the Don, Jilly was instead greeted by Queenie. Queenie remembered Jilly, like everyone in this household loved him, and more importantly, she didn't fear Jilly at all. The 110-pound Labrador retriever and mother of half the dogs in Casa Fanzi crashed into Jilly legs in that sideways manner Labs do and gave him a kiss as he leaned over to give her a good scratch.

"Queenie! Where are your manners?" Martin shouted. Queenie looked suitably shameful at Martin's admonishment but still wagged not only her tail but half her body as Jilly moved past her into the study.

On the far end of the twenty-foot-long room, with rear windows facing backward on a courtyard behind the study, sat a small man at a big desk. He was tapping on the computer sideways to the approaching Jilly and did not immediately look up. The Don was wearing a Paul & Shark quarter-zip sweater, Brooks Brothers flannel pants, black penny loafers, and a very simple Patek Philippe wristwatch (which actually cost more than Jilly's Continental with the suicide doors).

Jilly knew the least expensive thing the Don wore was the simple gold band he had placed on his finger a very long time ago when he married a woman he'd probably never loved in the traditional sense but was loyal to, supported, and deeply respected all of her relatively short and difficult life. Marino Fanzi did not discuss his deceased wife, hadn't even mentioned her name in nearly ten years. Neither did he discuss "Uncle" Martin, who was not his brother but rather his partner and had been for many years, before the term "partner" had become fashionable.

Jilly stopped and waited about ten feet from the desk. Martin had moved in quietly behind Jilly and closed the study doors. Queenie, most of the time given complete free reign to go where she pleased by virtue of her standing as Canine Emeritus, was relegated to the hallway and would not be part of this meeting. After a few seconds, the Don stopped typing and turned toward Jilly, his half-moon reading glasses on a cord around his neck.

"Martin, has our security degraded to the point you are allowing total strangers into this room? I don't recognize this man."

Martin smiled and stared at the floor.

"You're a big fella. Come closer so I can see you better," the Don said. "Age is hell on the vision. Gina Lollobrigida could walk in here and I'd mistake her for the milkman."

Jilly walked up to the front of the desk.

The Don squinted at him, cocked his head sideways and said to Martin, "No, don't recognize him. He looks vaguely like a street urchin I used to know from the Southside, but I haven't seen that kid in so long I'm not sure I'd recognize him."

Jilly, a small smile playing around his mouth, wandered left from the desk to a very large wall of shelves containing hundreds of books. With no hesitation at all, he reached to the third shelf, removed *The Good Earth,* turned, and handed it to the old man seated behind the desk.

Jilly said, "There is a lesson in Wang Lung, Don Fanzi. With love and respect, Julian."

The Don opened the book to the flyleaf, read it, and placed the book on his desk. "What have you done with my Julian, sir? I will pay any ransom, just let me know your terms."

The book was a first edition, signed by Pearl S. Buck, and she had underlined the mistaken word "flees" for her intended word "fleas" on page 100, pointing out the error that made the book identifiable as a first edition and thereby so valuable. The fact that Julian had inscribed the flyleaf, and by doing so reduced the value of the book from $10,000 to about 10 percent of that, was no mistake. He knew the Don knew the book's value, that the inscription was more valuable to the Don than money, and also that the book would never be sold.

The old man smiled. "It's nice to see you again, Julian. I was wondering if I might not. I'm not so young anymore, you know."

Don Marino Fanzi was a small man by any measure. At about five foot seven and a slim 140 pounds, he was trim and compact but not skinny or slight. He didn't look his seventy-eight years, perhaps ten less. He was tan, had the best teeth money could buy, and carried a quiet authority about him you could not miss. Presence was the word. The Don had a presence, and when you were in it, you sat a little straighter, listened a little closer, and thought about what you were about to say before you blurted out the wrong thing.

Don Fanzi liked finer things, unlike the Dons of an earlier age. He was by no means ostentatious, but he appreciated quality and had not been afraid to spend money on it. He liked the *Godfather* movies, but more because he was a Coppola fan than for the subject matter. He felt no particular kinship with Vito Corleone. Born in Pittsburgh in 1940, he had not been an immigrant. His father had fought, and died, in World War II; Marino had never known him. Raised by a strong mother, his family had survived by sticking together and living lean, always a little hungry but otherwise okay.

Like many children in one-parent households, the Don had been raised by community, and his Uncle Sal had been a major influence on the young Marino. Sal was an old-school wiseguy. He'd come over "on the boat" and did a little of everything—most of it not, strictly speaking, legal. Uncle Sal had been an affiliate of the Costanzo family whose specialty had been produce and unions when Pittsburgh was a big union town. Never big on what he saw as a non-Italian establishment, always suspicious of authority, Uncle Sal instilled in the young Marino a belief that if he was not careful and didn't protect himself, the "system" would give him the shaft.

Lacking a calmer influence who would have recognized the Don's inherent intelligence and thoughtful nature, he learned to scheme when he should have learned to study. He learned to be suspicious of outside opinions, and worst of all, that he was born with the odds against him and would likely not succeed by following the rules, working hard, and using his head instead of his back. This led him into the life that had defined his existence the past sixty years.

By keeping his eyes open and his mouth closed, the future Don Fanzi learned. He learned the biggest and meanest don't always win and that they were a dime a dozen, but the smartest often did win and there were far fewer of them in your average criminal organization. Uncle Sal used to say tough guys grew on trees but smart guys were like hitting a pick 6 out at the Meadows. Rare. Marino Fanzi showed his value and earned his way up the Costanzo organization by figuring efficiencies, understanding the logistics, and demonstrating even at an early age a skill for understanding people. What motivated a person, what his angle probably was, and more importantly where his weakness lay. While he was never violent himself, he understood violence was part of the life around him. He was ambivalent. People sometimes ended up dead. Sometimes good guys, sometimes bad guys; it was part of the process. Like any small company, you had specialists, and Marino was not in the muscle end of the business.

By 1976, the Costanzo organization was fading, the pater familias was dying, and Marino decided it was time to move. Some old-school guys died, some forward-thinking guys moved in, and just like that he was in charge. And nobody minded. Change had been long overdue. Although there was never any direct connection to Marino with the end of the Costanzo family and the beginning of the House of Fanzi, everyone knew what had gone down and who had engineered it.

"So, the Russians. Run at least here in Pittsburgh by our friend Alexi 'the Wolf' Volkov," the Don said when Jilly was comfortably seated in front of his desk. "I think they are our people a hundred years removed. They are fleeing something bad, and no matter how bad it might get here, it will always be an improvement over where they are coming from. They are desperate, they do not fear our prisons, and they are happy to use violence since that is what they understand. Frankly, they do as they please, when they please, and if one of them charges a cannon and gets blown to bits, another one fills his shoes in short order. There is no long-term thought, no plan, no business acumen.

"They are amateurs with guns, and until now have mostly confined their activities to the sort of vice we are no longer interested in, based on its inherent volatility. But lately they are getting involved with the unions, and have interfered with large construction projects that are important to the family and to me. I sent my brother Angie to talk to the Wolf. Volkov called him an old man past his time and told him to tell me he was not rich, old, or soft like me. That he would run his business and expected no interference. He added if the "queer old Italian on the Northside didn't like it, maybe he should pack his Louie Vuitton bags and head to South Beach with his boyfriend."

At the mention of the Don's "boyfriend," reflexively and without any conscious thought—for if he'd thought about it, he'd never have done it—Jilly looked at Martin. Martin was staring directly at him. Martin knew this part of the story, and he was angry in his protective way for the Don. He also understood that he was a liability in a violent world of very macho men. Martin held Jilly's gaze for a moment then looked away.

The Don continued, "The Russians are flies on our windshield; we roll on without regard to their existence. They are a corner grocer to our Giant Eagle. Until now. Last week they killed Charlie Katz."

"They killed Charlie?" Jilly blurted out, again without thinking. This was two unconscious actions in less than ten minutes. And the first two in about five years. Funny how being around the Don made him sometimes act like a teenage kid at a high school dance.

"Yes, they killed Charlie," the Don said.

Charlie Katz was an institution. You could not walk into Chupkas, or Donzi's, or Mario's, or Doc's out in Shadyside without someone knowing Charlie Katz. In a city with a very long union history stretching back to Carnegie and Homestead, Frick and US Steel, Charlie K was the union guy to see when you needed to see a guy. Everybody loved Charlie, and Volkov had killed him.

"Why?" Jilly asked.

"We said no on a concrete bid. It was a crazy demand, gangster stuff," Marino Fanzi said. "We assumed it was just an opening salvo, ridiculous ask and they'd back it off to something more reasonable. But they said it happens or it gets nasty. Again, this is not new ground; the Russians are a clogged fuel line to a master mechanic like Charlie. He told them to kiss his cabbage and make some borscht out of it while they were at it. And that if they wanted to fuck with him, he'd roll their nuts down Grant Street like a squirrel with a soccer fetish. They shot him twice out back of Primanti's in the strip then dumped his body, naked, with a cabbage up his ass on the front stoop of the Oliver Bath House."

Jilly's thoughts raced. A message? That particular place? Probably. The Russians are generally about as creative as a six-year-old fingerpainting with peanut butter, but that message was hard to miss.

Jilly looked at the floor. He couldn't have made eye contact with the Don under any circumstance, but more than that, he was angry. Charlie Katz had been a friend. A series of photographs flashed through his mind: Charlie taking him out on his twenty-first birthday, Charlie introducing him to Art Rooney Sr., Charlie taking him out on the ice at the Civic Arena to meet Mario when he controlled the guys who ran that venue. And now he was dead.

The Don said, "Julian, the Wolf is out of control. But this is a sensitive situation. I need it handled, but professionally. I understand your history, and I am respectful of what we've discussed in the past. But I need your help. I need Volkov taken care of."

Chapter Eleven

Back on the Southside, Leonard said "motherfucker" for probably the five-hundredth time that particular day. He was out of cash, and the dickhead manning the exit from the "T" wouldn't let him get off the light rail without paying.

"Look, Haji,"—the clerk was Indian—"I lost my wallet on the train, and I don't have the cash. So just let me slide here and I'll get ya later, okay, Lion King?"

"My name is Amir," the attendant said. "I don't get the Lion King reference, and if you don't pay two seventy-five, you cannot leave the platform, sir."

"Look, dickhead," Leonard said, "if I had two-fuckin'-seventy-five, I'd give it to ya, you cow-worshipping jagoff. I told ya, I was robbed on the way over from dahntahn. You can't get blood from a stone. You wanna handcuff me to the bench there and make me one of those pagan sacrifices you guys do?"

Amir Laghari was working on his master's in accounting at Pitt out in Oakland. He had been born in Pittsburgh, and he considered himself a native. He had watched the Grand Prix at Schenley Park, had Pirates season tickets, and knew what "yinz" meant.

"Well," he said after a moment's thought, "I might let you fly for free if I could convert you to my cow-worshipping religion. If you will take a brief oath, I think perhaps that would be okay."

"Listen, Sanjay, I'm all in. I'm an oath guy. Bring it," said Leonard.

"Okay," said Amir. "Repeat after me, and please with utmost sincerity: O wah."

"Oh wah," said Leonard.

"Ta do," said Amir.

"Ta do," repeated Leonard.

"Shiam," said Amir.

"Shiam," said Leonard.

"Again, and faster," said Amir. "O wah, ta do, shiam."

Leonard repeated, "O wah, ta do, shiam."

"Brother!" said Amir, smiling. "Welcome to our family."

"Great, have me over for curry rice sometime soon, Mowgli," said Leonard. He pushed at the turnstile, but it was still locked.

"One more thing," said Amir.

"What, for fuck's sake?" asked Leonard.

"This is how we know each other, brother." And reaching over with a red sharpie from his backpack, he put a red dot on the middle of Leonard's forehead. "Go with God."

Chapter Twelve

Jilly wiped the bar absentmindedly, his thoughts elsewhere. Angie Twice was seated across from Jilly, reading the *Post-Gazette*. "Heard you talked to the Don." Jilly said nothing. "What did he ask you about?"

"The weather," Jilly said.

"The weather, huh?" Angie said. "Well, it's gonna be partly cloudy with a chance of serious fuckin' thunderstorms if these Russians don't understand who they're messing with."

"Volkov surprises me," Jilly said. "Never took him for the impulsive type. He's nuts, they all are, but he's not stupid."

"Nah, not stupid," Angie said. "I heard he actually went to college in the USSR. For some kind of engineering. But those guys, if you're not always the biggest, baddest bear in the woods then you get eaten by a bigger, badder fuckin' bear. Those guys sleep with one eye open all the time. They are way more worried about their own kind taking them out than anyone else."

Further down the bar, Leonard was trying to look down Mandy Monroe's shirt every time she leaned over to wash glasses in the bar sink. Mandy was on the plump side, but at only twenty-three, she had not filled out the way she would later in life and was still attractive to a guy like Leonard. Of course, Leonard's standards over the years had been reduced to 1) the woman had to be conscious and 2) less than sixty years old for him to be interested. And number two was negotiable.

"Why do you have a red dot on your forehead, Leonard?" Mandy asked.

"Gang tat," Leonard said.

"Stop looking at my tits," Mandy said without looking up from her dishwashing.

"I wasn't looking at shit," Leonard said. "And your tits aren't anything to write home about anyway. Always been a melon guy. I go for cantaloupes more than oranges, if you know what I mean."

Mandy lifted a glass from the water and flicked half a cup of soapy water into Leonard's face, pretending it was an accident.

"Motherfucker!" shouted Leonard. "My eyes! I'm callin' Edgar Snyder, I'm blind!" Jilly and Angie both turned and looked down the bar at Leonard. Leonard shut up.

At the other end of the bar Jilly was lost in thought. So the Don wanted Volkov dead. It made sense. The Russians were getting out of hand, and no better way to kill the snake than chopping off its head. And Jilly had been an expert axeman in his day. The problem was, Jilly wasn't in the chopping business anymore.

Chapter Thirteen

Archangel Uriel stared at his computer screen and ground his teeth in that way he did when he was angry or frustrated. The more he saw of David "Dave" Brady, the more he was convinced he was the "AC"—the Antichrist of biblical prophecy. There was a great amount of material describing what the AC would look like, act like, what his mannerisms were, etc. The more Uriel saw, the more he was certain he was correct. From a biblical perspective, everyone in the Holy Host (HH) knew that the Rules dictated that He could not know who, when, or how the AC would evolve and arrive; they just knew it was going to happen sooner or later.

Uriel was certain this was the Guy. He felt he had a duty to address the situation. But there was a problem. The Rules forbade any direct interference with what had been foretold. Things were supposed to play out in the manner they were intended. Now, "direct interference" was open to interpretation, and Uri had his own opinion on exactly what that meant. What if he could "indirectly" address the situation? He felt he was not only uniquely equipped to handle this epochal occurrence, but that he had an absolute duty to do so.

In Pittsburgh it was Friday, Happy Hour, and Dave Brady was Rolling. He always thought of it that way. Rolling. When he was

Rolling, he was slick, he was cool, he was Jay-Z, Beckham, and a little Benicio Del Toro (you know, for the edge). Dave was a good looking, wealthy, still a fairly young man, and DB (he had a tendency to think of himself in the third person under that pseudonym) could still charm like a house afire.

"What can I get you?" the bartender asked him. She was halfway decent, maybe a 7.5 rating on a 10 scale.

"Sweetheart, I'd like a martini, and since I just got out of jail, I want you to surprise me and pour me whatever makes you hot and bothered."

This was, of course, pablum—the worst kind of bullshit macho male bravado—but DB got away with it. Always. He had no idea why. After a while, he just assumed he was born with some kind of Bogart-level charm that allowed him to smile and wink and say things that would have gotten Leonard kicked in the nuts.

"Bombay Blue, give it a look at the vermouth bottle, lemon peel," the bartender said.

DB put a hand over his heart and said, "My sainted aunt had that exact same concoction every day at precisely six p.m., never a minute before. She wasn't an animal, after all. Lived to be ninety-four. You will make me weep if you look me straight in the eye, as you bear a striking resemblance to her at age twenty-two."

The bartender, who was in fact thirty-one and an expert in all manner of patron flirtation, was nonetheless charmed. "Well, drink to her memory and my being hot and bothered."

DB smiled and toasted her. Boom. Rolling.

Dave Brady was a Certified Financial Planner. But not just any CFP. He was good. Really good. At least at making himself money. Born into a wealthy family (DB's father was also a CFP) and educated at first Penn and then Wharton, the future wasn't exactly in doubt for Super Dave. Played lacrosse, dated everyone, managed to graduate without trying too hard, got his MBA while summering in the Seychelles and came home to his father's company to take the reins.

He'd never married, which bothered the Fam, but they'd deal with it. Life was too short to commit to something like marriage. And lately, he didn't know how to describe it, but he felt he was going to be called to do something...significant. He had no idea what that was, but he felt he needed to be ready.

Just then, his cell rang. "DB?" said the person on the other end after he'd picked up.

"Yeah, it's me. Go," Brady replied.

"We got the meds back on Mrs. Epstein. She's got a variety of health issues, and at seventy-one, life expectancy tables say she's got five years max. We can roll that million-two into a life insurance contract, but she's going to get her ass kicked on the cost, and the issue is the longer she lives, the worse off she'll end up."

DB's assistant was a kid named Conor who was sharp and considered DB his hero. Brady had hired him straight out of Penn State where he had graduated with a 4.0 GPA and two misdemeanor convictions.

"We're doing her a favor," DB said. "Mill-two buys her two-point-five mill in face amount, and her heirs get it with a lot less tax ramifications than if she'd willed it to them. What are the odds she lives past seventy-five anyway?"

"Well," Conor said, "break-even is about seventy-nine. If we put that money in good mutuals, they'd get about the same, but of course she doesn't have to buy a product so the money is more liquid in case, you know, she ends up in a home or something."

"Conor," Brady said, "what's the commission on a one-point-two mill upfront life insurance buy?"

"Thirty-five percent," said Conor without hesitation.

"And what do we get with your good mutual fund?"

"Three percent," said Conor.

"Yep. See ya in the a.m., bro," said DB and hung up. Boom. Rolling. He touched his empty martini glass as the bartender came by. "Sweetheart, can you mix me up another Sainted Aunt?" He smiled in that DB way of his.

On another plane of the universe's dimension, Uriel had made a decision. You either sit on the sidelines, or you get in the game. He was going in. To Pittsburgh, Pennsylvania. Home of Dracula. He was ready.

"Oliver, ready my things. We're going in."

Oliver had suspected this was going to happen for some time

and was actually looking forward to it. You didn't often get to head down to Real Life, which was sort of like a TV show for the Holy Host. You watched it from a variety of angles and always with intense interest depending on your role, but actually going down there... Well, that was going to be interesting.

"Tell Manon I want to talk to her. She's going with us," Uri said.

Manon? The Black Death? How about that... *And away we go,* thought Oliver.

Chapter Fourteen

Jilly had decided to go see the Wolf. Maybe there was a way around the problem of the Don wanting the Russian mobster dead and Jilly's decision to no longer make people dead. Jilly didn't suffer fools, but he knew Volkov, and Volkov was no fool. He pulled out his cell, made a call to a Russian who was a respectable dentist, and told him who he was and that he was in pain and needed a visit. The doctor said he'd check with his secretary and call him back shortly. Thirty minutes later, he called back and said he had an opening in two days, 7 p.m. He didn't say where. He didn't need to.

He headed home at 1 a.m. He didn't need to close the register; he trusted his manager, and bar traffic at that hour was always winding down. Coming into the row house quietly, he left his shoes in the kitchen. It was sure to bother Anne, but in the past few years he had gotten the feeling she needed to be needed. So he played up his male oafishness. Pretend to not pay attention. If it made her happy, then so be it.

His relationship with Anne was complicated, although he would not have thought about it in that manner. At some point in their frenetic upbringing, he had simply started taking care of her. And he continued to. And would continue. Did they love each other? Of course, on some level. Did they ever use the word "love" as far back as either could remember? No. Did they ever hug, kiss each other on the cheek, cry together, or share emotions on any topic whatsoever? No. And they likely never would. Did they have a very strong bond? They absolutely did.

It was Julian's habit to get up around 8 a.m. There was no particular reason for this; it was just when he got up. He came home most nights after midnight, and at his age, he didn't like getting up early. Anne was almost always in bed by 10 and up at 6 a.m. for 7 a.m. mass. They'd see each other most days when she returned from mass and he was having his coffee. She'd make him something—usually eggs, sausage or bacon, and toast—and while cooking, air out her complaints about how much of a headache taking care of him was, who she had seen at church, and what was going on at Prince of Peace, Roman Catholic Church.

Anne always made the walk to Prince of Peace because she felt at home there. Of course, at 6:30 a.m. on the Southside, you could throw a hand grenade and injure nobody. The drunks had long gone home, and the normal working class weren't out for at least another hour. It was her time to enjoy her neighborhood. In 1992, the falling attendance, financial issues, and lack of priests had forced the consolidation of seven parishes on the Southside into one. But it was a good parish. Anne felt it held to the old values, and that made her feel comfortable. For reasons she could never explain, and would never, ever have discussed with Julian, the church was the one thing in her life she felt was solid and could be relied upon. And if sometimes late at night she wondered if she was worthy of her own religion, well, best not to dwell on those kinds of questions. She'd discussed this with her priest and confessor, and it was all good in the neighborhood.

That morning, eating breakfast with his sister, Jilly was still lost in thought, the events of the previous day on his mind.

"Marion Kelly showed up this morning with her whore of a soon-to-be daughter-in-law this morning, can you imagine? Tattoos all over the place. They aren't even sure her son is the father, and she has the gall to bring her to mass. And communion, no less!" Anne said. "The world has gone to hell in a handcart."

Julian did not look up from his eggs. He knew who the father of Angie Sedlak's baby was, and it was not Marion Kelly's son. But Charlie Kelly had a job and was convinced he was madly in love with Angie, and as far as Jilly was concerned, that was good for the kid. Angie occasionally worked shifts at J's, didn't steal, and Jilly always had a soft spot for kids who actually tried even though they'd never frame a degree from Duquesne or Pitt.

"I heard it's Charlie's kid," Jilly said.

"Well, could be *Wheel of Fortune* from what I hear." Anne replied. "Just spin the wheel and try to figure out who she slept with. Nobody has any morals nowadays. I wonder what Jesus would think if he came down here right now and watched all the tattooed kids vaping on Carson Street."

"I guess he'd want to know first if they were Steeler fans," Jilly said. "I think they get some kind of credit."

"I'm serious, Julian. I've been having this feeling that things are coming to a head. The Bible predicts these things. It's fashionable these days to mock the faithful, but it's all been predicted. You follow the Word, you will be rewarded. I know how things truly work, Julian. I have an inner sense. And that inner sense tells me God watches each and every single one of us, all the time. No baloney. You foul up, you burn in a lake of fire."

Anne could not, of course, know that at that very moment, an archangel, an assassin, and an assistant were preparing to head down to Planet Earth to facilitate the murder of an Antichrist without any particular business case, Ecclesiastical approval, Papal Bull, edict, writ, and sure as hell without the knowledge of the Holy Host and completely unbeknownst to the Chairman.

"Well," Julian said, "I'm not gonna argue with you on the church stuff. Things happen for a reason. God apparently wants the Patriots to win because he seems to keep getting involved and changing reality."

"Go ahead and joke, Julian. There is a whole higher plane of existence you don't understand, but I do. And there is judgment coming. I can feel it," Anne said and stared out the window as she wiped the breakfast dishes. At what? At nothing. Or maybe not at nothing.

Chapter Fifteen

Alexander "Alexi" Volkov sipped his vodka. It was cold, it was top shelf. It was not endorsed by a rapper and was not sold in the United States. It had been handed to him by a stunning twenty-three-year-old girl from a very poor area in the Carpathian mountains whom he owned. Literally. He had purchased her from her parents for 1,200 American dollars, which was 75,600 rubles. A lot of cabbage for the average peasant. All three parties felt it was a win/win/win. It was 10:30 a.m.

The girl had retreated silently to an overstuffed chair in a dim corner. The Wolf's cell phone rang. He answered it, spoke briefly, and hung up. So Jilly the Hitter wanted to see him. Not surprising, really. One doesn't wipe the street with Charlie Katz and expect that to go unnoticed. Not even by the gomik midget Italian on the Northside. Except word on the street was that the Hitter was retired. Or maybe not so retired.

"We'll see, I guess," he said out loud.

"What, baby?" asked the girl. Her name was Tatiana. They were all named Tatiana. He had nicknamed her Moushka (Mouse) since she had a tendency to scurry in and out of corners to avoid being stepped on. By him. He respected that.

"Moushka, the Hitter wants to see Daddy. Should we?" Tatiana had no idea who the Hitter was. Or what hitter meant. Or what peanut butter was, or twerking, or the infield fly rule.

"Yes. I think so, baby."

"He may want to kill Daddy," Volkov said.

"Nobody kills Daddy," Moushka replied.

"This is true," Volkov said. "Nobody kills Daddy."

Alexi Volkov was not crazy. He was not stupid, he was not a psychopath, he did not have a death wish, he didn't snort meth to speed metal music and then shoot people in the head. What he was, mostly, was bored. Although the Wolf was not born penniless, and had at some point hit Powerball, the story arc was pretty similar from a financial perspective.

He had been born to middle-class Russian parents near Moscow in the Lyubertsy suburb of that city. His father, a university professor, had made enough to feed his mother, him, and his sister, and although life was pretty sparse, they weren't starving. Then his father published a few articles critical of Andropov. And he disappeared. Literally. He left for the university one morning in 1983 and never came home. Eight-year-old Alexi had no understanding of what was occurring, but he certainly understood what happened next. He was an eyewitness.

Two days later, while he and his sister and mother sat in their three-room apartment wondering what the hell was going to happen next, there was a knock at the door. A man came in, followed by two other men. While he was gently but firmly held by a hand on his shoulder, his mother and sister were raped by all three men and then shot in the head. He was told to come with the men and given no choice. Men had value in the former Soviet Union. Women, maybe not so much.

The men were in the employ of a mid-level gangster named Uri Vasilovich. Not destined for the organized crime Hall of Fame, Uri "The Roach" nonetheless had a soft spot for boys. His family had been systematically murdered by Stalin when he himself was a boy, and he had been taken in by a kindly older gangster who brought him up in the business. Twelve-year-old Uri was occasionally required to put on a wig and a dress, and do things that he would forever block from his memory. Nevertheless, he still felt a kinship with boys cut adrift from their families at a tender age. Uri tutored young Alexi in the ways of crime, recognized his father's intelligence in him, and eventually sent him to university when he realized his adopted son was too smart for the muscle end of the business.

When Alexi was two years into the Advanced Engineering program at Moscow State University in 1994, Vasilovich got diagnosed with cancer. With a year to live and understanding the Russian Mafia rule was "you get sick, you get squashed," Vasilovich arranged for his adopted son to head to the United States.

Volkov went to New Jersey and, after quickly learning the ways of the American-Russian Mafia, was sent to Pittsburgh. Expecting to find mean streets and ruthless competition, he was surprised to find Pittsburgh was neither organized nor particularly deadly. With a crew straight from the worst places in the Soviet bloc, Volkov quickly established himself as a force to be reckoned with. There was money to be made in Pittsburgh, and he was going to make it. Quickly becoming known as "the Wolf" for his habit of howling loudly after doing shots of vodka, Alexi ended his first year in the Burgh with a crew of eight hardcore disciples, a very nice condo in Polish Hill, and about $800,000 between his official bank accounts and various shoe and safety deposit boxes.

It had only gotten better since then. Four million dollars in net worth later, the problem was he had become bored. Lean on a guy to get a contract, kill a competitor, blah, blah, blah. As a reasonably intelligent man, the mechanics of the Life weren't really that challenging. The Roy DiMeo's and Anthony Spilotro's of the underworld liked to kill people. It was in their DNA. If they had ended up firemen, instead of in the Mafia, they would have put out a fire, had a few beers, and then killed people.

The Wolf didn't particularly like to kill people. He could. He had. But really, it had lost its cachet. As had a lot of things. That really was the problem, wasn't it? At some point, probably about five years and two million in net worth ago, Alexi had started to lose interest. Booze, drugs, sex, cars, clothes, vacations—none of it excited him anymore. When you've watched the sun rise over the Mediterranean in an infinity pool after snorting about a half a pound of coke off the backsides of two stunningly gorgeous models, what the hell is left?

Food. That's what. In the end, a Russian kid raised on cabbage soup falls back on food. Rich food. Fatty food. And in this manner, the Wolf became big. Pretty goddamn big. Not later Orson Wells or later Marlon Brando big, but pretty beefy. My man was fat, and he knew it. He had taken to wearing color coordinated tracksuits although he knew they were Russian Mafia cliché, not because he wanted to fit a stereotype, but mostly because they were loose fitting.

Volkov decided he'd see Jilly. Why not? If the Italians were going to snuff him, they wouldn't do it by Jilly setting up a meet at his own dacha where he controlled the circumstances. If they wanted to kill him, they'd hit him somewhere else with no advance notice, somewhere he was exposed.

Chapter Sixteen

After his breakfast conversation with Anne, Jilly had asked Angelo Fanzi Jr. to meet him in a small office he kept at the back of his bar, mostly to have a door to close when counting the till or when he needed to talk to an employee about a performance or personal matter.

"We need to go see the Wolf," Jilly said to Angie Twice.

"When?" Angie asked.

"Tomorrow, about seven."

"Okay," Angie said. "With or without?"

"Well," Jilly said, "without. We won't get past his goons carrying, and this isn't about being heavy. I just want to talk to him."

"So, we're going in, unarmed, to see a crazy man who called the Don a homosexual, killed Charlie Katz and stuffed a cabbage up his ass, and is stupid enough to fly the bird at the most powerful crime family in the city. Swell. I love this idea. Afterwards, let's go to the Pittsburgh Zoo, rub our bodies in gravy, and hop in the lion pen."

"Ang," Jilly said, "Volkov isn't stupid, and he isn't crazy. I want to know where he's coming from. If I hit him, all hell breaks loose. You know that. Crazy Russians who want to impress Brighton Beach with rocket launchers will bury the Don's two blocks on the Northside and never give it a second thought. I love the Don, you know that. He and your father are family to me. But they are businessmen now. It's been a long time since they had nothing to lose. I don't think they understand where this could go and the mayhem this could cause."

"You know Leonid Spasilovich? They call him Spatz?"

"Yeah," Angie said, "the big Georgian. Missing a few cards from the deck. Muscle for Volkov, drives a gold, pimped-out '72 Caddy."

"That's him," Jilly said. "He was in here two weeks ago with three guys. Lit like a lamp. I don't know what he was on, but I took the .45 out from under the bar and put it in my pocket. I never do that, but he was just, I don't know, close to being out of control. You could tell, ya know?"

"Yeah," Angie said, "I know. Big smile on their face and then they smash their beer glass into someone's head."

"Exactly," Jilly said. "He was treating Mandy like a five-dollar whore, so I headed down and poured them shots of good vodka and said this is on me but behave yourselves. They calmed down, toasted me and Mandy, and I thought we were good. Then, about an hour later, Spatz starts raising his voice, yelling at one of the guys in Russian. I start down the bar, but before I get there, he pulls out a Glock and jams it under the guy's chin, screaming at him in Russian. I have no idea what the fuck he's saying, but I'm thinking this dumbshit is going to spray the guy's brains all over the bar in front of ten witnesses and either I shoot him or he goes away for twenty to life."

"I got down there, cocked the .45, and put it to the back of his head. Hard. Got his attention. I'm thinking, hell, I don't know what I'm thinking. You know how you get, kind of calm because you've moved and there are only a few outcomes at this point and the other guy calls the play. It's up to him. I'll shoot him. That's fine. I don't particularly want to, it's a lot of cleanup and then paperwork, but you never move like that unless you have to, and this night I had to. Didn't really think about it. He was gonna waste that guy. I could feel it.

"Anyway, my point is, you know what Spatz does? He sort of cuts his eyes back and to his right over his shoulder at me. I'm behind him. Just his eyes. Never moves his head. He has the gun under the guy's chin. Guy is about to faint. And real slow, he smiles. First just a kind of grin, but then all the teeth. Then he starts laughing. I'm about this close to offing him at this point, and I'd have gotten away with it, given all the witnesses. He eases the hammer down on the Glock, pulls it back from the guy's chin, slams it down on the bar, raises his hands for a second to show me he's done, then hugs the guy he was going to kill and kisses him on both cheeks. 'Vashe zrodovye!' he says. 'Bring the good vodka!'

"These guys, they live in that moment. Live, die, whatever. All I'm saying is the rules are different when there is nothing to lose, and these guys are living on fear and thrill. So before we go to war with that, I want to make sure there might not be a compromise in there somewhere."

"But the Don says hit him," Angie said. "What he did not say is 'let me know what you think about this' or 'give me a two-page synopsis about the pros and cons of hitting the Wolf.' He said hit him."

"I know," Jilly said. "But I also know I'm not in the business anymore. And the Don knows that. The way I see it, you're gonna ask me to work, I don't necessarily have to take the job."

"You sure you aren't just avoiding what you maybe can't do anymore?" Angie asked. "We can get someone else to do it, Jils. Out-of-town talent, it wouldn't be that hard."

For an instant, Angie Twice thought maybe he had gone too far. The look in Jilly eyes, just for a moment, was truly frightening. Not so much because it was a hard look, and a hard look at a man he had literally grown up with, but because in that moment Angie was afraid. And Angelo Fanzi Jr. was rarely afraid. And then it was gone.

"I want to talk to him, and I want you to go with me," Jilly said. "Not because I need muscle—you don't frighten anyone anymore except maybe your drycleaner, you salami. I need you there because if he offs me, he has to off you, and I don't think he wants to smoke the nephew of Marino Fanzi."

"Well, fuckin' fabulous," Angie said. "It's nice that my value here is as a hostage. Fuck you, Jilly. What time do you want me here? I'm gonna have to stop by my lawyer and update my will tomorrow. You are definitely out. Leonard is in."

"We'll go at six-thirty," Jilly said. "No hardware. I'm serious. If you want, have Jimmy Hallendorf nearby with some guys with autos in case they waste us, then it's the OK corral, but by then, it's too late anyway. Up to you on that. I don't care."

"I want to tell Dad," Angie said. Jilly was silent for a long moment. "Okay, go ahead. He'll tell the Don. If the Don says no, then I'm out and no hard feelings. Will make it easy for me."

"See you tomorrow," Angie said.

Chapter Seventeen

Leonard sat at the end of the bar playing video poker and sending tweets to a twenty-two-year-old girl whom he had told he was a thirty-five-year-old porn producer. From Leonard's perspective, the beauty of the internet was you could be anyone you wanted. Just create a person you thought was attractive to some moron and tell them what they wanted to hear. In the end, if they eventually met you and realized you weren't what they had expected, shame on them for being a loser jagoff. Hell, all the dating websites were doing the exact same thing.

@LenzTheProducer: *"You are exactly what I am looking for to star in my next movie. I need a fresh yung face to bust this shit out. Tired of older hags ruining my vision. Need a good yung body"*

(Leonard had learned younger types liked misspelling.)

@hotyungthang: *"I don't know, I think u playin me. You ain't real."*

@LenzTheProducer: *"Baby, the shit don't get realer than this. If you got the bodaaaay then you got the part. But I gots to see it up close and in it. Don't b bullshittin me."*

(Leonard had also learned younger hotties liked bad grammar, abbreviations, and language that made you seem like a sedated caveman.)

@hotyungthang: *"I done sent you nekkid pix already, creepo. If that ain't real whaaat is??*

@LenzTheProducer: *"ok. Damn baby, I ain't dissin you. But I got mad cash in this shit and I can't play with fakers. Let's meet and get this bitch done once and for all."*

@hotyungthang: *"I'll meet u but I think u shave that nastty beard."*

(Leonard had sent her a photo of James Harden.)

@LenzTheProducer: *"I may shave it, we'll see, sugar."*

At that moment, @hotyungthang, who was not hot and definitely not yung but rather a forty-three-year-old divorcee currently living in a trailer with her mother, closed up the bag of Cheetos she had been eating, moved her teacup Yorkie—named Precious, of course—off her ample lap, farted loudly, said, "Precious, you little gasbag! Shame on you," and headed to the bathroom. Precious sneezed, the flatulence making her tiny eyes water. She took an awkward step and fell off the recliner into a half full sixty-four-ounce Big Mutha fountain drink purchased just an hour before during @ hotyungthang's visit to the convenience store to purchase the aforementioned Cheetos, along with a carton of smokes (for Ma) and *People, Star,* and *US Weekly* magazines.

The one-pound dog had not been genetically engineered to swim. There was no lineage of sea-going, hummingbird-retrieving bloodlines to hand her down the inherited traits she needed to survive this situation. Her strengths were mainly being portable, easy to control, and creating the illusion of offering "therapy" to those whose lives held the kind of stress that could only be alleviated by hauling around a really small dog and making said canine's life miserable. She was drowning in fizzy Mountain Dew.

Sadly, the Big Mutha had no ladder on its inside to assist her. She flailed. She whimpered. With one last desperate jerk of her slightly orangey, Cheeto-dust-covered body, she created a sloshing wave of soda that tipped the cup over. Precious, about fifteen ounces of soda, and a few ice cubes spilled out onto the matted shag carpet beneath the recliner. Lying there, panting, all the carbonation she had swallowed during her ordeal created a belch that @hotyungthang heard while passing by the recliner from the bathroom. "Precious, you tiny pig!" she said as she picked up the dog, tossed her on the recliner, and headed to the kitchen to see if Ma had heated up the Totino's Pizza Rolls.

Chapter Eighteen

The Presidential suite at the Fairmont Pittsburgh was palatial. Wall-to-wall windows overlooking all three rivers, marble, thick carpeting, furniture that was a designer's dream. In short, everything you might ever want in a hotel room. Unless you were an archangel with an ego.

Oliver checked his room (fabulous), considered the possessions he had chosen to bring along, and reread the Rules of Holy Host Visiting Real Life. The rules were interesting. There were many, but the important ones were:

1) You were immortal, so you didn't need to worry too much about walking in front of a bus. The bus would hit you, but you'd sort of vaporize and then show up on the other curb, just fine. Can't die if you're dead.

2) You weren't a ghost. The Rules were consistent with a sort of understanding of fair play regarding interfering with human life in that they dictated HH visitors could be seen, could feel pain (to a degree), wouldn't necessarily be rescued in the event of issues (purgatory and other less attractive options were in play), but most importantly, that visitors should always be aware of not interfering with the Order of Things. They *could* interfere, but only

under certain, clearly defined circumstances. The assumption was they weren't there on a holiday to see Dollywood and had some important work to do, but HH always needed to be cognizant that the less interference, the better. Real Life needed to work out the way it was supposed to.

3) Since visiting Real Life was, to a certain extent, the result of important business that needed to be handled, it was also a kind of reward for those selected. This meant you could, while you were there, experience normal human pleasures. To a degree. Taste, smell, and touch were definitely in play. With no negative effects. If you decided to eat fourteen hot dogs, you could. And they would taste good. You had no human body and thus no real digestive system, just a sort of Hollywood stage set that looked like a digestive system but really wasn't. So the effects were very temporary. Sex was out. He wasn't going for that. He had always felt sex was less recreation and more reproductive, and since HH can't reproduce, no go. And He made the rules. The net effect was Oliver was way more interested in a chili dog with onions than he was in a tall, blonde twenty-three-year-old.

"Is this mattress filled with straw and goat shit?" Uriel said. "Complete garbage."

"Sir, I think it's fairly comfortable, by Real Life standards, of course," Oliver replied.

"I hate coming here," Uriel said. "It's like visiting children. No understanding of cause and effect, no concern for the next five hundred years, just live in the moment. Beasts."

"Animals," Oliver said. "Agreed. If you have no objection, Holiness, I'd like to recon the surrounding area to be certain it is secure. The Agency of Darkness is always present down here, as you well know."

"True," said Uriel. "Go ahead, and be vigilant, Oliver. We are here on serious, nay, likely epochal, business."

Manon Salle, the third member of Uri's team, had retired to her room without a word, as always. She was dressed in all black. The Rules suggested all white, all black, or exactly fifty-fifty and nothing else. But depending on your level, you could create your own look to a degree. Her bag contained little—some talismans from a very long time ago, some books, and a photo. She never went anywhere without the photo.

In 1789, Manon had been murdered in France. Born of a mother who had never known happiness and to whom survival was a daily chore, Manon had learned quickly that you considered life in terms of what the next objective was. In her particular case, that meant: *Get up. Try to find something to eat. Don't get raped. Don't get killed. If you have to pick, get raped but don't get killed.* Her life being more important than her body, and being a survivor, she had opted to focus on not getting killed.

She had ended up with a man who was an assassin, but who had grown to care for her. Older, but kind in his way, he had fed her, clothed her, and made sure she was educated, in a manner that gave her the skills to survive. Never a believer in religion, as it seemed to her God had not had time to be concerned with her struggles, Manon nonetheless had learned to live by her own rules. A code, if you will.

By 1788, she had become a proficient assassin in her own right, and at this point had been informed by her agent she needed to kill a particularly turbulent priest. Manon knew of this man—he had been kind to her, and she had watched him be kind to others near where she lived when he had nothing to gain. Of course, this very kindness was the issue, and it had been decided he was making life difficult for the corrupted members of his profession, and this had to be addressed. Manon had refused. She did not know this man personally, had no particular allegiance toward him, but her rules, which had never failed her, would not allow her to take the assignment. In the end, Manon had laid low after refusing the job, but some part of her understood she needed to keep an eye on the priest. And so she had.

Then, on a sunny day in the south of France, 1789, a slight girl had seemingly appeared out of nowhere to fire a very large pistol at a man who was preparing to shoot a priest in a village square. And Manon had killed that man. But another man, who had not been initially noticed by any of the witnesses, had killed Manon from behind with a single shot to the head. The killer, who had later been described as wearing "a red outfit, head to toe" had disappeared, never to be seen again.

In her room at the Fairmont, Manon stared out at three rivers. She was calm. She was always calm. But she also understood that this was an intersection of events, a confluence, that she could not deny. Her pulse, as it was, was elevated. She was not interested in a chili dog with onions.

Chapter Nineteen

Jilly and Angie Twice stopped two blocks from the Wolf's condo in Polish Hill. It was probably an unnecessary precaution as Volkov was not particularly worried about being taken down in a massive frontal assault on his condo.

"The play is I'm just feeling him out," Jilly said. "We're not committing to anything. We're here to discuss what happened and see where they are. There is no benefit in going in hard here; they already know who we are. We can squash them, they can call New Jersey and squash us, we can call NYC, and so on and so on. Don't fly our flag and just let me move with this. Like sixth grade. You remember?"

"No," Angie said.

"Bullshit, no," Jilly said. "Stewie Rose. You tell me you don't remember him, I'll tell you that you are full of shit. Class bully, hit his growth spurt early and became a superjagoff. He took your lunch money. I was four inches taller than him and twenty pounds heavier, and I talked to him in the cloakroom. Did I hit him in the head with a wooden hanger? No. Did I scream at him and let him know I was bigger and stronger? No. Do you know why?"

"Because you are a sissy at heart and don't want to hurt anyone," Angie said. But he wouldn't meet Jilly's eyes.

"No," Jilly replied patiently. "Because he already knew. If I back Stewie down that day, he just figures out how to get you later. I can't always be there. The key is not beating them down to dirt. The key is leaving them a little dignity. Letting them believe they decided for themselves they didn't want to get in a fistfight with a bulldozer. That maybe while you are bigger and stronger, that maybe you have some respect for them.

"We can crush the Wolf. He knows that. And if he was a methhead spending all day cleaning his guns, then I wouldn't be doing this. We'd call in the airstrike, Jimmy H would show up, and problem solved. For the time being. But Volkov is not stupid. And he's not crazy."

Jilly paused for a moment, and then amended, "Okay, maybe crazy, but not as crazy as the rest of that crew. This is about trying to figure out why they are pushing something they can't win. Hittin' Charlie Katz? Are you kidding me? While that is unforgiveable, I'm very interested in what the hell made him think he could do that. You understand, Ang?"

"Yeah, yeah," Angie said. "I get it. But I have this memory—Charlie Katz showing up at my twelfth birthday party with an autographed Terry Bradshaw jersey. I still have it somewhere."

"I know," Jilly said. "I loved Charlie like you do. But he is dead. And we have work to do." Jilly looked at Angelo in the eyes. "So let's go do that work. I need you for this."

"Okay," Angie said. "Okay, okay, o-fucking-kay. You're gonna get us killed. I'm only happy I changed the will to make sure Leonard gets your share. He can use it to pay off his tattoo bill."

Jilly said, "Let's go."

After a thorough pat down—"Igor, that's not a gun, sweetheart," Angie Jr. had said—they were escorted upstairs to the Wolf's apartment/office. Jilly surveyed the decor. Best he could do was strip club meets palm beach, or elderly millionaire retirement nest meets Sylvester Stallone's bathroom. If it wasn't glass, it was chrome, and if it wasn't glass and chrome, it was black enamel. And red enamel. There were Buddha statues. There were gilded mirrors, overstuffed chairs, Persian rugs, and chandeliers with crystals that had to number in the thousands.

"Welcome!" the Wolf said. "How do you like my little dacha?"

"Cher called, she wants her living room back," Angie said. Jilly threw him a look.

"Well, we Neanderthal Balkanites can't hope to replicate the sophistication of Rome, or the Jersey Shore chic, but we try. And Cher is Armenian, a daughter of Russia, so I consider that a compliment. Come, drink with me." Volkov moved his bulk behind an ornate bar which appeared to be supported by four gilded, naked statues of Jennifer Lopez. "I can tell you like them, Angelo Two Times, they speak to you. It's okay, they speak to me too. Late at night," Volkov said.

"Do they ask you why you wear canary yellow Run DMC outfits?" Ang said. Volkov was indeed wearing a matching Adidas tracksuit in what could only be described as canary yellow. With black stripes.

"Ah, you are jealous. I can hear it in your tone. I will send you two tomorrow. If you'd like, I will send another one to your uncle's boyfriend. He might like canary yellow, no? Perhaps with a matching purse."

"Go fuck yourself, Alexi. You buy another girlfriend, or did you decide it was easier and cheaper to just head down to the humane society and do your fishing there?" Angie said.

"You two want to get into a slap fight, or can we get down to business?" Jilly asked, tired of the predictable masculine exchanges.

"Jilly the Hitter," Volkov said. "Once feared. Now, not so much. How's the bar business, Charlie Brown? Duquesne college kids giving you some grief? How can I help you, barkeep?"

Jilly walked over to a side table and picked up what appeared to be a porcelain figurine of a dolphin having sex with a sheep. He looked at it and shook his head slightly, involuntarily, before putting it down. "You're an intelligent man," Jilly said. "Almost made it through Let's Be A Good Communist College. Somewhere along the line, reality smacked you in the face. I'm gonna guess when the Machine ran over bubba and poppa and you were raised by some kind of pedophile Russian Fagin. Okay. Life is hard. Shit happens. Cry me a river.

"I understand why you are in Pittsburgh. Jersey is a little too tough for your delicate university skin. Those Jersey guys don't care if they wake up tomorrow. You're not a big leaguer, so they sent you to our little city. Makes sense. You're not a franchise player, disposable. I'm Brighton Beach, I throw you in front of the machine guns in a new city, see what happens. You succeeded. Congrats. Wasn't that hard. It's not so difficult to be a small player in this city. And you are."

Jilly walked over to the J.Lo bar, picked up a glass, and poured himself a shot. Tito's. "Vashe zrodovye," Jilly said and tipped the shot glass. "Remarkable they can make a better vodka here than they do in the Motherland, no, Wolf?"

"Garbage," Volkov said.

Angie had already compiled an inventory of items in the room he might use as weapons: statues, candlesticks shaped like phalluses, etc. What the hell, he wasn't doing anything else.

"What I don't understand, Alexi," Jilly said, "is what makes you think you can hit Charlie Katz. Piss on Fanzi's shoes. Makes no sense. You know that we know who you are. We let you fly under the radar, run your little games. McDonald's is not worried about Joe's hamburger stand. And you're doing well. And now this. You're smarter than this."

"I am very, very smart. Agreed," Volkov said. He moved to the bar, lifted a bottle of Mamont, poured a shot, drank it, inhaled sharply, and said, "Not garbage," before continuing, "I am not stupid. I just want what everyone wants—a piece of the pie. I come here to survive, to prosper. I don't care about your silly Italian structure, your silly rules, your existence. I don't care. You stick a gun in my mouth, I'll care. Then I'll kill you. Or you'll kill me. Your self-image means nothing to those who have starved."

"Well," Jilly said, looking the Wolf up and down, "you don't appear to be starving lately. So good for you. Now, here's the thing. I'm not concerned about you. Really, I'm serious. Don't give two shits. As you've mentioned, I'm just a barkeep now. You want to sign your death warrant, hit a guy with real balls, a real gangster, shoot him in the back. Go ahead. You know there's going to be fallout. So I assume there was some method to this. Some bigger plan. That you can't be some stupid, fat, bored son of a professor pretending to be a gangster while not understanding that the world is going to fall on you for what you did, and that Brighton Beach won't give a flying fuck.

"My guess is they make your dog over there the new boss. Track suit would be a little smaller, and she's probably smarter than you, given she's worked this gig, but life will roll on without you, *Wolf,*" Jilly said with a quiet sarcasm that could not be missed. "So I'm only here because they want me to bury you under the Smithfield Street Bridge, as you know. And what I want to know, what was the plan? I want to know where you thought you were going with this. Why you, an overfed mosquito, decided to pick a fight with a freight train. Maybe there's something I can work with. Some negotiation that can be done. Is there anything I should know before you end up filler under a sidewalk in the Hill District?"

Alexi drained another shot of vodka. It made him feel better. "The plan," he said to Jilly, "is to win. And I will win."

"You will win, baby," said a voice from the shadows, like some kind of creepy Volkov Greek chorus.

"The plan is to move into your business and make it my business," Volkov continued. "And I will. And you won't stop me. Not you, a has-been hitman, not your spaghetti boyfriend over there, not your queer daddy on the Northside. None of you. I will win. Because I am hungry, and you are not." The Wolf slammed his shot glass on the J.Lo bar. "YOU ARE NOT!"

Jilly looked at Angie, who was trying to figure out which items he could reach that would cause the most cranial damage not only to Volkov, but to his two Frankensteins. Served him right, going to this without a gun.

"You are correct, Alexi Rostanovich. I'm not hungry. If you are, I'd recommend the wings at Fatheads down on Carson Street." He said this in very good Russian. Sighing because he knew this meeting had been a failure, he said to Angie in English, "Let's go." And they did.

His familial name being invoked in his mother tongue by the man he knew was from his neck of the woods had given the Wolf pause. Nobody knew much about Jilly the Hitter, but this much was true: he was eastern European. Best to keep that in mind, Volkov thought. A bulldog is a bulldog. They clamp on, you gotta cut their head off before they'll let go.

Driving back to the Southside, Jilly was lost in thought.

"Hey," Angie Twice said, "I was thinking, since that didn't go as well as you had thought, maybe you'd like to try and back up over the Liberty Bridge? Maybe if that risk factor doesn't give you the boner you are looking for, maybe blindfolded? Because, you know, I'm totally in. I have nothing to live for. What I like to do, really, these days, is get up, have a cup of coffee, and then put my nuts in the blender and flip a coin to see if I throw the switch. Gets the fucking blood flowing. What the fuck, Jilly?!"

"I gave him too much credit," Jilly said. "There had to be more to it than that. Charlie dusted for this? That's how you go out? Because a fat jagoff is trying to live out a gangster movie? Jesus."

After a few minutes of silence, Angie said, "I've known you almost forty years, Julian, so I can say this. You don't want to hit him, so you go up there and put our balls on the line to try and not have to hit him. I knew it going in, and if it was anyone but you, I wouldn't put up with this nonsense. He could have iced us both, you know that now. He's not afraid of me, you, or the Fanzis. He's nuts. Now he knows he's on a contract, so he'll be ten times more vigilant. Ten times harder to whack. And we look weak. We look weak, Jilly, and you know what that costs the family."

Jilly knew. It had been a mistake. A bad mistake. And it was his fault.

Chapter Twenty

Dave Brady finished his fourth martini, headed to the bathroom to do a little coke, and reflected on how life was pretty damn good. The eight-out-of-ten chick who was waiting for him to return to his bar stool offered endless possibilities for this evening, and Conor had closed Mrs. Epstein for $410,000. What the hell were the odds that old bag lived more than five years anyway? They were doing her (heirs) a favor. That's the business he was in. Making people happy.

Finishing at the urinal, he noticed a guy next to him. Normally he paid little attention to those around him, but this guy was different. It wasn't so much that he was dressed in red from head to toe—that was unusual but not enough for DB's time. No, it was more his...presence. Dave had the odd feeling that the man knew Dave was going to talk to him, that he didn't have much choice. Dave chalked it up to the coke, but still it bothered him.

Later, long after Dave Brady had retired to his condo for the evening, he continued to think about the Man in Red and the conversation they'd had in the men's room.

"I'm here to do your will, Lord," the man dressed in red had said. He had bowed to one knee. It was the beginning of a surreal conversation that would only get surrealer. Or more surreal, or freaking unreal.

"Uh, well, cool. Can you get me a cheeseburger?" Dave had said, his gut reaction being this dude was drunk and he needed to vacate asap. But some part of him knew it was more than that, and that the guy wasn't drunk. And that he was a pretty scary dude who also happened to be on one knee telling Dave he was there to do what he wanted him to. Oh, and the Lord thing. The mental noise of the past year was beginning to clarify. Things that had not made sense were not so senseless now.

"So you are, Minion, and you are the first." Dave said this without any thought whatsoever. He would later wonder why in the hell those words had come to his lips. But he wouldn't wonder too much. His newfound clarity was making what only a few days ago would have seemed crazy, not so crazy.

"I am the first, but not the last. We are Legion. And we are ready, Lord." The man had still not raised his head, let alone his eyes, to Dave.

"I am not ready. But soon. When I need you, I will summon you. Be ready and watchful as events are occurring according to prophesy," Dave said.

"As you wish, Lord." The Man in Red rose to his feet but kept his head bowed, backing out of the bathroom.

Dave would later not recall his exact words in that bathroom conversation, only that they seemed to be spoken by another person. Like something from a movie. One thing he remembered clear as a bell—since he had been mostly ignoring the girl he was with all night—was that he had left that bathroom with an erection. And that was strange. Or, not so strange.

—

Leonard entered Jilly's bar, pissed off. He plopped down on his customary stool and said to Mandy, "Gimme a double vodka and a beer."

He had noticed a mousey, brown-haired, middle-aged woman sitting by herself further down the bar and had mentally registered her. She was wearing a sweatshirt with the words "Pug Life" sewn onto it above a childish rendering of what Leonard assumed was a pug dog. He had seen *Men in Black*. Fucking Tommy Lee Jones. Awesome.

The woman was within earshot, and so Mandy, who knew that Leonard—the bottom-feeding, garbage-eating carp of the bar scene— would be sizing this woman up, said with a smile, "Grey Goose?"

Leonard, who would sooner get a Joe Paterno tattoo than spend the extra three dollars for Grey Goose, said, "Popov." This sounded Russian and expensive, but Leonard knew it was cheap and the well vodka for J's.

"Excellent choice," Mandy said with fabulous sarcasm. Leonard rested his head on the bar.

The brown-haired woman moved a stool down and said, "I'm sorry to bother you, but you look so upset."

Leonard raised his head and looked her mournfully in the eyes. "My dog died today," he said and burst into nearly real tears.

Chapter Twenty-One

Oliver finished his fifth "big beer" and burped. He felt fantastic. He had met new and wonderful friends at Primanti's on Market Square, and he was no longer, strictly speaking, doing reconnaissance work. He had decided it was all good. There was no Evil within two blocks. He would have bet his immortal soul on it. He giggled. He had decided he liked, in this order: cheese fries, beer, and more beer. He also liked TV weather forecasts, commercials for car dealerships and those humane society commercials where the pets look really, really sad and some singer sings mournful songs behind the pictures. In short, he loved everyone and everything. His new best friend was a woman who kept grabbing his leg. He liked her because she smelled nice and reminded him of his mother. The leg-grabbing thing didn't register with him, since, as a Lesser Angel, he wouldn't have felt any sexual interest. Her name was Anita.

Anita: "You going my way, sailor?"

Oliver: "Yes. I am absolutely going your way."

Anita: "I like pale, overweight men."

Oliver: "I am glad for you! Would you like some cheese fries?"

Anita: "I'd like your cheese fries, baby."

Oliver: "My cheese fries are your cheese fries. Help yourself."

Anita: "Oh, I'll help myself, you bad boy."

Oliver: "Okay!"

Manon entered the bar. She was dressed in black. All black. Manon's image was hard to describe. She was slight, but tall. Pale, but with some substance. Not diminutive. Nobody noticed her, yet everyone noticed her. Every woman in Primanti's on that night hated her, and were also afraid of her for reasons they could not explain. Every man was attracted to her, but at the same time knew that was never going to happen (and some part of them was relieved). Manon moved next to Oliver.

Anita had intended to say something like, "Hey, you moving in on my man?" but then Manon looked at her, and she forgot exactly what it was she was going to say. She decided her best move was to get up and leave. And she did.

"There is Evil here," Manon said to Oliver.

"You are absolutely correct," Oliver said. "Evil cheese fries!"

Manon looked at him, and Oliver sobered. A little.

"There is an agent of the Dark operating here," Manon said. "I can feel it, and we need to be aware."

"Where?" Oliver asked. "Who?"

"Not sure," Manon said. "But close. And strong."

"I will be vigilant," Oliver said.

"You will come back with me to the hostel," Manon said. It was not a request.

"Yes, of course," Oliver replied. Together they returned to their penthouse suite.

In a corner of the bar, a man in a red St. Louis Cardinals jersey with matching red pants and shoes watched them leave. He was not referred to by name. Had not been, in fact, for thousands of years. He was Cambion, and his fate had been sealed before the Son of the Carpenter had walked the Earth. As the St. Louis Cardinals were in town, his red outfit generated no more than a passing interest. But he was interested. Very interested. He had been surprised to recognize a member of the Holy Host in town. But not too surprised. Prophesy and signs had been aligning for a while now. What he had been shocked to see was Manon in person in this place at this time. He was familiar with the Black Death.

He left the bar. He had things to do. It had been a very eventful evening indeed. First, the man who might be the Antichrist. Although, truth be told, he had been disappointed in this man. He had expected to feel a more... dark sense about him. But he had not. And now Manon of Legend. Very eventful.

Uriel drank his bottled water and spit it onto the floor. Garbage. Where was Oliver? Undoubtedly checking local restaurants for evil spirits. He had been getting reports about Brady, confirming what he already knew in his heart. It was time to make a move.

He stared out at the city. What he saw was a Neolithic landscape of cretins who had no idea that the end of their existence was near. He would save them; it was his destiny. The idiots. If not him, who else?

"Yo, Cardinal fan," Leonard said. He had been eyeing the guy in the red outfit at Primanti's ever since the Carlow College chick had told him he was old, creepy, and should get lost. "We don't put up with Cardinal fan bullshit around here. This is Bucco Country, asshole."

Leonard was drunk. That was like saying it was dark, or the sun was out. Mostly a fifty-fifty proposition at any given time. Leonard was not having a good day. He had been late to family court, referred to the (female) judge as "sweetie" (a mistake), had returned to his car to find it booted due to about fifty unpaid parking tickets, and then gotten roughed up by a taxi driver (also female and mean as a snake) he had tried to stiff, telling her he had left his wallet at the veterinarian's office while crying so hard over the death of his maltipoo he couldn't see straight. He was looking for a fight.

Leonard assumed, incorrectly, that in a fight with an out-of-town sports fan, bar patrons would come to his assistance. Leonard moved down the bar next to the Man in Red, who had been ignoring him. "I was talking to you, jagoff," Leonard said. The Man in Red turned and looked at Leonard.

There had been maybe three times in his life when Leonard had been truly afraid. Okay, maybe four. Eighth grade: drank the whole bottle of Dekuyper peach schnapps, ralphed on the good couch. And the curtains. And the dog. The time he had been pulled over by the township cop with about a pound of weed under his seat and half a bottle of Jack he had jammed between his feet as the cop approached the car. The wedding reception where he had referred to ex number two as a "fat, hairy bitch." But other than those few times, he had never been truly afraid. Oh, he often knew he was probably going to get his ass kicked. But he'd had his ass kicked so many times it had become kind of like going to the dentist. *It's gonna hurt, so let's get this sonofabitch over with.*

When the Man in Red had looked up from his beer at him and made eye contact, Leonard had become very afraid. Very quickly. His bowels went a little loose, actually. Never a religious man, Leonard nonetheless automatically sent up a prayer for his aforementioned backside, the knee-jerk reaction of the Classic Loser since the dawn of time. It being after 11 p.m., his prayer went to a Night Shift member of the Holy Host, new to the job and more fascinated by one of hundreds of small video feeds of Real Life developing in front of her than Leonard's request for divine intervention that had popped up on her screen. Absentmindedly, she clicked her mouse on "Denied" and went back to watching a drunk man get mugged by three twelve-year-olds and a Labrador retriever in Brussels.

Leonard then fainted, dropping almost elegantly to the floor of the bar in his now urine-soaked jeans and Molly Hatchet concert tee (Flirtin' With Disaster Tour '79). A patron stepped over Leonard on his way to the bathroom. The Man in Red returned his dead gaze to the television set.

Chapter Twenty-Two

After his train wreck meeting with Alexi Volkov, Jilly dropped Angie Twice off and went home. He was completely lost in thought and not interested in heading to the bar. Entering his kitchen, he kicked his shoes off, got a beer from the fridge, and went to the living room to sit in his chair. Like Bogey in Casablanca, he did not drink with customers. But he was at home now and had much to think about.

Anne sat in her recliner, sudoku book in her hands. She found the puzzles mesmerizing and an escape from the troublesome thoughts that would crowd her mind, moreso lately it seemed. She frowned at Jilly's stockinged feet, knowing exactly where he had left his shoes, but a look at his face, blank with thought, made her decide to keep her comments to herself, at least this time. Jilly sat down with his beer and then seemed to notice her for the first time.

"You ever get a feeling like you are completely wrong?" Jilly asked. "Like everything you think you know, the things that give you an edge, what you are good at, is a pile of baloney? That you don't know jack? You ever feel that way?"

"Oh, I guess," Anne said. "I think we all do. It's not our place to always know everything all the time. Only God knows everything all the time. And he has a Plan. I always feel better knowing that."

"Well, yeah. The Jesus stuff," Jilly said. "But do you ever question that? What you believe deep down? The things that you don't usually question, that are bedrock, that make you what you are. Let you sleep at night? I mean, you don't want to question them—you may as well question whether you will remember to breathe—but have you been in a place where you questioned them anyway? Things happen and you think maybe I'm way off here?"

Anne's face had gone cloudy as she remembered a distant time. A time when everything could still go the way it did in fairy tales and she could still live happily ever after. She was young and had acted impulsively. She had made rash decisions, but she'd been deliriously happy. For a while, at least. Then it had evaporated like smoke. Some kid's dream. She had not been meant to be happy, so she had made the next few very difficult, but required, decisions and gotten down to the business of being unhappy for the rest of her life. It was okay. She could confess, get her forgiveness, and suffer courageously knowing that her reward lay down the road when she was freed from this tedious life. But some sins—and Anne knew this whether she chose to acknowledge it or not—are grave.

Jilly watched his sister's unfocused eyes and semi-catatonic state and waited. He'd been here before. "I think." Anne said, "that we need to believe. Believe that what we think is right and that it will all turn out in the end. Be the best person we can be, work hard, and think the best of people. And it will be all right. That's what I think." Her eyes were no longer clouded—they had become very clear. "Jilly, you have been a good brother to me. The only family I'll ever have. And I want you to know that God loves you. No matter what you have done. I love you, and He does too. Have you thought about going to see Father William?"

"I see Father Bill every month for lunch at Fatheads. Like clockwork. You know that, Anne."

"I know you give him money, Jilly, and that's nice. It really is. But have you ever, you know, really talked to him about spiritual things?"

"I have," Jilly said. "I've never discussed this with you, but..." Jilly paused, looked away, and then said, "I once asked him for absolution for wishing the Detroit Red Wings all died of syphilis shortly before the 2009 Stanley Cup Finals. Swear to God. He closed his eyes, said something in Latin, opened his eyes, and said, 'It's all good. Say two Our Fathers, read *Fighting Back,* light a candle for Rocky Bleier, and your soul is good to go.'"

Anne shook her head. "Go ahead. Laugh. But there are bigger things out there in this universe than you and I. I believe that. You should too."

Jilly got up from his chair, patted his sister on the top of her head, and went upstairs to his bedroom. But he would not sleep well. Several chapters of Steinbeck's *Of Mice and Men* didn't help. Anne, who almost immediately removed her brother's empty beer can and glass and put his shoes where they belonged, also went to bed, but she would also be denied a restful night.

Chapter Twenty-Three

"Team meeting!" Uriel said. Oliver sat to his left, Manon to his right. They were in Urial's palatial suite at the Fairmont. Uriel was wearing black pants and a white shirt. Manon was in all black, as was her custom. Oliver happened to be sporting a Primanti's t-shirt that read "Eat My Beef with Coleslaw and Fries" and sweatpants.

Uriel sighed. "Oliver, what can you report?"

"Well, sir, all is well as far as I can tell. I detected no serious threats, although, of course, we should continue to be vigilant," Oliver said.

Uriel looked at Oliver for a long moment. Then thirty seconds longer.

Oliver said, "Lord, tell me how I can assist you?"

Uriel surveyed Oliver's bloodshot eyes, puffy face, mildly shaking left hand and said, "Oliver, you have performed as I had expected."

"Thank you, Eminence," Oliver replied.

Uriel gave him one last look of disdain, then turned to Manon. "Report?"

"There is Cambion here. I felt it," Manon said.

Uriel was instantly alert. "Cambion? Are you sure?"

"Yes, they have a...signature. It is unmistakable. They are here, at least one. There is a sense here that forces are assembling," Manon said. "Moreso than would be the case in less...apocryphal times, Holiness." Manon kept her eyes downcast, as was her nature. Cambion were half-human, half-demon beings often associated with the Antichrist in ancient writings.

"You have seen this Cambion?" Uriel asked.

"No, Lord," Manon said. "But it is here."

Uriel turned toward the panoramic view the suite offered of the nighttime skyline. He decided he was not surprised. Not at all. If what he thought was occurring was truly occurring, then, well, the appearance of Cambion was only confirmation of what he already knew in his heart to be true. What he knew was he had been called to fight. All right, then. It was time to fight.

—

Holy Host hierarchy was complicated. Uriel "technically" reported to Archangel Michael, but only because, in Uriel's opinion, Michael was something of a suck-up. Michael was always the angel who agreed with HET (Holy Exalted Team), which included Abraham, Moses, some guys who had been eaten by lions, had limbs ripped off and then been burned as heretics, and, of course, Jesus. Uriel was a little intimidated by this group since, as previously mentioned, his faith hadn't "technically" been tested at a level commensurate with theirs. He knew this, he "got it." Okay. He had chosen to outwork those who may have had the luxury of having their entrails pecked out by vultures while singing his praises. Okay, okay, for Christ's sak—Nevermind. The point was, when Uriel was in front of HET, which was a precursor to getting an issue elevated to The Show, he always seemed to be slightly off his game.

"Uriel, report," Michael said.

"Yes, Lord," Uriel said, blowing it right off the bat because technically, as an archangel, he was at the same ecclesiastical level as Michael and as a peer did not have to refer to him as "Lord." Nuts. "As HET knows, we've been watching developments in Pennsylvania for some time now as things have boiled in that area. We have begun to suspect—"

"Isn't that where Dracula is from?" Moses interrupted. There was murmuring among HET.

"Actually," Uriel said, "that would be Transylvania, and Dracula is more of myth than—"

"Go on," Jesus said. And everyone shut up.

"We feel signs indicate the Antichrist may be in Pennsylvania," Uriel said. This was greeted by another murmur from HET, but this was not the first time Uriel had advanced this theory, so it was not so much a shock wave as an interesting development.

"Do you believe it's George Clooney again?" Abraham asked to snickers, which Uriel could hear even though he was on the Holy Host version of Skype and couldn't actually see the entire group he was speaking to.

"No, our reconnaissance indicates the presence of Cambion here," Uriel said, playing his hole card. Now the murmur was concerned. Uriel could tell. Emboldened, he continued. "We feel forces of the Dark are assembling in this place and are looking toward a leader to unfold events as prophesized. We believe the leader is a man named Brady."

"Tom, Wayne, or Mike?" a man interrupted, whom Uriel believed had been beaten to death, revived, burned, beheaded, and then drawn and quartered. Gotta be careful with that guy. J loved those dudes. Seriously.

"Actually, Saint Myron, his name is Dave Brady, and we feel he is exhibiting behavior consistent with what has been foretold regarding the AC." Again, the murmur was for real.

"Uriel," Archangel Michael said, "do you think this is an Alter Existence issue?"

"Brother," Uriel replied, careful this time to refer to him based on his correct rank, "I'd like another week to be sure."

"Fair enough, Uriel," Michael said. "We'll await your next report."

As the assembled participants began to move about and make noise signaling the meeting was over, a voice said, "Uriel." And it became quiet.

"Yes, Lord," Uriel said, recognizing Jesus' voice and using the correct salutation.

"Manon, what is her part in this?"

"It was she, Lord, who discovered the Cambion." There was absolute silence for perhaps fifteen seconds while everyone waited.

"I will await your next report with much interest, Uriel. And good work," Jesus said.

"Thank you, Lord," Uriel said and signed off. It was only then that he realized he had shredded the fancy hotel napkin he had been holding in his hands without realizing it.

Uriel then spoke with Manon for about thirty minutes, filling her in on his meeting and explaining what he wanted her to do.

Chapter Twenty-Four

Jilly stared at his newspaper, but he wasn't really reading it. Anyone who might have been watching would have noticed he hadn't turned a page in nearly half an hour. He had been asked to do something by a man he looked at as a father figure, who had been good to him. That thing was something he'd done many times, but he didn't want to do it. He could lie to himself and make an argument that resolving this without violence was a better way to go, often true, but after the meeting with the Wolf he knew that was baloney. Volkov had essentially called him and his adopted family soft and cowardly, and in that business, being perceived as soft was death. Hitting Volkov was now, more than ever, the only correct course of action. Anything else would only make them look softer.

"Hey, Jilly?" It was Mandy, just arrived for her shift. "I hate to ask you, but is there any chance you could advance me a little on my next check? I have a chance to get Chesney tickets for me and Amy, but if I wait, I'm going to lose them."

"How much?" Jilly asked.

"Well, two hundred would be great if you can swing it."

Mandy was a good kid at heart, as were most of the staff Jilly hired. He never liked the ones that had a long, sad story; he had lived a sad story and crying about it wasn't how he had survived. He liked the kids who had a little pride. Sure, maybe they lied about why they'd ended up where they had, but pride is an indication you aren't satisfied with where you are and you want to improve your lot in life. The ones who didn't lie a little about their background—and let's face it, if you are applying to be a part-time bartender in your mid-twenties then life probably hasn't worked out exactly as you had hoped—those were the ones who had given up. And he didn't hire those people.

"I've been meaning to give you this," he said, peeling two hundred-dollar bills from the wad of cash he always had in his pocket. It's your one-year anniversary bonus."

"I've only been here ten months," Mandy said.

"You get two bonus months for not having punched Leonard in the face." Jilly said.

"Are you sure?"

"I'm sure. Now get to work. Those two drywall hangers down there aren't making us any money while they sit there with no beers in front of them."

"Thanks, Jilly," Mandy said, smiling and heading to the other end of the bar.

"Russian Americans are no different than any other immigrant group; they want their piece of the American Pie," said Alexi Volkov.

Jilly was startled out of his daze and turned his head expecting to see a fat man in a green and blue Adidas ensemble with matching fur lid, two bookend bruisers on either side of him. His hand went without thinking to the small of his back where for a long time he would have found a pistol, but no longer. The thought flashed across his mind that he was about try and defend himself with the elastic band on his underwear, and he almost giggled crazily. And then he saw the Wolf. But not in person. On the bar TV.

The Channel 11 reporter was interviewing Volkov, and the script under their faces read: "Local Russian businessman speaks out." In the background was a carnival of sorts with Russian flags, rides, and food trailers set up, and Jilly remembered reading something about a Russian American Festival up in Polish Hill.

"Russian Americans are hardworking, decent, and very loyal

to the USA," Volkov said. "They just want to fit in and be afforded the rights other American minority groups have."

At this point, Manon walked into the bar. Jilly, transfixed by the man on the screen who had that very afternoon been occupying his thoughts, noticed her, but only in passing.

She sat down at the bar near Jilly. Mandy wandered down and asked what she wanted to drink.

"Nothing, thank you," Manon said, never looking at Mandy but keeping her gaze on Jilly. Mandy thought that odd, but for reasons she couldn't explain decided to return to the other end of the bar. There was a vibe about this woman that told Mandy to let her alone.

"You have a problem," Manon said.

Jilly removed his gaze from the TV and turned to her. What he saw was an attractive—if severe—woman, maybe in her mid-forties, hard to tell. She was dressed all in black so probably some kind of artsy type.

"Fair treatment and equal rights for the fastest-growing immigrant segment is what I'm talking about," Volkov said up on the screen. He was surrounded by Russians with their faces painted and with Russian flag t-shirts on, mugging for the camera.

"I have a problem?" Jilly asked, only now processing what the woman had said.

"Killing has become difficult for you. I am very familiar with that feeling, my friend," Manon said. "I can solve your problem."

"Killing is my problem?" Jilly said slowly, somewhat confused and completely transfixed by this woman who had such a presence about her.

"No. *That* is your problem," Manon said, inclining her head toward the screen where the Wolf was leading a "Russians for USA" chant.

Jilly, as if in slow motion, looked to the TV screen at Volkov, then turned his head back to Manon. This was all very strange, and he couldn't shake the feeling that he wasn't sure if any of it was actually happening. Manon made a very simple gesture with her right hand, as if waving off a waiter who had arrived at her table and was interrupting her. She sort of lifted her fingers and dropped them while looking at the TV. On the television screen,

Volkov dropped as if shot and someone screamed. Jilly turned again to the TV to see chaos as the camera tilted downward and people shouted. "Heart attack! Get an ambulance!" someone said loudly within the range of the microphone. And then a commercial for a Subaru dealership filled the screen.

Jilly was staring at Manon. "I don't kill people," he said.

"No, not anymore. I know. You quit after forty-six. Manuel Esteban Ortega, age forty-three. That is your problem. You are a craftsman who no longer has a craft. And your patron wanted one more commission." She said this looking him directly in the eyes with no sarcasm or judgment, her voice level.

"You just killed Volkov?" Jilly asked, his head still swimming.

"I solved your problem," Manon said.

"Who the hell are you?"

"I am a friend. And now you are in my debt."

"Your debt?" Jilly repeated.

"Yes. My debt," Manon said.

Along the wall and a few feet away, the Widow Antonucci, who had come into the bar unnoticed by either Manon or Jilly, listened intently.

Chapter Twenty-Five

Raconteur and potential Antichrist Dave Brady sat in his condo, with a bourbon rocks, and pondered life. The Man in Red had been unsettling. Dave, at first a little frightened but then strangely excited, hadn't been able to think of much else since the encounter. The guy had all the makings of a complete nutcase, but he was so... intense. And those *eyes*. There was only one word for them and that was dead. Dead as a doornail. And he had bowed to Dave. And then said things that you could write off as pure insanity, except... Except. Except the more he thought about it, the more some of it made sense. A lot of sense.

Dave had always felt he was different than others. Smarter, sure. Better looking? Of course. He had money, success, women, and on and on, but he had always felt, well, special. He was just never sure why. And another thing: almost all his life he had held certain contempt for the goody two-shoes types in the world. The big smile, empty-headed do-gooders who bee-bopped through life smug in their certainty that if they were swell eggs then everything would turn out just grand. Well, everyone knew that was horseshit.

And worst of all were the holy rollers. This bunch of self-righteous, judgmental pricks. Man, he hated them. Some part of him had always felt that they were cowards hiding behind their religion, masquerading as wonderful people when in reality they were stupid sheep who felt safe in their flock. Maybe they needed a little wolf pack smackdown. And maybe, just maybe, he was the leader some wolves had been waiting for. Dave smiled. Yeah. Leader of the Pack. He liked that. Maybe this was the logical progression. The next thing his life had been steadily leading him toward.

His cell vibrated and he looked down at the ID. Chenille. A solid eight-point-seven out of ten. He declined the call. Sipped his bourbon. Leader of the Pack. Yeah.

—

Back in his room at the Fairmont Hotel, Oliver stared at his screen. Not a computer, not in the Real World sense of that word, but good enough. Call it a Computer of All Computers. He was concerned. He was eating Cheetos. Which should not in any way suggest to the reader he was somehow less focused than he should be. But let's be honest, Cheetos are really good. So are Snickers. In any event, what he saw concerned him. He had been doing some research on Dark entities, their signatures, and then overlaying that on a map of greater Pittsburgh. His initial reaction was he had screwed up and picked Starbucks locations instead of Dark personas. There were thirty-seven pins on his map. Jesus Chr—nevermind. He went to find Uriel.

—

Following his surreal conversation with Manon, Jilly had walked aimlessly for about half an hour without really paying attention to where he was. When he had returned to conscious thought, he was standing in front of a bar called the Lamb, so he went inside. He did not, for a second, consider the irony of the name.

"Miller, Jack back," he said, not looking at the bartender.

"Coming right up. And it's on me. We don't get celebs in here very often so this is a special occasion, Hitter."

Jilly looked up instantly, and the look would have withered a bouquet of flowers or melted an ice cream sundae. He did not recognize the back of the bartender who had referred to him by a name he did not allow.

The bartender placed the drinks in front of Jillian with an enormous smile on his face. "Salud!" he said.

Jilly stared at the man. Elderly but not old, maybe mid-sixties. Skinny, cardigan sweater, five-ten frame. Reminded Jilly of Mr. Rogers. Thinning hair, kind, extremely inoffensive. Goddamn grandfatherly is what came to Jilly's mind. Which was still a bit off.

"How do you know me?" Jilly asked.

"Everyone knows Jilly the Hitter," the man said, smiling. There was nobody else in the bar. "Chances Are" played on a jukebox, although Jilly did not see one.

Jilly's mind swam. Under normal circumstances he would have, at a minimum, dressed down the bartender in profane fashion. At a maximum, he would have grabbed his wrist, in order to pull him closer, and punched him hard in the face. But none of those options occurred to him. He was fascinated by this man. What a day. First a woman in black who he had never met, who could drop Russian gangsters on TV with a wave of her hand. She knew him. Now Mr. Rogers was calling him "Hitter" and claimed to know him too. Like some kind of "This Is Your Life" on acid. He shook his head to clear it. It didn't help.

"I don't know you," Jilly said.

"Oh, we've met, my friend," the bartender said. "We've had a few conversations over the years. I'm sure you probably don't recall, but that's fine. Good bartenders are used to that kinda thing, as you know."

Jilly drank his beer, for lack of anything else to do, then drank his shot. At no time during these two actions did his eyes leave the bartender's. "Look," he said, regaining his composure with the help of a little Jack Daniels, "I'm sure I've never met you, and I don't know what Hitter means so..."

"I knew your father, Julian," the bartender said.

Jilly froze with his mug halfway to his mouth and stared as though he had been struck with a brick. He slowly put the mug down on the bar. His mind had decided to launch himself over the bar at this man. Done deal. Like when the door swings back and hits you in the head and your instinct is to punch that damn door right in its...door face. No thought at all. Pure reaction.

But Jilly couldn't do it. This man, who seemed to know him, although Jilly was sure he had never met him in his life. This man, who had insulted him and then mentioned his father. Unforgiveable. And yet Jilly could have no more attacked this man than he could have punted a puppy down Carson Street.

"My father," was what Jilly said.

"Yes. Your father," the bartender replied. "Not the waste of breath who your mother ended up with. Your real father."

"How..." Jilly managed.

"I've been around for a very long time, Julian Tetanich. Seen it all, really."

It would only occur to Jilly later that the bartender had used his surname. His real surname. Nobody knew his surname except Anne, because it no longer existed.

Chapter Twenty-Six

"Order!" the Man in Red said. "Order!"

He was standing in front of perhaps forty people in what would best be described in a Hollywood screenplay as "warehouse: vacant." There was a big, slowly spinning fan near the top of one wall. Somewhere, water dripped. Loudly. Of course. If the irony of yelling "order" at what was quite literally the photo next to Webster's Dictionary description of "disorder" struck him, you wouldn't have known it.

"Sons of Disorder!" he cried. "Agents Of Chaos! Our time is near!"

There was a roar among the crowd, who raised their fists. The sea of faces the Man in Red addressed was a montage of bad luck, bad news, bad breath, bad juju, and a little bad medicine thrown in. This was not a Victoria's Secret calendar shoot.

"Excuse me! Excuse me!" a voice said. The polluted sea parted for a misshapen man who appeared to be about four feet tall with an enormous wart on his forehead and a malformed horn growing above one ear. "We've been talking, most of us, and—"

"SPEAK, LITTLE MAN!" the Man in Red bellowed.

"Well, me and the guys, we decided we want to be called 'Sons of Violence and Anarchy,' not 'Sons Of Disorder.'" There was silence as the assembled crowd waited.

The Man in Red took a deep breath. "Can you spell Anarchy, Spokesman?" he asked. The misshapen man suddenly looked frightened. "Spell it!"

"Well, I don't see why I should..." the small man replied, but then he suddenly went silent.

The Man in Red had raised his hand and silenced him as surely as though a cork had been placed in his mouth. "Spell it, scum!" the Man in Red demanded.

"A-N-E-R-K..." the small man began.

The Man in Red smiled, waved his hand, and the little man began to melt away. Literally. He'd be reassembled in the lower regions from whence he had come, but for now, he was gone.

"Any other requests?!" the Man in Red bellowed. There was silence. Good. "Our time is at hand! I have met the Antichrist and he is nearly ready to assume his rightful place as the redeemer of all that we believe in! All that is Dark!" Again, a roar from the assembled crowd. "We will be ready to do what we have been called to do!"

"So...." a voice said when the roar had subsided. "When you say 'ready to do what we are called to do,' can you be more specific? I mean, some of us feel like we aren't really sure what exactly we're supposed to do, and others, they are totally with the movement, for sure, but they feel like, frankly, their needs aren't really being addressed."

The Man in Red looked down for a moment. Assembled his thoughts. Things used to be so much easier in the old days. Back when you were evil, or you weren't. Black and white. These new residents, these kids. Always with the questions, always with the arguments. He had begun to think, and this was sad really, that he might like to transfer over to a supervisor's job at the sulphur mines. Sure, it wasn't exactly challenging. I mean, you just mine sulphur—what's there to figure out? Buncha tortured souls with shovels. Bada bing. He knew one thing: nobody lifting a shovel in the mines was going to ask him what their motivation was.

Later, in an establishment called Happy Times where the patrons were trying desperately to get happy but mostly not succeeding, two dark minions conversed.

"How about Red melting Jon B.?" the large, fairly grimy man said while drinking his seventh beer. "Jon's a bit of midget, and a lying blowhard, but that never bothered me. Not sure he deserved the old McKeesport Meltdown, ya know what I'm saying?"

"Well, you don't argue with Red. Everyone knows that. Little man wants to argue, he's gonna get what he gets," said a second fairly grimy man while drinking his own seventh beer. They both turned as a man in a Foghat concert t-shirt (Fool For The City Tour, 1976) approached. He introduced himself as "Leonard."

Chapter Twenty-Seven

"Boss, we've got trouble," Oliver said to Uriel. He had fetched the archangel from yet another reality show on TV ("So much discord!") and showed him his overlay of Dark and the Greater Pittsburgh area.

"Thirty-seven?" Uriel said. "Far more than we had thought were here."

"Well," Oliver said, "here's the thing. I only get a strong Dark factor from about four of them, and maybe only one true Cambion as we would define the term. I've looked at some research, and those four are bad news for sure, definitely working for the bad guys and with serious cred, but the other thirty-three are kind of, I don't know, less dark. Sorta Dark wannabes, really." Oliver gave a sheepish shrug.

"Explain," Uriel said.

"Well, it's complicated, but using The System and an algorithm I've come up with, I can plot all their evilness throughout their existence and come up with a score of sorts. The score is generated from the worst Known Evils, those people who are documented in the historical one percent of the Dark. That's one end of the scale. On the other end are only mildly evil, let's say people who like to fart in an elevator or loosen salt shaker lids. People who enjoy making others unhappy, at least for a moment, to share their unhappiness with life in general. The important thing is most of this crew is in the lower twenty-five percent of the Dark scale. I'd call them 'shoving an old lady out of the way for a bus seat,' or 'taking money from a blind guy's cup' evil. No Adolph Hitlers in this crew. Other than those top four—they're serious. And one more thing."

"What?" Uriel said.

"On the intelligence scale, and this is well documented, Evil or Good, Dark or Light, tendencies run consistent with intelligence, weak to strong. That is to say, the more Evil or the more Good you are, the smarter you tend to be. The weaker end of the spectrum on both ends is sort of furniture from a mental perspective. The mildly Good and mildly Evil are sorta, you know, dumb."

"So, if I have this correctly," Uriel said, "we are dealing with four Himmlers and thirty-three elevator-farting morons?"

"Precisely," Oliver said.

—

In his garden on the Northside, Don Fanzi sipped his cognac and let his mind wander. He scratched Queenie's head but was unaware he was doing it. In this small green space off his office, an oasis in the middle of a busy city, he could think about the events of the day. He came here often. He would not be bothered.

So the Wolf was dead. Well, probably dead. There had not been confirmation he had actually expired, but from the video he was at least out of action for a while. This was good. Good for his family. Good for business. He had asked Julian to get involved. Asked over the objections of both his brother and Martin. It was his prerogative. It was easy for others, even beloved others, to second guess the hard decisions. It was his job to make them. Some part of him had hoped Jilly would refuse. He had never been a violent man and recognized in Julian the intelligence that made him trustworthy. Contrary to popular belief, the Don didn't think stupid animals were the most loyal. No, in his experience, this group could never grasp that true loyalty wasn't blind but rather the result of paying attention to events and making an intelligent decision when the time came to test that loyalty. And Julian was both intelligent and loyal. If he ever betrayed Mia Fanzi, he would know exactly what he was doing. And the Don would have had to have earned that betrayal.

But Jilly hadn't refused. Not exactly. He had deferred and asked for some time to consider the task. And now the Wolf was out of action. But something about it was off. Marino had trusted his instinct all his life, and it was screaming at him that this was not a hit but also wasn't a coincidence. Further, he had heard some talk of a woman in black in J's when this all happened. A woman who resembled some of the old stories his nonna had told him. Church craziness, for sure. But, if he was a dog, he was an old and wise dog, and sometimes if it looked like a tasty sausage had been thrown away in the garbage, but that sausage had just a little whiff of bad smell, it was best to leave it be. This Wolf thing had a smell. He wasn't sure what yet, but he wasn't buying this particular sausage.

"Martin!" he said. The garden door opened. He would not have known as Martin was, as always, almost soundless in his movements, but the bump against his leg and the creaking of a big, happy dog getting to its feet could not mean anything other than the arrival of the big man. "Tell Angie I need to talk to him." Martin, in his usual position—down on one knee with the big dog's head between his hands while making dog noises—appeared not to have heard. But the Don knew he had.

Martin got to his feet, turned, and left the garden without a word. Queenie followed. If he had said that didn't bother him a little, Mia Fanzi would have been lying. Goddamn dog. The dogs loved Martin. Everyone loved Martin. Who cared, really. He smiled.

Chapter Twenty-Eight

At the Prince of Peace Roman Catholic Church rectory, William "Father Bill" Wojtanowicz's alarm clock went off at precisely 7 a.m. He did not want to get up. He did not want to save souls. Hell, he didn't want to change his underwear. But, as the swallows return to Capistrano, and the Democrats win every seat in Pittsburgh politics, so did he have to perform his ritual duty: getting out of bed. And so he did. He had a bit of a gut. He was not exactly "in shape." He had been, once. He remembered it, albeit vaguely. He wore boxers. He was losing a bit of hair every day.

After showering and absolutely destroying a cup of black coffee, he looked at himself in the mirror. Other than all those negatives, he thought he was doing pretty well for forty(ish) years old. He did his best Magnum P.I. pose in the mirror. "I'm good enough, I'm smart enough, and goddamn it, people like me," he said, quoting the great Stuart Smalley. Then he let out his breath, which in turn released his stomach to its normal parameters, which he didn't particularly care for.

Eventually settled behind his desk, Father Bill looked at Pittsburgh Steeler Antonio Brown's stats and sighed. He was gonna finish last in the Holy Rollers Fantasy Football League yet again. This year, last place meant he had to get a tattoo. A small tattoo, but a tattoo nonetheless. Well, wouldn't be the first one. How the hell did he always seem to pick the wrong horse? He reflected on his life, as he seemed to more and more these days.

Back at the beginning, when religion had rescued him, literally, from Lord knows what horrible end, he had been so full of energy. Enthusiasm. Excitement even. These days... he had wondered, more so lately, when his enthusiasm had begun to wane. Sure, he could point to events that challenged his faith—the tragedy of 9/11, the increase of gun violence, Cleveland winning an NBA championship. Looked at individually, not necessarily so horrible. But together? Perhaps a sign of the End Times.

He had been able, when he was younger, to throw off these occasional depressive periods, but it seemed to get harder and harder. He looked at the TV. Sally Wiggin was talking about some Russian who had collapsed at an event in Polish Hill. He looked closer and realized it was Alexi Volkov. No loss there. He knew the Wolf. Everyone on the Southside did. Maybe things weren't so bad after all. Maybe, somehow, He (capital H) had something to do with a bad guy being removed from the equation. Yeah, and TMZ was going to be turned into a pillar of salt. He snapped out of it. When had he started to so openly mock divine intervention? He supposed he knew the answer to that question.

"Father Bill!" his secretary/assistant/housekeeper, Sister Mary Lee, called out from some distant place where there was zero possibility she could ever see, hear, or remotely imagine any part of Fathers Bill's morning bathroom activity. Lest her soul burn forever like a road flare after a Kenny Chesney concert.

"Yes, Sister Mary Lee, what is it?"

The nun entered his office. "The Widow Antonucci is here to see you. And she's upset. Sort of. Well, more agitated probably. She's wound up. What the hell do I know?" Sister Mary Lee said, quickly crossing herself for having uttered the word, which she tended to do at least twenty-five times a day on average.

"Wound up?" Father Bill said. "About what, pray tell?"

"Well," Sister Mary Lee said, dropping into the chair across from his desk and leaning forward, delight in her 65 year-old eyes. "Something about the Black Death in a bar on the Southside, that

Russian gangster, and, get this, the Apocalypse!"

"The Apocalypse?" Father Bill repeated.

"I shit you not," Sister Mary Lee said, crossing herself again (although, frankly, sort of halfheartedly—like a shortstop dragging his foot in the general vicinity of second base while turning the double play). Sister Mary Lee, a veteran of her own Holy Wars, crossed herself the way a gunnery sergeant with thirty years of experience salutes a young officer: purely out of habit and without any particular vigor.

"Well, if it's the Apocalypse, you better tell the Sisters of Perpetual Discomfort that the big used book sale is off."

"Your Holiness, I don't mean to speak out of turn"—she always did mean to—"and as a faithful servant of yourself and our Lord as his Earthly representative, I would never presume to offer my humble opinion"—she offered it many times daily on everything from teenagers to poor restaurant service—"but I think the Widow may be on to something here."

The Widow Antonucci entered Father Bill's study. The priest had risen from his chair out of respect and motioned for the woman to sit down in one of the chairs in front of his desk. Today, the Widow was wearing what can only be described as Spanish mourning dress circa 1875 meets Alice Cooper-inspired flamenco dancer. She was wearing some kind of head gear with a veil that Father Bill had not seen before, but he was certain it would have looked fabulous at a bullfight in the event one happened to break out on Penn Avenue.

He wondered if it had been handed down through the ages from mother to daughter, soaked in years of misery and mourning, a sponge of human agony. He shook his head to clear the thought and assumed his best "mildly disinterested but kindly priest who has heard it all" look, leaning back in his swivel chair and steepling his hands over his stomach. TWA settled herself in the chair, fussing until she was comfortable, and crossed a leg encased in support hose that had long ago given up the fight and a pair of light blue Crocs that definitely did not go with the rest of the all-black ensemble.

"The Antichrist is among us," the Widow Antonucci said. "It is true." Then she settled back in the chair and looked at Father Bill with a slight tilt of her head and a look of smug satisfaction Father

Bill could only envy. He was pretty sure he had never felt so confident he had been proven right in his entire life as the Widow did at this moment. It had to rank among the best days of her life. He knew this as sure as he knew the sun would rise tomorrow morning.

After pretending to give this news a moment of deep and careful consideration, the priest said, "Widow Antonucci, what you speak of is serious and perhaps of Papal importance. If it is true, I must immediately make a report to the Vatican in order that His Holiness himself be made aware the Rapture may be at hand. Please tell me all that you know. The fate of mankind may hang in the balance." Father Bill continued his admirable job of keeping the hint of a smile off his face.

"I was at that hired killer's bar on Carson," the Widow Antonucci began. "I went there to see Angie Sedlak. You know I don't drink." She crossed herself. "I was there to talk to that whore about changing her life. But she had not started her shift yet so I waited for her."

"Ms. Antonucci, whore is a term that degrades—" Father Bill started to say.

"She's a whore. Everyone knows it. She had a kid by some Casanova, and now she's trying to latch on to a nice boy who doesn't know better by swinging her ass in front of him and promising Lord knows what." The Widow sat back, and again that look of absolute affirmation, from whom Father Bill did not know, but he suspected probably the CEO of his own organization.

"Can we get back to the Antichrist, Widow?" he asked. "One more whore, more or less, really wouldn't change exis—"

"So I was sitting minding my own business," the Widow continued. "I'm watching the TV news and then the Angel of Death walked in." They both let that sit for a moment.

"Josef Mengele has been dead for forty years," Father Bill said.

"Who the hell is Joe Mengelez?" the Widow Antonucci said. "He a city democrat?"

"Never mind, Widow. Go on," Father Bill said. "You were saying the Angel of Death popped by for a drink."

"Everyone knows who the Angel of Death is, Father. Where did you go to seminary, maybe a correspondence course?" the Widow Antonucci said. "Manon, the Black Angel of Death, was in that bar talking to the hitman. I saw it with my own eyes."

Father Bill stared, forgetting all about affecting his "seen it all" look. "Manon?"

"Yes, that's what I'm trying to tell you. Manon, the Black Death. My mother told me of her, as her mother had told her in the same way. One of the angels who are the Right Hand of God. The hand that He uses to smite his enemies!" the Widow Antonucci said.

Letting the passing thought that he hadn't heard "smite" used in conversation since his second year or so of seminary slide right on by, Father Bill tried to assemble his thoughts. "Widow, surely you are not suggesting God has sent an assassin of the highest order to a bar on the Southside to have a casual chat with an ex-contract killer? Not that I'm agreeing Julian is any such thing. What did they discuss, Julian's views on the Pope?"

"They discussed a contract hit, you numbnuts! What else?" the Widow said. Outside the open door in the hallway, Sister Mary Lee, who was listening intently, crossed herself vigorously. She wasn't sure what the rules were on calling an ordained priest "numbnuts," but having heard it, she was taking no chances.

Chapter Twenty-Nine

Dave Brady buttoned his shirt (black) which he had tucked into his pants (also black). Somewhere in the background, Metallica played. Dave had cut his hair shorter, disdained bright colors, and generally stopped talking to people whom he felt had no ability to impact existence on a cosmic level. Two men, whom Dave did not previously know, had been hanging around him, and he had allowed them to serve as sort of valets. They did whatever he told them to do and didn't ask for any money, so he figured it was a pretty good deal. One was tall, one much shorter. He had named them Lenny. Both of them. He didn't really care who responded when he called, just that one of them did as he had ordered. That their names were, respectively, Asmodeus (tall) and Moloch (short) made no difference to Dave. That they had witnessed the fall of Rome, sacked villages in the Dark Ages, and worn the Stahlhelm of the Third Reich would have likewise not impressed the Almighty Dave. And he had begun to think of himself in this way. Almighty. He was thinking of a goatee. Yes, sort of pointed at the chin.

Dave entered Club Dormont flanked by the two Lennys. He had outfitted them in all black earlier in the day and the three of them looked kind of like a Johnny Cash tribute band, but Dave thought it very cool and hopefully a bit edgy. He sat down at the bar and ordered, his entourage content to stand behind him as they had not been asked to join him.

After a while, the drunk man next to Dave said, "You must be a big timer to have bodyguards, pal." Dave ignored him. The man was beneath his stature. "I'm talking to you, buddy," the man said, swiveling on his stool and putting his hand on Dave's shoulder. Big Lenny placed his hand in turn on the drunk man's arm and looked him in the face. The man's expression changed instantly to wide-eyed fear and he went limp. Big Lenny steered the man by his arm out of the bar to the street. Little Lenny crossed his arms over his chest behind Dave, ever vigilant. Dave smiled. He was starting to like this job.

Dave sipped his martini and awaited the man he was to meet. It was his second drink, and he was starting to feel pretty good. It is an odd feeling to sit in a club and know nobody in the entire place can mess with you and most of the women are looking at you regardless of who they are with. He sort of felt like P. Diddy.

Big Lenny touched his shoulder from behind, leaned in, and said, "He is waiting for you in a back room. When you are ready, come with me, Eminence."

"In a minute, Lenny," Dave said.

"By your command," Big Lenny said.

Fuckin' A, His Eminence thought. Goddamn right, by my command. He sipped his martini. The red guy could wait a bit.

—

Earlier that day, Leonard had sat near the stairs from the upper level of the train station by the county jail drinking beer from a large can concealed in a small paper bag and watching working women coming off the train, giving each a rating out of ten. As entertainment, it beat cable TV and cost him nothing. Between trains, he had time to ponder. The two goth guys in the bar the other night had him thinking. While it hadn't occurred to him until after his conversation with them, he had become aware of a lot more goth types wandering around the city the past few weeks. Like there was an Ozzfest in town or something. Normally that wouldn't have made any difference to Leonard as his taste tended toward classic rock and not that metal shit. Mostly loud noise as far as he was concerned. Led Zep, ACDC, Aerosmith—now those were talented bands.

Usually he dismissed the black-fingernail-polish-coated, tattoo-covered, Doc-Marten-wearing crowd as spoiled suburbanite kids trying to piss off their parents. These two guys were a little different. Mostly because they didn't so much affect the dark aspects of that crowd, but rather kind of projected it. They had dismissed his idea about the neck injury scam but had started to talk about "serving a lower purpose" and that there were "cataclysmic events coming" that would change history. Since they were buying and he had nothing better to do, he had hung around, initially thinking they were a couple typical douchebags talking big. But after a while, he started to believe these guys might be the real deal. It didn't hurt that they told Leonard they thought he should join them and that he was a "good fit for the Dark work ahead."

Leonard had not been complimented often in his lifetime. Frankly most people avoided him like the plague and treated him like some kind of parasite. He couldn't deny that, after a while, he had started to feel a kinship with these two misfits. He decided to meet them at Club Dormont as they had suggested and meet upper management. Who knows, maybe this was his calling. Either way, it was good for some free drinks. As the 8:15 a.m. train eased into the station, he was jolted back to reality. Showtime.

—

Dave Brady was ready. Finishing his third martini, he placed his glass on the bar, turned to the Lennys, and said, "I'm ready."

"Yes, Lord," said Big Lenny. "Follow me."

Across the lounge, Manon, in a black headscarf and sunglasses, watched unnoticed from a dark corner. Dave was lead down a hallway to a door, outside which sat a large man in a black leather motorcycle club jacket. Bowing slightly, he opened the door. Little Lenny preceded Dave into the room, and Big Lenny waited for Dave to enter the room before following him in, taking up a station by the doorway. *So cool,* thought Dave.

A small group of people were in the area, which resembled a living room more than anything else. Comfortable chairs, couches, and tables filled the intimate space. It was dark, but not too dark. Everyone held a drink. The clientele could best be described as circus sideshow glammed up for a night on the town. As people moved out of Dave's way, he eventually faced the Man in Red, who was holding court in a large wingback chair in a red velvet smoking jacket, red pants, and red Armani slippers embroidered with black skulls.

"Welcome, Lord!" the Man in Red said. "Our guest of honor!" He rose from the chair, went down on one knee, raised his glass, and said, "A toast! To the Lord of Darkness! To our Emancipator! The Apocalypse is at hand!"

A glass of wine was handed to Dave by a woman who would not raise her head but only stared at the floor and backed away. He toasted the Man in Red, then raised his glass to the crowd and drank.

Understanding some kind of speech was expected, Dave said, "Minions! Our time is at hand. There is much Dark work to be done!" There were cheers and more drinking. "This man," Dave said, motioning to the Man in Red as he had no idea what his name was, "and I are ready to embark on a journey that has been a long time coming. Too long. Soon all will be revealed!" Raising his glass, Dave toasted the room. A roar erupted and there was suddenly Motorhead blasting from unseen speakers. *Nice touch,* Dave thought.

At that moment, the door burst inward, and everyone turned to see Leonard land face down on the floor. The guard was standing in the doorway ready to grab Leonard and throw him back out into the hall.

Big Lenny placed his hand on the guard's arm. "He's with us," he said, and the big man nodded and went back into the hallway, closing the door. Leonard picked himself up, brushed the dust from his faux satin AC/DC Back in Black tour jacket and looked at the room, which had gone silent.

Noticing Dave Brady, he exclaimed, "Holy shit! Dirty Dave! How you been, bro? I haven't seen you since Pig Nite at Donzi's!

Man, that one chick you hooked up with, fuckin' cow had to go at least—" Leonard stopped suddenly, mainly by the look in Dave Brady's eyes but also as it suddenly dawned on him he should shut up, and quickly.

Switching gears, he said, "Dude! I love ya, man!" He then made a sudden move to hug Dave, too sudden. Big Lenny reacted by grabbing Leonard's arm, forcing him to the floor, twisting his arm behind his back, and placing his boot on Leonard's neck. "Not cool, man," Leonard said, which sounded vaguely like "no coo ma" as Leonard's face was once again pressed hard against a dirty, beer-soaked floor.

Everyone looked at Dave. There was silence. "Suffer the little children and forbid them not," Dave said, looking around at the crowd. Then he smiled and continued, "And neither the assholes. Get him a drink, Lenny. He's one of us."

There was a cheer as Leonard was lifted to his feet, dusted off, and given a beer. In the main room, Manon got up and left the club.

Chapter Thirty

Jilly awoke in his own bed, a bit of a hangover making his thoughts muddy. The ending of the last evening was lost to him. He remembered being at a bar called the Lamb and an old man bartending. An old man who had used his surname. What the hell had they talked about? He didn't remember, but he vaguely understood it had not been specific, just sort of grandfatherly advice. The kind of advice an older, wiser man gives someone who is facing a big decision. Not so much *do this* or *do that,* more *you were born to know what you should do, so just do it.* He couldn't recall a detail of the actual conversation, but he knew he had work to do and it might be the most important thing he had ever done in his life and maybe his sister's life as well.

Anne was in the kitchen when Julian came down to a late breakfast. "You must have tied one on last night," she said. "I gave up around eleven and cashed in." Jilly said nothing, still in something of a haze.

He sat down and said, "Anne, can you make me some eggs, sausage, potatoes, some of that Italian bread toast, and a bunch of coffee? I would appreciate it."

"Well!" Anne said. "Must have been a true bender. Yes, I'll make that for you, but I'd like to hear all the details, thank you very much, Party Boy. Did you meet a woman? Will some poor lass finally make an honest man of our Jilly?"

When she had placed the first cup of coffee in front of him, Jilly said, "I have a serious question for you, Annie."

The familiar form of her name gave Anne pause, although she didn't show it. With a man like her brother, a human Sphynx, when they very rarely decided to talk about serious business, they could be easily spooked.

"Well, a serious question from a hungover man. Quite a morning. Go ahead. I'm ready, brother," Anne said, smiling slightly.

"You told me you believe all this religious stuff. That it wasn't just a routine designed to give people comfort in a better life after this one, especially if this one wasn't so great. What I want to know is, what if that was tested? What if your faith was tested? And I mean truly tested. What if you were asked to do something to prove your faith? Let's say you had to push me off a bridge because some angel told you to. Would you do it?"

Anne said, "Well, that's ridiculous. Faith isn't about extreme tests, it's about daily commitment to—"

"Bullshit!" Jilly said, slamming his hand down on the table. Anne jumped as if stung. "Bullshit. Don't give me that tried and true baloney, Annie. Would you push me off a bridge? Yes or no?"

"Well, I—" Anne stammered.

"Yes or no, Annie," Jilly said.

Anne looked blankly at Jilly for a long moment, there but not really there, remembering things from a long time ago, a mixture of fear and calm on her face. "Yes," she said.

Angelo Fanzi Sr. sipped his expresso and waited on his brother. He was concerned about recent developments. His strength had always been knowing his landscape, applying his experience to situations and making an intelligent call on the probable outcome. Lately...well, lately it had become a bit more like trying to guess the outcome of a wiener dog race. He had seen mostly everything in his seventy-three years, but Angels of Death, crazy Russians, and whispers of an actual Antichrist showing up in Pittsburgh, well. Well.

His brother arrived, as always slowly and with dignity. As always accepting the adulation of those who recognized him. He was a celebrity, after all, in their little microcosm, and Angie Sr. didn't fault his brother for that. He had earned it. The two well-dressed but casual elderly men exchanged a slight hug and sat down again. The tables nearby were empty; it was understood at this place that when the Don was here, he wanted to be neither bothered nor overheard. Angelo had given them advance warning, as he always did, of their pending arrival. Once they had their drinks in front of them—anisette for Angelo, and a Tito's and soda with lemon for the Don—they got down to business.

"So we have a dead gangster, perhaps killed by the Angel of Death, or maybe Jilly, and the Antichrist walking among us, or maybe just some guy from Blawnox with good hair? An interesting week, I think," the Don said, a twinkle in his steel blue eyes.

"The Russian is not dead," Angie Sr. said.

"Really?" Mia asked, raising his eyebrows. "That's a shame. Charlie Katz was a good man."

"A good man," Angelo confirmed. "Volkov is at Mercy Hospital, an apparent victim of a stroke. At the moment, he can't speak very well and isn't particularly...focused. If you want it finished, we have two people who could do that fairly easily and with no connection to us."

The Don stared into the distance, thoughtful for a moment, then said, "No, I think that is best left for now. While he remains alive, there is no successor, so there will be confusion that will make them ineffective for a while. And from all indications, it was natural, so there shouldn't be any particular escalation in violence." He looked at his brother intently. "Was it natural?"

Angelo Sr. shrugged his shoulders. "The man had an apparent stroke, on TV, witnessed by thousands of people. Nobody touched him. What question could there be?" The Don continued to look at his brother, both men knowing Angie Sr. had not answered the question. "I haven't talked to Jilly," Angie said.

"Have you talked to Madonna Antonucci?"

"I have," Angelo replied. "She claims to have overheard a conversation between Julian and a biblical hitwoman arranging for a contract." The two men looked at each other.

"On who?" the Don asked, breaking the silence.

"The Antichrist," Angie Sr. said, deadpan.

"No shit?"

"No shit. Also that this Black Widow is responsible for the Wolf's stroke."

"Putting aside the question of why an alleged hall of fame Holy Hitter needs another hired gun to do her dirtywork, and the fact that Madonna Antonucci hasn't been playing with a full deck since about 1987, is there any reason to believe any of this silliness?" the Don asked.

"None whatsoever," Angelo Sr. replied immediately.

"So you don't believe any of it?"

Angelo looked at him, then said quietly, "I didn't say that. Things have been...strange lately."

The Don looked away again for a moment. He agreed with this assessment. As always, his brother was spot-on with his observations. "Go talk to the priest," the Don said.

At that moment, said priest was sitting at Fatheads with Jilly having an IPA and a kielbasa and pierogi sandwich. Most of which was getting into his mouth and not on his face or in his lap. As always, Jilly had handed him $500. As always, Father Bill had said it was not necessary. And as always, Jilly had insisted and waived the money away as though it was nothing.

"How's the soul-saving business, Father?" Jilly asked.

"Win some, lose some," Father Bill said. "We had a kid get into Harvard, that was a nice thing. Single parent, Mom works at Giant Eagle since Dad left town. Graduate of our summer schools and after school programs. Makes you happy when you feel like you made a difference."

"You do nice work with that stuff," Jilly said.

"Has nothing to do with me," his friend said. "Some sheep are destined to beat the shears. I'm just a lowly shepherd."

"Baloney," Jilly said. "The kids look up to you because you give a damn, just like Father Mike before you."

"He was a good teacher and better than I will ever be," Father Bill said, his eyes not meeting Jilly's.

"Also baloney," Jilly said. "And I only gave him three hundred a month." Father Bill looked up, startled. "I believe in paying for performance, and you are an upgrade, Padre. And besides, my sister thinks you walk on water."

"How's Anne?" Father Bill asked.

"She lugs that cross up Calvary Hill every day. Don't know how she does it," Jilly said, a smile at the corners of his mouth. "I'd like you to tell me when she becomes a saint so we can take out an ad in the *Post-Gazette* or something. Do it up right."

"She's good with the kids and the old folks," Father Bill said. "I'm serious. I think she missed her calling not having kids. She's a natural."

"That," Jilly said, "is a long story, Father, and between her and her Maker."

"Amen," said Father Bill and sipped his IPA. "I need to talk to you, Jilly, about a serious matter," he continued.

Jilly looked at him, but the priest did not meet his eyes. "Okay," Jilly said. "Shoot."

"Well, not here," Father Bill said. "Can you come to my office at the rectory this afternoon? Maybe around four?"

Jilly looked at Father Bill for a long moment. "Sure."

Chapter Thirty-One

Back at the Fairmont Hotel, a team meeting was in progress. Uriel, who had become addicted to Fox News and reality TV, was now certain an enormous conspiracy was afoot, very likely Armageddon. "Anyone see the billboard on Sixth Street?" Uriel asked. Manon and Oliver looked at each other and said nothing. "'The Time is Now'? Neither of you saw it? Am I the only one who is paying attention?"

"The advertisement for the wristwatch?" Oliver said carefully.

"I have no idea what goods are being sold, but I think the message is pretty clear," Uriel said. "Dark forces are being called to action. I believe by the Antichrist." Oliver looked at Manon, who was looking out the window. "Manon, report on the meeting at Club Dormont," Uriel continued.

"The one called Dave arrived with two guards. They were Ancient," Manon said.

"Ancient?" Uriel said. "Explain."

"They are very old—millennia. They are Dark."

"I knew it!" Uriel said. "Go on."

"There was a meeting, in a back room I could not enter. And—"

"And what?"

"I believe the Cambion was there, although I did not see him."

"Then why do you think he was there?" Uriel asked.

"I...I felt him. Felt his presence."

Uriel stared at Manon for a long moment. Then he got up and paced in front of the floor-to-ceiling windows overlooking downtown Pittsburgh. "Oliver?" he said, without looking back into the room.

"Manon's report is consistent with my assessment that we are dealing with a few Dark entities," Oliver said.

Uriel stared out at the city for several seconds. "Dark entities, including a true Cambion, bowing to a mortal human being. Thirty-three other soldiers of Evil suddenly in this place as well. Perhaps we need a billboard saying 'The Antichrist is among us'?"

"Sir," Oliver said.

"What?" Uriel snapped.

"This Dave Brady, I've been doing a lot of research on him and—"

"And what?" Uriel said irritably.

"Well, he's just, I don't know, he's just not really Evil."

Uriel, who still had his back to Oliver and Manon, looking out over the city, said quietly, "He's not Evil."

Oliver did not respond. After a few hundred years, he had learned to be careful around his master, and to be *very* careful when the archangel used that quiet tone of voice.

"Why do you think he's not Evil?" Uriel said, again quietly, calmly, his back still turned, arms across his chest.

"Well, using the System, I can pretty much look at Dave Brady's entire life. Minute by minute if I really wanted to. So, I didn't do that, that would have taken months. But using an algorithm I came up with, I can isolate Dark behavior. Using historical averages, the truly Dark are going to behave...darkly, if you will, in about thirty to forty-five percent of the time range. I just used a composite from 1200 A.D. to 1700 A.D. to get that number. You know, when things were fairly Dark. Not like today."

Uriel, his back still to Oliver and Manon, made a rolling motion with his right hand, signifying to get on with it.

"But that's just the Dark average," Oliver continued. "A true Cambion? That Dark behavior probably goes to sixty, maybe sixty-five percent. I'm extrapolating, of course, as nobody has ever verified a Cambion so obviously we have no historical tracking data and—"

"Oliver!" Uriel shouted, placing his hands on his hips and turning to face his assistant. "Will you get to the point?!"

"Yes, Lord," Oliver quickly said. "If you follow that logic—and it's conservative, believe me—then one would expect an Antichrist to exhibit Dark behavior, what, eighty percent of the time? Eight-five percent?"

"And?"

"Well, Dave Brady, in the thirty-six years since his birth, has exhibited Dark behavior about eleven percent of the time." Oliver finished and stared at the floor, afraid to meet Uriel's eyes. There was silence.

Then Uriel said, "Eleven percent?"

"Yes, Lord."

"Eleven percent?"

"Yes, Lord," Oliver repeated, still staring at the floor.

"Not possible," Uriel said. "Your numbers are wrong."

"Well, Lord, I—"

"You what?" snapped Uriel.

"I—" Oliver stammered.

"What?!"

"I counted, and I wasn't trying to fudge the numbers, honest I wasn't, but I knew you would be upset, and I wanted you to be happy so to make him seem more Dark, I counted—I counted—"

"For the sake of all the saints!" Uriel screamed. "WHAT DID YOU COUNT?!"

"I counted picking his nose," Oliver said. There was a silence. Manon continued looking out over the city, no expression on her face.

"You counted picking his nose as Dark behavior?" Uriel asked quietly. Oliver did not respond, only stared at the richly carpeted floor. "Not possible," Uriel muttered to himself, then headed to his bedroom.

—

Father Bill returned to the rectory, but before he could make his way to his study, he was intercepted by a once again excited Sister Mary Lee.

"You have a visitor, Father. A Mafiosi," she said, eyes sparkling.

Father Bill rubbed his face with his hand and said wearily, "Sister, I haven't heard the word Mafiosi since the Squirrel Hill Film Festival five years ago. Who is waiting for me? Don Corleone? Maybe Tony Soprano?"

"Angelo Fanzi Senior," said Sister Mary Lee, with gravitas.

Father Bill nodded. "Okay. Thank you, Sister. Did you offer Mr. Fanzi a beverage, or were you concerned perhaps that the seventy-something-year-old might garrote you with a teabag, given the chance?"

"He has coffee, Father," Sister Mary Lee said. "And no need to be sarcastic."

Father Bill sighed. He seemed to sigh a lot these days.

Having entered his office and settling in behind his desk, Father Bill said, "Mr. Fanzi, a pleasure to see you again. To what do I owe this unexpected surprise?"

Angie Sr., as ever, was looking calm, cool, and collected while wearing a wool suit. He said, "Father William, it's been too long. I wanted to stop by and see you. You know the Don supports the work you do."

"Yes, he has been generous in his support through the years, and we appreciate it," Father Bill said.

"I wanted to give you this, a small token of our respect for the good you do in the community," Angie Sr. said, handing Father Bill a check. Looking at it, Father Bill pulled in a breath. It was in the amount of $5,000.

"That is very generous..." Father Bill started.

"It is nothing," Angelo Sr. said. "We are all soldiers in His service."

Now, Father William Freelyn Wojtanowicz had been around the block. Hell, he'd been around the block, down the street, into the garage, and down to the basement underneath the garage. So he knew that when someone slides you a $5,000 check for no reason at all, that generally means there's a reason. Usually a big reason.

With a level of carefulness befitting discussing business with the Consigliere of the biggest, baddest Mafia Family in the 'Burgh, he said, "Mr. Fanzi, what can I, what can the Church, do for you?"

"Father William," Angie said, "I'm glad you ask. We're worried." And with that, Angelo Fanzi Sr. sat back in his chair and looked deeply into Father Bill's eyes.

"Worried?" Father Bill said.

"Worried," Angie repeated. "There has been talk, and we understand talk is often just that, talk. But there has been talk of ridiculous happenings on the Southside. Wives tales of angels causing heart attacks, contract murders being discussed with associates of our family. Craziness!"

"Craziness," Father Bill repeated, nodding.

"So you haven't heard anything about this?" Angie said.

"Well, I... This office, Mr. Fanzi, as you can imagine, it can be a... Well, it can be like a gossip marketplace. People are just comfortable talking to a priest, as though they are in a confessional and unconcerned about the consequences of what they might say. I hear so many things, most of which, of course, are inconsequential."

"So you've heard," Angie Sr. said, his gaze not moving from Father Bill's eyes.

"Well, I...I mean lately I have heard stories..."

"From the Widow Antonucci?" Angie said.

Father Bill immediately looked away, and that sealed the fact that he had, of course, spoken with TWA on this very topic. Damnit. Father Bill wondered absently how the hell they knew about that conversation over on the Northside.

"Well, I can share this with you, as you are man of discretion, Mr. Fanzi," Father Bill said. "Yes, the Widow Antonucci did come to discuss certain events she claims to have witnessed."

Angelo Fanzi Sr. stared at Father Bill unblinking, unperturbed, and in no hurry.

Father Bill continued. "Now, Mr. Fanzi, you know Madonna Antonucci is elderly. Bless her heart, she is in here once a month talking about everything from seeing her autographed photo of Myron Cope weeping blood during Steeler games to seeing the Crucifixion in her corn flakes."

"But you believe her," Angelo Sr. said quietly. "On this one, you believe her."

This guy, Father Bill thought. *This guy is good.* "Well, I don't know," Father Bill said, but again he did not meet Angelo Fanzi Senior's eyes.

—

Fifteen minutes after "the Mafiosi" left his office, Jilly arrived, four o'clock, on time as promised. "Julian," Father Bill began.

Jilly noted the formal usage of his name automatically, certain boxes in his mind being ticked, certain levers clicking into place. Subconsciously, as he had for more than forty years of survival, defense mechanisms were triggered, protective systems activated. His posture changed. If Father Bill had suddenly lunged over the desk at his throat, he would have been ready. But of course, that didn't happen.

"This is silly," Father Bill continued. "I understand that. I wouldn't even mention it, normally. I mean, I think sometimes the elderly, sadly, create melodrama in their waning years to make life more interesting. I certainly wouldn't bother you with the fantasies of a sad person who probably forgot what she had for breakfast the minute she..." Father Bill stopped and looked awkwardly at Jilly. He was babbling. This was not the way he had intended to approach this. Jilly sat stone-faced, no expression whatsoever creasing his chiseled features. Father Bill started again. "You know the Widow Antonucci?"

Jilly nodded, only slightly but enough.

"She visits me regularly," Father Bill said. "I think it's probably kind of like therapy blended with the son-in-law conversations she never had. Anyway, yesterday she told me she was in your place and she heard, well, she heard a conversation. You're going to think this is crazy." Father Bill waited for Jilly to say something, but the statue remained stoic. "She thinks a biblical angel assassin wants you to kill the Antichrist." This last was blurted out in a quick monotone that Father Bill thought absently was like telling someone a loved one had died. Just get it out there and then let's handle the blowback.

Jilly stared at Father Bill. They both waited until the silence became unbearable. "So," Father Bill said, just enough inflection on the single syllable to make it a question.

"So, what?" Jilly said.

Father Bill knew he was going to say this. He was pretty sure he may have mouthed the words at the exact same time Jilly said them, as though he was some kind of collar-wearing ventriloquist dummy. "So did that happen or not?"

"Did what happen?" Jilly asked.

"You know goddamn well what!" Father Bill shouted, then sat back in his chair, a little shocked at his outburst.

Jilly sat back in his own chair. His defense mechanisms had eased. He did not need to worry about a serious threat. Some part of him had expected this conversation since Fatheads, and he wasn't really surprised. "Father," Jilly said, "do you know who the father of Angie Sedlak's baby is?"

The priest became visibly uncomfortable. "Jilly, you know I can't—"

"Can't what, Father?" Jilly said. "Can't discuss what might have been said in a confessional?" Father Bill looked down at his desk, a smile just hinting at his lips. He knew where this was going. William F. Wojtanowicz reflected that anyone who thought Jilly the Hitter was a Neanderthal who lived in a cave was very likely to not realize they had underestimated the big man until it was far too late.

"Anyone who has had a drink..." Jilly said, pausing just long enough to make it clear both members of this conversation had imbibed their share, "knows that what is said in a bar, stays in the bar. I'd no sooner expect you to betray your confessional than you should expect me to betray mine, Father."

Father Bill looked at the big man, shaking his head slightly. "I think you could've made a helluva priest, Julian. You are a better bullshitter than most of them. I think maybe Bishop or even Cardinal."

Jilly rose from his chair, understanding the conversation was over. He took two steps toward the door, then turned back to the priest. "If an angel of death HAD asked me to take a contract on a man who might be the Antichrist, hypothetically, and you were me, would you do it?" Jilly asked. He turned his cabby hat in his big hands ever so slightly, a motion Father Bill noticed but was very careful to not telegraph he had noticed. On some level, he understood this was very, very important, and also in that moment understood the very conversation they were discussing had indeed taken place.

Father Bill looked out his window and paused a moment before giving his answer. "Murder, Jilly, is a mortal sin. You know that. I suspect Anne might have mentioned it to you at some point. I can't counsel you to commit a mortal sin."

Jilly nodded. "I am familiar with mortal sins, Padre. You may have heard," he said. "But, of course, Abraham took the contract on Isaac, didn't he? And Isaac was his son." Both men stared at each other in the silence.

"So you think this is a test of faith then, Jilly?" Father Bill asked.

Jilly smiled, then a bigger smile, and Father Bill registered the thought that he liked this man, no matter what the historical record might have to say. "Faddah," he said, adopting an Irish lilt, "my faith took the last train to Clarksville about twenty years ago." Then Jilly winked and said, "See ya in the funny papers," and walked out the door of Father Bill's office.

Three seconds later, just as Father Bill was exhaling deeply, Jilly popped his head back in the doorway. "And I got a good tattoo guy. I hear you're going to need one." And then he was gone.

The phone on the table in the rectory hallway outside Father Bill's office rang. Sister Mary Lee materialized, as she always did. Picking up the receiver, she said, "Ravenite Social Club, how can I help you?"

Chapter Thirty-Two

Dave sat back in his chair on the twentieth floor of an office building in downtown Pittsburgh. Very nice overstuffed leather chair, actually. Very nice panoramic view of the Allegheny River. He sipped extremely good bourbon he could not name from a crystal highball glass which was very heavy and felt extremely expensive. The Dark didn't fuck around, he mused.

He had been called and asked to come here, and he had. He had been advised to leave the Lenny contingent in an anteroom of similar quality and hospitality, and he had. And now he waited. He became aware of background opera music at a volume just loud enough to be heard. As he focused on it, he became involved in it, riveted by it, although he hadn't ever been to an opera in his life and had no idea of what the singer was saying. He became aware of the beginnings of an erection. The music was... the music was evil. It was evil, and it was building. Building to some kind of awful and wonderful climax. He sat straighter in his seat without thinking about it. His vision had become unfocused, which didn't matter at all since he had long stopped seeing anything with his eyes but was rather just sensing things and experiencing visions. Visions of unmentionable, awful things that he nonetheless wanted to see, wanted to see very much actually, and—

The large door to the room opened with what sounded like a crash but was probably a standard, run-of-the-mill creak. The opera music stopped immediately, and Dave vaguely wondered if it had ever been there at all. His eyes slowly focused. His erection evaporated. The Man in Red settled into the identical overstuffed chair facing Dave's. He was dressed in blood red jeans, no socks, dark red Footjoy moccasins Dave was certain were not for sale to the public, not even at Oakmont CC, and a red Vineyard Vines v-neck sweater with matching red polo underneath.

"I've never seen that shade of red before, I'm certain," Dave said, looking at the sweater.

"I'm sure you haven't," the Man in Red said, smiling. "I have a guy at the Vines." He looked at Dave pensively, a hint of a smile on his face. "We need to discuss some things," the Man in Red continued. "I think you're ready to take the next steps."

Dave suddenly said, "Who are you? Where do you come from? I don't even know your name. What should I call you?" Dave's posture had become anxious. He had moved to the edge of his seat, his eyes now darting around between glances at the Man in Red.

"Calm down, Eminence," the Man in Red said quietly. "There are things you are meant to know and things that will be revealed when it is time. You can call me Aza, Lord. It is a familiar form of Azael, which is what I was called a very, very long time ago."

"Azael?" Dave said.

"Google it," Aza said, staring at him with no expression whatsoever on his face. Dave looked at him for a long moment. Then smiled. Then laughed. Aza began to laugh with him.

—

At a corner table of the restaurant at the Fairmont, Jimmy Hallendorf sat and watched the entrance, as he had watched it from 8 a.m. to 11 a.m. the past three days since Angie Senior had given him his latest assignment. He was dressed in what he thought of as Artsy Guy Chic—yellow sportcoat, purple pants, purple scarf, yellow loafers, and black Buddy Holly glasses with clear lenses. (Jimmy's vision had been twenty-twenty as long as he could remember. Sort of a requirement in his line of work.) Looking like a flamboyant black man was a perfect fit at the most expensive hotel in Pittsburgh just as a Ben Roethlisberger jersey, jeans, and sneakers would have fit in over at Jerome Bettis Grille '36 on the Northside. In fact, it was not lost on Jimmy that had he shown up in his normal clothing, he would probably have been noticed by every diner in the place.

White people didn't bother Jimmy. He considered Mia Fanzi a businessman on the level of a Rockefeller and whose family had treated him with respect. Jimmy felt that, on balance, he had met an equal amount of what he considered black and white assholes in his existence, but sometimes white people did amuse him to no end.

Jimmy was looking for a woman. He had been told by Angelo Fanzi Sr. that she was staying at the hotel, was around forty to forty-five years of age, thin, and always dressed completely in black. He was also told by Angie Sr. that she would appear "serious" and should he engage her, he should be "very careful." Jimmy thought this advice cute. At six-foot-three and a still fairly solid 240 pounds at sixty-one years old, Jimmy was very comfortable he could handle a "thin, forty-five-year-old, serious woman." But right now, that didn't matter since he had seen nothing like that description in three days. His assignment had been to follow her if he saw her, that she was of interest to Fanzi business, but that he should not interact with her unless he absolutely had to. Given his time with the Family, Jimmy was afforded the respect of being allowed to ask questions junior associates would never have dared, so he said to Angelo Senior, "This woman dangerous, or what?" He had smiled a little, as he was wont to do.

"Very dangerous," Angie Sr. had said, and did not smile as he turned and walked away.

Very dangerous. *Well, we'll see, I guess,* Jimmy thought. He hadn't been involved with a very dangerous woman since Loretta VanCeil in the days when people in Pittsburgh still remembered Wiley Avenue. And Art Blakey and Billy Eckstine and Earl Hines. Those were the days. *Loretta,* he thought. *She was Damn dangerous. With a capital D. I wonder where you are now, Loretta. I wonder if...*

He jumped a little as a woman who had come from behind

suddenly sat down at his table in the seat opposite him. This happened so quickly he hadn't yet completely registered it when the woman said, "Hello, Mr. Hallendorf. Why are you looking for me?" She was dressed in a black pantsuit and short black jacket, black trenchcoat over it all, and a sort of headscarf holding her hair back (black, of course). She looked at him, squarely into his eyes, expectantly. There was no guile, no anger, no kindness, nothing at all in her expression.

"I..." he said. He couldn't think of anything else to say.

"Let's not urinate our lovely purple pants, Mr. Hallendorf. We don't need third grade all over again, do we? Miss Lowenstein's class, no?" Manon said, smiling slightly.

Jimmy simply looked at her, slack. It occurred to him in some distant part of his mind he probably looked like that damn RCA dog with his head tilted slightly. Third fucking grade? Miss Lowenstein's class? Nobody knew about that. Nobody. Yes, he had peed himself. Yes, he had gone to the boy's room and thrown away his underpants and spent the rest of the day terrified someone would notice. But nobody had. Nobody. He was absolutely certain.

"I'm supposed to follow you," Jimmy said, his expression still slack. He had no idea why he admitted this. He had no idea at this point why he was doing anything.

A waiter approached the table, two days growth facial hair, top knot on his head, slick. "Is there—" he began in a bored voice the less attractive are familiar with when they are in the eatatoriums of the upper classes. Manon, her eyes never leaving Jimmy's, lifted her right hand slightly from the table, her four fingers raising and falling in succession as though playing a saxophone.

The waiter wordlessly turned and left to attend to other diners. Jimmy's head tilted slightly toward the waiter, then back to Manon. Did she just do that?

"Don't follow me," Manon said.

"I won't follow you."

"Yes, I know you won't. Why do the Fanzis care about me?"

"Don't know," Jimmy said. Manon stared at him. "I think it has to do with Jilly," Jimmy continued. It was the damnedest thing, but he really, really wanted to give her the right answer.

"What do they know about Jilly?" Manon asked.

"Don't know, something about a hit," Jimmy said. "I'm supposed to follow you," he repeated.

"Yes, but you aren't going to follow me, are you, Jimmy?" Manon said.

"No, I'm not going to follow you."

"Good. We'll talk again."

"Okay," Jimmy said as Manon got up and left. It didn't occur to him to follow her. He sat there for several minutes, staring into space, slowly returning to normal. Angie Sr.'s words came back to him. "Very dangerous." No shit.

Chapter Thirty-Three

"It is written," Aza said, and he would say this repeatedly, Dave would soon realize in the days and weeks to come. "It is written that the Antichrist will rule the world."

"Yes," Dave said, "I know. For three and a half years and then be killed by Jesus Christ right before the Second Coming."

Dave was no idiot, and ever since all of this... all of this, what? His mind said "craziness." Ever since all this craziness had begun, he had spent a lot of time both at the University of Pittsburgh library and also online doing quite a bit of research. Say what you will about Dave Brady, he came prepared.

"Yes," Aza said. "That is written too. You do your homework, Eminence. But you will come to learn that what is prophesized does not always come to pass. It is, let's say, a blueprint. A plan. And a good one. Most often the building is built according to that blueprint."

"But not always," Dave said.

After a pause, Aza's eyes never leaving Dave's and looking bemused, Aza said, "No, not always."

"So, I may not rule the world," Dave said, a bit too petulantly for Aza's taste.

"You may not be the Antichrist," the fallen angel said, his eyes hardening. "You may be an insurance salesman who couldn't make the high school wrestling team no matter how hard you tried. You may be a complete goddamn waste of my time, and I have been around for a very, very long time." As the Man in Red said this, Dave realized this was a very ancient and very powerful spirit. And that he should be very careful.

Just as quickly, Aza's demeanor softened. He rose from his chair and then took a knee in front of Dave's chair, his head bowed. "Forgive me, Lord," Aza said. "I am an old man with a young man's task on his shoulders. It is no excuse."

Dave placed his hand on Aza's head. "The fault is mine. I am new to this, and I should trust in your wisdom."

"So, nobody knows what is going to happen next. Whether or not someone is the Antichrist, how it's all going to, I don't know, turn out? The whole world? Existence?" Dave said. "Not even you?"

"No," Aza said. "Not even me. Nobody. Nobody on this wretched planet. Nobody from the place I come from, nobody from what you would call Heaven. Nobody."

"Not even God?"

Aza looked up slowly, a mixture of sadness and the slightest hint of humor in his dark eyes. "We don't call Him that."

"You don't call him God?" Dave asked.

"No," Aza said. Seeing the confusion in Dave's eyes, he continued. "God is just a name. He has been called many things. He is the Creator. He is all powerful. He does not win or lose. You may as well fight the wind or the tides. It is believed among my people that the Dark was created by one of his disciples who thought he could challenge him and was cast out. With this casting out came an alternative to the Light. His people. You could choose Darkness."

"But if he can't lose, why would anyone choose to be on the wrong side of Him?"

"That is hard to say. But it is believed that in allowing for the creation of an alternative, He introduced an element of uncertainty to the order of things. To the outcome. Allowed it to be removed from his control."

"Why would he do that?" Dave asked.

"No one knows," Aza said, looking out one of the very large

windows at the city. "Perhaps boredom."

"Boredom?!" Dave repeated, incredulous.

For a time, Aza continued to stare out at this city, and it struck Dave that he was truly old in this moment. His eyes looked very tired. "Let me ask you this," Aza said. "If you had all the money in the world, all the power, anything you wanted, and could control outcomes, behavior, all the time, wouldn't you eventually become bored?"

"I'd like to give it a try," Dave said, flustered.

"No, consider it seriously," Aza said. "It is believed He decided to introduce an element of uncertainty, a scenario even He could not control the outcome of to make it more...interesting for Himself."

"I find that hard to believe," Dave said, shaking his head and sipping his bourbon. "Why would anyone do that?"

"Do you want my opinion?"

"Yes."

"Because we are a toy to Him. An ant farm. If you move a wall here, the ants will turn the other way. If you crush one of their tunnels and a hundred of them, they will build another tunnel in another direction. And you watch. For amusement. If you decide to see one day what will happen if you submerge the whole thing in a bathtub, what the ants will do, what do you care if they all drown? You just go get more ants. That is what I think," Aza said. "He has allowed the outcome to be out of his control because He doesn't care how it ends. He just wants to be surprised, and by being surprised, entertained."

"No shit?" Dave said, in awe.

"No shit," Aza said.

Dave also stared out at the city for a while. Then he turned to Aza and said, "So how did an old soul like you decide to go Dark? To fight the underdog fight against the forces of Good and Righteous? Why the hell would you do that?"

The Man in Red—Azael Al Amin, Aza to his pals, and at that moment around 2,023 years old—sighed. "Well, it involved a woman."

—

That evening, a clean-shaven Leonard sat at the bar at Morton's Steakhouse sporting a new black suit and a hundred-dollar haircut. He had tried to get the money for the haircut from one of the Lennys and instead go to HappyClips and pocket the eighty-dollar difference, but he had been thwarted. Dark jagoffs. He had been assigned to take care of a certain guy who was big in the Democratic Pittsburgh City Government political machine. And liked vodka. And maybe a little coke. And strippers. And some other stuff, if he was still standing upright after the aforementioned. Apparently Super Dave was going to run for mayor. Fine by him. Leonard thought it was funny how sometimes things just fell into your lap. He was born for this job. He felt like a duck that had been wandering around in a desert and was suddenly lifted up by the wind and dropped into a lake in Minnesota.

"Another Grey Goose, sir?" the bartender asked.

"Absolutely, Sparky. And easy on the ice, my man," Leonard replied.

—

Jilly wandered aimlessly through the bookstore that had always felt comfortable to him. The owner of Kosmos Tomes was a bit of a character whose hippy parents had named him Transcendental Kosmos, but whom everyone in Pittsburgh called TK. He knew everyone in Pittsburgh.

"You okay, big man?" TK asked Jilly. "Getting bad vibes off your person. Not bad like negative, just bad like confusion and chaos."

"I'm fine, TK," Jilly said in a tone that really didn't require a follow-up question. But TK's comment hit way too close to home. He was out of sorts.

Ever since the night at the Lamb, he had felt like events were not within his control. That things were moving in a direction that had been almost... No. He wouldn't use the word "preordained." Things had gotten so biblical lately, he simply would not use that word or any like it. He did not believe in any of that. Would not. If it nagged him somewhere in the back of his not-unintelligent mind that his rejection of a higher power would be typical of a man who had killed forty-six people, he pushed that aside too. That way lay madness.

When he was restless, he lost himself in books. To his stand-bys. Hemmingway. How could you not just immerse yourself in the *Old Man and The Sea*? Or Francis Macomber? Steinbeck? Those stories of heart-of-gold, hard-luck Tortilla Flat paisanos always made him feel good. More recently, James Lee Burke. John Grisham and Nelson DeMille's early stuff, when they were comets in the sky, and, of course, Stephen King. Best. Author. Ever. Not so much the scary stuff—after all, Jilly was a story guy at heart—but *Christine* and *Shawshank*, Ma McCausland and *Blaze*. He had read the *Gunslinger* series four times and listened to it on audiobook twice. He felt a connection to Roland. Surprise. And that girl who loved Tom Gordon. Weren't we all lost in the woods at some point?

He wandered the aisles. He had been about to lift a copy of Christopher Moore's *Fool,* which was flat awesome and which he had already read and then listened to three times, from the shelf when he heard, "You won't find your answers here, Hitter." He didn't want to turn around. He knew who he was going to see. But he did. Just like a goddamn Bogart movie.

Twenty minutes later, Jilly sat drinking coffee at Pamela's Diner in the Strip District. Pamela's was always busy and a good place to have a private conversation as the hustle, bustle, and general noise level of the place made everyone fairly invisible. If anyone noticed the large, middle-aged man talking to the slight, middle-aged woman dressed in black, they would have assumed a married couple was out having lunch.

Manon, as was her preference, ordered a few things and then didn't eat them. Jilly ordered several things and ate them all. Jilly had noticed, as it was almost impossible not to, that waiters and people generally didn't bother Manon. Not that they didn't bother her meaning she was okay with them, they didn't bother her meaning they often ignored her. Which is what she wanted. Frankly, Jilly felt that Manon could have stood up, done a pirouette, and flung her coffee against the adjacent wall and nobody would have noticed if she didn't want them to. And then there was that thing with her hand, the sort of finger-waving motion. That was downright scary, truth be told.

Jilly had long been a man who observed life around him with a sort of studied bemusement, feeling a little like he was watching a TV show—interested but not directly involved. Given the early life he had led, very little upset him. He didn't get all that excited, happy, sad, or angry most times. He had, he understood, lived a pretty moderated life the last ten years. This had all changed in the last few weeks. Jilly's personal EKG machine had gone from a nice, steady, narrow bandwidth to the peaks and valleys of the Himalayas in no time at all. Manon fascinated him. He tended to just stare at her; he couldn't help it.

In their first brief meeting at his bar, Manon had been somewhat evasive in her proposition, saying only that she was part of a team that had come in to disrupt events that had been foretold in the Bible involving the end of the world. A man in Pittsburgh was believed to be the Antichrist, and her team was to stop him. Rules of the Universe dictated that they could not interfere directly. Jilly, however, could. Manon knew a lot about Jilly's past and his vocation, and she referenced Anne as well. She implied she had been in the same business as Jilly in another time. That was really the extent of the conversation. No further details were discussed, including identifying her team. Manon had suddenly said she needed to go, but he was to consider what she had told him, and she would be in touch.

Jilly, mainly in a semi-daze during this prior conversation, felt Manon's abrupt departure had something to do with the Widow Antonucci, who had come in and sat down nearby unnoticed by Jilly initially, but apparently not by Manon, who gave her a direct look on her way out. The Widow had been sitting close enough to have heard at least some of the conversation, and Jilly registered that she crossed herself and mumbled something that sounded like words he had heard in grammar school Latin as had Manon left the bar.

"Have you given what I told you any thought?" Manon now asked. Always that very direct look, unblinking.

"Not really," Jilly said. "It's our busy season, and I also had to get my taxes done." There was silence as Jilly stared back at Manon with the same lack of expression. Then he smiled slightly.

Then Manon did the same. It was only for perhaps four seconds, but the effect transformed her into another person altogether. Instantly, it was gone.

"So you have, then," Manon said.

"I have."

"And?"

Jilly looked away for several seconds, then back at Manon and said, "First of all, what you described to me is nuts. Comic book stuff. I'm supposed to buy the fact that you and some God Squad has arrived from another dimension to save the world from End Times, that the Antichrist happens to be living right now in Pittsburgh, that he must be destroyed, and conveniently you can't do it but have selected me, a bartender, to take on this mission which will literally save mankind. That about it?

Manon stared at him and said nothing.

Jilly continued "You understand I don't even go to church, right? Given my history, if there was a God, I'd assume he'd drop a statue of St. Pete square on my head if I so much as dipped a finger in the Holy Water font at Prince of Peace. But I'm your guy?" Jilly sat back in his chair, the ball having been thrown directly back into Manon's court. "I'd be absolutely crazy to believe any of that. Certifiable."

Manon's expression never changed, her eyes never left Jilly's, as she said calmly, "You believe all of it. As does the priest and your adopted Italian family. Because it is true."

Chapter Thirty-Four

"Dave Brady is going to run for Mayor," Mia Fanzi said to his brother. "I don't think that's a good idea."

If it had crossed his mind, and it hadn't, to wonder how his brother knew that, Angie was not one to waste time moving backward. If Don said it, it was true.

"Okay," Ang said. If his brother had said "a meteor is going to blow Pittsburgh off the map in an hour," Angie would have said "you wanna fly out, or you think the Turnpike?" Already Angie Sr's mind was sliding through his mental Rolodex (did anyone know what a Rolodex was anymore?) and considering who they might reach out to. It was a big Rolodex. About sixty years' worth. "Why don't we like him?" Ang asked.

The Don did not answer for a while. "Talk to the unions. This is important." Angie understood his brother had not answered the question, and further understood this was an affirmation of something he had suspected and now knew was true. In a strange and oddly calming way, he was glad.

"Okay. You coming for Sunday dinner?"

"Of course," his brother said absently.

"Okay, see you then," Angie Sr. said. He had some phone calls to make and then some things to discuss that would not involve a phone.

—

"Things are being moved into place," Aza said to Dave, in a very nice boardroom that seated twenty around a very nice and very enormous mahogany conference table equipped with every conceivable gadget for conferences one could imagine. Leonard had the iPad he had been given plugged in and was watching Japanese cartoon porn with the sound muted. Awesome. Since it was just the three of them, there really wasn't much need for the gadgets, but Dave suspected that if need required him to, Aza could get Kim Jong-un or Vladdy Putin on the telepresence in about ten minutes. Dude had global swing.

"Leonard, we'll need your attention here. If you want to watch Asian cartoon characters getting laid, that can be arranged. While your entrails are being eaten by jackals," Aza said flatly without ever looking at Leonard.

This creeped Leonard out to the extreme. He had only known Aza (which he didn't dare call him, only "sir" at this point) for about a week, but the dude was, like, all-seeing. Leonard had never met anyone like this guy. To be fair, Leonard understood he had never met anyone famous either. Or rich. Or generally successful if you got right down to it. Hell, Leonard had been confined for most of his existence to hanging with the barnacles that tended to grow below the water line on the Cabin Cruiser of Life. But that was about to change, was changing already. Leonard needed to Not Fuck This Opportunity Up.

"Yes, sir. Sorry, was doing some research," Leonard said, quickly powering off the device and moving two chairs closer to the Power Couple.

"It is written that you will win over the people," Aza said. "It is my job to ensure this happens. Two days from now, you will be at Market Square when a crazed gunman decides to begin firing a pistol and getting his revenge on the world. You will save the world. Or at least those in Market Square."

"How exactly will I do that?" Dave asked.

"Don't worry, Leonard will handle it. He will give you the details you need to know. Following this event and the attendant media coverage, we will begin your campaign for Mayor."

"Mayor?" Dave said.

"Leonard," Aza said, "is there an echo in here, or is it just an old man's hearing going bad?"

Leonard, who was beginning to learn the value of keeping his mouth shut, said nothing and just looked at Dave.

"Mayor. Yes," Aza continued. "Then, once you miraculously turn this city's fortunes around, Governor. And once you miraculously turn the state around, President. These things are arrangeable, and the Dark's resources are unlimited." Aza said all this without even looking at Dave, mostly staring out the window at the cityscape many floors below. He seemed almost bored.

"You can arrange all that?" Dave, the erstwhile Antichrist and ruler of the planet, said.

Aza didn't respond immediately. He continued to stare out the large windows, his hands clasped behind his back. There was much work to do with this one, he thought absently. "Yes." He sighed, turning to face DB. "All of these things can be made to come to pass. And easily. We can always depend on the truly Dark. They are as predictable as dawn following the night."

Dave joined Aza at the window. Then he turned and faced the panoramic view of a city and three rivers below. "Then it's done," he said. "It will come to pass."

"Nothing," Aza said, "is done. Nothing is certain."

"Well, for fuck's sake!" Dave exploded. "You just told me you can make these things happen! You just sat there and said we can rely on the Dark! Can we or can't we? I'm the one who will be King and maybe squashed by Jesus in his Almighty second coming, and now you're telling me this epochal concert, this Apocalypse, this biblical cataclysm, might be derailed by some undependable roadies in the goddamn grand scheme of things?!"

During this self-righteous tirade, Aza continued to stare out the windows. His ward was validating things that had concerned him in the back of his mind where he could be alone with his thoughts. As a faithful servant of a Dark master, it was not Aza's job to question orders. He never had, he would not now. He had been told this could be the man who would change history. And Aza believed he would. But.

After a pause (during which Leonard had discovered he had been holding his breath. This was better than MMA chick fights. Fucking Awesome!) Aza quietly said, "What I said was, we can always depend on the truly Dark." He stared at Dave.

In the silence that followed, Dave stared at Aza, his righteous indignation slowly, very slowly, turning to fear as the realization of that comment eventually dawned on him. *We can always depend on the truly Dark.* He swallowed. Took a deep breath. There was no turning back now. Truth be told, he had known for some time he was committed to this odyssey wherever it might lead.

"Well, all right then," Dave said quietly, resolutely. And Aza took note. "Who fails us was never truly Dark, and I will make sure their souls burn as an example. Who fails me, fails the Dark. Failure will not be tolerated." As Dave said this, he moved to the window wall and his gaze became flat, not seeing anything in his field of vision but seeing perhaps his vision of the future. His voice, quavering at first, had grown firm and then angry. His hands, now fists at his sides, clenched as he said, "He shall intend to change times and law. The Saints shall be given his hand for a time, and times, and half a time!" Dave's voice rose, and now he was shouting. "And he was given a mouth, speaking great things and blasphemies, and he was given authority to continue!" As he said this, he raised his fists up and in front of him, clenching them so tightly his nails bit into his palms.

And then he relaxed. His back to both Aza and Leonard, he slowly turned and faced them but looked directly at Aza. "For forty-two months," Dave said quietly.

Aza looked at Dave. No stranger to the Bible—he'd been an angel once a very long time ago, after all—Aza recognized both Daniel and Revelations 13:5.

"Yes, Eminence," Aza said just as quietly. "For forty-two months. So it is written." And he bowed his head.

Dave nodded, more to himself than anyone else. "Then let's get moving," he said. "There's a lot of work to be done. Leonard!" Dave suddenly shouted. "Leonard, we're going to do great things, you and I." Dave moved to Leonard and put his hands on his shoulders, and moved in close to his face. "I will make you a king. I will. But if you fuck this up, I will make sure you burn like a road flare for a thousand years." He stared into Leonard's eyes for a few seconds, his eyes illuminated. Bright. Crazy. Then he slapped Leonard on the back and laughed.

"Aza, give Leonard a thousand dollars. Lenny, my friend, you go spend that money tonight. And I mean you spend all of it. Tomorrow, you sleep it off. Nine a.m. Tuesday I will see you at my offices, and you will be ready to go. Can I count on you?" Dave asked, smiling.

"Uh. Yes. I mean, definitely. Your Eminence," Leonard said, stuttering. He actually took a knee in front of Dave and bowed his head as he had seen Aza do. But it occurred to Leonard that the eyes, the eyes were, well, out there. In another place. And that bothered him a little.

Aza pressed a buzzer on the conference table, spoke into the intercom, and a little while later while all three men were finishing their drinks, the door to the room opened to reveal a very attractive twenty-five-year-old woman in a tight dress.

"I'm here for Leonard?" she said.

As Leonard stared at her, uncomprehending, Aza said, "Your maiden, Lord. For your pleasure," and smiled.

Leonard looked at Aza, then at Dave. Then a smile began to form on his face. No shit. He went to the girl, shook her hand awkwardly, and said, "You like wings and beer?"

"Of course. By your command, Lord," the girl said. Collecting an envelope containing ten hundred-dollar bills from the receptionist in the outer room and accompanied by one of the Lennys, Leonard left the building.

After he had gone, Dave looked at Aza and smiled sardonically. "How many buffalo wings will a thousand dollars buy?" he asked. Then his expression turned serious. "I must say, I expected a better supporting cast than an unemployed loser of bar fights. If he shows any sign of failure, I want him out."

Aza said, "He, like you, has been living his whole life for this exact moment. He is fit for the job."

"Very well," Dave said. "But it's your ass if he isn't. Let's meet here tomorrow morning to discuss next steps."

"Yes, Lord," Aza said. "Eight a.m."

Dave, on his way out the door, turned and said "Seven a.m."

"Yes, Lord. Seven a.m.," Aza said, bowing his head.

For a long time after Dave left, Aza stared out into the darkness. *Okay,* he thought. *Okay. We shall see.*

Three days later, Aza would see a very different Dave at what amounted to a staff meeting of about twenty-five of the Dark, in an ornate suite at the William Penn Hotel. Dave sat listening indifferently to the plans Aza was making for his ascendency. They were tedious recitations of meetings, rallies, etc. He knew they were designed to make him look good and get elected, but they bored him. Then at one point, a tall, very pale, slim man interrupted Aza's instructions regarding a city council member.

"Lord, he will not vote the way we'd like," said the slim man, known to the group as Silas.

"Why not?" said Aza, turning to face Silas and looking irritated.

"I offered him everything I could imagine, but he refused," Silas said. "He appears to be impervious to bribery."

"Nobody is impervious to bribery," Aza said. "Try again. We have unlimited resources. Have him followed. Every man has a vice. Your job is to discover his."

"I have followed him for two months now, Lord," Silas said. "He goes to work, he goes home to his family. He doesn't have vices I can see."

"EVERY MAN HAS VICES!" Aza screamed, upset that the meeting had been derailed in this fashion. There was silence.

"Kill him," Dave said quietly from his seat in the corner away from the table.

Everyone turned to look at Dave. Dave looked flatly at everyone. Dressed in a black shirt, pants, and vest, his outfit cost about $2,000 and was accented by a red carnation in his vest lapel. His expression could best be described as bored.

"An elephant doesn't step around an ant on the sidewalk. Squash him and let's move on. We are not here to win minor victories. We are not here to win major battles. We are not here to fulfill some fantasy all of you have had since you were able to get an erection. We are here to affect events of biblical cataclysm. Disruption on a scale that has not been seen but has been foretold. Is anyone unclear on this? Silas?" Dave said, turning his attention to the slim man.

Now, Silas was not a half-assed Darkster. He had earned his stripes in two former lives. He was not Cambion, and he was not truly Dark enough to stick out on Oliver's charts as the Lennys did, but he was not just doing this on the weekends, and he was not just farting in elevators. The man known as Silas had been involved with Stalin in the hard days, and before that a mid-level Visigoth during the most successful period of that people's era. In short, Silas was not one to cower.

"Lord," he said, but Dave noticed without much emphasis and not averting his eyes, a deferential practice Dave was becoming used to. "You'd have me kill a city councilman publicly outspoken in his opposition to you?" The sarcasm in his voice was unmistakable. He looked at Aza for affirmation, but Aza sat stonefaced. Aza was both wise enough and old enough to not interrupt, to let this play out. It was a watershed moment, even if nobody else knew it.

Dave took a deep breath, got up from his chair, and began walking around the table toward Silas, his hands clasped behind his back. "What I'd like, Silas, is for you to handle this. And if you can't handle this, we'll find someone who can. Perhaps we need a better Dark Angel," Dave said, turning to face a mirror above a sideboard, his back to the table as though he were giving instructions about cutting the grass.

The table looked at Silas, who was looking down at his hands folded in front of him. "Perhaps we need a better Apollyon," Silas said quietly, to no one at all. But not quite quietly enough for most to miss hearing.

Well, I'll be damned, Aza thought, instantly thinking he had underestimated Silas. Guy had serious guts. He filed that information, as he had for thousands of years. Everyone held their collective breath.

Dave looked into the mirror behind the sideboard at himself, the table to his back. He smiled. He liked what he saw. Still smiling, he turned slightly to his left to look at a heavy silver candlestick on the sideboard. He picked it up, turned, and in a fluid motion slammed it into the back of Silas' head. The four-pound, sharp-edged candlestick struck Silas' head in a manner that not only burst his skull but splattered bone, brains, and blood all over the table. It took only that one blow to kill Silas instantly—that much was obvious—but Dave struck him three more times, all in the head, and when he was done, dropped the candlestick on the floor. The smile had never left his face. Wiping his hand across his now blood-stained face, he said to Aza, "I'll be in my room if you need me to discuss any further business," and walked out. Elegantly.

Aza didn't need him. The rest of the meeting went remarkably well after Silas' body had been removed. Around the periphery of the table and along with two other staff, a slight woman dressed in a black maid's outfit cleaned up glasses and dishware, unnoticed by the room. Under different circumstances, Aza might have at least felt her presence, but not tonight. Tonight he had been too riveted watching his man come of age to notice Manon. The Black Death.

Chapter Thirty-Five

Leonard's world was filled with guys who were good at stuff. Not stuff you went to Craigslist for. If you needed a guy to get you hooked up to Direct TV, complete with brand new satellite dish for $200 and no monthly fee, ever, there were guys like that. If you needed a guy to get the boot off your car due to unpaid parking tickets, there were guys like that. For Leonard, who'd always known he had certain skills even if he wasn't sure what they were, he had discovered if you needed a guy to pull off a fake shooting in Market Square, Leonard...was your guy.

It took Leonard about an hour to assemble the group of losers, misfits, and potheads who would be the cast of his very own *Les Misérables* to be conducted in full public view. Sitting at a table in Primanti's looking out at the square, Leonard held court.

"I need you dirtbags to pay attention," he said. Looking around the table, he noticed Arnie, who was missing several teeth and always wore the same dirty YinzBurgh hoodie and corduroys, was nodding off. Who the fuck wore corduroys anyway? Leonard guessed they were available in many sizes and colors at Goodwill.

"Arnie!" Leonard yelled. "You fall asleep and I swear to God I will have you thrown in the river with a cinderblock around your neck, ya fuckstick." Arnie snapped out of it so quickly he nearly spilled his drink. Everyone at the table—and it looked like the Pittsburgh chapter of the Varsity Losers Club—had heard of Leonard's sudden rise to importance and likewise knew of Aza, this presence whispered about in the darker venues on the underside of the Steel City. Looking at them, Leonard reflected that every one of them had probably stolen money from their mother's purses. Fabulous. Well, truth be told, so had Leonard.

"Here's the way this is going to go down," he said. "Chooch, you are the key to the whole thing." Dave "Chooch" Jaworski straightened and beamed. "You're gonna have the gun."

And so it was that at precisely 11:36 a.m.—Chooch was six minutes late owing to the fact he had no wristwatch and had been distracted from his cue by a particularly fascinating pigeon who appeared to have a birthmark resembling the Stanley Cup on its chest—that Chooch stood up from the bench he had been seated upon and screamed loudly, "I hated my mother, and I hate all you mothers! I'll kill all of you!" He rushed at the center of the square, waving around a flare gun Leonard had located for him that didn't even have an actual flare in it.

At that moment, said center of Market Square was occupied by the Pittsburgh Chapter of Mothers for Motherhood Mothering Our Precious Children. The MMMOPC had invited Mayoral candidate Dave Brady to speak on Mothers' Rights, and, as such, he was conveniently located to intercept this crazed madman. Which he did. Spectacularly.

The news footage couldn't have been directed better if Leonard had held the camera himself. The Action4 News team was in the square anyway to cover the event and was conveniently rolling when it all went down. Chooch was seen running, waving his flare gun, and screaming about how he was going to "kill all you mothers!" Two apparent henchmen proceeded him into the square, and Dave karate kicked and judo chopped both of them to the ground. Dave launched himself at Chooch just as he was pointing his (empty) flare gun at a screaming woman holding a baby. Dave and Chooch hit the ground, and Dave came up with the gun which he uses to bludgeon Chooch unconscious. A third henchman, on cue, grabbed a stroller containing a baby and began pushing it towards the busy intersection. The baby's mother screamed, "He has my baby!" which News4 audio picked up clearly. Dave tossed the gun to a bystander and ran down the stroller roller, knocking him unconscious as well, and returned the stroller to the crying mother amid cheers and wild applause from the crowd.

Over the next forty-eight hours, Dave Brady is interviewed no less than fifteen times for various news outlets and gets nine full minutes on *Good Morning America*. During each appearance, the interviewer mentions Dave is running for mayor of Pittsburgh, and in every interview, Dave shrugs off any accolades, saying, "I'm sure anyone would have done what I did," as he looks boyishly into the camera. Dave's Q Score, which had to this point been nonexistent, goes to 73 percent.

—

At the Fairmont Hotel, Uri was finishing his morning meditation. In something resembling a cross-legged yoga pose (cross-legged but not with his hands steepled in front of him), he faced the floor-to-ceiling window of his hotel room that looked out on Point State Park. It was a pretty sight, especially with the sun rising behind him and lighting the view, but Uri may as well have been staring at the sheetrock of the Southside Budget Hotel for all that he was paying attention. His eyes were closed. He murmured his daily affirmation. "I am strong. I am wonderful. I am God's Messenger. I am not a dick." Okay, that last one was probably part of Oliver's Wish List for Uri, but let's not dwell.

In these moments, essential to his state of mind, Uri tried to carry positive thoughts to his vision of how the day might unfold. On this day he was particularly intense in his focus as he knew he had a conference call with the Holy Host. He never looked forward to these calls, but much like the degenerate gambler who knows he's probably going to lose, he nonetheless lived for the anticipation. Maybe it would go well. Of course it would.

During these sessions, always right after his morning shower, Uri wrapped a towel-like garment he had brought with him around his midsection in order that his skin, such as it was, would not touch the filthy Earthly fabric of whatever it was he was sitting on. Uri believed, deeply, that Earthly things diluted his post-Earth self. So, it was this scene that Oliver, frantically searching for Uri, stumbled upon when his knocks to the outer door of Uri's suite went unanswered.

"Lord, I—" Oliver said and then froze. He was looking at Uri, who appeared to be in a diaper, with his arms outstretched, and sort of, well, rocking from side to side while singing what appeared to be the theme from *Frozen*. Oliver loved *Frozen*.

Uri stopped singing immediately. His whole body shuddered, and he lowered his arms. He did not turn to face Oliver. He breathed in deeply. He bowed his head before lifting it again, took another very deep breath, and said, quietly, "Yes, Oliver?"

Oliver, who was frozen (no pun intended) into a state of shock and awe, only made a sort of guttural sound. Uri waited.

"Lord, I—" Oliver tried again. "I have the..." He searched for whatever the hell it was he had that he couldn't remember. It was just that the image of his boss, diaper clad, his arms outstretched, singing "The cold never bothered me anyway" had interrupted his mind the way a reboot would interrupt your iPad. He was still getting back online. "I have the—the reports..." Oliver said, slowly remembering what it was that had sent him to this room in the first place. Yes, the reports.

"And...?" Uri said, getting to his feet, the garment that had clothed him falling away.

Oliver averted his eyes so fast that he probably pulled some kind of optical muscle, his head turning so abruptly away from the vision of a naked Uri that his entire body essentially pirouetted, and he crashed into the glass dining table in Uri's suite. His papers scattered as he ricocheted from the table and fell to the floor, pulling the tablecloth—on top of which was a carefully presented breakfast of croissants, fruit, and coffee—with him. He didn't care, he was happy. Happy because his head, and by extension his entire field of view, was now swaddled in a tablecloth. He could see nothing. His body hurt, although he was pretty sure the twinge he felt was less muscle pain and more a bit of nausea.

Uri stared at the mess on the floor that was his assistant and said, "Clean that up, you idiot. I'll meet you back here in ten minutes, and I expect a full explanation."

As Uri stalked away, Oliver reflected that, much as he would try, perhaps for eons, to forget it, he had seen the Promised Land. And it was nothing. Nothing. His Lord and boss, at least on Earth, was a Ken doll down there. His entire body convulsed in relief. Thank you, Jesus.

Chapter Thirty-Six

Jesus checked his calendar. He knew what was on his calendar, he always did, but he checked it anyway. He was that kind of guy. Well, not guy, per se. Anyway, the point is, Jesus was thorough. When you are sent to a planet by your Dad where your goal is to pretty much get persecuted and die, you learn to cross the T's and dot the I's. And he had.

Jesus was a good dude. He just was. You'd pretty much expect Jesus to be a diva, but the fact was Jesus Was Not A Jagoff. And he had a right to be if he wanted, to be fair. As ecclesiastical rock stars go? Top of the heap. The Elvis of the afterlife. And yet, everyone—and by everyone that means not just the heavenly suck-ups and the groupies, but literally everyone—loved him. No, liked him. That's more important. He was the really good-looking captain of the football team you just wanted to hate but then he'd remember your birthday, or that you liked pizelles so he'd give you a bag his grandma made. That guy. You just liked him. When he blew by in a crowded place but patted your shoulder as he went past, you just felt good—*You see that? He knows me. I know that guy.* That was Jesus.

"Uri on the call today, from down there?" Jesus said to his assistant.

"Yes," his assistant replied. He was a eunuch who had been consigliere to a pharaoh a very long time ago. He did not say "Lord." Jesus forbid that with his staff. Of course he did. He would say, "There is only one Lord, and He is not me," and smile to put everyone at ease.

"The Antichrist thing?" Jesus confirmed.

"Yes," his assistant said again, handing him his robe.

The robe was simply fantastic. From ten feet away, you'd have believed it weighed thirty pounds, so ornate was the embroidery and quality of fabric. But in fact, it weighed exactly one and a half pounds. Jesus had maybe twenty of these. There was a valet whose sole job for eternity was to keep his robes looking showroom new—not *all* Jesus' robes, mind you, just the ones he wore to meetings. The fabric was fairly light and not particularly cumbersome.

All things being equal, Jesus would have preferred a simpler garment, as he'd had on Earth so long ago. After all, if Mick Jagger or Michael Jordan shows up in jeans and a white Oxford shirt, who really cares? But Jesus understood that the people wanted a little bit of pomp and circumstance. You want to stand outside Buckingham Palace for hours and then Queen Elizabeth comes out in sweats and a hoodie? No.

"Let's go with blue today, buddy," Jesus said, handing the robe back. His assistant bowed his head, stepped into the enormous closet, and returned with a royal blue robe that had been custom embroidered by a woman who had served as Genghis Khan's tailor back when Earth was a different place. "Ahh, I love that one. Thank you, sir!" Jesus said, pulling it on over his head and then patting his valet on both shoulders. "Perfect for today.

"Did you know that on this day in 337, a devout Christian man named Jerhousa—from Esterius, a province near the Mediterranean—was wrongly brought up on charges of theft when the local Majordomo decided to settle an old score and get Jerry stoned?"

"I was unaware of this," his valet said, brushing nonexistent dust from the shoulders of the garment.

"Yep," Jesus said. "But when they convicted him and took him to the quarry, guess what happened?" His valet just looked at him. "The stones fell to the ground and his accuser collapsed and perished of an apparent heart attack. I just love that He did that," Jesus said, inclining his head toward the offices further down the Executive Wing from his own. "So epic. So Him."

The Executive Wing (not an official name) contained Jesus' living quarters, some really sweet conference rooms, some support staff, and Him. Nobody called God "God." It was truly strange. Even if on Earth you had believed in God with every fiber of your immortal soul, once you died and came to this place, you stopped calling it Heaven and you started referring to God as "Him," or "He," as the case might be. First of all, the name "Heaven" seemed trite once you got here. A better fit to describe a good red velvet cake or a lyric in a lame country song. Blue Ridge Mountains, Shenandoah River. This place was beyond any Earthly explanation. It was like calling the Grand Canyon "neat." This place just Was. It was just referred to as Here. As was the guy in charge, the Creator. "He" was not an indication of sex, male or female. He had no sex, that would have implied "He" was like anyone else. He was definitely not.

This particular morning, Jesus had to see Him. In the general hierarchy of the afterlife, He and Jesus were different from everyone else. Jesus was different because he had not been born like every single other soul Here, save Adam and Eve (who ran a truly terrific Bodega somewhere West of St. Pete's Gate). If you read scripture, Jesus was the Son of God. So of course he was the number two guy. Or gal. Whatever makes you happy; it didn't really matter as Jesus had no sex, just as He didn't. If you were in the room with Jesus, did he look like a thirty-something, bearded, really cheerful male? Yes. He did. Turns out all those cheap dining room paintings are spot-on. Although the creepy paintings that also had the burning heart with a sword through it are waaay off. And he looked fit. Actually fairly muscular in a male gymnast sort of way. Not in a Mr. T sort of way. Not that ripped. But you kind of knew you were just seeing what you expected to see. What you had been taught. It was pleasant, and it put you at ease. In a similar fashion, and yet different, was Him.

Very few souls saw Him. And everyone was okay with that. Did you love Mr. Rogers? Yes. Did you ever meet him? No. If you had the chance to meet him, are you sure you would want to? What if that day he had some toilet paper sticking to his shoe or had missed a spot shaving? Wouldn't you rather have been content with your own image of the way you saw him? Forever a forty-something older-brother-looking guy in a sweater and Keds who you never, never had to worry was going to do you wrong. Who cared about you, even loved you. Even if you might have thought nobody else did. Even if you thought maybe you weren't worthy of that love. And in the same way, most never saw Him. They just knew He was there. Like Mr. Rogers every morning on your TV screen.

To those who saw Him—and this was not limited to the Holy Host, nor even to souls who had left Earth—he appeared as your interpretation of Him. If He decided you would see Him, then He wanted you to be comfortable. He had no particular reason to make you feel afraid. You couldn't have harmed him under any circumstance anyway, and his interest in you was mainly curiosity. Like a kid examining a ladybug. Well, this is interesting. Would you try to terrify a ladybug? Why? Contrary to the Brimstone School of religious doctrine, the Creator of All Existence wasn't too concerned about terrifying you into obedience. Too easy. Not interesting at all. No, he was more interested in presenting choices and then watching the outcome.

Jesus made the relatively short walk down the hall to His office. Nodding at the secretary outside His double doors (Jesus was the only one who didn't need an appointment), he knocked twice, as was his custom. After a few seconds, he heard a voice say, "Come in," and he did.

His office was very, very pretty. And light. Very light. All windows, outside of which were clouds and sun and the occasional very pretty bird way off in the middle distance. There was a large desk and a "man" seated behind it. There were very comfortable chairs in front of it as one would have expected. Jesus took a seat in one. To Jesus, He looked like a larger, older version of himself. This was Jesus' perception of Him. He saw a somewhat rotund, although not fat, bearded elderly man with half-moon reading glasses around his neck and a slightly distracted air about him. Think Santa Claus after a couple months on Weight Watchers. He was reading papers and had a pen in one hand which he occasionally stuck in his mouth. On some level, Jesus understood the vison in front of him was not, strictly speaking, real. Likewise, although he'd never discuss this with anyone, Jesus understood the Creator couldn't actually have a son. At least, not in the manner most would understand as offspring. But Jesus understood the concept that he had been Created on a different level than any other bird, or blade of grass, or human being. And that was good enough for him.

"Sir," Jesus began. And the man in front of him lifted one hand slightly in a "hold on a sec" motion, continuing to read the papers in his hand without looking at him.

Then, putting the papers down and turning, He said, "Honest to Me, I wish Brad and Angelina would get their act together. Seriously." Then a broad smile spread across his face and he laughed loudly. Jesus laughed along—he couldn't help himself. This entity always seemed so amused. Like a new grandmother watching a toddler. Even when that toddler started eating dirt from the potted plants. "Anyway, looks like Aza may be up to some bad business down there," He said, changing the subject, His eyes virtually twinkling. Jesus was always surprised at how He seemed to always know things even though that sorta made a hell of a lot of sense if you thought about it. "The guy has spunk, I have to give him that," He said.

"Aza's business is usually bad business," Jesus said. "What's he up to now?"

"Oh, you'll hear about it in your briefing this morning," He said. "I'll be interested to see what you think. But that's not why you came to see me."

"No," Jesus said. "I had a conversation with Michael yesterday. He's concerned about Uri."

—

Martin, the Don's "friend" and sometimes consigliere on the "softer" matters, hated hospitals. And doctors. And nurses. And that antiseptic smell, and all the very sad, old people in wheelchairs that always seemed to be sitting in hallways waiting to die. Every single time he left a doctor's appointment, he went and made it a point to spend a lot of money on something, anything: clothes, shoes, a really expensive haircut. Made him feel more alive. Today he wasn't sure he could spend enough. And he hadn't told the Don where he was going.

Emil Roth was a very good doctor. Martin had known Emil from way, way back. From grade school. From when Martin was known as Marty Epstein to those who knew him and cared about him. And those people were few. Both had taken alternate paths through life. Emil had become a doctor, which pleased his parents. But he never had children, and he had married a woman of Mexican heritage, which was something a bit avant-garde in his world and the closely-knit community of Squirrel Hill. Martin liked Emil very much, loved Juana Roth, and Martin trusted Emil. They were, had remained, very good friends.

But until today, Martin had never been in Emil's' office, had never asked his professional opinion, had never needed to. And today Martin hated Emil. Hated his office, the antiseptic smell, and the people in his waiting room whom he very carefully avoided making eye contact with. For Emil was a specialist, and a good one. Emil had decided long ago what field probably offered the best job security. Martin had not been able to miss the brass placard outside the office which read: Dr. Emil Roth, Oncologist.

Chapter Thirty-Seven

Uri was ready to go. He had been ready for about fifteen minutes actually, carefully going over what he planned to say again and again in his head. When the time came, he was staring at Oliver's computer, waiting for the red light to go on. Three o'clock came and went and no feed from the Holy Exalted Team. Always fashionably late, this crew. He shook that thought and told himself to concentrate.

At this point, Oliver came into the room and closed the door behind him. Uri glanced at him, annoyed. Manon had come to the room ten minutes early and sat quietly out of camera view in case she was needed. Oliver was also supposed to have been here early, but Oliver was habitually late and disorganized. Uri made a mental note to raise that issue on his next performance review. Oliver was eating some sort of conical orange crackers with a disgusting odor that reminded Uri of rotten cheese. If that wasn't bad enough, he was crunching them in a particularly disgusting manner that called to mind swine eating slop from a trough. Uri grew more annoyed by the second, trying to clear his head and maintain focus. No red light yet, no feed.

Oliver belched, giggled, looked at Uri's scowling face, and said "Sorry, I—" he began, interrupted when the bag of Bugles slid from his cheese-powdered hand. As he tried to grab it before it hit the floor, he smacked the bag out of the air, causing a shower of Bugles to cascade over Uri, one going into his mouth, which hung open in amazement as he watched this scene unfold. Oliver leapt to his feet and began brushing Bugles from Uri's white robe, the good gold-trimmed one he saved for occasions like this.

"Get. It. Out. OF MY MOUTH!" Uri screamed, trying desperately to not swallow the horrible Earth cracker that had invaded his oral cavity. "GET IT OUT OF MY MOUTH! ITS DISGUSTING!" Neither he nor Oliver had noticed the small red light come on in the corner of Uri's open laptop.

The Holy Exalted Team, for their part, saw a feed of Oliver's backside wiggling and his arms appearing to jerk back and forth as Uri, partially seen seated and at Oliver's waist level, screamed at Oliver to get it out of his mouth. Oliver's backside suddenly moved out of camera as Uri repeatedly spit and made hacking noises. Wiping his mouth and gathering himself, Uri finally looked up and noticed a feed of several faces staring at him from the laptop screen.

After a moment of silence while everyone digested what they had seen and Uri tried desperately to focus his mind, all the while processing what the scene must have looked like from the point of view of the HET, a disembodied voice from the computer said, "If you're busy, perhaps we could come back another time..."

There followed a few more seconds of silence, then a snicker. Then a snort. Then several snorts and giggles, and then wholesale laughter. Someone was laughing so hard, in a sort of high-pitched hooting, that everyone got going again.

Uri, forcing himself to try and maintain some semblance of dignity, could only manage, "I...I wish to report."

As the laughter slowly subsided, a voice that could only be Jesus' said, "Report, Uri." And the laughter finally died away.

Uri began. "I have reason to believe the Antichrist is among us and is readying himself to fulfill biblical prophecy." Uri paused to let that sink in and began to feel a little more confident in his serious message.

After his pause, another disembodied voice, which Uri was pretty sure belonged to a saint who had been disemboweled by hummingbirds in about 100 A.D., said, "Well, that's hard to... *swallow.*" And they were off to the races again, shrieking, howling, and again that high-pitched hooting that just made everyone laugh even harder.

"Please," Jesus finally said. "Please, let's have some quiet and allow Uri to report. Please."

Eventually the team quieted down again and Uri continued. "It is the intent of Dave Brady to become Mayor of Pittsburgh, then Governor, and eventually President of the United States. He is being assisted by a Cambion named Azael and approximately thirty of the Dark. Manon witnessed this Dave Brady murder one of his Dark henchmen at a meeting where the plans for his ascendency were being discussed. He is maturing in his Evilness and following prophesy, which we all know indicates one will come to power by appearing to be good before his true nature is revealed."

"Can Manon report?" Jesus asked.

"Yes, Lord," Uri replied.

Manon came and sat next to Uri in camera view. "I witnessed approximately thirty Dark at a meeting discussing plans for Dave Brady's ascendency. They appear to be organized, are backed by true Dark forces, and Brady..." Manon paused.

"Manon?" Jesus said. "Brady what?"

"He's becoming Darker, Lord."

"Darker? Explain."

"I watched him murder a henchman without remorse, and I think he, well... I think he enjoyed it.

"That doesn't make a man the Antichrist, Manon," Jesus said.

"No, Lord, you are correct, of course. But I don't think this man could have done that two weeks earlier. Maybe not two *days* earlier. He is growing more comfortable and confident in what he believes is his destiny."

"What he believes is his destiny may only be what Azael is whispering in his ear and not Prophesy," Jesus said. Manon said nothing. There was a silence as everyone waited for Jesus' response while he considered the information he had just been given. Eventually, he said "Uri, you and your team are doing good work. HET will consider what you have reported, and we will offer direction when that consideration is complete. Until then, we will consider this not to be an Alter Existence matter, and you are to stand down until further instructed. That is all."

"But, Lord, I—" Uri began, stammering, unable to believe the matter was not being taken seriously enough.

"That is all, Uri. And thanks," Jesus said.

Uri just stared at the laptop as robed people began to move out of camera view. Then someone said something Uri could not clearly hear, and the laughter erupted all over again. Then, mercifully, the screen went blank. Uri just continued staring at the black screen, a slack look on his face.

"Lord, I'm sorry, I—" Oliver began. Uri, not turning to look at Oliver, just raised his right hand in a stop gesture, and Oliver fell silent. Then Uri waved his hand in a motion clearly indicating Oliver should go away. He did, and Manon followed, closing the door behind her. Uri sat silently for a long time.

—

Anne and Father Bill watched the kids play in the Prince of Peace Rec Hall playground area. Father Bill was always impressed with the calm but firm way Anne handled the youngsters. It wasn't that she was sharp with them—at least, unless they had earned a rebuke. She was just no nonsense. But you could tell she genuinely cared for all of them, even the troublemakers. In fact, Father Bill thought sometimes she did her best work with the troublemakers, and Prince of Peace had its share. The Southside was mainly a blue-collar area, and at ten dollars a day, subsidized by the church, the day care was very popular, particularly with single moms who didn't always have the time to instill discipline in their high-energy five- or six-year-olds after a long day at work. All her young charges called Anne "Baba," which is an eastern European term for grandmother, and although Anne was only in her fifties, she didn't mind it.

Anne received $250 per week, the two younger girls who helped her on alternating days got $100 each. Father Bill knew Anne would have been a bargain at twice the rate of pay, but the reality was Anne did not have to worry too much about money as all her expenses were taken care of by Jilly, who also put $500 a month into her checking account even though she had long ago given up telling him not to. Anne never had been a person with champagne tastes and couldn't spend the money she had. She saw the reduced wages as a way of giving back to a church that had been a refuge for her when she felt there had been nobody else but God to talk to. But she was past all that nonsense now.

There was just no way around using the word "motherly" to describe how Anne handled the kids. That mix of love and discipline, born out of fear for the children's well-being, could not be missed even by a lifelong bachelor like Reverend William Wojtanowicz. The priest had broached the topic of why Anne had never married and had children of her own a few times but had always been immediately and firmly rebuffed, Anne's typical no-baloney response being something along the lines of "That's between me and my Maker, Father. No offense." Father Bill took no offense and eventually stopped asking. She was right, it was none of his business, and he was just glad to see the kids had such a valuable presence in their lives.

"I was thinking the other day—it's my nature to think about logistics, as you know," Father Bill said. "Kind of a hobby, I guess." Anne turned to look at him expectantly. "How do you think they handle the prayers up there?"

Anne squinted her eyes in a quizzical look. "What do you mean, Father?"

"Well, we live on a planet of billions of humans, and more than a billion of them are professed Catholics. Plus, you have to figure non-Catholics pray to God. We don't have exclusivity in that regard."

"Yes?" Anne said, still confused.

"Well, I just mean if each person in the group we are talking about throws up even a single prayer a day on average, that's more than a billion prayers a day that are directed at God. Even if He never sleeps and does nothing but listen to prayers, that's like forty million prayers an hour, six hundred and eighty thousand a minute, eleven thousand a second. I worked it out. Every second of every minute of every hour of every day. How can He handle that kind of volume? He's gotta have help. There's no other possible explanation."

Father Bill sat back and stared off into the playground, watching the kids. Anne continued staring at the side of his face for a long moment, then also stared out at the kids, although she wasn't really watching them. She was deep in thought.

Finally, still staring ahead, she said, "Well, that's ridiculous." Then suddenly realizing what she had blurted out, said, "No offense intended, Father," and crossed herself.

"None taken, Anne, and I hope I didn't upset you. It's just my nature to consider things like this from time to time. Keeps my mind from growing stagnant, I guess."

"Do you think he has a bunch of angels with headsets sitting at computers, Father? Listening to prayers as they come in? Maybe randomly answering them yes or no, or elevating the serious stuff to a supervisor?" Anne said, a smile widening on her face. "Kind of like the Jerry Lewis telethon, maybe, Father?" She was laughing now, tears in the corners of her eyes, her hand covering her mouth.

"Well, it's possible, isn't it?" Father Bill said, somewhat defensive and slightly embarrassed at being laughed at. "I mean, anything is possible, because we don't really know how it's all handled. Don't get me wrong—I am certain our prayers are heard and each considered seriously. I just wonder sometimes how that all works. That's all I'm saying," he said, still a little annoyed and embarrassed.

Anne looked at the priest, the hint of a smile still on her face, although she had calmed down. "I'll tell you what I think, Father. I think He hears every one of them and in his way responds to every one of them. Just as he hears and sees everything because he is everywhere, all the time. And He is a vengeful God, my God. He rewards, but he also punishes. His rules are strict, and he does not forgive unless the sinner truly repents her sin." Anne paused for a few seconds, then said, "I am very, very certain of that, Father. That is my God."

Father Bill noticed Anne was no longer looking at him, or the kids in the playground. Her gaze had become unfocused, staring at a middle distance but not really seeing anything. She was not smiling anymore, either. Although Anne would not recall it, Father Bill had not missed the use of "her sin" in the statement Anne had made.

Chapter Thirty-Eight

Leonard was living large. There was no other way to describe it. He was so far removed from his life just six months ago that it sometimes literally took his breath away. He had money, doled out by Aza. He had a car at his disposal—badass monster black Escalade that there was no chance he could park on the Southside, even at four a.m. But that was okay. Because he also usually had one of the Lennys. They drove him. They dropped him off. They did what they were told. They beat up guys who would have beat up Leonard only a few months ago. A guy who used to spend large parts of days at the race track picking up losing tickets and running them through the machines just in case someone threw away a winner, now tipped the valet guys at Morton's steakhouse ten and twenty dollars like it was nothing to him.

And the funny part about all of it was he really wasn't doing anything differently than he always did. Drinking, bullshitting, lying about himself, smoothing on women—it was all the stuff he had always done. The difference was he had guys behind him. He now had a rep.

If Leonard, for example, had even so much as asked City Councilman Barney "Busta" Nutt for a light for his cigarette a few months ago, he would have not only been completely ignored, but worst case one of Busta's goons would have probably told him to go pound sand and stay away from the big guy. Now, not only was he not shunned from this crowd, he was at this very moment buying Barney Jaeger shots at J's while introducing the politician to girls who, under any other circumstance, wouldn't have given either Leonard or the balding forty-seven-year-old the time of day. But that was thing about the Dark. It was like the women, the booze, the money just came so easily.

Jilly watched Leonard and his party from his usual stool behind the bar. The transformation of Leonard had been interesting to Jilly, but he wasn't entirely uninformed. Manon had mentioned Leonard to Jilly during their meeting. He was to be wary of Leonard, as he had gone over to the Dark. Jilly took this information with a little bit of humor as Leonard had been such a compete fuck-up for such a long time, it was hard to take him seriously. But watching him this evening, Jilly understood Manon was right. But what the hell, Manon was always right.

Leonard, as usual, had not gotten the memo. He had no idea about Jilly, Uri, Manon, or most of the grand plan. What he knew was he had stumbled into a very good thing, and if Super Dave Brady was buying, he sure as hell wasn't going to ask too many questions. Yes, Aza was a little scary, but Leonard had dealt with scary people his whole life. Yes, Dave Brady was probably a guy who was too pretty with too much money and whose ego was running his life, but why the hell would Leonard care?

"What the fuck is up with Leonard?" Angie Twice asked from his usual stool, end of the bar nearest Jilly, back to the wall. "He hit the lottery? Maybe marry a rich widow? What?"

Jilly didn't answer, just continued to watch the proceedings at the other end of the bar. Leonard and Busta Nutt. That was surprising. Or not so surprising.

Leonard came down to Jilly and Angie's end of the bar. "Gentlemen!" he said magnanimously. "Can I get a Crown, rocks?" Jilly looked at him and then turned to make the drink. "Would you guys do a shot with me? Crown? That stuff is golden," Leonard said. Jilly placed the drink in front of him. Leonard looked at both of them. "Yes, or no? C'mon, I'm celebrating."

Angie turned on his stool and looked at Leonard, putting his newspaper down on the bar. "Leonard, why don't you take your Crown and shove it up your ass." Having finished, Angie continued to look into Leonard's face.

"Hey, that's not cool, man," Leonard said. "I'm trying to buy you a drink here. Jilly, what's with him?" Jilly looked at Leonard with his perpetual stony expression, both hands face down on the bar.

One of the Lenny's, the bigger one, moved up from the other end of the bar, placing himself between Leonard and Angie Twice. "You okay, boss?" he asked. "Having any trouble?" As he did this, and facing Leonard to his left, he rested his hand on Angie's shoulder, who was seated to his right. The move was seemingly innocuous, but it was calculated to let Angie know the big man was going to protect his boss. Leonard was quietly pleased his bodyguard had moved in. Then he heard the click.

Angelo Fanzi Jr. might not be Dark and might not have been an evil henchman for three lifetimes, but he was in his element. His eyes had never left Big Lenny's, and he had never made a noticeable move, but he had carefully slid the bluesteel .38 from his waist and pressed it into Lenny's stomach while cocking the hammer. "You are invading my space," he quietly said into Big Lenny's face. "That is inconsiderate." And then Angie Twice Fanzi smiled. The big bodyguard/henchman moved his eyes down to his stomach at the pistol.

"Hey, hey, hey," Leonard said. "Let's all take it easy here. Just having a good time. No worries. Lenny, I'm good," Leonard said to his bodyguard. "I'm good. No worries." He patted the big man's shoulders. "Can you go make sure Busta is doing okay?" The big man looked at Leonard, then down at the pistol pressed into his stomach, and then slowly at Angie.

"Sure, boss," he said and moved away. In an instant, the pistol had disappeared from whence it came.

Leonard's eyes lit up as he looked over Angie's shoulder at the entrance to J's. Dave Brady had arrived. Leonard hustled him down to the other end of the bar and shouted at Mandy to get Dave a drink. "A toast! A toast!" Leonard said as Jilly and Ange watched from the other end of the bar. "To the next Mayor of the 'Burgh!" Everyone in their crew cheered, raised their glasses, and then waited for Dave to say something.

"Well," he said, "you are too kind. My opponent has a lot of support, and it will be an uphill battle to unseat the Honorable Charlie Connor."

"Ahhh," Leonard said, "fuck City Hall, fuck the Democrats, and fuck Charlie Connor. The son of a bitch is from Philadelphia anyway. Never swam in the Mon, wouldn't know a Primanti's sandwich from a cheesesteak and doesn't know the 'Burgh." Raising his glass, he said, "CHARLIE DON'T YINZ!" to the roar of the crowd as they all raised their glasses.

Back "upstairs" in the Executive Wing, Jesus said, "You had mentioned Michael has his concerns about Uri." He waited.

God, who was semi-watching his computer screen, said, "It's funny, those people on *Home Hunters* always seem to pick the place I would have never expected them to. This last couple picked a one bedroom in Saigon and they have, like, twelve kids. Can you imagine!" He laughed, as always amused by the actions of his ant farm.

"Anyway," God said, turning to face Jesus and reclining back in his chair, his arms folded across his stomach. "Yes. Michael is concerned, as we've discussed."

"Uri reported today," Jesus began, leaving out the embarrassing details. "He feels strongly that this Dave Brady could truly be the Antichrist." Jesus sat back, thinking he had delivered what he expected to be grave news.

The Creator nodded slowly. "Well, he could well be. Hard to say."

Jesus was surprised. Stunned, really. He had expected the Big Guy to be amused, maybe a little annoyed. After all, while Uri was an archangel and afforded the proper respect, we're talking about the Celestial All-Star Team here, and nobody was above criticism of a fellow who was acting a bit off his nut. Everyone knew of Uri's conspiracy theories; they were well documented. But for the Chairman to suggest that maybe he was right? Well, that was a bit surprising, to say the least.

"Michael believes that Uri may be on a one-man mission to save existence," the Creator said. "Michael is the most competent archangel you have. Best of all of them. His perception is usually flawless. He is emotionless when it is appropriate, emotional when it is appropriate. His judgment is outstanding, and his Corps would burn in Hell for him. If you can trust any being in the Universe's assessment, you'd trust his, no?" he said.

"Yes," Jesus said. "I have valued his counsel, and I will continue to."

"Uri, on the other hand, is more volatile," God said, now leaning a little forward in his chair, his elbows resting on his desk, eyes absolutely, positively alive, sharp. "Uri is almost as competent as Michael, almost as sound in his judgment, and if you wanted to take ten thousand angels downstairs to storm the gates, who would you rather have at the front, flaming sword in his hand, Righteousness sitting on his shoulder like a parrot, as he fought for everything we all believe in up here?"

"Well, I guess...I guess Uri," Jesus said.

The Creator nodded. "So, who's right?"

"I don't know," Jesus said, understanding he was stating the obvious.

"More importantly, is either of them right?" the man Jesus considered his father said. Jesus looked away, feeling like he was being given a lesson and wanting to give the correct answer to the teacher who already knew, but he just wasn't sure. After a while, looking out his endless windows at clouds in the near, middle, and impossibly far distances, the Creator said, "I imagine we'll eventually find out," and smiled.

"But," Jesus said, "if he were truly the Antichrist, this would be an Alter Existence issue of the highest order."

"Oh, I think so. Definitely," He said, turning his attention back to the monitor on his desk. "What do you think you're going to do about it?"

Jesus didn't know what to say to that, either. The entire conversation had him reeling. Sure, everyone knew Armageddon was an eventuality, but not this week. Or this year. Or for a very long time yet. Maybe next week was now.

After a while, his mentor seemingly absorbed in his screen, Jesus said, "I think we have some work to do. I think we need to give serious consideration to Dave Brady, and I think it might be a good idea to begin preparations for a battle against the Dark." The man staring at his computer did not appear to be paying attention, and Jesus understood he was really just voicing his thoughts out loud. But he added, "I think Dave Brady becomes priority number one, starting now." With that, Jesus got up from his chair and turned to leave. Walking the several steps to the door, lost in his thoughts, he almost missed the clearing of the throat of the man seated at the desk behind him. He paused without turning and waited.

"Son," God said, and although he wouldn't have admitted it even with wolves tearing his innards out, Jesus absolutely loved it when He called him that. He waited.

"Keep your eye on the bartender."

After a moment, Jesus said, "Yes, sir. Absolutely." Then he opened the door without turning and walked out. In the hallway, he smiled absently at God's administrative assistant seated at the small desk near the door and kept walking. The AA returned the smile, as always thinking that Jesus was just a damn good egg no matter how you sliced it.

Bartender? Jesus thought. *What bartender?*

Chapter Thirty-Nine

Jimmy Hallendorf shifted in his seat. He was in a position he was not only unaccustomed to, but which he had so limited experience in as to make him a babbling idiot. Completely uncool.

"You followed her," the Don said.

"Yes. Absolutely. I followed her," Jimmy said.

After a few seconds, the Don said, "And...?"

Jimmy cleared his throat. Again. "Well, it's strange, sir. I followed her, but she's hard to follow, really. She's—it's like you have her right there and then she's gone. She's, I don't know, she's..." Jimmy's voice trailed off as his hands did some kind of waving thing in the air and he just gave up.

The Don looked at Martin, leaning against the wall of the Don's office a respectful, but still relevant, distance away. Martin looked back but said nothing, understanding he wasn't supposed to; it was just his job to look concerned. "What do you think this woman, this specter, is up to?" the Don asked.

Jimmy thought a long time before responding. It was never a good idea to bullshit Mia Fanzi, but in this instance, it was an even worse idea. Lately, Jimmy felt this thing they were into was different than anything they had ever been into before. Way different. Fuck it.

Finally, he said, "Don, it's like this: I've never seen anything like this before. This woman scares the shit out of me. I'm sixty-one years old and I've seen it all. I've been mauled by police German shepherds back during the protests, I've got three bullet wounds in my body, I've climbed out of windows so close to getting my brains blown out you could have flipped a coin for my life, but I really have to tell you... I have to tell you..." He trailed off again, speechless. "Who the hell is this woman?" His look was so bewildered, so lost, that Mia had to stifle a laugh.

Of the very few people in the world Marino Fanzi would have entrusted his life to, Jimmy was one of those very few. Jimmy was unflappable. Sitting in his wicker chair on the Don's front porch, Hannibal himself with 150 elephants and 5,000 men could have rolled up and Jimmy would have said, "Zoo's over in Highland Park, G. About five miles from here. Now, let's keep it moving. Don't need a bunch of elephant shit ruining our front yard." But this woman had him rattled more than the Don had even seen. "You believe she's shadowing Dave Brady?" he asked.

"Yes. Absolutely," Jimmy said, getting his feet back under him. "I have people who have been keeping their eye out for him, and she seems to show up in places where he is. No question about that."

The Don looked again at Martin. "Do you think she's here to kill him?"

"Well, that's the thing!" Jimmy said, moving to the edge of his seat, very focused. "That's exactly the thing. I feel like this woman could kill anyone she wanted to in about two seconds, including me. But she isn't killing anyone. I don't get it. I can't figure why she's here." Jimmy looked at the Don, then at Martin. He had nothing else to say.

The Don swiveled in his chair to look out at his private patio and small garden, his hands steepled across his chest. He did this often, and anyone who had been in the inner sanctum knew to keep their mouth shut and wait while the Don considered his options. Sometimes those options meant life or death, and like a heart surgeon headed into the chest cavity, you didn't pick that moment to tug on his elbow.

After a few minutes, Marino Fanzi swiveled his chair back

around to face Jimmy and Martin. "She is called Manon. She is a hitter. She has been dead for more than two hundred years. She is known as the Black Angel of Death. In this thing, this thing that is going on now, her interests coincide with ours."

Jimmy tried to process what he had just heard. It was pure fourteen-carat bullshit. Not possible. And yet, on some level, he absolutely believed it and was completely unsurprised. Some part of him accepted this ridiculous explanation without any thought whatsoever. Because he knew it was true. And another part was relieved the Angel of Death was with them on this thing. Jimmy said, "Sir, if you don't mind my asking, what the hell is this thing that is going on now, exactly?"

—

In another part of the city Father Bill stared out the rectory window. Things had sure as hell changed a lot in the past few weeks. After being summoned to the Northside to talk to Don Fanzi (another $5,000 donation), he understood what he had probably already known for some time. Things were going down. This was not a drill. On one level, he was terrified. On another level, he was alive. Alive in a way he had not been for a long time.

—

Turns out the Wolf was also alive. Very much so. He had regained consciousness shortly after suffering what had been described as a stroke by his doctors, but he knew better. He had been concerned about Jilly on a level he would never have let anyone realize, and something he felt was like a series of events that had a commonality. He was, were he honest with himself, and he always was, a little scared. A paper gangster at best, he had always known he wasn't a tough guy. He was too smart for that. He had always played his cards the best way he knew how, maximized any advantage, and, eventually, had come out on top most of the time. But he knew there were forces at work here that he had not dealt with and which he couldn't handle by the normal Brighton Beach rules.

A loser named Leonard representing Dave Brady had approached his people shortly after Volkov had let it leak he was "recovering." In a nutshell, they wanted him elected mayor and knew the Wolf ran Polish Hill and other lucrative voting blocs within the city. They had met, Alexi had pretended to be more out of it than he was, let his people run the meeting, but had paid very close attention. Dave Brady was a piece of this confluence. He knew that on some level he could not have explained to anyone. But he knew it just the same. Dave Brady might become big. Very big. Or he might not. It was like a roulette wheel, and the Wolf knew he had a part in the eventual outcome, although damned if he knew what that might be. In the end, they had agreed to cast their lot with the Brady campaign. Why not? They'd keep checking the prevailing winds and could always decide they were out if they felt like it.

After the meeting, the idiot called Leonard had asked for a few minutes alone with Volkov and "Spatz" Spasilovich. He had cut to the chase fairly quickly, which the Wolf appreciated. There was a woman, a problem. Leonard described her as a do-gooder working for the opposition, although who exactly the opposition was had never been made clear. She had the potential to cause serious issues with the campaign and everyone felt that it would better if she was "out of the way." Volkov stared at Leonard vacantly and let a little spittle ooze from the corner of his mouth. No Academy Award winner had ever played a part so well.

Spatz said, "You want us to get her out of the way? What's in it for us?"

Leonard had gone on to imply that his boss, Dave Brady, would be eternally grateful and was the kind of man who did not forget favors. They left it at "We'll think about it and let you know."

Once Leonard and company had left, Volkov got up from his wheelchair, poured himself a vodka, and one for Tatiana and Spatz as well. Spatz was crazy, no question about it. And he liked to kill people. No question about that either. But he was street smart. Everyone was terrified of him, and he and Alexi had come from the same area of Russia. This meant Spatz afforded the Wolf a certain respect, and that was critical in Volkov's line of work.

"So, we're in bed with the cracker and his political machine?"

Spatz said.

Alexi looked at Tatiana, who was wearing a deep lavender Adidas tracksuit (size: boy's medium). Tatiana smiled at him. He liked that. Turning to his second-in-command, he said, "Leonid, we are in bed with nobody. We do what benefits us. Always. At the moment, we'll let them believe we are with them, then we'll see how the hand is dealt. Na zdorovie." They all tipped their very expensive vodka shots.

"This woman, why is she a big deal?" Spatz asked, wiping his mouth. "They're afraid of a woman?" He laughed.

The Wolf stared into the distance, seemingly without hearing the remark. Alexi knew this was no ordinary woman. He couldn't shake the feeling she had caused his "stroke." And she was working with Jilly. And the Italians. This he had heard on the street, and it jived with what he felt in his gut.

But Spatz didn't need to know it. "Spatz, droog"—Russian for *my good friend*—"we fear no woman, no bear, no gun. Na zdorovie!" and they drank again. "Well, we fear Tatiana," Volkov added, smiling at his girl.

"Fear the Moushka!" Spatz said and, skipping the shot glass, lifted the bottle of vodka and drank deeply from it.

Chapter Forty

Jesus called Uri. Now, "called" is a relative term. Speaking strictly metaphysically, there wasn't an actual "call" per se—at least, not at first—but as Uri was sitting in the penthouse of the Fairmont Pittsburgh watching season 14 of *Jersey Shore* (such discord!), his Earthly senses sort of blurred out and all background noise was cancelled. An image formed in his mind, and it was Jesus, and he wanted to talk to him. That's how it works. He turned on his computer, turned off the TV, took a quick look in the mirror, and prepared to speak to the big guy.

"I want to say, we all think you and your team are doing a fabulous job down there," Jesus said. "I couldn't have sent a better man given the very serious task at hand."

"Well, thank you, Lord," Uri said, being very careful as this was starting to sound like he was about to get canned. He wasn't sure he cared at this point.

"I've been thinking about this a lot," Jesus said. "I feel like there's more to this than might be right there on the surface. Do you know what I mean?"

"Yes," Uri replied immediately, although he had no idea what exactly Jesus was trying to say.

"It's just that, well, Alter Existence is such a serious category that I...I don't want to sound the alarm until I'm very comfortable we really have an AE event. I'm sure you remember the New Kids On The Block thing."

Uri's face turned crimson, and he sputtered, "Lord, I believed strongly then, and I still believe now, that Joey Fatone is working with the forces of Evil!"

"Yes," Jesus said. "Yes, well, the problem there is that we elevated that to an Alter Existence issue, and then it turned out the forces of Evil were an asthmatic janitor, two fourteen-year-old girls, and Joey's ninety-one-year-old grandmother."

"The grandmother is dirty!" Uri said, louder than he had intended.

"Then there was the Barney the Dinosaur thing," Jesus said.

Uri closed his eyes. "Lord, Leviticus makes clear reference to a 'crimson beast' who will come as a wolf in the clothing of a sheep."

"Yes, well," Jesus said, "some might say more purple than crimson, and perhaps less a beast than a stuffed child's mascot, but why split hairs? The point is that after these "incidents," we really do need to be careful before we declare that once again the forces of Evil are assembling only to discover we are dealing with elderly ladies and cartoon characters."

"Lord, I—" Uri began.

"Uri, credibility is a valuable thing. Once lost, it is difficult to recover."

Uri sighed. "Yes, Lord."

"Having said that," Jesus said, "I do feel that there is more to this particular situation than meets the eye. I agree Dave Brady warrants careful observation. I also agree that Aza doesn't show up because he's bored and looking for a good time." Uri began to feel some hope kindling. "But," Jesus continued, "given our credibility concerns, I think we're going to have to continue the operation more...quietly."

Uri gathered himself, for the first time feeling like just maybe someone was finally listening to him.

"I talked to Him today," Jesus said.

Uri immediately understood the implications of that statement. His pulse doubled. "He feels this could be a serious situation,"

Jesus said.

"He does?" Uri blurted out, immediately feeling stupid.

"He does." Jesus said.

—

The next day, Jilly stood behind his bar, lost in thought, absentmindedly cleaning things. It was 11 a.m. on a Tuesday. If you were drinking in Jilly's at 11 a.m. on a Tuesday, there was a good chance you had not cashed a ticket in life's lottery. There was only one person in the bar other than Jilly.

Leonard sat staring into space. He was wearing an $800 suit, no tie, and a starched white dress shirt that was moderately wrinkled from the antics of the night before. Some of those antics were a bit of a blur to Leonard. He had a Grey Goose and soda in front of him, which he really didn't want. Imagine that. It was not lost on Leonard that about six weeks ago, he might have sold one of his kids for that exact mixed drink.

"How are your new friends treating you?" Jilly asked. There was sarcasm in the comment, but only lightly and not enough to penetrate the fog swirling around Leonard's brain.

"Oh, okay, I guess," Leonard said. "You know them?"

"I know of them," Jilly said, being carefully non-interested.

"Brady is going to be Mayor. Trust me on that," Leonard said, taking a sip of his drink. "Probably bigger and better things after that too."

"You don't say," Jilly said, suddenly intensely focused on some shot glasses, his back to Leonard.

"He knows some powerful people. People who make things happen," Leonard said. "There's just some stuff going on, serious shit. Like extraterrestrial serious shit."

Jilly understood Leonard was mostly talking to himself. As a bartender, he had been in this situation before.

"It's just that they're, I don't know..." Leonard trailed off. Jilly waited. "Evil," Leonard said quietly.

"We're all evil," Jilly said, downplaying the comment.

"No," Leonard said, probably louder than he had intended to, "they're really evil." Jilly waited again. "I don't know..." Leonard said, his eyes distant.

The fact of the matter was, Leonard had become concerned about the whole operation. For a while, it had been really cool—the money, the women, the camaraderie (although Leonard would not have used that word, nor could he have spelled it). He felt part of something. And it was nice. His life had been a series of colossal failures; he was an experienced, full-time, Gold Medal Loser. And he had known it. And then, suddenly he was one of the Cool Kids. He had respect. People treated him differently than they had just a month before. Christ, his current wife decided she wanted to have sex with him. And he turned her down. Said he was tired. She got jealous. Jealous! Leonard had never experienced a woman being jealous in his entire life.

So, there was no question his life was much, much better than it had ever been. For sure. And yet... And yet, he couldn't shake this feeling that it was all wrong somehow. How come every time he woke up hungover after a night entertaining some politico, he felt like he had done something wrong? Leonard had woken up hungover so many times in the past thirty years it had become his status quo. But now it felt, well, wrong. Like kicking the dog wrong. He had no idea why. Sure, these guys weren't exactly Girl Scouts. He understood on some level they were kind of professional bad guys. But he had seen and been around so may lowlifes in his low life, what was the big deal?

Brady. That was the big deal. Brady was the thing. There were times Leonard felt, and he knew what he was talking about, that Brady was batshit, bus-window-licking crazy. The thing at the William Penn? Crazy.

And then there was Aza. Leonard had sort of blown off all this talk of "the Dark" as guys talking big. But he had come to realize Aza was on a whole different level. He had seen him do things, know things, and generally manage this game on a level that was more than human. Aza was the real deal. And he frightened Leonard. Hell, he frightened everyone. Super Dave Brady was crazy, but he was an egotistical jagoff. Without Aza, he was a blowhard talking big. It was Aza that lately had Leonard wondering if maybe he had signed on for something more than he had bargained for.

"Leonard, you goddamn little prick, how you been?!"

This snapped Leonard out of his daydream. Billy "Birdman" Piper had come into the bar and spotted Leonard (it would have been hard to miss the only other patron on a stool within the establishment).

Jilly turned and affected casual disinterest, but he knew an opportunity had been lost with the arrival of one of Leonard's old associates.

"Man, you look fan-cee, brother. You hit the big time or what?" Birdman said. "I heard you been running with the A-Team downtown!"

"Shit," Leonard said, immediately reverting back to his old schtick like Mr. Rogers throwing on that sweater and Keds. "Even blind squirrels find a nut once in a while. How you been, Birdman?"

"Not so good, brother. Been sick, and the family, well, you know how that goes. You think you might slide your brother a drink? You know, to celebrate your success and all?" Birdman said.

Leonard, who had actually been happy to see a lowlife from his old life, sucked in a breath. Of course. Everyone wants something. "Jilly," Leonard said, "can you get Birdman whatever he wants on me?"

Jilly looked at Leonard's friend. "As I recall, Bankers Club well vodka and soda?"

"Well," Birdman said, looking at Leonard, "let's make it Tito's today. Can't toast a top-shelf buddy without top-shelf goods, right?"

"Right," Leonard said. "Top shelf. All the way." He stared into the bar mirror at a man in a suit he wasn't sure he knew anymore.

—

Meanwhile, back at the Fairmont, Uri was on a roll. There were team meetings and then there were team meetings. Re-energized by his conversation with Jesus, he was like a kid headed to a toy store. "We have it on the absolute highest authority, and I think you know who I'm talking about, that stopping Brady is priority one," Uri said.

Manon and Oliver sat obediently on the couch in Uri's suite. They had frankly been convinced after the debacle of the Holy Host presentation that they would be shut down and recalled. Oliver looked at Manon, who looked at Oliver.

Uri said, "What?"

"Well," Oliver said, "it seemed like they didn't feel we had a serious threat. So, I guess we just thought…"

"Thought what?" Uri said, his irritation clear in his voice. "Thought that I was some kind of nutcase who couldn't be trusted to recognize a threat to mankind? That I saw the Antichrist in ex-boyband singers and was certain the Apocalypse would come in the form of a fat, purple, stuffed dinosaur who loved kids? Is that what you were thinking?" Uri said, his voice rising.

"Well, no, we—" Oliver began, but Uri continued.

"Maybe you thought the Holy Host didn't think I was capable of this assignment, that this is all some kind of prank to entertain them! Is that what you thought? That they sent us down here to serve as a kind of ecclesiastical sitcom live-streaming on HeavenTV?"

Oliver was no dummy. He recognized the signs his boss was tiptoeing on the ledge between rational thought and, you know, Looney Tunes. But the fact remained he had said the Big Guy was on board. Not the little big guy, the Big Guy. Well, that changed things. But here was the thing. Oliver wasn't a hundred percent sure the conversation Uri was referencing had ever actually happened. He'd been down this road before. Often Uri repositioned things to meet his needs. Oliver had overheard other conversations that Uri had later misrepresented in a way that suited Uri's position on things. Which was, well, a lie. For now, the best position was to fall back and get more information.

"I'm sorry, Lord," Oliver said. "I hope I didn't lead you to believe I have any doubt whatsoever in either your ability or your commitment to the good of mankind." As he said this, Oliver moved from the couch and took a knee, his head bowed. This seemed to placate Uri.

"And Manon, what are your thoughts?" Uri asked, his white, embroidered robe twirling just a little as he turned to face her.

Manon, in a sort of pantsuit-meets-J.Lo lounger ensemble

(black, of course), turned her head towards Uri and said, "I feel comfortable you would not risk us all based on personal aspirations or a desire to rectify past failures." She never for a second failed to meet Uri's eyes as she said this. So very Manon.

Oliver thought for the 1,257th time that he was madly in love with Manon. In a post-life, sanitized kinda way. He wished he had said what she said. But he hadn't. And so existence separates the celebrated from those who clean up behind the celebrated.

"Good," Uri said. His avoidance of Manon's comment was lost on neither Manon nor Oliver. "So, here's what we're going to do. Manon, you are our most critical asset. We need you to go in deep. I need you to get next to Brady so we know exactly what is going on and when is the best time to strike. With that bastard Aza whispering in his ear, the need for accurate information is very important."

"I have been around them frequently lately, Lord," Manon said. "I am concerned my presence may be known to them."

"They are so full of themselves, they are paying you no mind," Uri said. There was a silence, the kind of silence you get when a superior says something an underling doesn't agree with and is hesitant to argue, but also refuses to agree with.

"What?" Uri said, growing exasperated. This meeting was not going as he had hoped at all.

Manon collected herself and said, "I feel that Aza is aware of my presence and can tell if I am near him even if he cannot see me."

"And why do you think that?" Uri asked, his irritation now not masked at all.

Manon stared out the window, not meeting Uri's eyes. "Because we have met before, in a place where important events unfolded that would impact both our destinies."

"Explain," Uri said, only mildly less irritated.

Manon said nothing and continued to stare out the windows of Uri's suite, gazing at downtown Pittsburgh.

"Manon? Explain," Uri repeated.

Manon continued to stare out the windows, and Oliver was worried this was going to turn into a serious donnybrook, but then Manon said, quietly, "I cannot do that, Lord."

Uri thought for a long moment. Then, Oliver assumed, he

realized Manon was his only chance of success in this particular endeavor and so decided to let the refusal pass. "Well," Uri said, making an attempt at saving face, "I hope you can pull yourself together for the work I need you to do. It is work that may decide the future of mankind. We'll disguise you properly, don't worry. Oliver, are we ready with the comm device?"

Oliver, jolted out of his fascination with Manon, said, "Yes. Yes, Lord."

"Good," Uri said. "This device, implanted deep in your ear, will enable two-way communication with you regardless of where you are on Earth. In this way, we can tell if you are in danger."

Oliver understood that what Uri was really saying was "we can get critical information from you using this device, regardless of whether you are in danger," but he was already in the doghouse so he kept his mouth shut. Besides, he strongly suspected Manon understood the implications of what she was being asked to do as well. And then Uri explained what he wanted Manon to do.

Chapter Forty-One

Father Bill faced Jilly across the table at Hambone's in Lawrenceville. They had come here so they could have a quiet conversation. Father Bill had been nervously rotating his beer glass, something Jilly had noticed on many occasions in the past when something was troubling him. Jilly smiled at the thought that he sometimes functioned as Father Bill's confessor. The man the priest talked to about things he couldn't talk to others about.

"The Don called me to the Northside," Father Bill said, still not looking at Jilly. "He explained several things to me, some of which I find hard to believe." He looked at Jilly, who looked back at him, no expression on his face. "There is a lot of discussion in the Bible about Armageddon and the Antichrist. It seems all so...so, I don't know, like some kind of *Lord of the Rings* script. I have studied it since seminary and I know it backward and forward, but, I don't know, it's sort of like memorizing the protocol for a nuclear strike. You practice it, and you understand there is a possibility it could happen, but..."

"But you don't think it will," Jilly finished for him.

Father Bill looked at Jilly, then away, then looked at his beer glass. Rotated it. "Yeah," Father Bill said. "I feel like it can't be true, that this is all a bunch of overreaction." He stopped again, staring at his beer.

"But you think maybe not," Jilly said.

Father Bill looked up so quickly that Jilly almost jumped back in his seat. Almost. "Do you think it's real?" he asked with a look that Jilly could only describe as lost.

"I think," Jilly said after the correct amount of thoughtful delay, "we all see things through the lens time has created for our eyes."

Father Bill snorted, and his beer almost came out of his nose. "Well, my friend, that is some deep shit. You want to add we are clay from which the Potter of Life has forged in the furnaces of life experience? Maybe we are seeds of corn that life has watered with the occasional rain of discontent combined with the nurturing manure of social interaction? You wanna call up Dr. Freaking Phil and have him chime in that what we all need to do is calm down a little and love one another?

"From what I hear, people have been given heart attacks, melted, bludgeoned to death. We got a guy who may be the Antichrist, and I'm not talking about a Hollywood movie with some kid's head spinning around blowing pea soup; I'm talking about the end of existence as we know it. This guy has a...I don't know, Lieutenant or something, who may have stuck the spear in Jesus' side, and this guy decided to come back to Pittsburgh two thousand years later to bring about events of the Apocalypse, and the only goddamn clergyman in the vicinity who knows this is all going on fell asleep yesterday in confessions. What the hell am I supposed to do, call the Archbishop for Christ's sake?

"I'm supposed to be the flaming, righteous sword of God. I'm supposed to be ready for this. I'm the equivalent of the Catholic 'pull in case of emergency.' I trained for this. I want to smash them all to cinders. I want to save the believers. I have no idea what to do, and I feel like I absolutely need to do something!" Father Bill, spent after his tirade, sat back with a look on his face so completely forlorn that Jilly, although he tried not to, could not help but smile. And he did.

Holding his hands up with palms toward his friend the Holy Man, he said, "Whoa, whoa, preacher. When did you turn into Pale Rider? You Clint Eastwood now?" the big man said, smiling. Both men sipped their drinks and took some deep breaths.

"Can you sit tight for now?" Jilly finally said. "I need you to trust me on this. I have to think things through. I agree some things are happening that don't seem to add up. I don't know that I buy all this biblical baloney, but I can't dismiss everything either. I need a week, ten days at the outside. You think the trumpets are going to blow before then, Father?"

Father Bill sighed. "No." He stared out at the traffic on Butler Street and continued, "I don't think we're all in a lake of fire before the start of the football season." And then he gave Jilly a tired smile.

"Okay. Good," Jilly said, getting up from his stool.

"Julian," Father Bill said. Jilly turned at the sound of his formal name and looked at the priest. "That thing they want you to do. What do you think? Now, I mean. Now that all these things have happened. You going to..." He hesitated, then said, "Would you do it?" Father Bill did not meet Jilly's eyes as he asked.

Jilly looked at this man who was his friend. He felt sorry for him in a way he had never felt sorry for himself. Jilly knew answering "yes" would relieve Father Bill of his burden. He was smart enough to know that it shamed Father Bill to ask him. But he had been there, and he had learned that no man is always noble, no man is always honorable. Good men want to be, but when they are tested it is fear, in the end, that takes center stage. Jilly took two steps back toward the bar and leaned in close to the priest.

"What I think, honestly, is that if this goes down, and it may, I think I'd rather have you slugging away beside me than Archangel Michael himself."

Father Bill looked at him with relief and then something that looked like determination coming into his face. "No shit?"

"No shit, Padre. I think you got the goods," Jilly said, smiling. And then he turned and left.

The priest sat for several minutes just staring out at the sidewalk through the dirty bar window, rotating his beer glass. Well. Maybe he did. No, he definitely did. Maybe.

Jilly walked for a long time, his thoughts consuming him. Eventually he ended up in front of Kosmos Tomes. He was not surprised. When TK greeted him, Jilly absently petted the unofficial mascot of the store—an enormous tomcat sitting almost regally near the cash register in a basket that was even bigger than he was.

"My man, the thing I don't get," TK said, "is he hisses at ninety-nine percent of the people who try and pet him, but not you."

Jilly looked at the cat and then at TK. "Well, he recognizes a kindred spirit. I hiss at ninety-nine percent of the people who try and pet me, too," Jilly said, almost smiling but not quite.

Transcendental Kosmos said, "I held back a first printing of *Atlas Shrugged* for you. Just came in a few days ago. I know you're sweet on Rand, and this would make a nice compliment to that first edition of *The Fountainhead* you bought last year."

"Okay," Jilly said, still looking into the eyes of the cat, which were only half open as Jilly scratched his head between the ears.

TK said, "It's worth fifteen hundred, but for you, I'll part with this masterpiece for twelve hundred."

"For special friends of Rick, we have a special discount," Jilly said absently, still looking into the eyes of the cat.

"Done?" TK said.

"Done," Jilly said, now turning his attention to the bookseller. "Hey, I have a question for you. What have you got on how the world ends?"

TK looked at Jilly. "The world ends when the Browns win the Superbowl. Everyone knows that. It's in the Bible, I'm pretty sure," TK said.

"No, I'm serious," Jilly said. "I'm doing some research. I want to read up on it."

TK studied his friend for a long moment, his hands palms down on the counter. "And this wouldn't have anything to do with a certain mayoral candidate, some Italian friends of yours on the Northside, and a crazy old lady who might have our friend His Eminence Father Bill's ear, would it?" TK said, staring unblinking into Jilly's eyes.

As always, Jilly was surprised, but he should have known better. TK knew more people in Pittsburgh than anyone.

"Maybe," Jilly said. "So answer the question, yes or no?"

The big man stared back at the other big man for a moment, then moved with surprising grace to the front door and turned the

Open sign to Closed, pulled the door shade, and looked at Jilly with theatrical effect.

Jilly looked at TK, then at the cat, and said, "You think we should put the kid to bed? And do you have any wine, baby?"

"Shut up, ya jagoff." TK said. "Follow me."

In the back of the store and down a flight of stairs was the basement of Kosmos Tomes. Years ago, TK had enlisted a company to build a climate-controlled, spacious, and very secure vault to house his special treasures.

Though few knew his history, Kosmos' oddball parents had both been from wealthy families, and as an only child, TK had inherited enough money upon their eventual deaths to ensure he not only never had to work if he didn't want to, but that he could indulge his passion for book collecting. He had attended Harvard for two years and would have graduated had he not fallen in love with a pretty young Grateful Dead fan and followed her and the band for nearly two years before he gave up on trying to harness a shooting star. He returned to his hometown, eventually quietly finishing his degree in Library Science at Pitt and later his Masters.

Jilly had never been behind the scenes at the store. And if he hadn't, he suspected very few others had.

Using his body to (not so subtly) screen Jilly from seeing, TK entered a code into a key pad. It was twelve digits Jilly noted without really thinking about it, just counting the computerized "beeps" and observing, as was his nature.

After an audible click, TK opened the large steel door and stepped up onto the platform floor of the vault, inviting Jilly in with him. TK then closed the door behind them, and another audible click sealed them into the vault.

"If we get stuck in here," Jilly said, "I want you to know I will eat you before you eat me. I won't enjoy it, but I'll do it."

"You wouldn't like the taste, I think," TK said. "I've gone a little sour in my old age."

Jilly had never seen anything like the vault. It was essentially a square room, about twenty feet by twenty feet. Three of the four walls were lined with book cabinets that had glass fronts and temperature and humidity controls digitally displayed on the front of each. The fourth wall contained a sort of kitchenette with a refrigerator, sink, countertop, and cabinets with glasses and snacks. In the middle of the room were two setups.

The first was a very large, library-style high topped wooden table with four chairs surrounding it and what looked to be very expensive customized swing lamps at each corner that would enable the reader to carefully examine minute details of a book while comfortably seated.

The other setup was two very large and very comfortable easy chairs with a table in between with a large lamp. "Welcome to my man cave," TK said, motioning Jilly to one of the oversized easy chairs. "Sit down."

"So," Jilly said, "tell me what ya got on the end of times, the big enchilada, the final big boomba."

TK handed Jilly a glass of soda water with lemon before settling his bulk into his own chair, folding his hands across his belly. He looked at Jilly frankly. "There are several books on this subject, not least of which is the Bible, and I have four here in this room. One of them was written in 1245. No lie. But I can summarize it for you. Allow me to give you the short and sweet. Guy is going to show up. Difficult times. He will appear to have all the answers. Arrogant, boastful, full of himself. People will love him like Michael Buble and Michael Strahan combined.

"There will be a period of time where he appears to make the world a better place. Eventually he takes down the Church, whatever your interpretation of that is, and most would point to Catholicism, I assume. With Rome out of the way, he will eventually run the planet. Then comes what is called the Tribulation, a period of bad stuff. Eventually world war, as some don't buy what he's selling, and half the planet gets annihilated. Guy ends up kind of like Supreme Emperor.

"Then God gets involved and his boy Jesus plays a part, and in the end, the Antichrist is probably defeated and thrown into a lake of fire. How about that?" TK said sitting back in his chair and looking at Jilly.

"Probably?" Jilly said.

"The thing about the Apocalypse," Kosmos said, "is that there is no definitive account of what's going to happen. Not even in the Bible. Yes, there are general timelines and possible events, but there is a real lack of detail, and the overall impression is that some of it, or all of it, or the final outcome, are all kind of up in the air. Now, our friend Father Bill would disagree and say it is all very clearly explained, at least for the most part, but that's only if you rely on the Bible and then only if you look at it from a sort of slanted viewpoint."

"A slanted viewpoint?" Jilly said, feeling like he was becoming an echo.

"By that, I mean you interpret the Bible's words with a predisposition to how you'd like it to end."

Jilly looked at him vacantly.

"In other words, if you are true believer that everything is pre-ordained, and if you drink your milk and don't lie, cheat, or steal and love your mother and Jesus, it's all going to work out, then yes, you can interpret what the Bible says in such a manner that it will work out a certain way and good will triumph over evil."

"But you don't see it that way," Jilly said.

"What I see, and this is considering several accounts outside the Bible itself," TK said, "is that the whole thing is up in the air. Anything can happen and impact the outcome. In fact, there seems to be, in my opinion, general agreement among scholars that God is just going to sit back and watch what happens to see how his whole experiment turns out.".

Jilly, his face a mask of concentration, stared at his friend. "Is there anything you've read about, you know, a contractor getting involved to stop this guy?"

Kosmos looked at Jilly for a long time, no expression on his face.

"What?" Jilly said, for a second losing his normal ability to present a stoneface to the world at large.

"No," Kosmos said, smiling.

"No," Jilly repeated, deflating, sitting back in his chair, not sure if he was relieved or not.

"Somebody want you to punch Dave Brady's ticket?" TK asked.

Jilly should have learned by now to not be surprised at the things TK knew.

"That," Jilly said, "is a very long story." The two men looked at each other.

Then TK got up, put on a pair of white linen gloves, moved to one of the glass-fronted cabinets, and opened it. He removed a small book and brought it over to the table. He showed it to Jilly but did not hand it him. The leather cover, which appeared in good condition but was very old, had gold leaf lettering on the front that said "Fine Temporum."

Jilly looked at TK.

"Latin," TK said. "'The End of Times.' This was written by a monk—well, sort of a monk. More a guy who had the most horrible life and ended up in a Neapolitan monastery on a cliffside in the 1300s. He was known as Giglio."

"Guy only had one name?" Jilly said. "Like Cher?"

"It wasn't his name, just what history records he was known as. It means 'lily' in Italian. Let's not get sidetracked. I like this book because it is one person's interpretation of how it all ends. Giglio was by all accounts basically batshit crazy. He talked to goats, had conversations with invisible friends, preferred a loincloth to a monk's habit, you know, all the stuff from the Religious Fanatic Handbook. He claimed to have had a conversation with Archangel Uriel himself during a two-week fast where the end of times was explained to him." TK sat back in his chair and looked at Jilly.

"So?" Jilly prompted.

"So, what?" TK said.

"So, who shot JR? What the fuck do you think? How does it end, you jagoff?!" Jilly shouted.

TK just smiled at the outburst of a frustrated man. "Well, that's the thing. As with all this stuff, it isn't exactly clear, just more a set of clues to look for that will come into play."

"That isn't helpful," Jilly said.

"Look," Transcendental Kosmos said, "there is no definitive roadmap. Every version I've read basically says it's not a foregone conclusion. Antichrist may win, lose, or draw. It all depends on the actions of the principals when it goes down."

Jilly suddenly straightened. "Who are the principals? In Giglio's version."

"Well," TK said, "let me think. There's a priest. There's a man Giglio calls 'the Slav.' There's a 'white family that wears a dark costume.' There's a 'fool who becomes a prince.' And, of course, an Angel of the Apocalypse. Oh, almost forgot, there's a woman."

"A woman?" Jilly said.

"Yes. A woman who is the right hand of a vengeful God. I love that," TK said. He looked at Jilly. "What? You okay? You look like you're gonna pass out, my friend."

Jilly was staring at TK but not really focusing, his eyes vacant, lost in thought. He shook his head to clear it. "No hitter, though?"

"No, not that I recall," TK said. Jilly stared up at the ceiling as TK continued, "No hitter. But my favorite part is that in the end it kind of comes down to one man. The whole megillah. Comes down to one guy who ultimately determines the fate of the world. The book refers to him as 'the judge.' Not in those words—the book was written seven hundred years ago, so it's more like 'the arbiter,' but same basic meaning. This guy will eventually have to make a decision that will impact the final outcome. Imagine being that guy." He looked at Jilly, who turned his attention from the ceiling to his friend's face.

Then, slowly, Jilly began to smile. And the smile became a laugh. Then Jilly was laughing so hard he had tears streaming down his face. Gasping for air. TK became alarmed, never having seen his stoic friend in this condition. He moved toward Jilly to do... what? Something. But Jilly held up a hand and collected himself, eventually calming down and wiping his eyes, a big smile on his face. He stared at TK.

"What?" TK said. "Tell me."

Jilly said, still smiling, "Here come da Judge." and pointed a thumb back at himself. And then he was lost again in a fit of laughter. After a while, TK joined him. Somewhere in the store upstairs, a large cat opened his eyes in sudden alarm, then, after a moment, closed them again and settled back to sleep.

Chapter Forty-Two

Dave Brady sat nursing a martini and pondering his future. He came to this bar when he wanted to get away from everyone else and think. Wordlessly, the bartender removed the nearly empty small bowl of cocktail peanuts and replaced them with a fresh one. She was very pretty. No, he thought pretty wasn't the right word. Sexy? Well, yes, but...that wasn't right either. Exotic? Maybe "worldly"? Yes, he mused. Both of those too, but they weren't strong enough words. He watched her mixing someone else's drink, her back to him. He was mesmerized. That was it. She was mesmerizing. He had no idea why. But she sure as hell was. Were he honest with himself, he'd admit he had been to this bar three times in the last week and she was the main reason. He did not bring his bodyguards here, nor Aza. There were times, more times lately, that he just wanted to be alone. This bar was a block from his condo, and more importantly, its back door, mainly used by the staff to empty the garbage, faced an alley which shared an obscure service exit from his building. So, once he had cut the Lennys loose for the evening, he'd go into his building, through it, and in through the back of this place, taking a seat at the back end of the long bar, unnoticed in the fairly dark ambience.

During his first visit here, he had tried one of his very best and always successful lines on her. Something about asking her to be careful handling his olives as she made his drink since "a man's olives bruise easily." It was the kind of flirty line said with a hint of a smile that always charmed bartenders.

She had looked at him flatly, not bitchy really, not irritably either, just in a way that made him sort of feel stupid for saying it. When she had mixed the martini, she took three olives and dropped them into a small mortar, then took a pestle and ground them into a pasty sludge. She poured the paste into a strainer, turned to face Dave, and filtered his martini through the olive sludge into a martini glass and placed it on the napkin in front of him.

"That's how we handle olives where I come from. Let me know if you like it."

Again, flatly with no inflection in her voice, just that hint of some kind of accent he couldn't place but was definitely European.

Dave looked at her. "And where do you come from?" Not flirting now, curious, although careful. For some reason he couldn't put his finger on, he just did not want to piss this woman off.

"Far from here," she said, her dark eyes meeting his and looking essentially through him. He was pretty sure that was when he fell in love with her. Her look, her manner, and that undeniable aura of danger that surrounded her were...mesmerizing.

And now he was back at the bar, happy because it was a Tuesday at ten o'clock so the bar was nearly empty.

As she placed his second martini in front of him (without asking if he wanted it), he said, "What do you think about good versus evil?"

She placed her hands on the bar and looked at him. "I think it is a silly concept for those with too much time on their hands."

"Really?" Dave said. "You don't believe in the idea that there are two opposing forces at work in the world, the universe?" As he said this, he carefully rested his left cheek on the knuckles of his left hand, his elbow on the bar. This move was designed to make him seem like he was just a curious person after some casual conversation, harmless, definitely not on the make. Heavens no.

She looked at him, her face slightly tilted to one side as though really seeing him for the first time. After several seconds, she said, "I believe in what is. Call it reality or 'the truth' if you want. When

I leave this place, there are some people who would want to go to bed with me and some people who would as soon kill me. The rest don't give a damn about me either way. Tell me who is good and who is evil?" Again, that flat look.

"Well," Dave said, "there are like six billion people on this planet, and you just put the whole damn herd into three simple categories. I don't know if you are a genius, or if you just need to get out more. What about the jagoffs? You skipped that whole group and there are like eight million of them in Pittsburgh alone. Everyone knows they are evil. Absolute fact."

"Absolute fact, huh?" the bartender said.

"Absolute," Dave replied. "I know what I'm talking about. I was orphaned at a very young age and raised by jagoffs from Swissvale. Hand to God. I wouldn't lie to you," Dave said, raising his actual hand.

The bartender shook her head slightly and turned to go wait on a new customer who had just come into the bar. But Dave was absolutely certain he had seen just the slightest hint of a smile on her lips as she turned. How 'bout that? Later, when she returned, he said, "Would you consider having dinner with me? No strings attached, and I can meet you wherever you'd like. I'd like to discuss good versus evil in more detail with you."

She looked at him for a long moment. "I don't think so. Perhaps it's best if we have this bar between us." Then, after a pause, she added, "For now, Dave Brady."

Dave smiled. Then it struck him. "How do you know my name?" he asked. The bartender placed Dave's credit card on the bartop in front of him. "Ah. Of course." He held out his hand. "Dave Brady, nice to meet you."

She shook it and said, "Jeanne," but she pronounced it more like a French person might say "John."

"And your last name?"

"Dark," the bartender said.

"Dark? Really?" Dave said, smiling. "I like that."

He did not know she had meant "d'Arc" any more than he would have understood who Jeanne d'Arc was, even if she had written it out on a bar napkin.

Up in the suite atop the Fairmount three blocks away, Uri high-fived Oliver. They were both wearing headphones and had listened to every word of the conversation.

"Manon is awesome," Oliver said. "Joan of Arc. Just awesome."

"Exactly." Uri said. "I was right to bring her here."

Eventually Dave left, understanding he was going nowhere that particular night, but also happy as he had been given at least a little piece of hope by the mysterious woman who was occupying his thoughts so much lately.

Later, Manon closed the bar and left via the very same back service entrance Dave was so fond of. It was three a.m. on a Tuesday and the city was quiet. Entering the alley, she was lost in her thoughts, playing back the conversation with Brady over in her mind, pleased with the way she had played it.

She did not notice the two large men near the dumpster until one of them said, "Well, hello, little lady. Our boss wants to talk to you. Why don't you come with us?" The voice was heavily accented Russian.

Manon froze, her mind immediately considering several possibilities. She understood the rules of interference very well. There were things she could and could not do. She also understood that Volkov had a part in this. She was not sure what it was, but he had a part. She could not kill him; killing anyone was expressly forbidden and why she had only temporarily disabled him to make her introduction to Jilly. Killing one or more of his henchmen was also out, since killing anyone was verboten. She could put them out of action, easily, but here again she had to be careful. If they also had a part in this, and they might, if she interfered, it could have serious consequences for her. Like 500 years in purgatory serious. She hesitated.

"I have pepper spray," she said. It was lame, but it was the best she could do until she had a moment to collect her thoughts.

"I don't think you do, pasha," said Spatz Spasilovich. "Be a good girl and come along. There is nothing to fear. We will talk, have a drink. Then we will take you home."

Manon knew the man was lying. She knew if she left with them it was likely they would try and kill her. She did not want this to happen. She also did not want to stop them from killing her in such a way that she broke rules and thereby removed herself from the series of events she was certain were coming. She felt she also had a part to play, a part that was connected to events from her Earthly life a long time ago. A part that might swing the final outcome of the good versus evil battle of the ages. She decided to humor them for now and take her chances. It was a low-percentage move, but she didn't feel she had many options at that moment in a deserted alleyway. "Just talk?" she said, trying her best to sound fragile and uncertain.

"Yes, yes. Just talk. I promise. Scout's honor," said Spatz, holding one palm up as though being sworn in. The Russian smiled at the other man who laughed. "Come, come. We have very nice car, Cadillac, just around the corner. You like good vodka?"

As they began to walk, an African-American man suddenly walked into the alley toward them. Spatz said something in Russian to his henchman who reached into his coat and walked quickly ahead of the group.

"Easy does it, Boris. You just keep that piece where it is if you know what's good for you," the man said, raising a pistol and racking the slide to cock it. The henchman stopped, his hand frozen inside his jacket. Spatz stopped. Everyone stopped. High noon.

"What are you boys doing with my girl? Just walking her home, I assume?" Jimmy Hallendorf said, the pistol still leveled, waist high, at the first Russian closest to him. Manon automatically noted there was no shake at all in that gun hand. It was held firmly but casually. Could have been a flashlight, or a camera, or anything, but only an idiot would have missed the professional manner in which the firearm's owner presented it.

"Well," Spasilovich said, "if it isn't the mafia's shoeshine boy. How are you, Grandfather? Why are you poking around in others' business in alleyways in the night? You looking for a bottle of Night Train? The liquor store is nearby. We'll get you a bottle," Spasilovich said, smiling.

Jimmy knew this man was crazy; that was well documented. He understood that Spatz got fired up for this kind of crazy bullshit, didn't mind rolling the dice, enjoyed the uncertainty of the outcome.

That made him extremely dangerous. Guys like that don't always apply logic to a situation. Guys like that are like giving a six-year-old boy the circular saw and seeing what he'll do with it.

"You know how us street negroes like to cruise the alleyways, always slinkin' around looking fo' trouble. Sho 'nuff," Jimmy said, smiling, the accent suddenly appearing to make his point.

"Well, you found some, Foxy Brown," the Russian said. "Now, would you like to leave us to our business, or would you perhaps like us to put that pistol up your ass the way your boss the Godmother does after a nice plate of pasta on Sunday evenings?" The look in Spatz Spasilovich's eyes was literally gleeful.

Batshit crazy, Jimmy thought. At this point, three men entered the alley behind Jimmy. One racked a shotgun slide, the sound unmistakable. Spatz' eyes narrowed as he knew the men were not his. Then a second shotgun was cocked from behind him, and Spatz cocked his head in that direction, not turning, to see three more men standing in the other end of the alley.

Spatz returned his gaze to Jimmy. He stared. Everyone waited. Then he smiled. "I think maybe you win today, Oprah. I think maybe we'll walk past you and leave," Spasilovich said. "Unless you want to go for it. Maybe we all pull and see what happens?" The smile never left the Russian's face.

That's what he wants, Jimmy thought. *He knows it's suicide but he'll go out the way he wants if we make the play. Stone-cold nutjob.*

"Tell you what, Ivan. You put your pieces on the ground, slowly, and put your hands on your heads. You do that, and I think I'll let you walk out of here. Walk out of here and go back to that fat excuse for an LL Cool J impersonator you work for. Maybe he'll give you a bone and pat you on the head. That's what you do with dogs. What do you say, Fido?" A broad smile creased Jimmy's face. He knew this was the moment it went one way or the other.

Spasilovich stared at him, and for a second, Jimmy thought it was going to go down. That he had pushed it a little too far.

Spatz smiled again. "Fido, eh?" he said. "WOOF!" he yelled and suddenly reached into his jacket.

Jimmy's men all brought their shotguns up, and Jimmy, no

newcomer to how things worked, hit the ground as he waited for his men to open up in what would be a hell of a crossfire. But Spasilovich only pulled a pack of cigarettes from his suit jacket pocket, and he held it up in the split second before he would have been summarily executed along with his boy and probably Manon too. Then he put a cigarette into his smiling mouth and stuck a match to light it. As he walked past Jimmy, still prone on the ground, he dropped the extinguished match on his back and walked out of the alley singing a song in Russian, his man trailing behind him.

Goddamn crazy Russians, Jimmy thought. *I'm getting too old for this noise.* After a few seconds, it occurred to him to look for Manon. But of course, that one, that ephemeral ghost, was gone. *Of course*, Jimmy thought.

Chapter Forty-Three

BradyFest was in full swing. The Dave was, frankly, kicking ass on all levels and exceeding any expectation. Aza stood on the balcony of the ballroom at the William Penn, looking down on the celebration going on. Dave had just been elected Mayor. This had been expected. Soon Governor would be expected too. Then the Presidency, and eventually Emperor. In Aza's mind, this was a small victory, virtually assured before the race began. His job was not to celebrate sure things. But it was going well. According to prophesy, these things were to happen if the Apocalypse was at hand. They were not guaranteed. There were never any outcomes you could depend on, and as Aza knew, this was the nature of the universe He had created. In his very old heart, he was still not sure. Every time he had his doubts about the way Brady acted, there would be another instance where he was pleasantly surprised. And vice versa. For the moment, he was comfortable it was the Time. All his communications with his superiors indicated this, and he had no reason to believe otherwise. Still...

A hand clapped Aza's back, and he knew it was Brady—not only because no other person would dare come up from behind, let alone ever touch him, but because he had that sense.

"A fabulous night," Dave said, handing Aza a champagne flute and toasting it with his own.

"Indeed. A great day, Eminence. I am pleased for you," Aza said, drinking from the glass. Looking out over the floor, he said, "There are some things we need to attend to, things that are not... pleasant."

"Yes, yes, I know. The Italians, some suspected femme fatale. They will keep. Until tomorrow, Aza. Until tomorrow," Dave said, smiling and draining his glass.

"Until tomorrow, yes, Eminence," Aza said, slightly bowing his head.

"It's all happening. All of it," Brady said, his eyes scanning the revelers below. "I'm going to do great things. As has been prophesized. I am."

As Brady's eyes met Aza's, the fallen angel's thought was: *I, not we.* "Without a doubt, Eminence," Aza said.

—

It was not often that the Don met Jilly away from his stronghold on the Northside. Today it was the bar at Max's Allegheny. The lunchtime crowd was thin, and they had the booth Art Rooney Sr. used to have, set in such a way that it was difficult to approach, more difficult to hear the conversation. Among the locals,and there was nobody *but* locals in Max's, sort of like the Pope's booth. You don't ask the Pope for an autograph, and you sure as hell don't bother him over his bratwurst and potato pancakes.

The Don had neither sausage nor potato pancakes, but rather a cup of coffee and a highball glass of Galliano and ice—a liqueur which Max's kept in a cupboard for the Don, the tall bottle not fitting their hundred-year-old back bar. Jilly was eating. He loved the German food that was Max's specialty.

"Jimmy said the Wolf moved on the female hitter last night, as we had suspected," the Don said casually and quietly, his eyes scanning the barroom like always, not meeting Jilly's own.

The "Jimmy" who the Don had just mentioned sat near the end of the bar, a glass of Diet Coke in front of him, pretending to read the *Post-Gazette* while watching anything and everything. At his age and with the Kangol on his head, he could have passed for Samuel L. Jackson, although Jimmy would have said SLJ was bush league. Were a movie ever made about Jimmy's life, he liked to say it was Denzel he wanted to play him. All *Training Day* badass with a little Frank Lucas style thrown in.

"How'd that go?" Jilly asked, his mouth full of lightly breaded, pounded veal cutlet most knew as Weiner schnitzel.

"It was handled," the Don said, not one for getting into the details.

"Spatz?"

"Yes."

Jilly paused, looked at the elderly Italian gentleman across from him, the obvious question on his mind but of course not asked. Not here in this public place, anyway. The Don looked at Jilly directly, and Jilly remembered why this man had kept his position for so long.

"You don't need to take our Russian friend off your Christmas card list," the Don said. "I'm sure he's at Kennywood this morning riding the carousel." The Don's eyes were once again on the room and not on Jilly's own.

Interesting, Jilly thought, making a mental note to ask Jimmy about that little rodeo another time.

"We have a new Mayor," Don Mia said. "Not the candidate I voted for. This was a failure. I think I may have underestimated some of our competitors." Jilly was surprised, although he was careful not to show this. He waited.

"I think we will need to be more proactive," the Don continued. It's important this man not become Governor, and that is their plan."

After a silence Jilly interpreted as his opportunity to ask a question, he said, "Why is that important?"

Neither man looked at each other during this conversation. An onlooker might have assumed they were discussing the weather, or the pine-scented urinal blocks Max's had recently begun using in the men's room (much to the chagrin of the regular clientele).

"It's important," the Don said. In that simple statement, Jilly understood there was more to this than a turf war with the Russians, the making of money, or the Don's legacy. Things that Jilly had started to understand himself were being validated by his mentor.

There was more to this than met the eye or could be explained to the casual observer.

"Okay," Jilly said. "What's the play?"

The Don turned and looked at Jilly. "He doesn't become Governor."

Jilly looked back at the Don. He nodded slowly. "This is important to you."

The Don looked back over the barroom, not saying anything for a while as Jilly waited. Finally, the older man said, "It's not important to me. It's important to us."

With that, and without looking at Jilly again, he moved slowly from the booth and left, taking his fedora and saying his goodbyes to the waitresses and the manager, as was his custom. When he reached the front door, Jimmy got up from his barstool and followed, tucking his newspaper under his arm, a slight nod of the head to Jilly as he passed the booth.

Later, in his study, the Don was reading. He did this often, mostly when he wanted to stop thinking about things and be distracted for a while. This particular evening, he was reading *To Kill A Mockingbird*. The book was signed and had some collector value, though the Don cared little for these things. But his mind kept slipping to the problem at hand, the problem that had occupied most of his thoughts these days. He heard, but did not react to, the noise of the door to his study slipping open. He heard the padded feet on the hardwood and knew that a dog was coming to him but also that Martin was with the dog. He closed the book, turning from his couch.

"We're interrupting you," Martin said. "I'm sorry, your girl would not be denied. Throws herself at you like all of them do." The Labrador moved up to Mia's side, entire body wagging.

"Dammi un bacio," the Don said quietly and leaned his head toward the big dog, who licked the side of his face. The dog did not understand Italian, but when the Don wanted a kiss, she understood that well enough. Martin came and sat down across from the couch in a comfortable chair and waited.

After a while, Marino Fanzi said, "How was the doctor?"

Martin, who had become accustomed a long time ago to the

Don knowing things he shouldn't have been aware of, took a deep breath and said, "I'm fine."

"You're fine," Mia echoed, staring at Martin with those steel blue eyes.

Martin stared back. In his way, Martin was as much, if not more so, a rock than the Don. To those who knew them both, Martin was always the ever-present assistant, the second to the Great Man, but in private, Martin understood that his value was not in treating Mia Fanzi as some kind of God, but rather treating him like someone who was loved and cared for. And sometimes, most of the time, that involved straight talk.

"It is what it is. It's not worse, it's not getting better. If it gets worse, we'll talk about what we need to do. I'm not happy about it, but I'm not digging fucking ditches either, and I have no complaints." As he said the last, he placed his palms on his thighs and leaned forward, defiant, ready for a counter argument. Martin did not cry or get emotional; it was not his way. He would not, not ever, be the big, emotional, flamboyant man. Didn't need to.

The Don digested this last comment, then nodded ever so slightly, mainly to himself.

Then Martin changed directions. "This Brady," Martin said. The Don said nothing, but his look said, *I'm listening.*

"I think we need to talk to the Widow Antonucci."

Chapter Forty-Four

That day's team meeting was held in the Fairmont's tenth-floor conference room. Oliver wasn't sure why as it was only, as always, just the three of them and Uri's suite had a separate dining room where they usually met, but then again, he wasn't sure why Uri did a lot of things, especially lately.

Oliver was wearing what had become his favorite outfit—a pair of what looked like pajama bottoms, this particular pair orange with black cartoon wiener dogs on them with mummy-like bandages and the phrase "Happy Hallowiener" under each dog, and a t-shirt emblazoned with the phrase "Jesus Was Not a Jagoff" with a big smiley face. Ragg socks and Birkenstock sandals completed the look that could only be described as either Silicon Valley Billionaire or Thirty-Something Unemployed Slacker. He had arrived early. Ten minutes early, actually. He played *Grand Theft Auto* on his computer while he waited.

Manon had arrived five minutes early, was wearing black jeans, a black v-neck sweater with a black t-shirt underneath, and black pennyloafers, no socks. Her hair was pulled back into a simple ponytail. She was wearing virtually no makeup but did have on lipstick, which she did not usually wear when it was just the three of them. She was not playing a video game and did not, in fact, have a laptop with her. Oliver thought she looked beautiful.

Oliver became aware she was looking at him. He paused the video game, the room suddenly becoming silent. "What?" Oliver said. Manon continued to look at him flatly, saying nothing. "What?" Oliver said again, with more urgency. He looked down at himself, expecting to see some big stain on his shirt or that his fly was open, but neither was the case. As they heard the door open, Oliver looked back up at Manon and raised his eyebrows, turning his palms upward as if to silently say "What?" for the third time. He saw her just slowly shake her head and turn to look out at the city through the ever-present floor-to-ceiling windows which seemed to be in every room of this hotel.

Uri breezed in. Today's look was sort of Elton John meets Lawrence of Arabia. White, the idea of a caftan but with more layers, complete with white headgear. Oliver, a big Peter O'Toole fan, wondered if there was a camel somewhere. He liked camels.

Uri went straight to a wall-mounted whiteboard and began writing on it, his back to them. "Manon, report on Brady," he said as he wrote.

"He wants to have dinner," she said.

"Good," Uri said. "Very good. Agree to it."

"He will expect physical favors eventually," Manon said, her voice maintaining that same flat tone as she continued to stare out the windows.

Oliver cringed. It was almost physically painful for him to imagine some human being touching, or rubbing against, or... whatever, with Manon. You just didn't do that with goddesses. They were...well, they were holy.

"I think you can handle his advances, Manon," Uri said. "We need him to open up about his sinister plans, verify what we already know in our hearts. Verify it so we can convince that crew," he said, pointing a finger toward the ceiling, "that we need to take action. Direct, decisive action before it's too late to take it." His eyes were glittering.

Crazy Eyes, thought Oliver absently, only partially aware of the thought.

"I can handle his advances," Manon said, turning to look at Uri.

"Not that way. You know I don't mean that way," Uri said. "If you lose control and kill him now, before we can prove he's the Antichrist, they will decide we were all blowing this out of proportion, and we'll have a nice time playing checkers in purgatory for a few hundred years. You're a professional, and I expect you to act like one."

Manon stared at Uri. "I am a professional," she said, but this time not exactly flat and with just enough inflection, for Oliver at least, to swear there was a hint of sarcasm in there. Uri did not appear to catch it. If he did, he chose to ignore it.

A professional assassin or a professional whore? Manon wondered to herself. Seduction was not her game. It was beneath her. But she was bound to serve, and disobeying an archangel of Uriel's level was like a corporal telling a general he didn't like the order he was just given. So, serve she would. But she didn't have to like it.

Uri was done writing for the moment on the whiteboard. Down the left side of it, he had written a column of names: Leonard, Russians, Italian Don, Priest, Widow. He then drew a line to the right of the column, top of the whiteboard to the bottom, creating an empty column to the right of the list of names. "What do all of these have in common?"

There was silence.

"The bartender," Manon said.

"Yes!" said Uri excitedly, pointing his dry erase marker at Manon. "Exactly right. Our bartender. The hitter. Have either of you read *Fine Temporum?* By Giglio?" Uri asked.

Oliver looked confused, which did not surprise Uri one iota. He turned and looked at Manon, who was looking at him strangely, a light of understanding coming into her eyes. Uri smiled.

"You think Julian Tetanich is the Judge," Manon said.

"Tell me it doesn't all fit perfectly with that prophesy," Uri said.

"It's a book, not prophesy. One of many books and interpretations of the Apocalypse," Manon said. But she didn't sound like her normal disinterested self. She sounded unsure.

"He's the Judge," Uri said. I'm certain of it." Uri also did not mention he had pretty much dictated the very book he was referencing to a crazy man wearing a loincloth on a mountainside in Italy about 700 years earlier. "At first I thought the bartender was just a convenient tool in our mission to stop Brady. We have some... info, intelligence if you will, on him that we can use to motivate him to do what we are prohibited from doing. But as events have unfolded, I am convinced he's more than just that. It's all in the prophesy. Not just the Executioner, I am certain this man is the Judge who must make a decision and decide the entire outcome. He's more important than ever."

Manon had turned again toward the windows and she stared out of them, lost in thought. It had been a long time since she had read *Fine Temporum,* but she had to admit there were striking similarities to the characters in this current drama.

"What Judge?" she heard Oliver say as the meeting ended.

—

In the Prince of Peace Rectory, Sister Mary Lee stuck her head into Father Bill's office and said, "Sir, do you have a minute?"

Father Bill was sitting in his desk chair, his back to her, staring out the small window that faced out onto the playground of the daycare center the diocese operated. His reading glasses were resting up on his forehead. His hands were steepled on his stomach. He looked very far away. So far away, in fact, that Sister Mary Lee had considered not interrupting him. But not for long. She had sort of expected him to be jolted out of his trance by her interruption, but she was wrong. He just blinked, sighed, and turned to face her, almost as if he had known she was there all along.

"Sister," he said, "please sit down."

Sister Mary Lee did just that. She had expected him to say something like "What can I do for you?" or "How can I help you?" but he didn't. Just looked at her. Calm. It was pretty creepy. This was a guy she didn't seem to know lately. He wore his collar and blacks all the time. No jeans or sweatpants. He spent hours in his office reading a variety of documents that didn't seem to have any association with each other. Not that she checked the titles or anything when he was out of the office. A lot of it was old stuff, many of the titles in Latin.

And he was praying. Now, to the layman this would seem unremarkable. But to a bona fide, genuine, brains-behind-the-collar sidekick such as herself, this was a change from the norm. Not that Father Bill didn't pray. Not at all. But lately, he was putting on a bit of a clinic. He prayed early in the morning (before 7 a.m. Imagine!). He prayed late in the evening when everyone had gone home and the vast nave of the church was empty. She had no idea what had come over him, although she had her suspicions.

As a dutiful sister of the diocese, she regularly visited elderly shut-ins. Okay, some more than others. Okay, the Widow Antonucci a lot more than others. The nun had expressed her observations regarding a certain lately pious priest to The Widow on a few occasions the past few weeks. The Widow had been completely unsurprised. Leaning back in her chair, her ever present cigarette always just microns away from lighting whatever imitation lace concoction headgear she was wearing into a Hindenburg-esque conflagration, she'd just smile and nod and say, "Yes, yes. As has been foretold."

When pressed as to what exactly had been foretold, who had done the foretelling, and what the hell happened next, Madonna Antonucci would only smile and nod and say, "In time, in time."

With all of this in mind, Sister Mary Lee said to the priest, "You doing okay?"

"I'm fine," Father Bill said. "You?"

"Fine," she said. The ornate mantel clock across from Father Bill's desk, a timepiece he had inherited along with all the other furniture in this office from prior occupants, ticked loudly. She waited. He stared at her. Calm.

Finally, unable to bear it anymore, Sister Mary Lee began, "The Widow Antonucci thinks—"

Father Bill interrupted her, saying, "The Antichrist is among us and it's the End of Times. As has been prophesized. I know." He gave her a tired smile.

The nun stared at him, digesting this. "Do you..." Sister Mary Lee started again. "Do you believe her?"

Father Bill sighed again and picked up the baseball from the holder it sat in on his desk. Autographed by the great Roberto himself, he liked to toss it from hand to hand when he needed to concentrate. "Maybe," he finally said. Then, after a pause, "I don't know." He looked at her, then said, "What do you think?"

Sister Mary Lee's mind whirled. She had not expected this answer. "She's nuts," she said quickly. "Everyone knows it."

Father Bill just looked at her, a hint of a smile on his face. Again, that tired smile.

Sister Mary Lee felt nervous, the foundations of her entire belief system shaking a little in a manner she did not like. No sir, she did not like this one little bit. She continued quickly, gaining the speed she reflexively felt would make the argument that would preserve her sanity, "She once told me Pee-Wee Herman was also the Antichrist. She believes water from the Monongahela has curative powers, so she dunks herself in it once a week. Naked. Right by the Mon Wharf where everyone parks. And Justin Timberlake has the mark of the beast on him—six-six-six tattoo, just under his hairline, left side, behind the ear." She had blurted all of these observations out, machine gun style, and now she took a deep breath, realizing she was sweating a little. She had moved to the front edge of her seat and was clasping her hands together so hard that her nails were starting to hurt her own palms. She looked so forlorn Father Bill could not stifle a smile. "What?" Sister Mary Lee said.

Father Bill, leaning forward and lowering his voice in a conspiratorial tone, said, "To be honest?"

"Yes?" Sister Mary Lee whispered, her voice literally trembling.

"I think it's Kim Kardashian that has the mark of the beast on her," Father Bill said.

Sister Mary Lee digested this comment, then blurted out, "THAT IS NOT FUNNY!" and collapsed back into her seat, covering her eyes with her hands.

After a few seconds of silence, Father Bill began to laugh. After a while, the nun joined him. Hearing the laughter as he ran his mop over the mosaic floors of the nave, Charlie, the church's cleaning guy and maintenance man, wondered if they were hitting the sacrificial wine up there in the rectory.

Chapter Forty-Five

Jilly opened the very nondescript, but heavy, black-painted door on Smallman Street and entered. It was 2:30 in the afternoon on a reasonably sunny day, but the instant the door closed behind him, the room returned to that kind of hazy, neon-lit darkness cockroaches and alcoholics love.

Touchtunes played "He Stopped Loving Her Today." There were four people in the bar not counting the bartender. Three sat at the bar, none next to each other. One sat at a hightop table by himself. All turned and looked at Jilly as he paused inside the door. All then turned back to their drinks, their reverie, their lost lives, their melancholy. All of them knew the big man who had returned to this place after a long absence. None of them had any interest in challenging his right to be here, among them. Jilly had earned his Players Card. Hell, the fact of the matter was his visit was kind of like Derek Jeter showing up at the local sandlot. Royalty was in the house.

Jilly took a barstool and seated himself. He said nothing and looked at no one.

The bartender—a 300-pound, six-foot-three, bald, heavily tattooed man—walked down and said, "Jack and Coke?"

Jilly nodded slightly, then turned to look at the man at the hightop table. A small man, half hidden in the shadows, but Jilly knew who he was. He turned back to the bar as his drink arrived. Taking a sip, he stared into the mirror behind the bar and breathed deeply. And waited.

After a while, maybe five minutes, he heard a voice say, "Long time, Hitter. Come talk to me."

Jilly smiled to himself, aware of how easily this life returned to him, and not minding it either. He eased himself off his stool, turned, and took the few steps to the table. All three patrons on their barstools noticed, although you could not have determined this from their demeanor, nor any perceptible movement at all.

The man was slight, balding, and wore horn-rimmed glasses. He was wearing slacks (worn but clean), loafers, and a cardigan sweater over a button-down shirt. He dressed this way as he didn't want the general public to believe him riffraff. He was no animal, after all. If you passed him on the street, you would not have noticed him. He was completely unremarkable. This was intentional. As of this particular day, his career stats indicated he had killed sixty-four men and was worth 2.7 million dollars.

"How's business, Julian?" the man asked.

Jilly smiled slightly. "Business is good, Cheech. Good. You?"

"Oh," the little man said, "I'm retired, like you. Just living the good life. Grandkids keep me busy, but I'm old and I'm tired." Both men knew this was bullshit. Manuel "Chi Chi" Vasquez had his hand in many things and wouldn't retire until they pried the gun from his cold, dead fingers as the bumper stickers indicated. "What brings you here, friend? A little thirsty maybe? Just need a drink?" Chi Chi smiled a little, not making eye contact, knowing that the need for a drink was absolutely not why the big man was in this bar at this particular time.

"You know about Dave Brady?" Jilly asked, sipping his drink, also not making eye contact.

The small man paused for a while and then said, "You remember Pauli Sistilli?"

After thinking for a few seconds, Jilly said, "Teamster guy? Crewcut?"

"That's him," Chi Chi said. "Ruled the roost for a while back in the late nineties." Jilly waited. This was part of the process. Anything less than an air of absolute disinterest meant you were a poseur, a jagoff. "Thing about Pauli was, after you got past all the big talk, he was a paper tiger," Chi Chi continued. "But he had muscle behind him, so everyone was careful." Again silence. Jilly sipped his drink. Chi Chi lit a cigarette. The smoking ban in Pittsburgh bars was not enforced in this place. "This Brady, he's like Pauli. Lotta noise but no sustancia, no substance, behind it. But he does have some muscle."

Jilly now turned fully on his stool and faced the man directly. He leaned in and spoke quietly but intently. "Cheech, who's behind Brady? That's what I want to know. Who is his muscle? Your guys involved?"

The little man took a long drag on his cigarette. "I am a little crazy, it's true, but I am not insane. I consider Don Mia a friend. And I don't associate with paper tigers," he finished, looking directly at Julian, his eyes hard.

Jilly nodded slowly. "Then who? It's not the Wolf."

"No, not the silly Russian," Chi Chi said. Again, Jilly waited. Eventually Manuel Vasquez said, "There is talk of a man, a devil." Neither man looked at each other while Jilly sipped his drink and Chi Chi exhaled another plume of smoke. "They say he is a diablo, works for Satan himself."

Jilly turned back to Chi Chi and stared. "A devil." he said.

"A devil." Chi Chi repeated.

"You've seen this man?" Jilly said. Again, he waited for Chi Chi to respond. This time it took a while longer.

"Yes, I've seen him. He dresses in red. He fears no one. He is frightening." As Chi Chi said this, he silently crossed himself, never taking his eyes from Jilly's, this man who had killed so many, completely unembarrassed at doing so.

—

Across the river from downtown Pittsburgh, there's the Southside and then there are the Southside Slopes. The Southside has Carson Street with its bars and shops, skews younger, trendy but in a blue-collar way. Springsteen had jumped onstage here to sit in with local bands in small bars earlier in his career. Southside is legendary. The Slopes sit behind the Southside, further from the river and Carson, residential and a bit of a walk to the action but with a decent view of the Monongahela river as you elevate up the slope. Then, as you drift out of the Slopes and the only view is of the Rite Aid, you come to Arlington. It was here that the Widow Antonucci made her home. And it was here on this cloudy afternoon that a priest, a nun, and a consigliere made their way up the sidewalk to the entranceway of a squat, two-story, red-brick apartment building called Skibo Castle.

It is a fact that Andrew Carnegie never visited this place, named optimistically after the ancestral home he had purchased in his native Scotland. He was long dead when the frame butcher shop that had existed to serve the Polish steel mill workers nearby was bulldozed to make this apartment building, and though the owner had named it in a grand style, it had become old, run down, and a bit of an embarrassment. Much like The Widow herself. Pausing after climbing the six concrete steps to catch their breath, the group was startled to hear a cracking voice from the tiny speaker near the row of small mailboxes built into the front facade of the building.

"The three wise men! Park your camels, bring your frankincense, myrrh, and especially your gold!" the voice said, breaking into tinny laughter. Then the front door buzzed, and after a cursory look at each other, the three walked in. The door at the end of the first floor hallway stood partways open, and they made their way in that direction.

"Come, come, children!" they heard a female voice say.

As a visitor entered the Widow Antonucci's apartment, they could not help but be struck by two things. First, that every conceivable space, every inch of wall and every square foot of floor, was covered in something. Anything. Postcard pictures of Europe were tacked to the walls everywhere, reproduction paintings of saints, popes, Frank Sinatra, Venice, Florence, Spain, Paris, Cleveland. Cabinets and shelves of figurines, statues, imitation crystal, animal figurines of every type were represented. There were more statues of the Virgin Mary in varying sizes in this apartment than the group had collectively seen in their lives.

And crucifixes. Had Jesus been forced to carry the combined weight of the crucifixes in TWA's apartment, he'd have gone two blocks and died of a combination hernia/heart attack before he ever had the chance to be crucified.

The other thing was the smell of cooking. This kitchen was used. A lot. Fabulous smells of Italian cooking were layered over each other like the eight coats of paint on the walls. It occurred to Father Bill that this home probably smelled better than any seventy-five-year-old osteria in any part of Italy.

And then there was the apartment's sole occupant. Seated in an imitation Louis XIV chair complete with imitation gilding—her Croc-clad feet propped up on an imitation gilded and red imitation velvet upholstered footstool—was The Widow herself. No imitation here. The genuine article. All three simply stood, processing the view. Today Madonna had gone with a blue turban complete with jewel, chandelier earrings the size of silver dollars, a light blue caftan that was interwoven with what appeared to be dragons either fighting or procreating (Sister Mary Lee could not tell which and dared not stare too long). Completing the look were black and gold Pittsburgh Spirit indoor soccer league knee socks and gold Crocs. The look was, in a word, heartstopping.

Fanning herself one last time with what appeared to be a Giant Eagle sushi bar grand opening paper fan, the Widow Antonucci gestured the group forward. "Come, come!" And so they came.

Father Bill, Sister Mary Lee, and Angelo Fanzi Sr. found seats. This was easier said than done as, although there were several chairs and couches, the surface areas of most were covered with pillows and cushions, many embroidered with words of wisdom like "Home is where the Braciole is" or "If You Won't Kiss The Cook, Then Kiss My Ass." The Widow waited expectantly.

"Madonna, we're here to—" Angie Sr. began.

"I know why you're here, Angelo," the Widow interrupted.

"You do?" Father Bill said.

"Of course," the Widow said.

"Of course she does," Sister Mary Lee said without thinking, then sat back, shocked she had spoken that thought out loud.

Father Bill looked at her. She looked at him then quickly looked away at what appeared to be a paint-by-numbers rendering of "Madonna and Child" by Salvi. Mentally, she rated it a four.

"Yes, I know why you are here," the Widow Antonucci said with a knowing and wise look at all three of them. She paused for theatrical effect, then lifted an imitation bone china teacup from its imitation (almost) matching bone china saucer and sipped it delicately, frowned, searched the folds of her caftan and removed a plastic pint bottle of Old Grandad. Tipping a generous dollop into her teacup, she sipped again and let out a satisfied "ahhh" before continuing:

"You have problems. Big problems. The Widow sees this." All three looked at each other and then just waited. "You are worried about that donkey who was elected mayor. You are worried about the fool Russian. You are worried about the Man in Red." The Widow paused. Carefully, slowly, she looked each of them in the eyes. "Aren't you." It wasn't a question.

"We're concerned—" Father Bill began.

"Concerned?!" the Widow erupted, eyes blazing, nearly spilling her teacup onto the imitation Persian rug at her feet.

Sister Mary Lee reflexively crossed herself, then felt kind of stupid for doing that, given there was no particular evil in the room at the moment. Unless you counted the imitation Picasso painting of Tom Brady staring at her from the wall next to the piano, one large eye and one small eye following her every move.

"Concerned," the Widow said again in a quieter tone, her eyes still ablaze. "You're not concerned, you're terrified. As you should be."

Chapter Forty-Six

Julian had left the bar in the hands of his night bartender Mikey P. Mikey was a good-natured guy who had made some bad decisions, had three ex-wives and probably five kids, but the funny part was everyone loved him. There are guys like that. They can walk on three loans from you and yet the fourth time you'll say, "Well, I got a good feeling about this one." That was Mikey P. Like many who knew Jilly's legend, he was terrified of Jilly, and Jilly was okay with that. A crooked bartender will steal you blind, and Jilly didn't need that.

When Jilly needed to think, he often walked, and at this moment, he turned off Carson Street, the main artery of the Southside, his mind working. When he reached the river, he walked over the Hot Metal Bridge and then turned and walked back, because after all, where the hell do you go once you walk over the Hot Metal? You gonna walk the Parkway east to Monroeville? Jagoff. It was in this frame of mind he once again found himself in front of the Lamb. *Odd,* he thought. *Never been to this bar in thirty years and now twice in a month.*

Same bartender. Surprise. Nobody in the joint. Surprise. And yet he seated himself. He was powerless not to. "Miller, Jack back," the bartender said, setting his bottle and shot glass in front of him.

"How's life, Hitter?"

Jilly didn't bother to offer payment; somehow he knew it wasn't necessary. He didn't like the reference to the name most used behind his back, but not as much as normal. This was becoming familiar to him. He was very comfortable with this old man, though he could not have explained why if his life had depended on it. After his second round, he said, "You knew my father? My... my..." Jilly stuttered, sort of making a rolling gesture with his left hand.

"Your real father?" the bartender said, polishing a highball glass and smiling in that grandfatherly way. "I knew him well. I know everybody, Julian."

"What was he like?" Jilly asked.

"No bullshit," the bartender said. "A no-bullshit guy. Big son of a gun, like you. I see him in you."

"You think he would've, you know...would've..."

"Approved?" the bartender said.

"Yeah," Jilly said, wiping the back of his hand across his mouth. "Yeah. Approved. You think he would have approved?"

Now, this was a topic Jilly had never, and would never, discuss with anyone on the planet—not Anne, not Don Fanzi, not even Angie Jr.—and here he was discussing it with a bartender he didn't know at all. Or did he? Who was this guy?

The bartender flipped his towel to rest over his left shoulder and placed his hands flat on the bar, a move Jilly couldn't help but recognize as he had done it himself a thousand times. He looked at Jilly and said, "I think, Julian, he'd have said it's not what you do exactly, it's why you do it that really matters."

"Yeah," Jilly said, absently watching the bubbles in his glass. "I agree, but it's a soiled choir you're preaching to this evening, Reverend." Jilly gave a wan half smile at the old man behind the bar who was watching him with no expression on his face. "The Bible says thou shalt not kill. I know this to be true as my sainted sister has advised me of the commandments on numerous occasions," Jilly said.

The bartender looked at Jilly, then picked up a glass and absently began polishing it. He said, "I like the Bible. It's well written. Considering, of course, it depicts events that happened years before it was written. Still, it's a good working guide to the history of Christianity and has a lot of good advice."

After several seconds, Jilly said, "But…" and looked at the bartender.

"But," the bartender said, "my feeling is—and this is just me, an old man with no existential relevance at all, mind you—the book is more of a guide for human coexistence than a collection of inviolate laws."

"A guide?" Jilly said.

The bartender smiled and nodded. "A guide. Yes. After all, if you created the world and mankind, would you want to create some kind of massive owner's manual of everything your new creations might need to do in every possible circumstance? Wouldn't that pretty much defeat the experiment of creating mankind? Boring!" The bartender smiled and leaned against the back bar, not really looking at Jilly.

The jukebox Jilly never could seem to find played "Up a Lazy River" by Bobby Darin. The bartender continued, "You want my opinion, I think God puts us in situations and then watches to see how we handle them. That's what I think," and winked at Jilly.

—

Father Bill was not accustomed to debriefings at the Don's home on the Northside. He wasn't accustomed to any of this, really. He felt like an understudy who'd spent his entire career being ready, but not really expecting, to have to go deliver his lines in front of a live audience. He felt, truth be told, like he was a fraud. He was no Laurence Olivier, no Michael Jordan. He was more the overweight guy wearing the safety glasses, terrycloth headband, and knee brace trying to get into a pickup basketball game at the rec center.

The Don motioned he and Angelo Fanzi Sr. into his study. Martin removed the Labs and closed the door to stand near it but out of the radius and relevance to the conversation at hand.

Once Father Bill and his brother were comfortably seated in front of his desk, the Don began, "You understand this conversation is privileged and confidential. It does not exist." He was, in theory at least, speaking to both of them, but he was looking directly at Father Bill.

Processing this, the Polish son of a street-fighting father suddenly grew annoyed. Forgetting he was sitting in front of a man who could control life and death with a phone call, or sometimes just a nod of the head, all the stress of the last few weeks that had been building up inside him welled to the surface.

"I have a lot of privileged conversations, Mr. Fanzi," Father Bill said, purposefully opting to use "Mr." instead of "Don." He continued, "Usually Monday, Wednesday, and Saturday mornings from eight to ten, and three o'clock to five. You should stop by. Certainly, it's mostly mundane stuff, but I'd say it's pretty confidential to those who confide in me and ask for penance." He took a deep breath and then sat back, staring down at his pants and smoothing them, his energy spent. He was beginning to think that outburst may not have been a good idea.

Nobody spoke. The Don stared at him. Angelo Sr. stared intently at a brass reproduction of Michelangelo's "David" on a bookcase back and to the left of the Don. A clock ticked. The Don shifted his gaze to his brother. His brother stared back. The Don rubbed his temples, quietly said something that sounded like "tipo tosto," under his breath, stared at nothing for a moment, and then looked to the rear of the room at Martin.

"Can you bring the anisette, if you don't mind? And four glasses. Thank you, Martin."

The anisette was pretty good. Although Father Bill would not have known, Angie Sr. knew it was a Pernod and thought probably early sixties. The bottle was worth maybe $800. When they had finished their glasses, each with their own version of a deep sigh, they waited for the Don to get back to the topic at hand. Eventually he did.

"So," the Don said, looking at his brother, "Madonna Antonucci..."

Angie Sr. smiled slightly, shifted in his seat to become more comfortable, and ended up leaning to his left in the corner of his chair, his eyes distantly focused on that David statue in the bookcase. "The Widow believes Dave Brady is the Antichrist the Bible has foretold," he said. "She is certain of this. Stories her mother handed down from her mother before her and back many, many years lead her to believe this is the man who will lead the end of the world as we know it. She references the Black Angel of Death. She says forces of evil she alone senses are gathered here in Pittsburgh at this very moment. Led by a mysterious Man in Red."

Here Angie paused and everyone gave that last some thought, nobody meeting anyone else's eyes. Angie continued, "The Widow believes it's up to us to stop this man." He shifted his gaze to look his brother directly in the eyes. The Don looked back. Nobody spoke.

Father Bill stared down at his glass, now just ice cubes, and wished there was some Woodford Reserve in there. Martin looked at the Don, knowing he could say something, but as he had hundreds of times before, simply held his counsel and waited.

The Don looked at the ceiling for what seemed a long time but was probably only fifteen seconds and said, "How does Madonna feel we should help?"

Angie Sr. sighed. He looked down at his shoes, then back at his brother, then the briefest glance at Father Bill, and said, "She says it has been foretold that there will be one opportunity to stop the Antichrist from bringing about the end of the world. She says it involves a Wolf, a Weasel, and a Judge." He paused and looked at his brother. When the Don simply looked back with no expression, he continued. "She says the Man in Red can be stopped, but only through 'betrayal by one of his own.'"

When Angie Sr paused and took a sip of his drink, the Don said, "Is that all?"

"Well, no," Angelo said. "There's something about a childless mother and an angel who makes an offer that may sway the outcome."

Angie stopped here, again staring at his brother flatly, no sign of the fear the Don was used to when others addressed him. The Don felt that stare and, not for the first time in his life, thought perhaps the wrong Fanzi kid had become King of this particular fiefdom. But that was crazy.

"That all?" the Don said again, steepling his fingers and trying to maintain an air of control over this surreal meeting.

His brother, again staring annoyingly off into space at the bookshelf to the right and behind the Don said, "Almost. She also feels strongly there is a priest involved in this outcome." Silence ensued. They all looked at the priest.

The priest, who was not looking at anyone but knew without any doubt whatsoever that they were all looking at him, looked again at his glass and sent up a silent prayer that it be magically filled with bourbon as with the loaves and fish. Somewhere far above, in the sprawling (but bright and comfortable) offices of the Holy Host, a Junior Listener (it was nowhere near Primetime, when more senior staff would be manning the Prayer Line) logged the prayer and, seeing on the video feed that it had been sent by an earnest-looking, middle-aged man in a cassock and collar, clicked immediately on "Approve."

A hand appeared over Father Bill's shoulder, taking his glass. Martin went to the sideboard, placed fresh ice, a generous pour of Pappy Van Winkle, about fifty dollars' worth, and handed it back to Father Bill. There had been no sound in this entire exchange.

Understanding it was his turn to talk, he took a generous sip from his glass, wiped his mouth with the back of his hand, looked up at the group, took a deep breath, and said, "There's a book, written by a zealot a long time ago, about 700 years or so..."

Chapter Forty-Seven

Brady was dressed well. Damn well, actually. Not all black tonight. He had the black suit jacket and trousers, of course, but this was now his style. He was trying to affect a slightly softer image, a half step away from the Prince of Darkness look he had draped about himself since he had become aware he was going to rule the world. So tonight he had a charcoal shirt and vest combo on—a little gray to offset the black—and in his lapel, a red rose, a nod to Aza. Jeanne would dig it, he was certain. Chicks dug Dave. Always, really, but even more lately.

He sat at a corner table at LeMont on Mount Washington, the restaurant windows directly overlooking downtown Pittsburgh and the confluence of the three rivers. The view was the best in the city, especially at night. And he wasn't at *a* corner table, he was at *the* corner table. No other tables in front of him to spoil the view. No bodyguards tonight; he was off the grid for this. He had told Aza he had some deep historical reading to do and that he would be at his apartment with his phone switched off.

He was awaiting a lady. Not a normal lady either. He had pursued Manon/Jeanne relentlessly over the past few weeks, and eventually, as he knew she would, she gave in. To his charm, he liked to think, but he suspected it was his looks and his raw sexuality.

That's what got all of them, and frankly, since his ascension, as he considered it, his natural attractiveness had gone into overdrive. But he had to play this one carefully because this woman was different. He would have had a hard time explaining it, but this woman was exciting to him in a way no other woman had ever been. It was a combination of things he couldn't quite put his finger on. She was pretty, of course, but he had been with prettier. She was smart, but he had dated smart women. She was just kind of generally, well, dangerous. That was it, really. This woman was dangerous.

And that made her exciting. And if he were truly honest with himself, and the eventual Emperor of the Planet always was, he was a little afraid of her. Not that he'd ever admit that to any woman. And then here she was. His pulse quickened, and without consciously thinking about it, he sat a little straighter in his seat. He tried to affect a cosmopolitan, uncaring demeanor but didn't pull it off.

For her part, Manon did a much better job affecting disinterest, mainly because she was disinterested. Solidly disinterested. Not only was this because in her post-life state, sex was of no interest to her, but also because when she *had* been interested in men many, many years ago, she would not have been interested in a Dave Brady. He was not an ugly man, of course. She understood in this time and place he was probably a catch, but he lacked a certain...manliness about him that she found offputting. He was too pasty, too fussy, too put together, and particularly too in love with himself to ever have attracted a woman of Manon's composition.

But tonight she had a job to do, a job of celestial importance and possibly one that might impact the outcome of humanity and the Apocalypse, so although she was not thrilled with the role she had to play tonight, she reminded herself she was a professional. She would deliver.

She was wearing a black bolero suit, pants, and short jacket with some exquisite white embroidery on the lapels and cuffs, white blouse, black heels, and makeup. A black bolero hat would have blown the doors off the look, but it would have attracted more attention than she was already generating, so she wisely went with a side ponytail that fell around the left side of her neck and lay on her breastbone. Dave was speechless. Most of the restaurant was speechless. But as she settled into her chair across the table from Dave, it was as if someone hit the "play" button from "pause," and the other diners went back to their conversations as though Manon did not exist. He thought she had that ability and wondered how she did it.

Dave stared at her.

"Sometimes a gentleman rises and offers a lady a chair," Manon said, no inflection at all in her voice, no expression on her face.

Dave smiled, jolted out of his momentary shock. "Yes, my, uh, my apologies," he said, flushing. It's just that you...you look, uh, well. Beautiful." He knew that was fairly lame and that he was completely out of his normal Rico Suave mode, but he couldn't help it. There was just something about this woman...

Fortunately, a waiter appeared and asked if the lady would like a drink. The waiter had a French accent, not unusual among LeMont's staff, and so Manon switched to French and ordered champagne. The waiter lit up like a sparkler and began speaking in rapid-fire French, all the while gesturing with his hands. Eventually, he kissed Manon's hand and promised to come back with the very best bottle he could find. Dave was not jealous, only amazed. This woman.

Manon stared out at the city. "Best view in the Burgh," Dave said.

"Yes, it's pretty," Manon replied.

"Yes, pretty," Dave said, "but it doesn't compare to you."

Manon turned and looked Dave in the eyes. At this moment, Dave had two thoughts: First, he'd give anything in the entire world, betray any friend or relative, beg, borrow, steal, or murder to sleep with this woman, and second, he was terrified of sleeping with this woman, and on some extremely deep level he'd examine later by himself, he knew this was probably never, ever going to happen. And he was relieved. But that was nonsense. He was Dave Fuckin' Brady. The Antichrist. The Johnny Carson of the goddamn Apocalyptic *Tonight Show*. He gathered himself, took a sip of his martini, and smiled.

Manon steeled herself and thought, *Je suis une professionnelle.* And she became a professional. She looked down at the table, took a deep breath, and when she looked up again at Dave, her eyes had softened. "So tell me, who are you and what were you before? What did you do and what did you think?"

Dave just stared. If he had looked her square in the eye and said, "We said no questions," Manon might have had some respect for him, since, of course, that was what Ingrid Bergman had said to Bogart when he had posed those questions to her. But he didn't.

Over the course of the next two hours, a very good dinner, and four additional martinis, Dave talked. A lot. He didn't give specific details, of course, but he made it very clear he intended to become President of the United States. And maybe even a bigger job, although he would not elaborate. He talked about "very powerful friends" and "forces outside normal boundaries" that were assisting him. He talked about his "destiny." He occasionally let slip that things were "as had been written."

Manon listened with a look of rapt attention on her face, nodding where appropriate, not overreacting but exhibiting the correct level of awe at the future of the man she was seated with on that particular evening.

When the waiter had retreated with the check, Dave looked at Manon and said, "Do you believe in good and evil?"

"That is the second time you've asked me that, Dave Brady," Manon said.

"It's an important question," Dave replied. "Myself, I think it's less good versus evil, as much as those in the know and the sheep who will be herded. So, Jeanne, are you a sheep or more of a shepherd?"

Manon looked at him. A thousand thoughts ran through her mind in three seconds. She said, "I think I am neither. I watch the sheep, and I watch the shepherds. Sometimes, if I feel strongly, I stop the slaughter of the sheep. Other times, I don't." She looked out at the city below her for a long moment. "And sometimes I slaughter the shepherd," she said, her gaze returning to Dave. He thought he saw just the hint of a smile around her eyes.

What a unique woman, thought Dave. What a pistol. He would lay awake for a long time after he got back to his apartment. In her room at the Fairmont Manon was asleep just minutes after her head hit her pillow.

Back at the Fairmont, Uri looked across the large dining

room table where he and Oliver had been listening to the entire conversation between Manon and Brady. "I knew it," Uri said. "Absolutely, positively knew it all along. Nobody believed me, but I knew he was the Antichrist. And this is the proof. You heard him yourself. It's time, Oliver. It's time to move. Before it's too late."

—

Unable to sleep, Jilly lay awake in his bed trying to summarize events into some kind of logical order. The way things were going, the sort of tidal swell he had begun to feel, led him to believe that just about everyone he had been in contact with over the past two months or so was being carried forward on some kind of strange wave that none of them were capable of stopping no matter how hard they might try. Here, he had some kind of Heavenly Hit Team in town with the Michelangelo of historical assassins wandering around the Strip District. Over there, he had an otherwise unremarkable insurance agent who might play some part in the end of the world. He had a villain. (Wasn't there always a villain? Deep down, he was glad this time he wasn't the villain.) A Man in Red straight out of Central Casting who was helping the insurance agent become the Lord of Darkness. Lovely. Leonard had become some kind of John Malkovich character with bloodshot eyes in a wrinkled suit. *Leonard,* for fuck's sake. Jilly had watched Leonard take, and swallow in one gulp, half-full vodka tonics sitting in front of passed-out patrons at Jilly's very own bar with no shame. Jesus Chr...

The Don was involved—how deep, Jilly wasn't sure. He was never sure in matters pertaining to Mia Fanzi. But there was no question he was with the Eradicate Brady faction. Except the Don had apparently been powerless to handle that particular job himself or with his crew. Then there was his friend Father Bill. Also on the Home Team sidelines like some kind of Holy Offensive Coordinator, a man he had known a long time and, though he'd not likely admit it, was his moral compass, had more or less begged him to take the heat off everyone else (including the planet) by doing that voodoo, that he do, so well.

His buddy the bookseller had the script (sort of) and a bag

of popcorn, pretty much content to watch this whole thing play out with a Macanudo and a bourbon sitting in an air-conditioned luxury box in the basement of his bookstore. Somewhere in the background was a crazy Russian gangster wannabe who Jilly had sensed had something to do with this whole mess. But he had no idea what the Wolf's part was.

He knew he should go slow. He had no idea why, but on this point he was absolutely sure. That was fine—it suited his nature. Jilly had watched a target go to the same grocery store six days in a row at almost the exact same time before deciding that on the seventh day he'd make his move. He also knew he didn't have all the info yet. There were pieces to this that he felt strongly had yet to be revealed, and would be revealed, soon. He knew this "in his bones," as the old timers would have said.

The thing was, if he were honest with himself, nobody had asked him for a decision. Not yet anyway. The Super Hitter in Black had said this was what was going to happen, and Jilly was certain it was going to, and probably soon, but it hadn't. Not yet. He had gathered all the info he could. He had become as familiar as possible with the terrain, the habits, and the overall situation. And now he waited. And waited.

Chapter Forty-Eight

Oliver had been doing some research. A lot, actually. On Dave Brady. The results would not make any headlines on the Hell version of TMZ. As the nerd of the group, Oliver understood that his value, where he could add any, was in analytics. Much like Eliot Ness bringing down Al Capone via tax evasion instead of murder, Oliver knew he wasn't going to "smite" anyone with a flaming sword anytime soon. But. If you took Wikipedia, and the whole internet, and then combined that with every library on the planet, then every newspaper ever written, then added in the fact that his "System" could track movements and actions of every human being who had ever lived (don't ask, it's a God thing)... Well then. That's a lot of data. And, with this kind of data, Oliver was in his element. Immersed in the data, he was Einstein. He was Botticelli, Toscanini, Frank Lloyd Wright—pick your genius. The Cake Boss. And this evening he was buried deep in his data.

He was wearing a Snuggie. He liked it. He'd had a cheesesteak (his twenty-seventh in three weeks) an hour earlier at Primantis. They knew him now and assumed Oliver was some kind of code-writing software genius since he kept showing up in pajamas, buying twelve-dollar sandwiches and handing them old hundred-dollar bills that appeared to have been in a cardboard box in Andrew Carnegie's basement for 100 years while saying, "That's for you. Grab yourself a beer after work." Oliver loved this line; it was from a movie he had watched called *The Pope of Greenwich Village* on his room TV, originally thinking any movie about a pope had to be good.

While he was confused that there were never any references to a real Pope, the Holy See, Rome, or even an actual church of any kind, he had been fascinated with Mickey Rourke and particularly Eric Roberts in the role of the likeable but hapless sidekick. Occasionally he stared out his window at the city, grabbed his (towel-wrapped) left hand, and screamed, "Charlieeeeeee! They took my thumb! Charlieeeeee!" But we digress.

The data was strange. As he had mentioned to Uri already, Dave Brady didn't really fit the profile of what Oliver felt a true Antichrist should. If he were a seismologist, he would have been looking for the San Andreas Fault. Earthquakes leading up the to the Big One. In this case, a nice increasing trend line of Dark Behavior he could reasonably extrapolate to an explosion of chaos in a nice bar graph. But it wasn't there. Davie B. was not a good guy. That much was easy to see. He was self-centered, had a superiority complex, had apparently murdered a henchman (Oliver loved that term and secretly aspired to be a henchman), and Dave had told Manon in so many words he intended to rule the world. But from a purely evil standpoint—and we're talking the Antichrist here—his stats just didn't hold up.

If Dave were a fantasy football QB, you'd have him like eighth on any given Sunday. Sure he might win a game, but that assumed some injuries, cheesy pass interference calls, and a tailwind. This was not the stuff biblical prophesies had foretold. In Oliver's opinion, anyway. Dave Brady was going to rule the world and bring about the Apocalypse? At best, the guy was Gong Show Evil.

Uriel had requested a meeting with Jesus. In fact, he had made the trip back upstairs for this specific reason. It was time to fulfill his destiny. He had the data, he had the experience, he had the tools, and he had the talent.

"The thing is, Lord," Uri began, "we have been assembling information. Our team has infiltrated the Dark Forces, and we feel certain the Antichrist is walking the planet right now."

Jesus looked at Uri, eyes widening. "No shit?" Jesus said, then covered his mouth and grimaced, looking around as if a nun was about to come over and slap his hand with a ruler. "Sorry," Jesus said, then continued, "The real Antichrist. Like, the Guy?".

"Yes, Lord," Uriel said. "The Guy."

"Wow." Jesus swivelled his chair to his right and stared out at the clouds. "Well, we always knew it was going to happen. The Book says so. Was always just a question of when."

Uri's mind still swirled. This was too easy. He awaited the next thing Jesus might say as a man in the middle of a minefield, not sure where to place his foot next.

"Of course," Jesus began, "we'd want to be absolutely certain." He swiveled and faced Uri again, his gaze suddenly more intense. He leaned forward, his elbows on his desk, hands interlocked under his chin. "We'd *need* to be absolutely certain."

Uri looked at Jesus, not sure what to say, so he didn't say anything at all.

Jesus raised his eyebrows "Are we certain, Uri?"

Uri looked at Jesus and suddenly realized he wasn't going to get the green light. He knew it in that instant. "Well, Lord," he stuttered, "when it comes to the End Times, nothing is certain. You've said it yourself."

"Oh," Jesus said, his face comically falling into a frown of consternation. "So you're not certain."

"We..." Uri's voice trailed off. The thing was, he *was* certain. As certain as he'd ever been about anything. But somehow, in this place, his arguments seemed thin and silly. "Manon—" Uri began, and Jesus suddenly became more focused.

"What does Manon think?" Jesus asked.

"Well, she—she has been around Brady and he...has taken her into his confidence," Uri said, looking desperately at Jesus.

"Aaand...?" Jesus said.

"And he told Manon he will rule the world."

"I see," Jesus said.

Instantly Uri knew it was the wrong thing. It sounded silly even to his own ears.

Furious, Uri walked the gardens around the executive wing.

As very few souls had the stones to head out here, he had the place to himself. Once you have your meeting with the President, you don't wander around the Rose Garden. The place was gorgeous. To anyone who had wandered the Vatican Gardens, it would look remarkably similar. Firs, pines, green grass—you would not know you were in the middle of Rome. Streams babbled. Birds chirped. If Bambi walked out with Thumper, or Snow White with a cadre of singing bluebirds, it would have been perfect.

Uri noticed none of this. His hands clasped behind his back, muttering furiously to himself, he walked. He was angry. At whom he wasn't exactly sure. You couldn't really be mad at Jesus. It wouldn't have crossed his mind to be mad at God. That would be like being mad at the rain. But he was still mad. Furious, actually. He had no idea what to do. Never in his long existence had he been so sure of something he couldn't seem to make people understand. He felt it in his bones. Deep in his bones.

Angry, he swung his fists at imaginary foes and hit them, hard, until he tired out. Then he collapsed on a bench and placed his head in his hands. He knew he was right. He knew the big guy knew it. This was His Test, Uri's time to shine. He knew that now, and he would go it alone.

A few hundred yards away and a few stories up, a lone figure watched Uri's odd behavior, then turned away from his window. It was a fellow archangel who had been advised, quietly, to keep an eye on Uriel.

Back in his suite at the Fairmont, Uri paced back and forth liked a caged animal. Oliver and Manon sat and watched him, waiting; they knew better than to interrupt an archangel when he was in this kind of mood.

"I went Upstairs today," Uri began. "I talked to Jesus." He looked at his team, hoping this statement would lend him gravitas. Oliver looked impressed and nodded. You know, for emphasis. Manon looked bored.

"Jesus…" Uri said, now turning toward the windows and facing the city, pausing. "Jesus is on board." He suddenly turned and faced them both, looking expectant, hands on his hips, defiantly awaiting their reaction.

Oliver understood in that instant that he had only one job to do. Like millions upon millions of subordinates over thousands of years, faced with a boss who they instinctively knew was wrong and also lying to their face, did the one thing subordinates like him had been born and bred to do. He agreed. Enthusiastically.

"That is awesome!" Oliver said. "Totally awesome."

Uri was nodding. "Yes. Awesome." Uri looked at Manon. Manon looked at Uri. The silence went on for what seemed like hours.

Then Manon said, casually and while turning her head to also look out on the city as though absorbed in the Gateway Clipper boat fleet navigating the rivers below her, "What did Jesus think about Brady being male?"

Uri simply stared at the back of Manon's head. Oliver realized he had been holding his breath for about thirty seconds and would have to breathe soon, but not just yet.

"Brady being male?" Uri said, quietly.

Manon said nothing and continued to stare out at the city.

When he realized she was not going to elaborate, Uri said, "What do you mean?"

Manon did not turn or reply for several seconds, then, taking a visible deep breath, she turned and said, "*Fine Temporum* makes it clear the Antichrist will be a woman."

"MAKES IT CLEAR THE ANTICHRIST WILL BE A WOMAN?! WHAT ARE YOU TALKING ABOUT?!" Uri screamed, totally losing any semblance of cool he may have had.

Manon, unmoved by this outburst, said, "Chapter fourteen, page three hundred and seventeen: 'And it will move with an uncaring hand, its love only for the spawn of its polluted womb, seeking only to set that spawn on the throne of a destroyed and soulless world.'" Manon turned and looked directly at Uri. "Sounds like a chick to me."

Uri stared at Manon for a long time. Oliver finally decided he had to breathe and broke the silence with a gasping deep breath that shattered the stillness. It didn't matter. He could have done cartwheels around the room for all Uri and Manon paid attention to him.

Uri collected himself with an extreme show of control, turning around, his back to them, and placing both his hands on the sideboard, wide. He lowered his head.

They waited.

Eventually Uri turned and looked at them. Well, at Manon, anyway. Then he said, evenly, "Dave Brady is the Antichrist. Jesus agrees. Our job is to eradicate him and save mankind." Then he smiled. Oliver cringed. Uri never smiled.

Manon continued staring at him, her gaze ever calm.

"AND I AM DAMN WELL NOT GOING TO PUT UP WITH ANY UNBELIEVERS IN THIS CAMP!" Uri screamed. "YOU ARE WITH ME, OR YOU ARE AGAINST ME. AND IF YOU ARE AGAINST ME I WANT TO KNOW THIS INSTANT!!"

With this last exclamation, Uri raised both his fists and all the windows in the suite blew outward. Furniture was thrown about, glasses smashed, potted plants defiled. The sinks ran blood-red water for a time, and Oliver's bladder let go. A few blocks away at Primantis, the TVs suddenly switched from a Sophie Masloff biography to a replay of a limping Sid Bream, literally dragging his leg, beating out an awful Barry Bonds throw in that National League Championship Series. In a nondescript bar in Dormont, Father Bill suddenly took a sharp breath and immediately wondered if someone had died. Above the Southside Slopes, the Widow just nodded and sipped her tea, rocking quietly in her chair, one Croc-clad foot crossed above the other.

Manon continued to stare at Uri.

"With me, or against me?" Uri said. The wind blowing in through the window spaces this high above the ground gave a surreal quality to the conversation.

Manon, who had never flinched, never moved at all as this cataclysm roared around her, was now framed against the open night sky, her back to the city. She looked at Uri and said quietly but firmly, "With you."

Uri nodded slowly. "Good," he said. Then he turned and left the room.

Oliver, urine-stained and trembling, crawled from beneath the coffee table where he had flung himself. Getting shakily to his feet, he looked at Manon and said, in a whisper lest he be heard,

"He's just not evil enough."

Manon, whose eyes had been distant, now focused on Oliver. "I know," she said and left the room. Oliver watched her go and then, realizing he was alone in Uri's suite, quickly got up and headed to his own room.

Chapter Forty-Nine

The bar at Palomino was upscale. Artglass and impressionist paintings adorned the walls. At three o'clock in the afternoon, it was mainly empty. Lunch was long over, and even the happiest of happy hour guests had not arrived yet. Leonard sat miserably nursing a vodka soda, dressed in a blue version of his now standard Brooks Brothers suit and wrinkled, white, starched shirt (no tie, as always).

The thought of paying someone $3.50 to launder and iron a shirt for him would have been akin to him paying $3.50 to buy a steamed coconut milk latte three months ago. Unthinkable. Laughable. Christ, he wasn't sure he owned a shirt three months ago that he would have taken to a drycleaner's, and he was pretty sure if he was honest with himself, he would have probably stolen $3.50 from one of his kids' wallets given half a chance.

He had at that moment about $2,000 cash in his right front pocket. And he didn't even care. He wasn't sure who he was anymore, what his role was, and why he was even involved in this goat rodeo at this point. A man in a trench coat and fedora walked in and seated himself two stools down from Leonard. Leonard glanced at him and then ignored him. Dude looked like some douchebag attorney.

The bartender got the man a drink, vodka. Leonard had gotten a cryptic text message asking him to meet here. This was not unusual as Leonard had become Dave Brady's de facto fixer of sorts. Your son got a DUI, but you're a ward boss and you need a judge to throw it out? Call Leonard. Steamfitters Union Rep's daughter got her car towed after twenty-seven unpaid parking tickets? Call Leonard. He assumed this was more of the same. Fuck-A-Rama.

"How have you been, Leonard?" the man in the trenchcoat said, not looking at him. The thick Russian accent was unmistakable as there was nobody else in the bar, and you didn't have to talk too loudly to be heard over the dulcet tones of Al Jarreau playing softly in the background.

Leonard turned and faced the Wolf. "How you doin', Alex?"

Volkov continued staring into the mirror behind the bar and not at Leonard. He asked the bartender for another shot of Stoli, which was delivered.

Leonard, taking his cue from the Russian gangster, also stared into the bar mirror. "Alex, when the hell are you going to get on that Tito's train? Stoli is for losers, babydoll."

The Wolf smiled into the mirror. "Well, I guess you are an authority on what losers drink, eh, Leonard? No Popov here though, huh? Maybe if you ask them nicely, they will send someone down to Walgreens to get a plastic pint bottle." Volkov laughed but toasted Leonard in the mirror.

As always, these days Leonard was just too tired to rise to the bait. He remembered when he thought Alexi Volkov was the epitome of cool. A real gangsta. Now he thought of him as just another parasite with an angle. It occurred to Leonard that the Man in Red would wipe his ass with the Wolf while reading the morning paper. Funny how times change. A small smile crossed his lips.

"I heard the Fanzis cleaned the street with your pitbull last week," Leonard said quietly, not looking at Volkov, no expression on his face. "You trying to bite off a little more than you can chew, Wolf?" Leonard said, still quiet, surprised at how little he cared about what his former icon thought.

Volkov tried to show no emotion, but Leonard saw for just an instant that this particular comment had hit home.

Leonard, emboldened, turned in his seat and said to Volkov,

"If you are trying to hit Manon the Black Death with anything less than a Navy Seal Team, then you have no idea what you are dealing with." And with that, he toasted Volkov right back.

Volkov stared down at his glass, no reaction that Leonard could see. Then the Wolf called the bartender over. "Do you have Popov?" he asked.

"I'm afraid not, sir," the bartender said.

"Ahh, okay. Stoli then. One for me and one for my friend," Volkov said, gesturing toward Leonard. The bartender looked at Leonard, who nodded slightly. Alexi toasted Leonard in the mirror and threw his shot back. Leonard did the same. After a few minutes, this showdown settling in, Volkov said, "And so what, Leonard, am I dealing with?"

Leonard took a slug of his vodka soda. He laughed a little to himself.

Volkov stopped staring into the mirror and turned to look at Leonard. "You and I are the same, pasha. We didn't expect to succeed, not at this level. That's okay. No crime, eh? Khoroshaya zhizn. To the good life." He toasted Leonard. Leonard toasted back. Why not. "But here, we are just the same," the Wolf continued. "I'm not a religious man, Leonard. One tends to lose faith in God the first time he is bent over the kitchen table. But we digress, eh? This Brady, he's the real deal, huh?"

Leonard stared into space. It was a pretty good question. After a while and another slug, Leonard said, "He's the real deal." And then, after a pause, "But..."

Neither man spoke. Volkov waited as Leonard collected his thoughts.

After a few minutes, Leonard said, "But the guy you need to worry about is Aza."

"Aza," said Volkov. "I've heard of this man. Everyone seems to fear him. I don't even know if he's real." Volkov smiled and motioned the bartender.

"He's real," Leonard said, lowering his voice without even thinking about it. Neither man said anything for a while.

They sat by themselves in a fancy bar they would not have dreamed of occupying many years ago, money in their pockets their parents had never contemplated.

Eventually, Volkov said, "So I feel like there is a thing, a thing that is going to happen. I'm not sure why, but I am sure, more sure than many things I have known for a long time." He sipped his drink.

"What does it have to do with me?" Leonard asked, careful. He knew the Wolf.

"Again, I don't know, Leonard." Volkov said. "I just know you are in it. And so am I."

Everything Leonard had learned over the past few months, all the craziness he had seen, screamed at him to deny this, laugh it off, make a sarcastic comment and tell this crazy Russian he had to go, but deep down he knew what Volkov was saying was true. Something was going to happen, and they were in it.

—

"The Archangel will summon the bartender., the Widow had said. This pronouncement had been roundly discussed in the Don's study. Various theories had been advanced. Many were dismissed. Eventually, this being a spiritual thing, they looked to their spiritual leader for some kind of wisdom.

This was Father Bill. Understanding the gravitas of their situation (and understanding he was sitting drinking very expensive bourbon in the study of the last true Don in Pittsburgh), Father Bill ruminated, rubbed his temples, and shifted his underwear (casually and with a certain dignity he had learned through years of speaking at bake sales). He settled and then faced the group. It was time to talk about what he thought.

"They're gonna ask Jilly to hit Brady," he said, then took a deep breath as though he just revealed the whereabouts of Jimmy Hoffa to a national TV audience.

There was silence for several seconds.

Eventually, Angie Sr. said, "No shit?" He looked at his brother then crossed himself, saying, "Begging your pardon, Father."

"We didn't think Jilly was involved in this because the forces of evil want free beer," the Don said, not sarcastically, although the comment was patently sarcastic.

Father Bill focused and tried to find firm footing. None of these people had gone to seminary. Jagoffs. "It's not as simple as that. I've been doing a lot of research, and, well, initially I wanted to think this was just a lot of baloney. But now...now I don't think it is."

He had the group's attention. "I'm going by a combination of things written about the End Times—the Apocalypse, if you will. The way I see it, there are a few key points. First, we need the bad guy. Maybe in Brady we have him. He has met some important qualifications. Next, we need a general status of mankind that might warrant the Big Guy turning out the lights. He has to be on board, and this is a key point."

Father Bill looked at the group. "You think we're there? As a world society? Damned?"

The Don looked at Martin. Martin shrugged. Angie Sr. looked at his shoes contemplatively and also shrugged.

The Don said, "Well, there's Trump."

Everyone nodded.

"And Reelz," Angie Sr. said.

Everyone groaned and nodded.

"I heard they now sell avocado pierogis at St. Stanislav's," Martin finally said.

"No fuckin' way," Angie Senior said without even thinking.

"Way," Martin said, shaking his head sadly.

Tacitly, without any verbal communication at all, the group agreed the Big Guy might be considering pulling the plug.

"So," Father Bill continued, "let's say, for now, we have a bad guy and we have circumstances where the Kahuna decides to clear the pool. Just for argument's sake, mind you."

They all waited.

"This is a very complicated series of events that has to happen before it all goes to hell. Biblical scholars agree God takes this seriously. My point is," Father Bill continued, "there are a few more pieces, and this is where I'm not sure."

"Pieces?" the Don said, his hands steepled under his chin. Everyone looked at the Don, then pivoted, as though watching a tennis match, to Father Bill.

"Yes. Pieces. There seems to be agreement that there is an

offer to the Judge. The offer is contingent on rewards to the Judge, but there is universal agreement the conditions of the offer can be mitigated by the actions of 'the Slav.'"

Everyone pondered that.

Eventually, the Don said, "Volkov."

Nobody argued.

"I don't think it's just that," Father Bill said. "There's also a woman and, this is one I don't see, 'a man who must decide to be an unlikely hero.'"

Nobody had a guess on that one.

"So that's everything?" Mia Fanzi said.

"Well, almost," Father Bill said. They waited. "In the end, it comes down to the Judge. And there is just no agreement."

"No agreement?" Angie Sr. said.

"Well, everything I've read says there is no certain outcome. The Judge will watch and the Judge will decide."

Chapter Fifty

Jilly sat on his stool behind the bar. His mind was miles away. It was Thursday night—busy but not crazy busy. As he contemplated possible outcomes of what he figured was coming, he paid no attention to the little guy in the pajamas who entered the bar and sat down on a stool across from him. The guy waited. Jilly ignored him.

Mandy was down at the other end of the bar pouring shots for four women who were so clearly a bachelorette party that aliens from Jupiter who landed on Earth twenty minutes earlier would have walked into J's and said to each other, "Bachelorette party," without even knowing what that meant.

"Jaeger!" one of the women shouted, one of the supporting cast with the "Fuckin' Bridesmaid" t-shirts on. Innovative.

Jilly processed all this peripherally; he was a veteran, after all. He had seen variations of just about every barroom scenario one might imagine. But his mind was elsewhere.

Oliver cleared his throat. It didn't register with Jilly even though he sat directly across from him.

He tried again. Zip.

Jilly continued to stare down at the other end of the bar where one of three guys who appeared to be fraternity brothers had removed one of the bridesmaid's tinfoil tiaras and placed it on his own head. Groundbreaking.

Oliver said, "Manon sent me."

Jilly was still looking away but now at least registered that Oliver had said something. He looked at Oliver. Oliver resisted the urge to release his bladder. He was on a mission. Jilly's impression was that this was some goofball Carnegie Mellon student or, at best, some trust fund loser who had wandered too far from the more chi-chi places further down Carson. Who the hell goes to J's in pajama bottoms?

"Manon sent me," Oliver squeaked again.

Jilly looked at him. "Manon?" he said.

Oliver just shivered. Then the name clicked to Jilly, and he looked closer at this kid. Oliver inadvertently kicked his foot against the bar. Jilly looked at him as though at wilted brussels sprouts.

Oliver said, "Can I use your restroom?"

Jilly stared at Oliver, then cocked his head slightly to his right. Oliver nodded furiously, removed himself from his stool, and rushed to the bathroom. Jilly watched him go.

Jilly went down to the end of the bar where the bachelorette party was playing out. He stopped and looked at the participants. One of the fraternity brothers removed a two-dollar tiara from his head. One of the girls stopped mid "woo!" (which, as everyone knows, is not easy and hurts the esophagus).

Jilly looked at this crew and then at Mandy. Mandy looked back, slapped Jilly on the meaty arm and said, "All good here, boss!" Jilly looked at Mandy, back at the (less) festive crew, and then headed back to his stool at the other end of the bar.

Oliver returned to his seat. Jilly looked at him.

"We...I...I mean, Uri..." Oliver began.

Jilly stared, no emotion on his face.

"I..." Oliver continued, "I was sent to let you know we...we, um, want—no, wait. We'd like to ask you to meet. With us. Not me. I mean with Manon. And Uri."

Oliver looked at Jilly, his expression so hopeful that Jilly wondered where they had gotten this kid from. The Mouseketeer Club? Who was he dealing with?

"Why?" Jilly said, his expression stone.

"I...we...I mean, we have a proposition for you," Oliver said, not quite willing to meet Jilly's eyes.

"What proposition?" Jilly asked, his hands palm down on the bar, his voice still emotionless.

"Don't ask me—I mean, please, I can't. I don't know, and..." Oliver's voice trailed off. They should have sent Manon. He had no idea why they had asked him to do this. This man was terrifying.

Jilly looked at this trembling doofus, thinking this kid was probably like a thousand years old. He shook his head to clear *that* particular thought from his mind, said "Oh for fuck's sake" under his breath, looked up at the ceiling, and said, "Where?"

Since Jilly said it to the ceiling, it took Oliver, his head down trying hard to not shake, a moment to realize the question was asked of him. "Where?" he repeated dumbly.

Jilly lowered his gaze from the ceiling to Oliver and said, "Where?! Where the hell is this meeting supposed to take place for Christ's sake?"

Through supreme effort, Oliver focused. What would Manon do? He slowly raised his eyes to Jilly's and said, slowly, "At the Fairmont. Tomorrow afternoon. Two o'clock."

Jilly sighed. He looked down the bar. At the far end, the subdued bachelorette party and their new friends had left. An old man was watching *Wheel of Fortune,* nursing a bottle of Iron City and laughing at everything Pat Sajak said. Jilly absently wished his life was simpler.

"No," he finally said.

Oliver just stared at him. He opened his mouth to speak, but Jilly got there first.

"If you repeat what I just said, I'm going to throw you out into the street. Hopefully in front of a speeding dump truck," Jilly said, lowering his face to Oliver's own.

Oliver, who had been about to do just that, clamped his mouth shut. He wasn't sure exactly what a dump truck was, but he suspected it was big and would squash him. He nodded silently at Jilly.

Jilly nodded slowly and said "Good. Tell your boss I said no. Tell him, it, whatever, I said I'll talk to Manon."

Oliver looked at Jilly and started to repeat, "Man—" when Jilly slammed his hand, palm down, on the top of the bar. The old man at the other end of the bar turned and looked disapprovingly at both of them. Jilly ignored him.

Oliver, recovering, said, "I'll tell him."

"Tell her Pamela's, tomorrow, two o'clock. You got that?"

Oliver, afraid to repeat what Jilly had just said, managed a nod.

Jilly nodded back. "Good," he said. "Now get out of my bar."

Oliver processed he had just been dismissed and scrambled to get off his stool and out the door.

"Kid!" Jilly said and Oliver turned.

"Get some jeans or something. Nobody goes out in public in their pajamas." Oliver looked down at his outfit, then burst out the door.

Jilly watched him go. *What the hell have I gotten myself into here?* he thought. Turning back to look down the bar, his mind racing, it occurred to him the old man was gone, although he had not passed Jilly and left through the front door. His bottle was gone. The TV was off. Jilly wondered if he had ever been there. Strange days indeed.

—

As Brady's star had risen, the Wolf had silently watched, trying to figure when and what his best move would be. More importantly, as things had unfolded in ways he would not have expected, he had wondered when to play his hole card. He had information on this woman who might be some kind of ecclesiastical hitter that had real value in what he felt was coming. Info from a very long time ago and obtained at a very high cost. *Leonard, where does your loyalty lie?* he wondered.

Leonard walked Penn Avenue, his hands thrust deep in his pockets, absently feeling the wad of cash with his right hand. It occurred to him in the swirl of his thoughts that three months ago had someone suggested he commit murder for $2,000, he would have given it serious thought. Now he had $2,000 in his pocket, but he hadn't killed anyone. Had he? Well, not really. And not yet, anyway. Volkov had suggested an alliance with Brady. He had professed his undying love and support for Dave on prior occasions. He said he could deliver votes, muscle, cash, and more.

Leonard didn't trust Alexi as far as he could throw a case of Smirnoff. Then, at Paolmino, the Wolf mentioned Manon. He said, "Tell your boss Red I have information he'd be interested in."

Now, Leonard didn't tell "Red" anything. Aza made him very nervous. But he also thought that if he withheld information from Aza, he'd be in the shit for that too. Thanks, Wolf. He sighed and headed for Brady headquarters.

In said headquarters, the Honorable Dave Brady was meeting with publicists hired for his coming Gubernatorial Campaign. Although two years away and at this point a closely guarded secret, his campaign for Governor was moving quickly. Standing at the head of the enormous conference table, talking and gesturing with his hands, Brady was focused on three consultants seated in suits and ties to his left at the table. On the right side of the table were his secretary, personal assistant, hairstylist, personal trainer, and one of the Lennys, the big one.

Aza sat and listened to His Highness spout his views on how he wanted to be perceived, how he'd like his fan clubs set up, how he'd like to structure a variety of social media platforms, etc. In a corner, dressed in red slacks, red turtleneck and red vest, Aza sat watching from a distance. He felt Brady was good at this stuff, good at creating a false image of himself. And that was not a bad thing. But as Aza continually tried to interest Dave in the less glamorous aspects of their mission, he was finding Dave putting him off, making excuses, delegating. This was troublesome.

In their daily morning meeting yesterday, Aza had said, "Eminence, there are three men interfering with our plans in the north of the county, the power plant thing. I'd recommend we remove them from the situation and in a manner that discourages others from interfering in the future."

Brady, who was looking at a selection of tuxedos he needed to choose from for his upcoming speech at a gala fundraiser, didn't reply.

"Eminence?" Aza said.

Brady looked at him. "Do you think the black or the grey?" he said, turning his phone toward Aza to show him the photos.

Aza, not looking at the photos but continuing to look at Brady, said, "I'm sure either will be splendid, Lord."

Brady nodded. "Grey, I think." He returned his attention to his iPhone.

After about thirty seconds, Aza said, "Lord, about these three men... We are thinking hanging them from the main gates at the power plant construction site should send a strong message to those who might consider interfering in the future."

Brady did not respond. Finally, he said, "I guess you wear black shoes with a grey tux, no?"

Aza realized he wasn't really asking him, just thinking out loud. He sighed. Given a choice between a party outfit and the murder of three interferers, the Antichrist should have relished destroying his foes, should have chastised Aza for letting them off easy with hanging. Not this guy. Aza's mind wandered back about eight hundred years to a time when he had ridden with the Mongol Emperor Genghis. He remembered how the Khan had understood the value of instilling fear in your enemies, how so many times the battle was won before it began because the enemy was so afraid they gave up before firing an arrow.

He saw Leonard standing inside the door to the conference room, leaning against the wall but looking at him. Aza motioned him over and got up and went into a side conference room. Taking a deep breath to try and calm himself, Leonard followed.

Aza settled into a conference chair and leaned back, his hands behind his head. Looking up at the ceiling as Leonard took a chair, he said, "So how is our friend the Wolf?"

Leonard, who had gotten at least somewhat used to the fact that Aza always seemed to know everything, nonetheless swallowed hard and then tried to proceed casually. "Oh, he's fine," Leonard said. "He, uh, he said he wants to join our cause."

"He did, did he?" Aza said, still staring at the ceiling. "I'm not surprised. What does he offer?"

"Well," Leonard said, "he says political influence, votes, muscle, and money."

Aza didn't say anything for a while and Leonard waited, now a veteran of exchanges with this creature.

"We have all that," Aza eventually said, still leaning back in his chair and looking up at the ornate plaster ceiling. "Why do we need him?"

Leonard wasn't sure he was supposed to answer; in any event, he wasn't sure he knew exactly why they did need the Wolf, but the man said he had some additional information he felt certain Aza would want to know. He waited until Aza spoke.

"I think the move is to agree to take him in, make him feel like he has some influence, and then when his resources are ours, we murder him, very visibly and very violently. This accomplishes two things. First, it removes any possible threat to His Eminence, and you and I know Volkov does not really believe in our cause. Second, it makes true believers out of his resources when they see our power, the thing that attracted them to Volkov in the first place. I don't see any downside," Aza said, continuing to stare at the ceiling, lost in thought.

Leonard thought he wasn't in Kansas anymore, Toto. The discussion of murdering Volkov was casual, as if talking about the best route to the Allegheny County Airport.

"There's another thing," Leonard said, not looking forward to this next part at all. Not one little bit. He looked absently around the room for a wet bar, but this room was a side room and had no such amenities. He licked his lips and waited.

Eventually Aza seemed to remember Leonard was in the room. "Yes, what?" he said.

"Well, Alexi said he has information about Manon." The impact of that statement on Aza was both immediate and frightening.

—

The team meeting at the Fairmont was calm, at least for the moment. Oliver hadn't said anything yet. The three-member team sat around a new dining table in a new suite, slightly smaller than the last but still lushly appointed. Manon had gone to the front desk visibly upset, claiming all the windows in her and her husband's suite had suddenly blown outward and the resulting vacuum had smashed furniture and destroyed their possessions, that it had been a miracle no one had been killed.

As the explosion Uri had generated had been heard and felt by other guests and reported to the police by many on the ground below, the management had apologized profusely and, fearing litigation, promised to move them immediately, issue them a check for several thousand dollars for the loss of their possessions, and comp their entire stay. Uri was upbeat. An impatient person by nature, he was at his worst during the tedious work of planning but at his absolute best when it finally came time to act. And that time had come. It was time to make a decisive move: eliminate Brady and prove to his Creator he was worthy of His love.

"Oliver, report," Uriel said.

Oliver—today dressed in jeans and a white Oxford shirt, albeit untucked—looked unusually solemn. Manon felt he looked suddenly older. Oliver was not looking forward to this. He decided the best way to go was straight to the truth.

"He won't meet with us."

Uriel stared, then repeated slowly, "He won't...meet with us?" Uriel was not angry, at least not yet. He hadn't even considered this outcome as a possibility. The bartender wouldn't obey a summons to meet with an archangel. "Did you explain to him who I am?" Uri said.

"I, uh, yes," Oliver said. He was learning that if you were going to lie, it was better to lie immediately and firmly.

"And he said no?"

"Well, not exactly," Oliver said, then quickly added, "Eminence."

"Not exactly?" Uri replied, a touch of irritation creeping into his voice. Oliver, realizing he was lapsing back into the hesitant style that got him in trouble, plowed ahead.

"He said he'll only meet with Manon. And not here, someplace to eat called Pandora's at two o'clock tomorrow." He turned to Manon. "He said you've met there before."

Uri looked at Manon.

Manon said, "Pamela's."

Oliver said, "I'm sorry, that's right. Pamela's."

"You've met him there?" Uri asked Manon.

"Yes," Manon replied.

Uri got up, paced the length of the room, then back again, his lips pursed, bouncing his steepled fingertips together as he thought this through. "Okay," he finally said. "Yes. Good."

Uri turned to Manon. "I should have sent you in the first place. He's a simple killer. He's afraid of me, as I represent the wrath of God. He likes you. Birds of a feather and all that. Meet him. Explain who we are, what is at stake, and what we need him to do." Oliver cringed inwardly at the criticism of his failed effort.

Manon crossed her arms and turned to look out the window, not wanting to show the anger that had crept into her countenance at Uri's implied insult of her and her profession.

"Yes, Lord," she said, not turning.

Uri, now upbeat, said, "Excellent. I appreciate the work you are both doing." Looking at Oliver, he said, "Let's go have dinner somewhere they don't just serve roasted cow dung and fermented hops. Is there a place like that around here?"

"Yes, Lord," Oliver said, his eyes on the floor.

Chapter Fifty-One

In the Don's study, Jilly sat comfortably in a butternut leather club chair across from the Don who was seated in an identical piece of furniture. Jilly felt certain the chairs were probably around five grand each. He had accepted a beer to the Don's scotch, but he had not touched it. It sat on his side table.

The Don sipped his drink and then set it down. Queenie lay next to his chair, asleep. Jilly was a little surprised as Mia Fanzi rarely allowed this kind of potential distraction when talking serious business. And this was serious business. Perhaps the Don was getting older and a little softer, Jilly thought. He knew that ten years ago, maybe even only five, the killing of Charlie Katz would have required a swift, clear, and very violent response. And this regal old man seated in front of him would have ordered it without a second thought. But instead, he had asked Jilly to do it. Why? Jilly felt sure both Angie Sr. and Martin likely counseled the Don against asking him. Hell, probably Angie Jr. and Jimmy H. too. So why? Maybe he wasn't the only one who had lost his taste for killing.

"You should know, Julian," the Don began, interrupting Jilly's thoughts, "I don't make decisions based on crazy old ladies, ghost stories, the Bible, or parish priests." Marino Fanzi turned and looked directly at Jilly now. "You know our business. I've never thought of our life as good or bad. I've never felt I've damned myself, my family, or anyone else I associate with because of the life I've chosen to lead." Jilly held the Don's gaze, unblinking, and waited for him to continue. It was not his place to interrupt.

The Don went on, "I say this, only because I wouldn't want you to think you are talking to a frightened old man ashamed of his life who might just be looking for some kind of eleventh-hour redemption when he realized the curtain would be coming down soon on a long and sometimes vicious tragedy."

Jilly continued to look at the Don.

"I apologize to no one. Including an almighty Creator, if one exists. I am at peace with my decisions and what motivated them."

Jilly saw the old fire in the Don's eyes as he spoke that sentence. He thought he was glad this man had been a part of his life and at least on some level that there was a bit of Mia Fanzi in him. The Don sat back in his chair and stared off into the distance while Jilly waited. He had been part of these discussions on a few occasions. Admittedly not lately, but old habits come back quickly. He waited for the Don to get to where he was going. He suspected he knew that destination anyway.

"Someone is going to ask you to kill Brady," the Don continued. "Maybe they already have." The Don said this as though this thought had just occurred to him. He turned again and looked Jilly straight in the eyes. Jilly stared back, stone-faced, and waited. The Don slowly nodded and then smiled slightly, mostly to himself, before continuing. "You may decide to do this, you may not. Of course, the choice is yours, as I believe the choice of taking another man's life must always be taken with free will and not under coercion."

The Don sipped his drink. Queenie snored quietly at his feet. The Don stared at his bookshelves.

"My gut tells me Brady must die. It has told me this for a while. Every time I try to intercede in this matter, I fail. Failure doesn't come easy to me. After a while, I have come to think that maybe there are...forces...at work here. That I am not permitted to be... involved...in this outcome, whatever it may be. But I suspect you are." The Don looked at Jilly.

Jilly said, slowly and evenly, "Permitted by who?"

The Don looked away, sipped his drink, and calmly contemplated his bookshelves again.

Eventually, it struck Jilly that he wasn't going to get an answer because it was a stupid question, and Marino Fanzi didn't answer those. After a few minutes of silence, the Don said, still not looking at Jilly, "If you need anything, anything at all, in this thing..."

Jilly heard, processed the meaning of the offer, and slowly nodded, although the Don did not see him do this. Then, their business done, he slowly got to his feet and passed the Don's chair on the way out of the study, lightly resting his hand on the old man's shoulder as he did so, a right he had earned, saying nothing.

—

Aza was unsettled. Well, frankly, he was as unsettled as he could ever get, which is to say, not extremely unsettled. Maybe "uneasy" was a better term. When you've seen it all, you don't get too shaken up about much. But these were definitely strange times. Leonard had relayed a conversation with Alexi Volkov that had surprised him. He had known of course that Manon the Black Death was here. It had confirmed, to some extent, the seriousness of the situation and given Brady a bit more credibility. He was concerned about Manon, but not overly so.

The Good couldn't directly impact events. He was not afraid she would kill Brady; it wasn't permitted. Everyone knew the rules. Still, he would be wise to be aware of her presence, and he was. Manon was not here to take selfies in front of the fountain at Point State Park. Leonard had told him Volkov had information from contacts in Russia, handed down and going back many hundreds of years in the church, that the Fallen Angel Aza had "killed" Manon many years ago when Manon was mortal. Volkov said the way the rules worked, Manon having ascended, Aza was now vulnerable to Manon. This idea of "payback" was also articulated in *Fine Temporum.*

Aza had not, until this information had been passed to him, remembered he had killed Manon. She had been one of many, and he had not given it a second thought after a few hundred years. The rules for Dark and Good were not the same. Dark could take life as situations required since life was not sacred to them, only to the Creator's crew. But, as with everything, there were Consequences. One of those consequences was that if you took a life, the trade-off was you were then vulnerable to that person in the afterlife.

Of course, there were other rules. Your vulnerability was cancelled if you could cause the death of a direct descendant—two negatives equaling a positive. Aza, as always, could only marvel at the Creator's creativity. His vulnerability to Manon was a problem, and he now understood why she had been selected for her role in this. Manon could destroy him forever if he was not careful. To resolve this problem, he had to cause the death of a direct descendant. He'd have to work on this.

—

Jilly sat at Pamela's drinking coffee. He felt alive in a manner he had not for a long time. He'd have been lying if he had said he was not looking forward to this meeting. Manon fascinated him. He knew in some area of his mind that this whole thing, this whole last few months, was coming to a head, a conclusion. He was unsurprised when Manon slid into the seat opposite him from behind him. He would have been surprised only if she had walked in the front entrance like any other customer.

"A franc for your thoughts," Manon said. As always, she wasn't smiling, but Jilly could not have said she wasn't *not* smiling, either.

"Sausage." Jilly said with no hesitation, the hitter returning the hitter's stare.

Manon kept his gaze for a second, then, looking away, said, "Un homme pensant à la saucisse."* Turning back to Jilly, she continued, "What a surprise."

Jilly, nonplussed, said, "I think sausage omelet." and then smiled a little. After the waitress had taken their orders, Jilly said, "So tell me what it is that's so important."

With no hesitation, Manon said, "You are to kill Dave Brady."

Jilly, who had been ready for this, said "Why?"

"Because it is important." Manon said.

*A man thinking of a sausage.

Jilly thought she sounded a lot like Don Fanzi. "Not good enough," Jilly said.

"Not good enough?" Manon repeated.

"Not good enough," Jilly said again. "Why is it important to me?" He leaned back in his seat and crossed his arms. This was a question that had been bothering him for a while now.

"He is the Antichrist," Manon said. "He will bring about the fall of mankind."

"Maybe he is, maybe he isn't," Jilly said. "Even if he is, I'm not young anymore; I'll probably be dead before the four horsemen show up. This Apocalypse thing takes a while from what I understand, so what do I care?"

"Do you not care for your soul?" Manon asked.

"Not sure I have a soul."

"You do."

"So you say," Jilly returned. "Even if souls exist and I have one, I'm not headed to Heaven anyway, so what do I care?"

"That is not necessarily true," Manon said. "Anyone can go to what you call Heaven, regardless of what they may have done."

"Not hitters," Jilly said with finality.

Manon stared at him flatly for a moment, then said, "Where do you think I live? Beltzhoover?"

Jilly processed this, the truth of the answer finally hitting home. He would not concede the point that he had clearly lost, but he could not help himself from looking away as a smile involuntarily played across his mouth. This woman. Something else.

"I'm not sure you are getting this," Jilly said, "but based on my track record, we're not on the same team in this whole good versus evil thing."

Manon stared at him. "We are on the same team and you know it. You knew it yesterday and you knew it last week, and I will not waste my time explaining something to you that you already know!" Manon slammed her coffee cup down on the table, breaking it. Her eyes were fierce. Coffee spilled, spreading over the table. Not a single diner noticed.

Jilly thought this woman would have been a force to be reckoned with in her day.

"What's in it for me?" Jilly asked after a while.

"For you?" Manon repeated.

"No, not for me, for Leonard the Wonderboy. Yes, what's in it for me. I do this for you, what do you do for me? Quid pro quo."

"Perhaps something can be done about your soul, Julian," Manon said.

Jilly stared back at her. This was also an offer he had expected to be floated, and as such, it did not surprise him. Eventually he said, serious, "So, if I take forty-six lives for money, then I am not welcome in God's kingdom, but if I take one life for your God Squad, then all is forgiven? Seems a bit hypocritical, you'll forgive me."

Manon understood the truth of Jilly's statement and had never been comfortable with the offer. But she had obeyed Uri's request and Jilly's insistence he meet with her only. The future of mankind might be at stake here, after all.

"It is not a simple explanation. The pathway to what you call Heaven is not simple."

"The offer sounds simple," Jilly said.

"I can't promise you anything," Manon said. "I am only sent as an emissary to let you know what is asked and how it might benefit you, should you agree."

Jilly looked at her a moment longer, then looked away. Eventually, he said, quietly, "How does one get to what I would call Heaven?" then added, "hitter."

Manon considered this question and replied, "It is always the decision of the Creator. There are no hard and fast rules."

"But the Bible says—" Jilly began, but Manon the Black Death interrupted him.

"The Bible says many things. It is a good guide. But it is not the rulebook."

"Every single person roaming around up there is in because He decided it? Every single person?" Jilly asked.

"Yes," Manon said. "Every single person based on each individual's actions and merit, character, inherent goodness, and propensity against true Evil."

Jilly nodded slowly. "I'm going to have to think about this."

"Certainly," Manon said before adding, "You have forty-eight hours."

"Thanks," Jilly said sarcastically. "I get forty-eight hours to decide if I want to try and kill the Antichrist. What if I fail?"

Manon only shrugged her shoulders. "Hard to say. The Dark would not be happy with you."

"And the Creator?" Jilly said. "Would he protect me? On this Holy Mission?"

Manon looked away, and for the first time, Jilly sensed she was not comfortable with the task she had been given.

Eventually, she said, "The Creator does not usually get involved. He watches. And I did not say this was a Holy Mission. I am only relaying to you what I have been asked to by a very high-ranking member of the Holy Host. This is all I can say."

Jilly nodded slowly, suddenly understanding. Getting up from his seat, he said, "You can have my answer now. I won't need the forty-eight hours. Tell your high-ranking member of the Holy Host that my answer is no." Jilly looked at Manon, and Manon looked back.

"Very well," she said.

Chapter Fifty-Two

In a fabulously appointed office high above the city, a minion bowed and left Aza's presence. Reading the report in front of him, Aza smiled. A direct descendant of Manon the Black Death. Right here in Pittsburgh. Who'd have thought it? This was going to be easy. Mentally checking that off his list of things to do, he moved on to other more pressing issues.

—

"He refused," Uri said.

Manon, seated in front of him, met his eyes. "Yes. He refused."

"You explained the gravity of the situation to him?"

"I did."

"And he refused."

"He did."

Uri paced. Then he paced some more. Manon awaited the inevitable outburst. Oliver, seated in a corner, cowered, hoping his preemptive action to remove all the glassware in the suite would pay dividends when Uri blew like Vesuvius. Oliver was, however, still worried about the windows. Finally, Uri stopped pacing, faced the windows, and took a deep breath.

"As I expected," he said, essentially to himself, though Manon and Oliver had no doubt he was also speaking to them. They stole a glance at each other and waited. "It is written that the Judge's decision will be hard won. But in the end, it must still be the Judge; no other can stop the Antichrist. I have prepared for our bartender's obstinance. I will meet with him." He turned to Oliver and said, "I'll need to be dressed. Something low-key—I don't want to frighten him to death." Oliver, still processing that Uri was going to meet with their hitman, just stared at him for a moment. Uri stared back. Then he shrugged his shoulders, fingers pointing downward with palms facing toward Oliver, and said, "What? Are you deaf, boy? Move!"

Oliver moved.

—

Leonard sat at a bar that appeared to be supported by naked Jennifer Lopez statues, drinking the best vodka he had ever tasted. He was getting drunk. He was trying to process the fact that he was doing shots with Spatz Spasilovich. He was having difficulty with this. Best he could come up with was that it was like working in the Zambelli Fireworks factory out in New Castle, PA; you were very close to things that fascinated and amazed you and had tremendous power, but one wrong move and you might blow your hands off. For probably the fiftieth time that evening, Spatz clapped Leonard on his shoulder. Hard. He knew he'd be bruised the next day. But truth be told, he liked these guys.

They were easier to understand than the Dark crew he was running with. They were Bad Guys straight out of central casting, sure. He assumed they got up every day trying to look the look and probably practiced their Bad Guy moves in a mirror. Had "The World Is Yours" tattooed on their shoulder. But Leonard had seen and been around bad guys all his life. He knew the language, the protocol, and had no problem deferring to those who would otherwise kick his ass. Hell, he'd been married four times. This was not complex; it was comfortable.

The Wolf rolled in with his girl. "Wolf!" Leonard yelled, maybe a little too loud.

"Leonard," Volkov said. "The Prince of Darkness. We are flattered by your presence in our little dacha."

"Sheeeiit," Leonard said, "I'm more like the guy who walks behind the Prince of Darkness' dog sweeping up his shit."

There was a moment of silence. Then Spatz yelled, "To shit sweepers!" and toasted. All laughed. Shots were consumed. Leonard's shoulder was slapped again. Hard.

—

On the Southside, Jilly sat behind his own bar, deep in thought. A veteran of the Life, he knew his decision would have repercussions. But in this scenario, he had no idea what they would be. He felt on some level his decision was the correct one. He'd been flying on gut instinct ever since his meeting with TK. He had a feeling everything was preordained and in that damn book. But somewhere deep down, he knew there was more than one possible outcome. So he would proceed carefully.

A man took a barstool right in front of him. Jilly jumped a little, shocked out of his thoughts. The man was wearing a clerical collar and black shirt. Jilly took a deep breath and said, "We don't serve clergy here."

"The hell you don't," Father Bill said.

Jilly turned and poured a Miller Lite, placing it in front of the man. "One and done," Jilly said. "I don't need you scaring my clientele."

Father Bill took a long sip. "So," he said.

"So, what?" Jilly said.

"So where are you on Tesla stock. What the hell do you think, what?!" Father Bill hissed in a whisper.

Further down the bar, customers turned and looked at a priest giving what appeared to be an angry lecture to an ex-contract killer. All was right with the world. They went back to their drinks.

"They ask you?" the priest said. Jilly looked at him and said nothing for a while, to the point where Father Bill thought he might not answer. Then Jilly said quietly, "Yes. They asked."

"And?" the priest said, nervous, his eyes widening. Here was the big decision that might alter the outcome of mankind.

"And I said no," Jilly said.

Father Bill stared at him. "You said no."

"I said no," Jilly repeated. He walked down the bar, drew a beer for an empty patron, cleaned some empty glasses off the bartop, and began washing them near Father Bill.

William Wojtanowicz sat stunned. He was trying to process this outcome. He had not expected it. He had always just assumed on some level Jilly would play his part in stopping the end of the world. After a while, Jilly looked at him and said, "What?"

"I, um, nothing," Father Bill stuttered. "I, uh, I support your decision. Up to you. Of course. Completely up to you…" He trailed off. Jilly looked at him and nodded.

Later that day, it was a Tuesday and Jilly would remember it was shortly after 2:00 because at 2:00, after the lunch crowd departed and at the start of a normally dead period, Mandy had headed home for a couple hours before coming back for the evening turn, so Jilly was alone in the bar. He had been absently reading his *Post-Gazette,* but not really. He was thinking he had let Father Bill down and maybe mankind. In the periphery of his consciousness, he heard the front door open and a customer come in, but he didn't immediately look up. Then, suddenly feeling a cold rush as though the AC had just been turned on, he raised his eyes.

The man standing before Jilly was wearing a suit—three-piece with tie, all in white. "Immaculate" was an appropriate word choice. He was fit, tall, probably six foot one. He appeared to be maybe thirty-five, though Jilly wasn't sure; he was never good with ages. The guy looked young, but not a kid. Beard, moustache, carefully trimmed. Dark hair, thick. Dark eyes that bored into you. No watch, no jewelry, no earrings or cute little tattoo. Nothing. Jilly thought absently, *Good-looking dude. Movie star good-looking.*

The man did not sit down. He stared at Jilly and said, "I am Uriel."

—

Leonard felt good. Very good. He was with his newest, bestest friends ever. He was an honorary Russian. He was really drunk. Spring Break drunk. Vegas drunk. He would not remember most of this part of the evening. He would not remember putting his arm around the Wolf and telling him that Aza was going to take over his operation and kill him. And that the two of them needed to stop him from doing that. And taking over the world.

But the Wolf would remember.

—

In a small café in what we'd call Heaven, Archangel Michael was doing some Jesus-suggested investigating. He sipped a latte and spoke quietly to a woman he'd spoken to many times before.

"Uriel..." the archangel began.

"Yes, Lord?"

"Is he...is he on the right path?"

The woman did not meet the man's eyes, since she'd been taught as a child that archangels were not to be looked upon. She said, "He is on a path. I cannot say if it is the right path."

The archangel said, mildly irritated, "Saldone, I am not here to see if our friend is enjoying the weather. You know why I am here."

"I know why you are here," the woman said. "Everyone here knows what may be happening. We all watch, and we all wait."

There was silence. The archangel waited, knowing the conversation was not over.

After a while, the woman spoke. "It is not clear. The outcome is difficult to see, but it has been foretold the outcome would be this way. It is possible. More possible than it has been in the past."

"Go with God," the archangel said in Hebrew. To the woman, it sounded like "Geyn mit got"* in her native Yiddish. The archangel got up with a sweeping of his ornate robes and left.

"Got vet bashlisn," the woman said quietly to herself.

*God will decide

—

Jilly wasn't sure what to say. He looked at this movie star in a white suit standing in front of his bar and—

"Do you know who I am?" the man said to him.

"You are Uriel," Jilly said after a second's hesitation.

Uriel mumbled something Jilly thought sounded like "oxen," then said, impatiently, "Yes, yes. Uriel. I just said I was. Archangel. Supreme Council, Holy Host. General, Ecclesiastical Grand Army. Deputy Minister, Holy See. And on and on." Uriel paused and looked at Jilly. "Ringing a bell?"

Jilly could only manage "Uh..." while thinking it was strange there was nobody else in the bar.

"We need to talk. Pay attention, peasant," Uriel said. Then he sat down. Sort of. Jilly thought he still was too tall to be seated. But the archangel continued.

"We have asked you to perform a great service to our Lord and Creator. And you, swine, mercenary killer for money, have refused. You had an opportunity to redeem your sad, sorry, worthless life. And you have decided against this. Explain."

Jilly wasn't really prepared to make an argument for a decision he just felt in his gut. He began, "I don't think—"

The archangel interrupted him. "Of course you don't think. You are an ox!"

Jilly stopped, unsure what to say next. This was surreal. He had never felt as helpless as he did right now.

"You will kill Brady," Uriel said.

Jilly just looked at him. On some level, he understood this wasn't really a command, that the angel couldn't actually make him do it. That there were Rules. He took a deep breath and said, "No."

Uriel stared at him. "No?"

"No," Jilly repeated.

Uriel turned and faced away from the bar, muttering something that sounded vaguely like Latin to Jilly. He stalked up and down the bar for a while. Eventually, he turned and, placing his hands on the bar, said, "Why, bartender?"

"I don't kill anymore," Jilly said. It was the first thing he had said with any conviction in the last twenty minutes.

Uriel stared at a Budweiser mirrored sign with seven bikini-clad models staring over their shoulders whose bottoms spelled out BUD 4 YOU. "You don't kill anymore," he repeated quietly. Jilly waited. Uriel breathed deeply several times. Then, composed, he looked at Jilly and said, "So, just to make sure I understand... You have killed for groceries. You have killed for some ducats. You have taken men's mortal lives to please a gangster."

Jilly, his mind swirling, said "I...I..."

"Did you, or didn't you?!" Uriel demanded, his voice rising.

"I guess I—" Jilly started.

"Guess nothing!" Uriel cried. "You killed your father!"

"He was my stepfa—" Jilly stammered.

"AND YOU WILL NOT KILL THE ANTICHRIST?! THE BEAST WHO WOULD DESTORY MANKIND?!" Uriel raged.

There was a roaring in the bar, like a wind tunnel. Uriel stared at Jilly, his eyes burning. Then he lifted his hands, palms up, and Jilly was literally lifted off his feet. Uriel swiped his arms left, and all 240 pounds of Jilly flew down the bar and was slammed against the refrigerator that marked the southern end of his domain. He fell to the floor. Uriel roared. Every bottle behind the bar exploded. A cascade of glass and liquor drenched Jilly as he lay stunned.

"You have twenty-four hours to change your mind, assassin." Uriel said and left the bar.

Chapter Fifty-Three

Manon sat on a bench at Point State Park. She watched the birds and children, but only absently. She was sad. She was not sure what she had expected when she left for this adventure, but it had not been this. She knew there was something going on, an Event. She wasn't sure if it was the Apocalypse; she leaned against that. Surely someone more impressive, more frightening, more Evil, more......just More had to be the Antichrist. Surely not Dave, the better-dressed Lounge Lizard. And yet, she wasn't sure. Nothing about this entire engagement had gone as she might have expected. She had always been sure of herself, always prepared, knowledgeable. In this thing, however, she was flying by the seat of her pants, and she didn't like it. Part of her felt this might be the enemy's plan. She wondered if they were more prepared, whether they were succeeding where her team was wandering around blind with no support from above.

"I thought you'd be bigger," the woman said from the other end of the bench. Manon jumped. And she had not jumped in probably 150 years. "And prettier," the woman added.

Manon could only look at this woman while she tried to gain her footing. Most on this planet didn't even see her at all, let alone comment on how she looked. The woman was wearing what looked like a dead animal around her shoulders, and a tricornered hat combined with some sort of skirt that appeared to be made of crocheted yarn and pieces of what Manon assumed were tin alcohol cans that had the words "Olde Frothingslosh" printed on them.

Manon said nothing. She would not have known what to say.

The woman looked out at the park, one leg crossed over the other, some kind of sandal made of rubber on her feet. She bobbed her foot and said, still not looking at Manon, "Manon Salle. The Black Death. Not so great."

Madonna Antonucci sniffed and held her head high, waiting.

Manon was not exactly sure how to proceed. She was out of her element.

Fortunately, the odd woman took the initiative. "I know why you are here. I know you think the End Times are upon us." The woman paused and looked at Manon with gravitas.

Manon, lost, dumbly repeated, "End Times?" It was all she could think to say. She was still lost, unsure how this woman could even see her, let alone know her surname.

"End times. *Fine Temporum,*" the woman said. Then she crossed herself and looked toward the heavens. "What the hell did you send down here? The Junior Varsity? Against Aza? Idiota!" She crossed herself again.

In a very well-appointed office among the clouds, an old man watching a video feed who bore a striking resemblance to a skinnier Santa Claus smiled to himself. This was getting good.

Later, alone in her apartment, her dinner eaten, her dishes washed, the Widow Antonucci settled into her chair. She had brand new editions of *Star, People, US Weekly,* and the *National Enquirer* in a neat pile next to her chair. She loved these magazines, but tonight, her mind was elsewhere. She had been aware since her youth that she had special qualities. She knew things others didn't, saw things others didn't see.

Perception was the word. She could watch a news broadcast and see behind the story to what was really happening. She couldn't explain it. She just knew. And she was right. Well, she was right most of the time. At a certain point, she had come to realize her perception transmitter—a very finely tuned instrument, she felt—

was sometimes out of tune. Who could blame her? Who is right all the time? Who doesn't get older? What equipment doesn't get slightly worn with time?

Yes, Ronald Reagan was not the reincarnation of Vlad the Impaler. She got that. Sure, she had missed the mark on her interpretation that Beanie Babies were devil spawn introduced to turn children to Satan. Okay. Hell, even Ted Williams only batted .400. But she wasn't wrong on this one.

A creak sounded from her kitchen floor—she knew this as she knew every creak and noise in this apartment she had lived in so long—but she did not react. Things she had long suspected would happen, had long seen coming, were now happening. She had tried to tell them, had tried to explain this to her parish priest. Did anyone listen to her? No.

Another creak. She grew tired of the intrigue. "Come, sit," she called out. "I'm an old woman; I'm not going anywhere. You think I got a ball bat here under my housecoat? Come out here, you coward."

Big Lenny moved into her line of sight from the kitchen. Sheepishly, he walked to within a few steps of her chair. In his hands, he had a short length of rope with a knot at each end.

"Garrote," the Widow said. "Come to kill an old woman with a rope. Your mother must be proud." The Widow's chin, as always, raised in a manner the Duce would have admired.

"I gotta kill you," Big Lenny said. "Aza said so."

"Did he tell you why?" Madonna Antonucci asked, her bobbing right foot crossed above her left knee like always, today in a flaming red Croc. "He, uh, he said...well, he said..." Big Lenny stammered.

"He said you have to kill her because she's a direct descendant of mine." The comment came from behind Lenny, and he turned to see a woman dressed in a black ninja outfit, complete with black slippers and headgear, showing only her eyes and nose.

"Do you know who I am?" the woman asked.

Lenny would not look her in the eyes. "Yes," he mumbled.
"Who?"

"You're...you're M-Manon. The B-Black Death," Lenny said, his eyes fixed firmly on the carpet.

"Correct," Manon said, moving further into the room. "The

Black Death. You will leave now, or you will be destroyed."

Big Lenny took a step backward, confused. "I...I have to kill her," he said weakly, unsure of himself now, some fear in his voice.

"You will kill nobody," Manon said. "Be gone."

Lenny processed this, looked at the Widow, who returned his look with one of her own that reminded him of his grandma's look the time he had eaten both the blueberry pies she had made for his sisters eighth birthday.

"I..." he said.

"Go," Manon said firmly.

And Lenny went. Or at least, he started to go. Two steps toward the door, a thought sliced through the fog of confusion swirling through the meatloaf that was his mind. He stopped. "Wait," he said.

They waited.

Lenny turned. "Aza said...he said you can't stop me. He said you can't...interfere?" He raised his eyes hopefully to Manon's face. "You can't interfere," he repeated.

Manon, surprised by this turn of events, hesitated just a beat too long. Her eyes betrayed the truth of Lenny's statement. A huge smile appeared on his face, the look similar to a poorly cut jack-o'-lantern.

"You can't interfere!" he cried, nearly skipping across the room. Gleefully, he leaned down into the Widow's face. "She can't interfere!" he shouted. "Ha! She can't interfere!" He danced over to Manon, leaned down, and literally sang, "Yooou caaan't interfeeeeere!"

He turned back to the Widow, twirling the garrote with one hand and sashaying back to the Widow's chair. Dropping to one knee, the six-foot-four, 300-pound behemoth waved it in front of her face and continued, "She can't interfere! Happy New Year! I want a big beer! Because she caaan't interfeeeeere!"

Then, pausing and giggling, he reached out one finger and tapped the Widow's nose on each word, and three times on the syllables of the last "int-er-fere." He smiled a big goofy grin in the Widow's face. Manon looked on helplessly, her fists clenched.

Lenny, overjoyed he wasn't going to have to face Aza and explain why he had failed in his mission, never saw the bowling pin swung from the shadows over his left shoulder. One moment he was smiling ridiculously into the Widow's face, and the next moment the left side of his temple exploded and his world went black. He crashed to the carpet.

Manon looked at the Widow. The Widow looked at Sister Mary Lee. Sister Mary Lee, the bowling pin now swinging at her side, looked at Manon with no expression on her face.

"You can't interfere, but I can," she said. "Nick Perry himself gave me that bowling pin. He signed it." Sister Mary Lee flipped it expertly in the air and caught it. "You know, before all his troubles."

They all sighed and nodded, remembering the local TV celebrity host of the *Bowling for Dollars* game show who later went to jail for fixing the Pennsylvania Lottery Daily Number.

Chapter Fifty-Four

Jilly had lost consciousness for a few minutes after his flight down the bar and collision with his refrigerator. Coming to, he eventually remembered where he was and what had happened, which wasn't really that hard considering he was still lying in a pool of glass and hard liquor. Then he was out again. Then he was back. He looked up and tried to focus his eyes. There was a blurry haloed image leaning over the bar, peering down at him.

"God?" Jilly murmured.

"Uh, no," the head said.

Jilly shook his head, and it cleared a little. "Not God. Leonard," he said to himself. This struck him as funny, and he stifled a giggle and rolled onto his side. This created a crunching sound, and he remembered all the glass he was lying in. He quickly decided that maybe he better not move so much.

"Jesus. Someone throw a hand grenade in here?" Leonard asked.

"Wasn't Jesus," Jilly said, "but I think one of his crazy relatives."

Leonard tried to process that and decided Jilly probably had some kind of concussion. "Hang on, don't move," he said and went to get a broom.

Eventually, he got Jilly up and seated, having swept much of the glass into a large rubber trashcan. "It's gonna take a while to get that booze mopped up, chief," Leonard said.

"Don't worry about it," Jilly said. "I have a night crew that cleans once a week; they can handle it. We are officially closed for the day."

Leonard turned the front door sign to "Closed," then closed the blinds and flipped the front door deadbolt. He made himself a generous vodka soda and poured Jilly a beer, placing it in front of him, then went back around the bar to the customer side and sat in front of Jilly, who was seated on his usual stool.

Leonard took a long drink of his vodka and wiped his mouth, his eyes never leaving Jilly.

Jilly drank half his beer in a gulp and then, closing his eyes, took a deep breath. Eventually, he opened them again and looked at Leonard.

Leonard could tell Jilly was shaking off the shock of whatever it was that had happened. He waited. He had learned long ago that you needed to be careful with wounded animals (and ex-wives).

"Thank you, Leonard," Jilly said.

Leonard just nodded slowly, still staring at Jilly.

Jilly looked at the chaos that was now his back bar, then returned his gaze to Leonard. Leonard could see the big man was mostly back to normal.

"You're aware of what's going on," Jilly said.

Again, Leonard just nodded slowly. Jilly nodded too, mostly to himself.

"Why are you here?" Jilly asked.

Leonard had to give that one some thought as he had been thrown off track by the bomb site that had greeted him upon entering the bar, but quickly said, "I, uh, I was sent here."

Jilly smiled sardonically. "Of course you were."

"I, uh," Leonard continued, "I'm supposed to ask you to meet with my boss."

Jilly nodded slightly, then drained the second half of his beer. "Your boss," Jilly said, "is a halfwit insurance agent. Nothing more."

Leonard looked confused for a minute, then understood and said, "Oh, uh, no, not Dave, uh, Mr. Brady. No, I meant..." and he trailed off. Leonard did not like to say Aza's name out loud as he had this creepy feeling that when you did, some kind of eye opened on you and Aza knew what you were saying and doing.

"Aza, then," Jilly said, and Leonard flinched involuntarily.

"Yes," Leonard said, then repeated, unnecessarily, "Yes."

Jilly could see that Leonard was terrified of this man, this entity, he had heard about. "Why, Leonard, does the Almighty Aza want to see this lowly bartender?"

Jilly said this in a mostly tired tone, and Leonard thought he sounded a lot like his second wife had sounded when she had asked him—on one of the many occasions she'd had to post his bail—why he had hit the cop. Or maybe it was why he had run his car over eleven parking meters in a row on Carson Street at 3:12 a.m. Or maybe it was when they had found two cases of knockoff Justin Timberlake concert t-shirts in his car when he had been drunk enough to lock his keys in it, and then dumb enough to call the cops to jimmy open the door for him. He couldn't remember.

The point was, Jilly asked in that tone that said, *I already know the answer to this, and it's sad, and you are performing as the professional-grade loser you will always be, so let's get it over with*. A few months ago, Leonard would have missed the tone, the sarcasm, the whole burrito. Not now.

"He, uh, my boss... He'd like to talk to you. He would like to... to explain some things to you," Leonard said carefully.

Jilly nodded slowly, tiredly. Of course. The White Team had talked to him, now the Black Team wanted an audience.

Leonard noticed the big man had glass in his hair. Jilly closed his eyes again, and for a while, Leonard thought maybe the effects of whatever had blown up this bar were returning. He waited.

Eventually, without opening his eyes, and in a quiet voice, Jilly said, "Should I go, Leonard?"

Leonard was not prepared for this question. Every self-preserving sinew in his emaciated body screamed at him that there was absolutely only one answer to this question, and it was yes. Like a cockroach, self-preservation was Leonard's wheelhouse. He was the Hank Aaron of self-preservation. You need a homer in the ninth of the Self-Preservation World Series, you need it to be absolutely certain, you send Leonard to the plate. It was like Jilly had asked him "You wanna get high?" or "You want a free ticket to

Ozzy Osbourne?" Iron-clad, double-platinum no-brainer.

Leonard waited before answering. He thought for a while, the events of the last few months flashing through his mind. Meanwhile, a chorus in the style of "Bohemian Rhapsody" thundered in his head with the obvious answer.

"No," he said simply, not meeting Jilly's eyes. He distracted himself by looking at his vodka soda. "Don't go."

Jilly opened his eyes and looked at Leonard, things almost audibly clicking into place that made perfect sense, in a way. He nodded to himself, the conversation with TK about *Fine Temporum* resonating in his mind. He ran a meaty hand over his face, sniffed, and placed his hands flat on the liquor-soaked bar in that familiar gesture. "Leonard," he said, "you tell your boss I'll see him. Tell him the Judge will see him. You tell him that. He'll know what that means."

"The Judge?" Leonard said, looking at Jilly, confused.

Jilly just looked at him. "Now get out of my bar." Leonard processed this and quickly got up and headed toward the door.

Before he could grab the deadbolt, Jilly said from behind him, "Leonard." Leonard stopped but didn't turn, just waited. "You're going to tell yourself later you made a mistake today. Telling me not to go. You'll be tempted to try and fix it by bullshitting your boss. Don't do it."

Leonard considered this, still frozen a step from the door.

Jilly continued, "Everything you think, everything you are beginning to suspect about yourself, is true. You can fail your whole life and then maybe fate gives you a chance to succeed. Or maybe not fate."

After a while, Leonard just nodded and then as he turned the deadbolt and opened the door, Jilly said, "Be careful."

At two in the afternoon the next day, having headed home exhausted and slept for ten hours, Jilly went back to Pamela's. Something told him to, the same intuition he had been relying on and was now taking over events. He scanned the restaurant and saw nobody he recognized. He sat down. He ordered coffee and an omelet and waited. His mind was busy, but he was strangely calm. Things were coming to a head. He was pretty sure nothing would surprise him at this point. A hand brushed his shoulder, and he jumped a little as he had been more lost in thought than he realized.

Manon sat down across from him. Today, she was in a black sweatshirt with black jeans, a black hairband keeping her hair from her face. She smiled, sort of. Jilly just looked at her, not sure exactly what to say, as always.

"You look like the weight of the world is on your shoulders, mon ami," Manon said.

"Funny you say that," Jilly said, smiling in spite of himself. He just couldn't help it. He wondered if he was flirting with a 300-year-old woman. That made him smile even wider and almost laugh.

Manon, as always, stared right into his eyes and said nothing, but he wondered if she could read his mind. It wouldn't surprise him. Hell, it wouldn't surprise him if she pulled a thirty-pound cod from her purse and the fish asked for directions to Wholey's fresh seafood market down Penn Ave.

"Your boss came to see me," Jilly said, figuring he may as well start the conversation.

Manon nodded. "Yes, I know."

"He seems to think I need to whack our Mayor."

Manon nodded again and repeated, "Yes, I know."

Jilly nodded back then looked away for a while. "Should I?" he asked.

After a pause, Manon said, "I think that decision is yours, and yours alone."

Jilly smiled wanly and said, "Yes, I know."

The hint of a smile on Manon's face went away quickly as she said, "I have information I have been asked to relay to you."

"Asked by whom?"

Manon ignored the question. "What we have asked of you does not come without its rewards."

Jilly looked at Manon, and, for the first time, she was not meeting his eyes, instead staring at the tabletop. There was not an occupied table near them, no waiter had approached, and Jilly was certain none would until Manon was done. Manon's demeanor was now no nonsense, all professional.

She continued, "In addition to your soul being cleansed of your former profession, I am advised to also offer you an Intervention." She raised her eyes to his.

He waited.

"Under the Rules, we can intercede to stop the normal course of events. Only where the action is positive and where extreme action is warranted in an Alter Existence situation." Manon folded her hands and looked at Jilly.

Jilly raised his eyebrows. "I have no idea what all that means."

Manon took a deep breath, then said, "Don Fanzi's friend Martin has inoperable, terminal cancer. He will die within the year. We can help."

Jilly processed this stunning news slowly and sat back in his chair. His mind whirled. This kind man, an uncle to him, who had never hurt anyone his whole life, was dying. Scenes of Martin's kindness to him and Anne flashed through his mind.

He raised his eyes to Manon. "He's dying? You're sure?"

"He is. We are," Manon said.

"And you can stop this?"

Manon just nodded, again not meeting Jilly's eyes.

Jilly tried to process the myriad of thoughts going through his mind. He looked at Manon. He said slowly, almost to himself, "So, I kill Brady, I'm forgiven everyone else I killed, and instead of dying, Martin lives. That about it?" The expression on his face was a cross between bewilderment and confusion, and Manon felt for him, this kindred spirit.

"That's about it," she said.

Jilly nodded. Manon waited. After a while, he said, "Would you do it, if you were me?" He looked Manon in the eyes.

Manon returned his gaze. "I have killed for less," she eventually said.

"That's not what I asked you."

"I know."

He held her eyes for what seemed a long time. Then she said, gathering herself and rising from the table, wanting this business to be over with, "You will need some time to think, of course. Archangel Uriel would like to see you tomorrow morning at nine a.m. Fairmont Hotel." She waited, but Jilly just looked at her, so she continued, "It is not an invitation; it is a command."

Jilly's eyes hardened, and, seeing this, Manon quickly continued, "Uriel's methods have served him well for a thousand years. Agree with them or don't, but do not underestimate him. He is an Archangel of the Holy Order, and history records his performance. You would be wise to proceed carefully."

She gave a short nod to Jilly and left the restaurant. Instantly, a waitress appeared and asked Jilly if he needed more coffee. He stared at her vacantly until she backed away from the table.

An hour later, he was seated in front of Father Bill's desk. The priest had listened with growing incredulity at the story Jilly told him. When Jilly was done, he sat back in his seat, looking exhausted. Father Bill looked exhausted. Out in the hallway, leaning against the wall, eavesdropping and unseen by either man, Sister Mary Lee looked exhausted.

Father Bill waited, knowing better than to ask Jilly what he was going to do. He knew Jilly would tell him if he wanted to, and if he didn't want to, asking him wouldn't help. Sister Mary Lee appeared with a tray of coffee and cookies. She nearly dumped the tray on Jilly and appeared somewhat unsteady. She poured coffee, her hands shaking slightly, and when she poured a third cup, Father Bill realized she wouldn't be leaving the room to allow them to continue their discussion.

She took her cup, took the second chair in front of Father Bill's desk, sat back, and looked at them both. "So, what's the plan?" she said.

Father started to speak, afraid Jilly might decide to brain her with the coffeepot, but surprisingly Jilly interrupted him and said to Father Bill, "I want you to go with me."

"Me?" Father Bill said, startled. "To see—"

"Yes. To see Uriel."

Father Bill just started at Jilly for several seconds. Then he spoke again, though more in Jilly's general direction than talking to him.

"An archangel." Father Bill shook his head, then looked Jilly in the eyes properly as he said, "You know, you read about them from the earliest days of seminary. It's like reading about Napoleon or Julius Caesar. Almost comic book heroes. Not real."

His eyes shone with a wonder that surprised Jilly, this somewhat jaded man of God who may not have seen it all but had definitely seen a lot.

"Oh, he's real," Jilly said. "He's real, he's movie-star pretty, and he likes playing human pinball with bartenders who piss him off." Father Bill nodded.

"So," Sister Mary Lee said, drawing out the vowel, "like Clint-Eastwood pretty or more like Brad-Pitt pretty?" She leaned forward in her seat, both hands clasped around her coffee cup. Jilly just looked at her and shook his head. Sister Mary Lee looked at Father Bill, who also shook his head.

"What?" she said.

Chapter Fifty-Five

That evening, seated at his kitchen table, Jilly was lost in thought when Anne said to him, "I heard a rumor someone wrecked your bar."

Jilly looked at her, distracted. "Shelf collapsed," he said.

"Uh huh," Anne said, busying herself with a plate of raw chicken breasts over the kitchen sink. Ten minutes later, she went out to the living room for a while and then returned, saying, "You order a limo by any chance?"

Jilly looked at her, saying nothing, as the question was ridiculous.

"I'm serious. Go look for yourself," Anne said.

Jilly went to the window and looked out. Sure enough, a fire-engine-red stretch limousine sat idling right in front of their row house. Big Lenny, in a suit complete with peaked drivers cap, leaned against the front fender, arms crossed and staring at Jilly's front door.

"Oh, for Christ's sake," Jilly mumbled. "What next?"

Jilly let the car and its moose of a driver sit for a while as he changed clothes and cleaned up somewhat. Coming down the steps from his bedroom in a jacket and slacks but no tie, he asked Anne, "How do I look?"

Anne tried to form speech, but her mouth only formed indistinct noises. She was lost.

"Going to see Aza," Jilly said, suddenly cavalier as this whole passion play had started to become surreal to him.

"Aza?" Anne said.

"Aza," said Jilly. And then, after a few seconds, "Azael, actually. At least, Father Bill says so. Google it."

He opened the front door and descended the always-present Southside row house double steps to the sidewalk. Only then did he look at Lenny. He kept his expression neutral; he would not give this lesser henchman the dignity of recognition. Sort of like sending a driver for Sinatra, Jilly understood he was the star of this particular play, at least for the moment.

They drove. Jilly couldn't get the Stones song "Sympathy For The Devil" out of his head, and it made him smile. Sure as hell was appropriate. They arrived at a large office tower and the limo pulled to the curb. Lenny got out and opened Jilly's door. Jilly moved to the front door of the office building, and it was opened by a security guard who neither asked Jilly to state his purpose nor anything else for that matter, just motioned him toward a bank of elevators and said, "You'll want floor thirty-two."

Jilly nodded at him. As the doors opened on the designated floor, the lobby Jilly had expected to step into was instead replaced with an entry covered in rose-colored flagstone, leading to an enormous open room that had to be fifty feet wide, two stories high, its windows opening on a terrific view of the city. He stopped, taking in the spectacle. He had expected a glass and chrome lair of evil.

What he was looking at was beautiful, airy, comforting, and actually inviting. There was a floor-to-ceiling fireplace, and brightly colored rugs (mostly shades of red) everywhere. There was furniture, very comfortable-looking furniture, everywhere. Jilly tried to take it all in while remaining cool. He suspected he was not really succeeding.

"Can I get you a cocktail, Judge?" he heard from behind and slightly right of him.

He turned, the turn too jerky to be cool. The woman who had asked him for his order was beautiful. She was exactly what Jilly would have created with a Perfect Woman App if such a thing existed. He knew she was probably a reflection of his own preferences. He was not sure he cared. He managed to say "Yes. Please. Maker's and water."

"Yes, Judge," she said before moving away silently, elegantly.

Jilly looked around for Aza and saw nobody. He moved into the room and toward the windows as he had nothing else to do and the view was spectacular, thirty-two stories above the city lights and the confluence of three rivers. He wondered what it would be like to live here. Not that he cared. Okay, he cared. A little. He figured Ben Roethlisberger probably had a place like this. He wondered if Ben was on Aza's payroll. He wondered if—

"The Judge!" he heard from behind him. "Welcome!" He turned and saw Aza, thirty feet away and approaching slowly. The Perfect Woman handed him his drink, appearing silently and handing him a glass that was heavy crystal yet not too heavy, and cool but not too cool. Dark Life.

"Please, please, Julian, come and sit, be comfortable," Aza said. Jilly took in the man approaching him. His impression was of a man in his sixties, fit, greying, and tall. Aza moved with a fluid, confident step, and everything about him suggested movie mogul or CEO Fortune 500 company. But there was more than that.

"Sit, sit, Jilly, please. You are my guest," Aza said, motioning him toward a very comfortable couch. "I will sit with you." And he did, collapsing into a double chair across from the very couch Jilly had chosen to sit. "Damn," Aza said, settling back, a big smile on his face.

"Janice, Julian is hungry. Bring him what he likes. Quickly." Aza clapped his hands.

"Yes, Lord," the perfect Janice said and removed herself silently.

Jilly looked at Aza. Aza smiled at Jilly as if waiting for the inevitable question. Eventually, Jilly asked it.

"How does she know what I like?"

Aza smiled. "We all know what you like, Judge." His smile grew broader. "Antipasto, potato soup, chorizo sausage on anything, potato pancakes." After a second, he added, "And with bread, Mancini's, or if not them, Cellone's." Aza leaned back. He did not ask if he was correct. He knew he was.

"So how the hell have you been, brother?" Aza asked, huge smile on his face. "I've been waiting to meet you, I really have." As he said this, Aza leaned forward in his chair. "I can't imagine having this much shit dumped on me as has been dumped on you, and I've been around for a long time." Then Aza sat back again in his double chair, smiling, waiting for Jilly's response.

Jilly was no babe in the woods. He tried to compose himself. He adopted his stoic look—the best he could, anyway. The problem was, and this was a serious problem, he was not ready for the way this sit-down had gone. He had come in ready for a battle royale, a test of wills, or at least a pretty angry argument. But that was not the way this was going. First Uriel, and now Aza. Jilly was beginning to understand these guys were good. Really good.

"What do you want?" Jilly asked. It was a line that he hoped would buy him some time to collect his thoughts.

Aza nodded and smiled benevolently. He said, "Fair question." Then he got up, went over to one of the floor-to-ceiling windows, and looked out at the city. After a while, he said, "You can see both inclines from here." He waited, but Jilly did not respond. "You like the inclines. Both of them. And the twenty or so others that are no longer here," Aza said. "The big ones are gone that used to take horses and wagons up the hills before the roadways were built into the hillsides." Aza turned and looked at Jilly. His smile was not what Jilly had prepared himself for. It was not oily or evil. "You like dogs. Not just any dogs, but the Labradors Marino Fanzi keeps on the Northside. And the color blue. Dark blue, I think. It makes you happy, and you can't even explain why." Aza smiled again, sat down and sipped his drink.

Jilly sipped his drink too and waited. He had no idea what else to do. Everything Aza had said was absolutely stone-cold true. His mind whirled. At the moment, he wasn't sure he could have recited the Pledge of Allegiance, or even his home address, if his life depended upon it. He knew he was lost, and he knew Aza knew he knew. Again, the feeling he was a minor leaguer dealing with professionals.

"So," Aza said, settling back in his overstuffed double chair.

"They are telling you Brady is the Antichrist, you have to kill him, and if you don't, it's the Apocalypse and the end of mankind. Do I have that right?"

Jilly just looked him.

Aza asked, "What's your end?"

Jilly said nothing, processing the question.

"Just curious as to what's in it for you. You're not exactly a religious man, no offense," Aza said, smiling. Jilly was starting to like him in spite of himself, but Jilly knew better than to show his hand at this point. "I assume Uri has sweetened the pot with something. Save your poor damned immortal soul, of course. But that's easy. Maybe something else? You have a kid or a relative dying? I assume it's something like that."

Jilly got up from his couch and walked toward the windows, his drink in his hand. The move was mainly to be able to turn his back on Aza while he processed that this man seemed to know everything or, at a minimum, was a damn good guesser. He took a big sip of his drink to try and clear his thoughts, then a deep breath as the cold bourbon shocked his system. He felt a little better.

Somewhere in the back of his mind, he listened to a voice nagging at him that if all these Masters of the Universe, these Archangels and Dark Angels, were so slick and knew all the answers, then why were they all asking him for favors? They shouldn't need him, should they?

Eventually, Jilly said, "How do you know all this stuff about me?"

Aza looked out over the city and sipped his drink. Instead of being condescending or sarcastic, he said quietly, "Jilly, we know all about you. It's the game we all play and have played for a few thousand years." He sipped again. "You want me to tell you that you stole five dollars from Jerry O'Banion in fourth grade from the cloakroom, or how happy you were in eleventh grade when Lisa Slovensky had her period after missing one?"

Jilly's eyes widened at these truths, although he would not have known it. He took a big sip of his drink.

Aza settled back into his chair and looked at Jilly. "Of course we know these things. So does Uriel. You are being played. You just are, pal." Aza smiled, but it was a sympathetic smile and did not offend Jilly.

"What is your impression of Uriel?" Aza asked, suddenly shifting gears.

"Uriel?" Jilly repeated, not ready to answer.

Aza just smiled and waited.

"Uriel is apparently a player upstairs," Jilly said and looked at Aza.

"He is," Aza said, nodding. "He has a great resume. His exploits are told in song and story. He has my respect. And I am no slouch, an ex-archangel myself, you know. Or did you not know that, my friend?"

Jilly shook his head slowly, thinking he probably should have Googled this guy as he had suggested to Anne.

Aza sighed and shook his head but retained a wry smile. "We lesser angels don't get the press, I guess. It's funny, but you know the kind of person who does an internet search on me? Usually a bunch of angst-ridden, acne-covered sixteen-year-old boys in Suburbia who have decided to hold a Black Mass in their dad's garage around Halloween. As though I can be summoned for weddings and Bar Mitzvahs."

Aza stared at the floor, shaking his head, and for a moment, Jilly felt he wasn't getting the slick sales pitch, that he was getting just a quick look at the soul of this man.

Just as quickly, that glimpse was gone as Aza collected himself and said, "Anyway, Uriel is A-list, but in my humble opinion, headed toward retirement. His judgment has become...unsound."

"Unsound?"

"Unsound," Aza repeated. Sitting forward in his seat and looking directly into Jilly's eyes, he continued, "You see, Uriel is a warrior at heart. But there haven't been any wars to fight for a long time. His skills are unnecessary. The Creator is content to watch life play out for the moment. When it is business as usual, who needs Genghis Khan or Napoleon? Nobody. So Uriel is resigned to the back bench. And what happens? He begins to long for the next war.

"He thinks that Armageddon would suit his talents nicely. He dusts off his armor. He warms up his flaming sword of retribution. And he starts to see the Antichrist everywhere." Aza smiled again, shrugging his shoulders. "He sees him in a blowhard insurance agent from Pittsburgh. The Rules say he can't get directly involved, so he decides he will come down here and use you to meet his needs. As I say, you are being played." With that, Aza sat back and spread his arms out on his couch cushions, a sympathetic smile on his face.

"I'm being played," Jilly repeated. Aza nodded slowly, and Jilly mirrored it.

Lest this become a bobblehead doll convention, Jilly decided to switch the gears on Aza. "If Brady isn't the Antichrist, then what are you, Dark Superstar that you are, doing here exactly?"

"Ha!" Aza exclaimed, laughing and getting out of his chair to refresh his drink at the wet bar. "Another fair question from the assassin!"

Jilly noticed Leonard enter the room from an unseen door and quietly take a chair at the small bar that was, for the moment, out of Aza's sightline. Jilly met his eyes, but Leonard betrayed no emotion or acknowledgment.

As he put ice cubes in his glass, his back to both Jilly and Leonard, Aza said, "Why am I here? If Brady isn't the real deal, then why am I in Pittsburgh?"

Everyone waited.

Jilly again looked at Leonard. Leonard again did not meet Jilly's eyes.

"It's my health," Aza said. "I came to Pittsburgh for the crystal-clear waters."

After a moment, Jilly said, "The crystal-clear waters? In the Monongahela?"

For the third time, Jilly looked at Leonard, who had apparently found something fascinating on the ceiling as he continued to not meet Jilly's eyes.

"I was misinformed," Aza said, his back still to them. The silence went on a for a period as Aza sipped his fresh drink, and then, without turning around, said, "Leonard, why am I here?"

Jilly nearly spit out his own drink as he knew there was no way Aza could have seen Leonard; his back had been to them both since Leonard had entered the room, and there was no mirror on the wet bar. Leonard was not similarly shocked—he had been around this block a few times.

"Pierogi Fest?" Leonard ventured.

Aza laughed loudly and turned to face them both. Leaning on the wet bar, he said, "Look, Julian, my job is to keep an eye on things that might impact my employer."

"And Brady might?" Jilly said. "Impact your employer?"

Aza again shrugged his shoulders. "Might," he said.

"But you think he's just an annoying insurance agent?" Jilly asked.

"Yes," Aza said. "Most likely."

"But you don't know for sure," Jilly said.

After a pause, Aza said, "No. Not for sure. Nobody knows for sure."

"Why?" Jilly asked.

"Because, Jilly, nobody knows what the Creator will do at any given time." Jilly processed this as Aza continued, "You think Brady is the only guy I'm looking at? He's not. I am monitoring two others—one in Canada and one in Egypt. Could they be the Antichrist? Maybe."

"But you're here," Jilly said.

"I am here. Yes," Aza said. "Uriel is here, so I am here. When Bill Belichick shows up at a high school football game, we pay attention."

Jilly nodded. "But you don't think he's the Guy."

Aza smiled sympathetically and collected himself before saying, "Jilly, I don't want to lessen your importance at all. Really, I don't. But reliable sources tell me Uriel is a bit of a laughingstock among the crew upstairs at the moment. The boy who cried 'wolf' one too many times."

Jilly, who had been a bit mesmerized by Aza, suddenly snapped into focus. He would later think it was the reference to "Wolf" that had done it.

"Not the Guy, though. You're saying you don't think Brady is the Guy," Jilly said, looking out at the city. As he turned back to Aza, his eyes rested, just briefly, on Leonard's. Leonard stood behind and just slightly to the left of Aza. As Aza began to speak, Jilly saw Leonard's head shake almost imperceptibly from side to side. Just one shake.

"Brady is very likely not the Guy," Aza said. "You can kill him. Maybe they will save your soul and your friends, maybe they won't. As I say, sources tell me Uriel doesn't have backing at higher levels, but that's your call. It's not that important to me. I'll be moving on soon."

Jilly looked at Aza. "But you wanted to talk to me. Before you left." Aza smiled, and it occurred to him as it had to many others and usually far too late, that this big man was no idiot. But Azael the Fallen Archangel had not gotten to his place in the Grand Scheme by not having talents of his own.

Like a cat getting his feet under him prior to hitting the floor, he said, "Yes, Jilly. I wanted to talk to you. I think we have things in common, that we may be kindred spirits. I think you may have a misperception of how things work. What you would call Heaven is not filled with the Righteous and the Good, and what you would call Hell is not filled with murderers, thieves, and rapists. It doesn't work that way. It's not cut and dried, and it's not really a question of good versus evil. That's the Bible, which was written by a bunch of zealots based on their utopian version of things and Hollywood nonsense."

Jilly looked at Aza and said, "Did you kill Manon?"

The effect was immediate and impressive. Aza's entire spine stiffened, and his fists clenched the pillows of the couch they had been so casually resting upon just seconds earlier. Jilly (mentally, at least) took a step back as he watched what he had suspected become confirmed.

Leonard, who both Jilly and Aza had essentially forgotten about, tried to control his bladder, and it occurred to him he'd not lost his bladder (against his will) since that Crüe concert when the goddamn bathrooms were out of order at the Civic Arena. He thought that Jilly didn't truly understand what he was up against.

The erstwhile cool Aza stared at Jilly. Jilly stared back. He was beginning to understand the Rules of this thing. Aza's eyes turned a glowing yellow. It was just for a moment, but Jilly saw it. He had hit a nerve. The urbane, slick, sophisticated man was evil. Some part of Jilly understood he should press. To say he was flying by the seat of this pants would have been akin to saying Lewis and Clark needed a map. He didn't care.

"You did," Jilly said quietly, nodding.

What clicked into place at this moment, and Jilly had probably known it all along, was that he was going to determine the outcome. In that instant, he understood he was untouchable. This entire silly cast of some reality show, *Good Guys, Bad Guys*, had all been assembled to function as lesser lights to the Judge. And he, Julian Tetanich, was the Judge.

He wondered if his mother would have been proud. He remembered he had, you know, killed a bunch of people. For money. He took a deep breath. Okay, maybe not so much proud, but maybe impressed. He then wondered if his mother was in "Heaven." This thought lead to wondering if she wasn't in Heaven, maybe he could work a deal whereby she—

"Julian," Aza said, snapping him back to reality.

Jilly focused on Aza. He said nothing. Well, hell, that was his specialty.

"I think..." Aza began, and Jilly knew he was about to hear a bunch of baloney. "I think you expect to hear a bunch of baloney." Jilly processed this, surprised and suddenly a little worried that Aza could read his mind.

"I'm not going to give you baloney," Aza continued, his voice suddenly softening. "This is beyond you and me. This is beyond whatever you think of as Order. There is no Order." Aza sat back in his very comfortable chair. "There has always been Disorder. The Creator doesn't mind it. What remains is whatever He thinks should remain. He'll decide. Not you. If you think, for a second, that you, the orphan son of an illiterate millworker, could somehow decide what He will do next, then you, my friend, are very, very wrong." Aza smiled a tired smile.

As he said this, Aza leaned in closer to Jilly, and the very old man's features (and Jilly now understood he was very, very old) weren't so hard. "I don't envy you," the fallen angel said. "I'll be here when this is done. I'll be here when your bones, and your time, have passed into dust. Do you know why?"

Jilly did not respond, just waited.

"Because He likes it this way," Aza said, his right index finger pointing slightly upward. He sat back.

Jilly sat back as well, not so much because he wanted to, but because he understood much of what Aza had said was probably true, though not all. His illiterate millworker father hadn't raised a moron, after all. Had he?

Aza looked out onto the lights of the city.

Jilly took a deep breath. "I kill Brady, and I know you can't stop me from doing that. I know you can't like I know the sun will rise tomorrow. I kill Brady, and they save my soul. My polluted, son-of-an-illiterate-millworker, contract-hitter soul."

"Now, why?" Jilly continued, leaning forward and feeling like he had the advantage for this first time in this whole thing. "Why, on Earth, wouldn't I?"

Leonard, who had realized he hadn't really soiled his pants, considered the question. He felt that, like Aza, he was kind of a fallen angel. He understood he'd never be perceived this way, but if he had nothing at all, and he didn't, what he (probably) had were street smarts. So he knew the answer to Jilly's question.

Aza looked at Jilly. He took a deep breath, then a deep drink. He sighed and said, "I've known the Creator for a very long time." Jilly noticed he was no longer looking directly at him. Aza studied the lights of the city below him. "He enjoys the drama. If he didn't, then what fun would all this be?"

Jilly tried to look neutral but felt he wasn't pulling it off.

"Do you remember Arnie Gold?" Aza asked. He waited. Understanding Jilly was not going to respond, Aza continued, "You let him get eaten by the sharks. You did." Aza used his drink hand but still managed to point one finger at Jilly, a slight smile on his face.

Although Leonard wondered what the hell all this had to do with Armageddon, he, oddly, did remember Arnie Gold.

"You let him get his ass kicked by those metal shop guys in eighth grade when you knew you could have stopped it. He begged you to help him." Aza turned and looked at Jilly. *"Begged* you. Do you remember?"

Of course Jilly remembered. He liked the poor bastard. But

he had been distracted by some Anne thing. An emergency. And Arnie, until the very last second waiting for his hero to save him, had gotten his ass kicked.

"It still bothers you," Aza said. Jilly turned his head away, but he knew he had conceded the point. Of course it still bothered him.

"Let me tell you about Arnie Gold," Aza said. "He runs four tanning beds in LA, married the girl of his dreams, and has three kids—two of whom are at USC and the third married to a dentist.

"He never thinks about you or eighth grade. You've kicked your own ass about that for how long now?" Aza smiled. "And it never mattered."

Jilly, irritated at this truth and the occasions when he *had* beat himself up about that incident, said, "What the hell does Arnie Gold have to do with me killing your boy?"

"Because if you kill "my boy," Aza said, making air quotes around Jilly's words, "it will bother you. Not because you are worried about burning in Hell or wandering through gardens in Heaven. Even though now maybe you know they actually exist. Probably not because you want to redeem yourself and save your uncle and your sister. No, if you don't kill Brady, it will be because you have, always have, had your own idea of what is wrong and what is right. It saved you when you were young, when you could have gone the way of madness. It has governed you your whole life. If you kill Brady, especially if you feel you were coerced into doing it, it will bother you." Aza finished and sat back almost regally in his chair.

Leonard's mouth hung open without him even realizing it. "Close your mouth, Leonard. You catching flies?" Aza said, never turning, still looking at Jilly. Leonard closed his mouth. Damn.

Jilly continued staring at Aza for a long time. Finally, he said, "Well. Thank you, Dr. Phil, for the analysis, but if the Creator, as you call him, is the puppeteer pulling the strings behind all of this, why would he care if it bothered me?"

Leonard, his mouth closed tightly, wanted to answer this question for Aza but wisely did not. He might be the dumbest guy in this particular three-man band, but he knew the answer before it left Aza's somewhat-lizard-like lips.

"He cares, because it makes you the perfect Judge, my boy!"

Aza exclaimed, spreading his arms, a broad smile spreading across his face. "Don't you see? If you were a lowlife, like Leonard here"—Aza swept a hand behind him in Leonard's general direction—"well then, the outcome would be predictable. As you say, why wouldn't you dust Brady? Save your soul, your friends, get the girl, the fame, the money, live happily ever after. Or," Aza continued, "if you were your pal the priest, you couldn't possibly kill a man, no matter what was at stake. Also predictable."

Aza, the smile still lighting his face in the way smiles do when they are coming from people explaining something that truly delights them, continued, "You know what predictable is? It's boooooring!"

Jilly looked at Aza, then at Leonard. Leonard looked back at Jilly, but his mind was elsewhere, wondering if being called a lowlife by a fallen angel was an insult.

"Boring?" Jilly said, repeating the word as he digested the thought.

"Boring," Aza said. "You are the perfect Judge because you have a decision to make. And it's not easy, my barkeeper friend. It's not easy because, on one hand, you are an expert killer and you have killed many, so what's one more? But on the other hand, you have stopped killing. And you were never Dark at heart. And you know that once you had your epiphany, the decision to stop killing was the correct one by your standards, which is your code of conduct. But now an archangel descends from Heaven and tells you can help your friends, redeem your former wicked ways, and maybe rid the world of a man who will destroy everyone."

Aza smiled again and continued, "But if you do, it will bother you. Have you any idea how interesting that dilemma is to the Creator?"

Jilly did not.

"Very interesting," Aza continued. "That's why He picked you. For pure entertainment value. To make it more fun, Uriel rushes down here without any official clearance to try to coerce you into 'fulfilling biblical prophecy,'" Aza said, smiling, his fingers again making lazy air quotes around the words. "Hell, your friend the priest has had an erection for the past month that Cialis would like to sell to the elderly."

Jilly thought that might actually be true.

"But there is no Biblical prophecy," Aza said. "The Bible has been making people do stupid things for two thousand years. I can tell you. Brother, I've been there."

Jilly's mind was spinning. A lot of what Aza had said rang true. By the same token, he knew Aza was a professional liar of the highest degree. Aza got up and walked toward the windows.

Jilly said, "I have to go."

"I know," Aza said. "I had them bring the car around ten minutes ago. It will take you to the Northside. You'll want to talk to your uncle."

Jilly was not surprised, only mildly numb at the idea that Aza knew exactly where he had intended to go. Jilly set his drink down and got up, smoothed his pants, and collected his thoughts. What a night. He began to turn toward the elevator, Perfect Woman having hit the call button already as if by telepathy.

"Jilly," Aza said, facing the floor-to-ceiling windows, his back still to him. Jilly stopped but said nothing. "You're not going to do it," Aza declared.

Jilly still said nothing but now looked at Leonard, seated on a barstool directly in front of him.

"You're not going to do it because my guy is not the Guy."

Jilly remained silent and continued looking at Leonard.

"Not the Guy," Aza continued. "We discussed it this morning in our staff meeting." Jilly looked at Leonard, who was blocked from Aza's view by Jilly's own not-diminutive body. Leonard, his eyes locked with Jilly's, gave just the slightest shake of his head. "Didn't we, Leonard?" Aza asked.

Leonard, his eyes never leaving Jilly's, said in an even tone he was very, very proud of, "Sure did, sir. Not the Guy. That's what you said."

"And you know it too, Jilly. False alarm. And He knows it too, because He knows everything. He's waiting to see what you'll do. If you'll be flimflammed by a con man with wings on his back straight out of Hollywood. Good luck, my friend," Aza said.

Jilly turned and looked at him, then as the elevator arrived with a pleasant tone, he turned back and got in without another word.

On the way down, he realized something that had been nagging him like a fly buzzing around his head. Aza's words suddenly came into focus. *Be the good guy and save your uncle and your sister.* His sister? What the hell was that about?

When Jilly had gone, Aza, still facing the city, said to Leonard, almost absently, "Have the Russian kill him."

Leonard processed this command, then repeated, "Kill him. Jilly?"

Aza nodded and said, "Yes. I don't want to leave this to chance. He was listening tonight, and I think I got through, but I'm not going to leave this to a killer's decision. If our esteemed Mayor is the White Horseman, and I think he may be, I'm not going to sit by while some idiot bartender fucks this up. I'd prefer history not to record me as the guy who let Armageddon go off the rails."

Leonard listened, thought it through for a few seconds and then said "The Wolf then. I'll talk to him. What are we offering?"

"Tell him we'll get rid of the Italians and five million," Aza said, his hands still clasped behind his back, seemingly not paying full attention.

"Five million dollars?" Leonard said. Aza didn't answer, just continued looking out the windows at the city, his back to Leonard. After a while, Leonard left without another word.

Chapter Fifty-Six

Jilly's mind was racing. As he sat in the limo, he replayed the conversation with Aza over and over, each time remembering a nugget here and a phrase there that he had not recollected initially. Uriel didn't have backing at higher levels. The Creator was watching this like some kind of ecclesiastical dice game, maybe with a bag of chips and a beer. Jilly remembered the stickers on his very own video poker machines in his very own bar: "For amusement purposes only" (wink, wink). Is that what all this was?

And Aza saying Brady wasn't the Guy. Or maybe he was. For some reason, although he would no more trust Leonard any further than he could throw him, Jilly's gut told him Leonard was telling the truth. Why would he lie? Hell, to that end, why would he tell Jilly the truth? He had to be playing with the prospect of a very painful death to even risk the slight shakes of his head while Aza was speaking; that guy seemed to always know exactly what was going on.

And then the limo was stopping in front of the Don's block. As Jilly got out of the car, the driver's window rolled down slowly and Big Lenny, the large bruise on the side of his face from the bowling pin now a beautiful plum and orange, said, "You can get an Uber home, Big Time. I got shit to do."

Jilly looked at the man, then looked away, a small smile playing on his lips at this pretend gangsta. Then he turned back and, leaning down, put his hands on the driver's door sill. "I don't know your name, so let's just call you Meathead. You know whose house this is, and you know who I am. And do you know, Meathead, who you are?"

Lenny just looked at him.

"You're the guy," Jilly said, pausing for emphasis, "who drives guys like me to houses owned by guys like the Don on the orders of guys like Aza. Have a nice evening, Meathead." Jilly stepped away from the car.

Lenny performed the absolutely predictable tire-squealing exit, to the degree you can in a stretch limousine. Jilly just shook his head and smiled as he watched the taillights disappear into the night.

"I have no earthly idea why, but I am absolutely unsurprised you are here," said a voice from a wicker rocker on the front porch.

"Well, that's funny, because neither am I," Jilly said.

Once inside, Martin came down the main stair, casual this evening as he had not anticipated the visitors, but still put together in slacks and a cardigan sweater, reading glasses on a string around his neck. "Julian! A pleasant surprise. How have you been?"

The big man looked like he had lost some weight. Jilly registered this as he placed a smile on his face and said, "I'm great." Two Labs padded into the entry hall and sniffed Jilly, tails wagging furiously. Jilly petted each absently, looking into those guileless eyes and thinking life would be a hell of a lot easier if people were like dogs.

"Don't get me wrong, Jilly, I'm glad you're here, but the Don is in Philadelphia on business. If you had called, I would have told you and saved you the trouble of coming over."

"I didn't come here to talk to the Don, Martin," Jilly said, straightening from the dogs and for the first time looking the big man directly in the eyes. "I came here to talk to you."

Martin, no stranger to conversations that needed to be conducted privately, never hesitated but rather just said, "I'll get us a drink."

Ten minutes later, seated in a comfortable reading room, doors closed, dogs removed, Martin said, "Did you know Andrew

Carnegie's nephew once owned this house?"

"Did not," Jilly said, sipping his drink and looking at Martin, although Martin was not looking at him.

"Yes, nephew. Rumors from that time say he was gay." Martin laughed, but it was a humorless bark more than a joyful exclamation.

Looking at his drink so he would not have to meet the gaze of his "uncle", Jilly asked, "Do you have cancer, Martin?"

Martin took in an audible sharp breath and got up from his chair. He walked slowly toward the large, curtained window at the south end of the room. Jilly waited. The lack of an immediate denial pretty much told Jilly all he needed to know.

Martin faced the window, his back to Jilly. He sipped his drink. "Do you remember when you were, oh, I don't know, maybe sixteen? Seventeen?" Martin said after a while, his back to Jilly. "You had gotten into a fight at school because some kid had been saying you smelled bad." Jilly remembered. Martin continued, "When Angelo Jr. told me, I called you over to this house, and we spent some time talking about the importance of bathing and deodorant, laundering your clothes.

"I told you men of character and respect, like the Don, for example, need to be dignified, to be the kind of men other men looked up to. Do you remember that, Jilly?"

"I remember," Jilly said, then added, "Had anyone else tried to give me that speech, they would have been punched in the mouth, I guess."

"It wasn't your fault," Martin said. "You had nobody to teach you, having to take care of your sister, too. I always thought God dealt you a bad hand, Jilly. That under different circumstances, had your father lived..." Martin trailed off.

Jilly waited.

"I hope I helped you, even in my sad way," Martin said. "I would have liked to have kids of my own. But I think I'm better with dogs, you know." Again, that short laugh.

"You helped a worthless kid far more than many, and unlike anyone else, without expecting anything in return. And I have always appreciated that," Jilly said. He watched Martin as the big man nodded.

Then, a sob, just a single one on a sharp intake of breath, as though resisting every effort of a very determined man, escaped Martin's lips.

Jilly waited as Martin collected himself. When Martin eventually turned to face him, the big man's eyes were red, but there were no tears on his face. No blubbering, no melodrama.

"I've had a good life, Julian. Nobody needs to feel sorry for me." Then, resolve changing his face into an expression Jilly remembered when he was about to smacked across the backside or the side of his head, Martin continued, "And nobody better."

Jilly got up and nodded, smiling at this gentle giant. "You roll your dice..." Jilly said.

"You move your mice," Martin finished, smiling. This exchange was an old and familiar one for them both.

"Give me a hug, kid," Martin said, opening his arms, and Jilly did just that, not remembering ever having hugged anyone else in his entire life. Martin stepped back and looked Jilly up and down. "You turned out good. Don't let anyone tell you differently."

After a pause, Jilly said, "So did you, Martin. So did you." He turned to leave the room, and as he left, Martin said his name quietly. Jilly turned.

"Good luck, Jilly," Martin said.

Jilly nodded, the understanding passing between the two men without needing to be explained. He left without another word.

The next day dawned bright, clear, and a bit cold. Jilly had slept poorly—not really a surprise. He'd had odd dreams, none of which made much sense. There were angels and demons, vague recollections of his parents, and, of course, an appearance by Leonard. He'd woke to that one, shivering slightly and never so happy to be in his own bed. After coffee and an untouched breakfast, served by Anne who was oddly silent this morning, he'd left the row house. He beeped the horn twice outside the rectory at Prince of Peace, but nobody came. He waited ten more minutes. Then he parked the Lincoln, annoyed.

He headed in and said, "Yo, anyone home?"

Hearing nothing, he headed toward Father Bill's office. As he approached, he heard noises, and upon entering saw Sister Mary

Lee trying to cinch a red sash around Father Bill's waist. The priest's black cassock was immaculate and clearly never worn. On Father Bill's head was a black, four-peaked hat with a kind of pom-pom on top.

The priest looked at Jilly, slightly embarrassed, and said, "What?"

"I, uh, nothing," Jilly stuttered, unaccustomed to seeing his friend so formally garbed.

"Biretta," Father Bill said. Jilly tried to process why the priest would be carrying a gun. He was confused.

"No guns today, Father," Jilly said. "I don't think it's a good idea, and—"

"Biretta, not beretta, you numbnuts. The hat. It's called a biretta. Jesus."

"Oh," Jilly said, then added quickly, "Looks good. On you, I mean. Can we go?"

"Yes, yes," Father Bill said, checking himself in the mirror. He really was going to do that carb thing. Next week. "Let's go."

As they moved from the room, Sister Mary Lee, leaning on the wall near Father Bill's desk, said, "Guys." They stopped and turned. Sister Mary Lee looked at them for a long moment. Then she said, "I know this is kind of like going to meet a rockstar." She was talking to them both but looking at Father Bill exclusively. "I was taught that archangels were God's messengers and the holiest of the holy."

Jilly looked at her, then at the priest, who was looking at his assistant, mildly confused.

"Please keep in mind that there are an awful lot of people who did their catechism this morning and had their coffee, you know, just got ready to have a normal day. That don't, you know, don't know that maybe, just maybe, the future of the entire world they think they know might be in the balance. Today. They just assume, they've been taught by the Church to assume, that the Good Guys will always win, will do the right thing."

Jilly noticed Sister Mary Lee was wet-eyed, and he turned to Father Bill, whom he now noticed was also a bit wet-eyed.

"Just normal," the nun continued. "But they believe. Strongly. Just like me." This last sentence came out a little shaky.

Father Bill smiled and took a deep breath, wiping his eyes. He looked away into nothing, and Jilly waited. Then he said, sort of sang actually, "Always look on the bright side of life." He looked at Sister Mary Lee and waited for her to finish the line.

After a few seconds, she pursed her lips and whistled the ending of their favorite Monty Python song.

He gave her a hug and said, "If I don't come back, burn my collection of vintage *Playboy* magazines. They're in—"

"In your closet, in the crate marked 'Donny Osmond Albums.' Who'd look there?" Sister Mary Lee finished.

Father Bill smiled, took another deep breath, and then said to Jilly, placing his palms on his shoulders, "Sancho Panza, let's go," and strode out.

Jilly looked at the nun, who looked right back at him. "Don't get him killed," she said.

Jilly considered this, then said, "No promises." Then he strode out too.

When they were gone, the nun headed to a second-floor balcony and taking a crumpled pack of Marlboros from her skirt, lit one and inhaled deeply. Staring up at the statue of Mary that sat atop the day care attached to the rectory, she exhaled and then said, "Mother, I'm getting too old for this stuff," then quickly crossed herself. Of course.

In the car, Jilly said, "You thinking this is a photo shoot for *Priest's Monthly Magazine?*" Jilly asked, keeping his eyes on the road and trying not to smile.

"Screw you, Jilly," his friend said, smoothing his cassock, annoyed and, Jilly understood, embarrassed.

"Don't get me wrong—it's a good look on you," Jilly said, and Father Bill turned slightly in his seat, hoping Jilly was sincere. "I'm serious," Jilly continued. "We get you a couple of orphans tugging at your skirts, slide in a Bing Crosby soundtrack, and I could almost believe you didn't damn Rob Gronkowski's soul to Hell last fall when he dropped that sure TD pass and effed up your fantasy league."

"Look, goddamn it," Father Bill started, and Jilly quickly crossed himself, which pissed off the priest even more. He clenched his fists in his lap and took a deep breath. "Look," he started again, "I'm not going to apologize. I don't need to apologize for…" The priest trailed off as Jilly drove, thankful he didn't need to make eye contact. His friend tried again. "Did you ever have a hero?" Father Bill asked.

Jilly considered this. "A hero," Jilly said.

"Yes," Father Bill said. "A hero. Someone you looked up to when you were younger."

"Sure," Jilly said. "Of course I did."

"Who?" the priest asked.

"Well…" Jilly began and stopped.

After a moment, Father Bill asked again, "Who?"

Jilly drove, his eyes on the road, and eventually said, "Lassie."

Father Bill considered this. "Lassie," he repeated. "Lassie." They drove in silence. "Why? Why the hell Lassie?!" Father Bill eventually said, annoyed he couldn't take this conversation where he wanted it to go.

"I liked Lassie," Jilly said, "because she just did the right thing always. Even if her own life was in jeopardy. There wasn't any of that moral dilemma baloney; she was a dog, after all. She just did what she thought was right." He drove on. Both men sat in silence. Eventually, Father Bill nodded quietly. Jilly noticed but pretended he didn't.

"Well, my heroes were archangels," the priest said. Jilly turned and looked at him. Father Bill continued, "My parents were religious, so they didn't tell me cowboy stories or Batman stories; they told me archangel stories. About David and Michael and their flaming swords and the thousands of Angels in the Army of the Holy Host. I grew up wanting to be an archangel."

When they pulled up to the Fairmont's valet parking area, Jilly noticed Jimmy Hallendorf's deep green 1968 Shelby Cobra sitting across the street and down a block—exactly where Jilly would have parked if he didn't want to be noticed. Of course, when you were driving a $95,000 vintage sports car, you were probably going to get noticed. Jilly knew this. Jilly knew that Jimmy knew this, too. This was just a show of solidarity, a gesture from a man who knew he probably wasn't going to have an impact on the outcome but nonetheless wanted Jilly to know he was there. He nodded in the direction of the car.

"Who's that?" Father Bill asked, noticing Jilly noticing.

After a few seconds, Jilly said, "A friend," and tossed his keys to the kid in the valet outfit. Then he stared up at all thirty stories of the Fairmont. He looked at Father Bill, who was looking at him. "You ready, Padre?" he asked, a slight smile on his lips.

Father Bill looked up too, then, smoothing his skirts, said, "Well, I guess as ready as I'll ever be."

Jilly, his smile widening to a grin, said, "Well then, let's go do this, babydoll. I have a lunch reservation at Rosa Villa I absolutely refuse to miss!" He put his arm around his friend as they entered the building.

Chapter Fifty-Seven

Outside the suite, Father Bill again straightened himself, brushed nonexistent dust from his cassock, and said to Jilly, "How do I look?"

Jilly, who had probably a dozen great sarcastic lines come to mind, instead just turned and said, his face serious, "You were made for this." The priest exhaled so loudly Jilly thought he might trip some kind of security sensor.

"You really think so?" Father Bill asked. The look he gave Jilly was more than just a guy searching for affirmation. It was a guy searching for affirmation for a life lived in a manner that the liver of said life often wondered if he had made a horrible mistake. If, on one hand, all this was a bunch of religious baloney, then he was a fool. A ridiculous fool. A ridiculous numbnuts fool who had missed a whole hell of a lot of sex and booze and...and nevermind. Like Linus in that pumpkin patch. Idiot believer. On the other hand, if all this was not baloney, then he had likely not ever quite believed enough to earn his golden ticket and would probably burn ad infinitum. He looked nauseated.

Jilly waited for a few seconds for the brilliant, confidence-inspiring comment from his spiritual adviser that never came. Then he said, "Besides, if we blow this, we'll have plenty of time to discuss where it went sideways as vultures rip at our entrails in a lake of fire for the next five hundred years." Jilly smiled at the priest and hit the room door buzzer.

Oliver answered the door. He was wearing some kind of white robe with gold embroidery that was a bit too big on him, and, as such, he looked a little like the Charmin toilet paper teddybear. Father Bill, so nervous he was stopped from kneeling down and kissing Oliver's feet only by Jilly placing his hand firmly on the priest's shoulder and saying, "Oliver, good to see you. We're here to see Uriel."

Oliver moved to his left and, with a sweeping gesture, bowed slightly and motioned for them both to enter the room. They did, down a short hallway to a much larger living room. They saw Manon first, seated in a comfortable chair near the windows. She was dressed in black slacks, black shoes, black hairband. All business today, Jilly registered. A straight-up professional—no robes, no baloney. He nodded at her, one professional to another. She looked at him flatly, no sign of recognition, then turned and looked out the windows at the rivers and the city below. It would occur to him later, when he ran the events of this very, very interesting day through his mind, that his expectation of any recognition from Manon the Black Death was akin to a well-decorated high school quarterback going in for the high five when seeing Patrick Mahomes in an airport concourse. There are hitters and then there are Hitters.

"Can I get you a drink, or something else?" Oliver asked as they made their way into the living room. "Uriel will be here shortly."

"You have bourbon?" Jilly asked.

Turning to look at him, Father Bill said, "It's nine a.m."

Jilly looked at the priest, then at the assistant. "Beer, then?"

Oliver said, "We have bourbon and beer. Which do you prefer, Judge?"

Jilly looked at Father Bill and said, "You see? These people know how to treat a VIP," and smiled. "Oliver, gimme an IC Light".

"Of course," Oliver said, now a veteran of Primanti Brothers' beer list and familiar with Iron City Light. "And you, Father?"

"Diet Coke?" Father Bill asked, still trying to digest that he might, at this very moment, be in a hotel room with people long dead and maybe also a historical assassin he had only read about in textbooks.

They sat down. Oliver prepared and delivered their drinks. They waited in silence. They sipped. They looked out at the city. Father Bill kept stealing glances at Manon. Manon refused to look at either of them. After about the exact time someone would keep someone waiting if they were keeping them waiting intentionally, a door opened. Jilly, who had been waiting for this, did not turn but kept looking out the floor-to-ceiling windows, carefully sipping his beer. Father Bill turned immediately toward the source of the sudden break in the silence.

Uriel swept into the room with decorum—not too slow, not too fast, but with gravitas. No question. Jilly had to give him that. He was wearing the equivalent of a four-star general's uniform if Heaven issued that kind of gear. White on white on white suit, various and sundry markings on it that were not medals exactly, but he had no doubt whatsoever they signified battles won and campaigns successfully waged. Father Bill got up from his chair, Diet Coke in hand, and then just sort of stopped, staring at Uriel. Jilly turned and looked. Uriel surveyed the room.

Father Bill said, "Eximietatem, tuam a servo Dei vestry ac Nobili Domino,"* and fell to one knee, his head bowed.

Uriel, placing his hand on the priest's head ever so gently, said "Servum autem Domini non oportet quod ante arcum me,"** and raised the priest up with a hand, motioning him to a chair.

Father Bill sat, starstruck, his pom-pom'ed hat slightly askew. "It's a…it's an honor to meet you," the priest stuttered.

"It is an honor to meet you, Father Wojtanowicz," Uriel said, sitting across from the priest. "You've saved, by my count, twenty-six kids from heading to the Dark. Probably a hundred more from making very bad decisions that would have made their lives on this planet miserable. We keep track of these things, Father. Oliver, am I wrong?" Uriel said over his shoulder.

"Not wrong, sir!" Oliver said with vigor. "Twenty-six saved from the Dark, one hundred and seven influenced positively, sir!"

*A servant of God kneels before you.

**Servants of God need not kneel before me.

For the first time, Jilly began to understand the enormity of the situation. That this angry angel wasn't just some blowhard who was trying to bully a few more people to make himself feel better. That he might instead be dealing with people, or entities (who knew?), that had a much greater significance than he had imagined. He took a step back—mentally, at least, the hitter in him incapable of ever taking a step back lest he show fear. Jilly waited. They'd get to him in time, he suspected.

"Please, both of you, come, sit," Uriel said, gesturing toward the very comfortable furniture. They settled in, Manon refusing a beverage and staying on the perimeter, although never out of Jilly's sight or mind.

Uriel said, "So, you have met my old friend Azael, and you know what is happening here." Uriel gauged the response from his guests but mainly from Jilly, who did his best to keep a stoneface. "I want to say... I want to say I'm sorry," Uriel said, approaching Jilly, a glass of red wine in his hand. "I am...passionate." He said this last with a shrug of the shoulders. "I admit it, no question. I believe..." he said as he passed Jilly and headed toward the floor-to-ceiling windows in the suite, "I believe in the Good. Or the Light, if you prescribe to the Light versus Dark idea. I am on the side of the believers in the Creator. God, as you like to call him down here."

Jilly waited for Uriel to get back to his apology.

"And I overreacted. For this, I am sorry." As Uriel said this, he turned toward Jilly and looked him in the eyes. "I'm sorry," he said again. Turning back toward the windows, Uriel said, seemingly more to himself than to his audience, "I am built for war. I am best in a fight." He paced some more, not looking at anyone and instead looking out over the city below him. Then, taking a deep breath, he turned and looked at Jilly. "I know only action, not words. Perhaps we are the same in this regard? I don't know."

Jilly met the angel's eyes, and he'd have been lying if he said they didn't have that mutual understanding at that moment. Yes, they both understood action over words. Damn skippy.

"Why do you need me?" Jilly asked, choosing not to acknowledge the apology (probably the right move).

"Why do I need you?" Uriel repeated, musing on the question, a small smile playing at his lips. The feeling Jilly got was that this epic, rockstar archangel had asked himself this very question several times. "Oh, I imagine, strictly speaking, I don't need you at all," Uriel said, sipping his wine while looking out over the city. They all waited.

Jilly stole a glance at Father Bill, whose attention was still glued to Uriel as though in a room with Julius Caesar or Abraham Lincoln. Damn glad the guy who was supposed to have his back was starstruck like a teenager at a Taylor Swift preshow meet 'n greet...

"But there are Rules." The comment came quietly from Uriel's left. It was Manon, who also continued to look out the windows. They all waited again. Jilly caught the look Father Bill's gave him from the corner of his eye.

"Rules. Yes," Uriel finally said. "There are Rules." Turning to address the room, Jilly specifically, he said, "Our Creator has decided he enjoys an uncertain outcome. Agree or disagree, we all must consider the Rules."

Jilly immediately picked up on the use of that word and said, "Consider or obey?"

The angel laughed out loud. "A man after my own heart!" Then, after a pause, he said, "Consider." Oliver looked at Manon, who looked back at him, her expression flat.

Uriel crossed the room to Jilly, moved a large ottoman across from Jilly's chair, and sat down on it, only a few feet from Jilly. "If you embrace the idea that the Creator likes an uncertain outcome, that He likes to put events in place and see how His creations respond to them, then one must accept that I am included in the uncertainty of that equation. As is Manon, as is Oliver." Uriel said this with a sweeping gesture of his right arm, indicating his team. "There are Rules, yes," he continued. "Father Wojtanowicz can give you the ten big ones right now, beginning with 'Thou shalt not kill.'" Uriel smiled sardonically at Jilly. "And yet, here we are."

Jilly considered this. His mind was working quickly to try and process what Uriel had said.

Father Bill said, "But surely our God would not condone killing."

Uriel did not turn to look at the priest; his eyes never left Jilly's as he said, "I have killed thousands in His name, and I am revered for it. Did your GI's come home from your Great Wars and throw themselves at the confessionals of their parish, asking absolution for all those they had killed? Of course not. Because it was war. Not only war"—the archangel's eyes had grown brighter as he warmed to his speech—"but a just war. And this..." he continued, leaning closer to Jilly, "This is war."

"War," Jilly repeated.

"War," Uriel echoed. "Perhaps the greatest war of them all. And you think," he said, getting up from his seat, unable to contain himself anymore, "that our Creator sits and watches, hoping we obey some set of ephemeral, undefined Rules that will allow the Antichrist to rise and fulfill prophesy? I think not. He waits to see if anyone will fulfill their destiny and act in His name, fight in His name, destroy in His name THE EVIL THAT WE KNOW IS AMONG US!" This last was said while Uriel raised his fist in the air, the look on his face so severe and focused that Jilly was for a moment awed by it and understood at least a little of what Father Bill so revered in this apparition.

Uriel bowed his head, spent, and dropped to one knee, his back to Jilly. He held his glass out with one stiff arm, and Oliver rushed to take it from him, nearly tripping over his too-big robes as a child trips over his Halloween costume. Silence filled the room.

Father Bill looked at Jilly. Jilly looked at the kneeling archangel. Manon raised her eyes toward the ceiling, or perhaps higher if one assumed she had no particular interest in drywall with a coat of interior latex on it. Oliver looked from Uriel, to Jilly, to Manon, his head careening like a pinball.

Somewhere in a light-filled office, a slightly rotund or thin, elderly or middle-aged, depending on your taste, man (or woman) watched a large computer monitor in earnest. His focus was laser sharp, his eyes bright as he awaited the outcome. Across from his desk, another archangel watched with him, his expression neutral. Nothing he was seeing surprised him.

Uriel finally said, quietly, his back still to Jilly and everyone else in the room as though shamed at having to beg, "Will you Judge him? Will you kill the Antichrist in the name of our Lord, the Creator?" Everyone waited.

Jilly looked down at the carpet, mostly to avoid looking at Father Bill. Jilly was sure, although he couldn't see him, that the priest was drilling him with that look you give someone when someone says, *Do you want to meet Mick Jagger?* As if in a vacuum, the room, to Jilly, seemed to go silent. He felt alone, and that was fine.

He was thinking about a time when he had stumbled across a sick dog in an alley near the house he and Anne had shared a long time ago. The dog was old. It was clearly suffering. Younger then, Jilly did not dwell much on the finer points of compassion. He had his pistol, he removed it from his waistband. He pointed it at the dog, but he didn't immediately shoot it. The old dog convulsed and shook, and for some reason, Jilly could not bring himself to fire his gun. Eventually, he walked away, not sure why, but later feeling better that he had removed himself from involvement in the fate of the animal. The next day, he could not help himself from checking the alleyway as he left the house that morning. The old dog was there, stiff and dead, a froth of blood around his nose and mouth. Some other hungry animal had damaged the dog's body at some point in the night. Jilly absently hoped the dog had been dead when that had happened.

He sighed, a full body sigh that he was not aware of. "No," he said quietly, although everyone in the room heard it clearly.

Uriel made no movement at all for a moment. Manon stiffened, ready for something, anything. She was also secretly thrilled, for reasons she was not sure she understood at the moment. Oliver cringed. He was a Hall of Fame cringer, Oliver. He awaited the windows blowing out. He awaited Uriel casting the occupants of the entire room out the windows and down thirty stories to their deaths. He waited for... He wasn't exactly sure what he waited for.

For his part, Father Bill had a bit of an epiphany. Initially shocked that anyone, any mere mortal, could have refused the archangel's request, his emotion quickly turned to awe at his friend and admiration of his courage. Jilly had said no. A man who had killed many had decided not to kill one more. The priest figured they were all done for, but oddly a strange calmness had come over him. He was ready for that eventuality. It seemed right somehow. He didn't know it, but he was smiling. Jilly looked at his friend, thinking his buddy had finally lost his mind, but smiled back. He figured there were worse ways to go out as a collar-wearing messenger of the Creator Himself.

"Leave us," Uriel said, also quietly. He still had his back to the room, still on one knee. Nobody moved. After a pause, the angel roared, "LEAVE US!" Glass broke, although not the windows. Furniture moved, but not too much. They all moved, including Jilly, who got up from his chair.

"Not you," Uriel said evenly, although he could not have seen Jilly. Jilly looked at Father Bill whose eyes had become big. The message was clear: "Let's make like a newborn baby and head out." And they did. Or, at least, they started to. Uriel simply raised his left hand and made that same finger-waving gesture Manon had used, and Jilly's body froze. He could not move. The room had now emptied except for Uriel, Jilly, and Father Bill. The priest stared at his friend. Jilly shrugged his shoulders. Sort of.

Uriel walked up to the pair and, looking at Father Bill, said, "You can go, Father. Your friend will not be harmed." Placing his hands on the priest's shoulders, Uriel looked into his eyes and, smiling slightly, said, "Go. Peace be with you. He will meet you downstairs." Father Bill looked at Jilly. Jilly nodded. Sort of. The priest looked back for the last time at a real-life, honest-to-God archangel, then nodded to him and turned toward the elevator.

His mind spinning, he hit the call button. As he waited, Uriel said, "Father?"

The priest turned. "The cook's assistant? He would have killed you," Uriel said. Father Bill simply looked at him in confusion until the understanding dawned on him. "He would have killed you. You did the right thing."

Father Bill just stared at Uriel until the elevator bell dinged and he almost jumped out of his shoes. Uriel made a slow sign of the cross and smiled. "Go with God," he said. Father Bill went.

When the elevator had left, Uriel absently waved his left hand again, and suddenly Jilly could move. He took a deep breath and stock of all his moving parts. They all seemed in order. Good. Uriel had seated himself away from Jilly, again with his back to him and again gazing out at the city below. He said nothing.

Eventually, Jilly said, "The cook's assistant?"

The archangel said nothing for a while, then he said, "He'll explain it to you." Jilly nodded, then he waited.

Uriel moved to the sideboard and poured himself a fresh glass of wine, taking a deep drink. He then turned and faced Jilly. He looked at Jilly for a long moment. "Whether you believe in what I have been sent here to accomplish, or not, is not important. I understand that you may not understand. A general doesn't explain to a sergeant why he is ordering him to lead his troops to a certain place."

"I'm not in your army," Jilly said quickly, a little surprised at his own chutzpah.

"No, you are not," Uriel said. Then he added, "Definitely not. But I feel like I need to deal with you. I don't know if you are the Judge," Uriel said, studying Jilly then turning away. "When I dictated that to Giglio, I wasn't sure then, and I'm not sure now, if it was real or not. Maybe it is."

"Dictated?" Jilly repeated.

"Yes," Uriel said, his gaze moving into the distance. Jilly felt like the angel was remembering events that had long since passed. Uriel said, "In Italy, on a mountain—or maybe it was more of a hilltop—I appeared to a man who was half out of his mind, and I talked to him. I was younger then. I had visions of the future that I believed in very strongly. I thought I..." He trailed off. Jilly waited.

"I thought I knew everything." The archangel squeezed the wine glass he had taken up in his hand, but it did not break. At least, not that Jilly could see. It just sort of crushed, and wine slipped between the angel's fingers, creating a stain on the white carpet beneath his hand. He seemed not to notice, his gaze still far away.

Eventually he turned back to Jilly. "So," he said, seeming to refocus, "you will not destroy Brady. Not for your soul, not for your friend." That seemed to sum it up pretty well, so Jilly said nothing and returned his gaze. "You are willing to burn, and you are willing to let your friend die. I guess I respect that. What about your sister?" This last, the archangel said looking directly into Jilly's eyes.

Jilly returned the stare, trying to process the words, and understood at this moment that he was looking into the eyes of a Field General who had waged, and won, epic battles. Had commanded men, legions of them. Had made decisions and took chances and had won again and again. He understood this was no buffoon sent on a fool's errand. Aza was wrong. And Jilly's resolve cracked a little. If all of this was baloney, why was this man, this level of Ecclesiastical Royalty, here? In Pittsburgh?

"What about my sister?" Jilly croaked, disappointed at how his voiced sounded. Uriel looked at him for a few seconds. Then he got up, went to the side bar away from the windows, and set the crushed wine glass down, looking at it with amusement as if just now noticing it. He rinsed and dried his wine-stained hands, selected a bottle of Jack Daniels, and poured two generous shots into heavy crystal highball glasses. He returned to his seat in front of Jilly and handed him one.

"Na zdarovje," the angel said and toasted Jilly. Jilly looked at Uriel and then at his bourbon. "Drink," Uriel said. "Go ahead. You're going to need it."

With that, Uriel downed his and took a deep breath. Then he waited. Jilly thought for a moment that this was getting surreal. He was now doing shots with an angel who had been dead for nearly 2000 years. His next thought was that it had been surreal for a few weeks now. Why not? He drained his glass and winced as the alcohol burned. Uriel smiled and nodded slowly. "You ready?" he said to Jilly.

"Ready for what?"

"The truth," Uriel said. Jilly turned his gaze away and smiled, then he laughed, a short bark. "What?" Uriel repeated.

Jilly returned his eyes to the archangel's. "I haven't seen anything resembling the truth in so long, you could tell me today is Tuesday"—it was, in fact, Tuesday—"and I'm not sure I'd believe you, archangel."

Uriel smiled. In that moment, Jilly understood why men had gone to battle with Uriel. They had not liked Uriel, but they'd believed in him, in his bravado, in his confidence. Jilly understood this and also that he needed to be very careful.

"I'm ready," Jilly said.

Uriel nodded. "In 1992, Anne had a relationship with a man

named Anthony Colavito. They were intimate. Anne became pregnant. Mr. Colavito, who is now dead but at the time was very much alive, decided he had urgent business out of state and disappeared to handle that business. Anne didn't know what to do. She dared not consult her spiritual advisor and admit she'd had relations out of wedlock. She needed to make a decision. She did. That decision to abort the unborn child doomed her soul and excludes her from what she would call the Kingdom of Heaven. She can be the most wonderful day care, book sale, bake sale penitent on the planet until the end of her days, but she's going to burn. Those are the Rules." Uriel's gaze never wavered as he explained this to Jilly. It was flat and emotionless, a gaze Jilly might have recognized had he looked into a mirror when he sat behind his own bar.

He thought back, almost thirty years back. He vaguely remembered a guy named Tony. He had been around for what seemed like a minute, and then he was gone. Things clicked into place like gears. His sister never marrying, never really trusting men. Things she had said, comments she had made. It was probably true. And maybe he had known it all along.

His shoulders slumped a little with an exhale. He breathed and raised his eyes to Uriel. "But you can help."

Uriel smiled. "Oh, I can help," he said, nodding. "Definitely."

In an alcove off the main living room, Manon listened. Then she turned and headed to her room and her own Holy Host communication device. She had a call to make.

Chapter Fifty-Eight

Leonard sat on a stool at a brewpub that had been built inside an old, decommissioned church. He thought Aza would probably like it here, bars located in churches being right up the Red One's alley. He stared at the enormous stained-glass windows in what had once been the nave of the church. He had gotten a text asking him to be here at 9 p.m. without much other detail except that it was both urgent and important. What wasn't, these days? Leonard wondered.

An overweight college kid in jeans and a wrinkled white Oxford shirt sat down next to him. Leonard glanced at him and said, "I'm meeting someone, buddy. Need that stool."

The kid said, "You're meeting me, Leonard. Sir, I mean. You're meeting me, sir. I texted you."

Leonard looked him over. "What'd you do, knock someone up?"

"No, I—" the kid began, but Leonard interrupted him.

"So, what is it then? You got pictures? Let me guess, you and an important person? Intimate pictures? That it?"

As a bona fide fixer, Leonard had become used to this kind of thing. For a while, it had been intriguing, but now it was just annoying, and Leonard was tired of it. Tired of every weasel with an angle looking for money, favors, needing something, some mess they had created, fixed.

"Tell you what," Leonard said, "I'll trade your pictures for a better set of the Mayor at the zoo after hours. Good quality. What do you say, kid?"

"Well, I love animals, but I—" Oliver began.

"I bet you do," Leonard said. "You look like the type." Leonard sipped his drink.

"Thank you, sir," Oliver said.

Leonard just shook his head.

"Sir, I need to talk to you," Oliver said, attempting to start over. This was not going the way he had hoped.

"Get in line, kid," Leonard said. "I'm on sabbatical. Taking some time off to find myself." Leonard wasn't really talking to Oliver, more to the stained-glass windows showing saints and sinners, angels and devils. He couldn't stop staring at it.

"It's about Jilly," Oliver said. That got Leonard's attention. He turned on his stool and studied Oliver closely.

"What about Jilly?" he said, suddenly serious.

"He, um, he needs your help."

Leonard looked at Oliver, his face a mask of suspicion, almost a sneer. Then he repeated slowly, "He needs my help."

Oliver nodded vigorously.

"Help with what?"

Oliver looked around, comically, as though in a spy movie. Then he leaned towards Leonard and whispered, "With the thing."

"The thing?" Leonard repeated, squinting his eyes even further than they already were.

"You know, the thing he's being asked to do. That thing." Oliver raised his eyebrows in what appeared to Leonard to be a bad Groucho Marx impersonation. This was turning into a B mafia movie.

"Who are you?" Leonard spat.

"I'm Oliver."

Leonard had pretty much had enough. "Look, Oliver, I think you're batshit crazy. That's fine. Seems like half the city is these days. Get some help, a fuckin' shrink. Go to a pro. I have to go and meet some people," Leonard said, draining his drink and getting up from his stool.

"I work for Uriel," Oliver whispered quickly. Leonard froze and looked at him. "Like you work for Aza," Oliver added.

Leonard slowly sat back down.

"I was sent down here. To Pittsburgh," Oliver said.

"So you're...dead?" Leonard asked slowly.

"Well, I guess technically I am. Yes. I am," Oliver said, again looking around furiously to see if anyone was listening. He just wasn't good at this cloak and dagger stuff.

"Jilly needs my help. Why?" Leonard said.

"I think Uriel talked him into doing the thing"—again Oliver raised his eyebrows—"to the guy"—again the eyebrows—"because he thinks the guy is the Guy." As he said these last two words, Oliver used the first two fingers of each of his hands to put air quotes around them.

Leonard looked at Oliver and nodded slowly. Surreal. He motioned the bartender over and ordered a double vodka. Once delivered, he took a generous swallow. Oliver watched all this and felt that, at best, this man was an unlikely hero. Leonard continued his study of the stained glass. Oliver rattled off every single name of every one of the fifty-plus figures pictured in the window, occasionally throwing in personal observations like "It was actually a tiger not a lion that ate him," and "He's a good guy," or "He doesn't have the beard anymore."

Eventually, Leonard said, "So, *is* my guy the Guy?"

Oliver exhaled loudly. "I don't think so."

"But you don't know?"

"Well, nobody knows for sure. Except Him, of course. That's the problem."

"Him," Leonard parroted.

"Yeah. The Creator."

"Oh. Him. Of course."

Oliver continued, "Uriel wants him to do it because, well, it's a long story, but anyway, the algorithms all say he's not the guy, not evil enough. But I think Jilly now thinks he is the Guy. Or at least, Uriel convinced him to do it for a big reward."

"A big reward," Leonard said, thinking he was starting to sound like an echo. "What kind of reward? Money?"

"No, not money." Oliver said quickly. Then he looked away.

"Another long story?" Leonard asked.

"Yeah," Oliver said miserably.

Leonard nodded. Of course. "So how is it you think I can help Jilly?"

"You need to take a message to him," Oliver said. "I can't do it, but you can."

"A message," Leonard said and decided that was the last time tonight he was going to repeat what this dead kid had just said.

"Yes. A message," Oliver said. "Tell him Oliver and Manon don't think he's the Guy. Can you tell him that?" Oliver looked pleadingly at Leonard.

"Look, kid, I don't know if you've noticed, but I play for the other team here. Why would I help you?"

"You'd be saving your guy," Oliver said earnestly.

Leonard considered this. "I'm not sure my guy should be saved," he said finally, looking again at the stained-glass windows and seeming to talk more to himself than to Oliver.

"Exactly!" Oliver said excitedly.

"Ex—" Leonard started to say then clamped his mouth shut. Not doing it.

"You're on the wrong team!" Oliver exclaimed.

"Kid, if there is one thing I'm sure of anymore, it's that I am definitely on the right team. I'm pretty damn sure I've been on the right team my whole pathetic life."

But Oliver was shaking his head. "Not true," Oliver said.

"Why not true?" Leonard asked.

"Because the algorithm is never wrong."

Leonard raised his own eyebrows this time—not so much like Groucho, though.

"Also because of ninth grade," Oliver said.

Leonard waited, proud of himself for not repeating this. He had no idea what this batshit ghost-kid was talking about.

"In the ninth grade, you said the cigarettes they found in Marty Milstein's locker were yours."

Leonard just blinked. "There were mine," he eventually said.

"Yes, of course they were. But Marty was going to take the rap.

And you told the principal they were yours, and you put them there."

"They were, and I did," Leonard said.

"I know, but the point is, you didn't have to admit it. And you got detention. It's all on the System. We keep track of these things," Oliver said.

"Oh bullshit," Leonard said. "That doesn't prove anything. Kid, I'm a stone-cold loser. A bad guy. And I've ended up with the crew I was destined to. I think you should take a hike and leave me alone. Jilly can take care of himself. So can Dave, and Aza, and Uriel, and the whole damn soap opera. I'm pretty goddamn sure the fate of mankind isn't coming down to anything a guy like me says or does. Christ, I hope not." Leonard got up again to leave, but Oliver grabbed his wrist firmly.

Leonard looked back at Oliver and was surprised to see a look of resolve in the pudgy kid's eyes. "Marty was your friend," Oliver said. "He was your best friend, but his father was an alcoholic and beat him. You knew that. You knew if Marty got detention for something you did, he might end up with two black eyes and maybe worse. You did a good thing. And truly bad people don't do good things. The algorithm is never wrong."

Leonard looked at this kid, then back up at the stained-glass windows. "That so, huh?"

Oliver released Leonard's wrist. "You're on the wrong team, sir," Oliver said.

—

Back in the car, Father Bill waited for Jilly to say something. For a while, Jilly seemed lost in thought. "I'm at peace with it," the priest eventually said, eyes forward on the road just as Jilly's were.

After a moment, Jilly said, "With what?"

"With your decision. And the fact that we may be witnessing the start of the end of the world. I really am." As Jilly considered this, Father Bill continued, "I was proud of you today. You made your decision based on principle, regardless of the consequences. I'm not sure I would have done the same if I were in your shoes." Jilly said nothing. They sat for a while. "Sorry if I acted like an awestruck kid in there. It's just that the entire scene in that hotel suite was a validation of things I have been told my entire life but was never sure were really true, a validation of my chosen profession. It was a little overwhelming."

Father Bill turned at that point to look at Jilly. He was a little embarrassed at the honesty with which he had just confessed to his friend. Jilly continued to stare out the windshield. Then he said tonelessly, "Uriel told me Anne had an abortion thirty years ago. That she will burn."

Father Bill stared at the side of Jilly's head, shocked. "Do you believe him?"

"It's probably true," Jilly said.

The priest returned his gaze to the street in front of them, thinking about Anne and how she was, things she had said. Jilly was probably right that Uriel was right. "Wow," he said.

"Of course," Jilly said, "should I decide to assist General Moses up there on the thirtieth floor of the Fairmont, guess who else gets forgiven for their life of sin and a free pass to the Kingdom along with me?" Now Jilly turned his head to look at his friend.

"Anne," Father Bill said. It was not a question.

"Bingo," Jilly said. "This gets better and better."

The man in the pom-pom'ed hat waited to see if Jilly would comment further, afraid to ask him what he had told the archangel, if his decision had changed. Jilly just shook his head silently.

Later, Jilly and his sister sat together on a bench at the school playground behind Prince of Peace and watched the kids. Anne waited for Jilly to get to his point. He rarely visited her here, and today there was something about him that made her hesitant to talk much. She knew he had something to say, and she also knew he'd get to it in his time.

"You believe in absolution?" he finally said.

She paused. She was surprised by the question. After a minute, she said, "Yes. Yes, of course. A principal tenet of Catholicism is that Jesus died for our sins. The idea that anyone truly sorry for their sins can be forgiven."

"What if it's a big sin?" Jilly asked, not looking at her.

Anne felt she understood what her brother was asking, this man who had probably taken so many lives. "Jilly," she said, "all sin is forgivable if the sinner truly repents the sin." They both stared at the playground. Eventually, Anne gathered her courage and added, "Even murder."

Jilly nodded slowly. Then he said quietly, "Even abortion?"

Anne said nothing for a long time. She continued to stare at the kids playing. Her brother waited.

"Yes," she finally said. "Even that." Then she turned and looked at Jilly, who was looking at her. "If the sinner is truly sorry for their actions." She smiled a sad smile and got up, patting his shoulder as she did so. She walked slowly to a group of children playing on a swing set, not looking back.

Chapter Fifty-Nine

Jilly had searched frantically for the Lamb. He could not find it. It was ridiculous to think in an area like the Southside, where he'd spent his entire life, maybe ten blocks by thirty blocks, he could lose a bar he had been to twice in the past six weeks, but it was true. It did not exist. Sitting instead at the Corkscrew, a bar he knew very well, he got drunk. He pondered existence. He pondered good versus evil, right versus wrong. When he wasn't furiously pondering, he was furiously drinking. Why was this his problem? Why dump the potential future of mankind on his doorstep? It wasn't fair.

When he left, he was a bit worse for wear and unsteady on his feet. As he walked, he began to absently sing a polka he knew well. "We're from the town with the great football team. We cheer the Pittsburgh Steelers! Gerela's Gorillas are here for the show, and so is Franco's Army..." He stopped and looked up. He was in front of the Lamb. "Son of a bitch," he said and went in.

The bartender was new. Not the grandfatherly guy he had come to expect, but rather a clean-cut, maybe mid-thirties guy, fit and looking like he had just slapped on some Aqua Velva. "Miller, Jack back?" he said with no expression at all.

Jilly just nodded. "Where's, uh...where's..." It occurred to Jilly that he had no idea what the elderly bartender's name was.

"Florida," the young bartender said. "Everyone goes to Florida. He's no exception."

"He the boss? The owner?" Jilly asked, taking a sip he didn't need from his beer.

"He's the boss," the bartender said, a slight smile on his face. "No doubt about that."

"Then who are you?" Jilly asked. "And how do you know what I drink?"

"Call me Michael," the bartender said.

They had a very long conversation that Jilly would not recall the next day. He wouldn't recall being in the Lamb, or how he had managed to get home. But he awoke in his own bed, fully clothed and, surprisingly, with no hangover at all. He actually felt pretty good. He got out of bed and went to the shower. Although not really aware he was doing so, he was absently humming a polka.

Back behind the bar at 9 a.m., Jilly reviewed bills and receipts. Although he wasn't scheduled to open for two more hours, the front door wasn't locked, and when he heard the door open, he looked up. Leonard was wearing jeans, a Black Sabbath hoodie, and an Iron City baseball hat. It occurred to Jilly how far Leonard had come in such a short time that he considered this outfit out of character for Leonard, now often in suits and dress shirts.

"Casual Day, Big Time?" Jilly said, his eyebrows raised.

"We need to talk. That okay?" Leonard said, ignoring the comment. Jilly nodded, and Leonard closed the blinds on the door and flipped the deadbolt, locking it.

Recognizing the signs of a sit-down, Jilly went into high alert. He wasn't concerned about Leonard shooting him, but he knew to get his guard up and keep it up. Placing his hands flat on the bar, he leaned slightly toward his guest and waited. Jilly was truly a Rembrandt in the art of silence, and Leonard didn't even bother to wait for Jilly to say anything, instead getting right to the point.

"I'm supposed to deliver a message to you," he said.

Jilly waited.

"The fat kid and the hitwoman don't think Brady is the Guy. But they do think you'll get paid whatever reward you have been promised if you snuff him."

Jilly stared at him. Leonard sat back on his stool, his message delivered. There was silence. Eventually, Jilly looked away, toward his front window and the street. Leonard waited.

Jilly looked back at Leonard and said, *"Is* Brady the Guy?"

Leonard sighed and rubbed his face with both his hands, pushing his ballcap upwards. "I don't know," he said, the words slightly muffled between his fingers.

Jilly got a glass and the bottle of Tito's from behind the bar, put some ice in it, and then vodka and soda water. He placed it in front of Leonard. Leonard took a deep drink without looking up.

"Thanks," he said.

"You don't know." Jilly repeated Leonard's earlier response.

"No." Leonard replied eventually. More silence. Jilly rolled his eyes, although Leonard could not see this as his doleful gaze was focused only on the glass in front of him.

"No, he's not the Guy, or no, you don't know if he's the Guy?" Jilly asked, annoyed.

"He might be, he might not be," Leonard said, taking another drink from his glass. "I don't think anyone knows." More silence as Jilly considered this. "I have a theory though," Leonard continued. Jilly wondered if Leonard could spell the word "theory." Leonard pushed his now empty glass across the bar and waited.

Jilly frowned, thought about it, then refilled the drink.

"The fat kid said the Creator is the only one who really knows anything. I figure he means God." Leonard hit his vodka soda again. "The way I figure it, I'm not sure it really matters if he's the Guy or not."

This was an angle Jilly had not considered. "Why is that?" he said, breaking his silence.

"Well," Leonard said, "let's say he's the Guy. The Antichrist the Bible talks about, or something near enough. Let's say he's a super bad guy at least, and he wants to try and rule the world. Maybe you stop him from doing that and he fails. Maybe you don't and he succeeds. Maybe you try and fail, and somewhere down the line, he fails some other way. If any of these things happen, then I think that would just create a bunch of new possibilities for what happens next."

Jilly stared at Leonard, aware that this line of logic had crossed his own mind, at least obliquely, in the last few weeks.

"I guess what I'm trying to say," Leonard continued, "is I don't think how it all turns out is a foregone conclusion. You know, written down somewhere in a book a long time ago. I don't even think it's really good versus bad or right versus wrong. Not anymore. I think situations arise and people react to them according to their own, I don't know, moral code maybe, and then the next thing happens which creates a whole new set of decisions that have to be made."

Leonard drained his second vodka in a long sip and said, "I'm not gonna lie to you, Jilly, I feel like a laboratory rat in some kind of science experiment. I've seen and done things over the last six months I would have never imagined a year ago. At first, it all seemed like hitting the lottery. Everything was a stone-cold no-brainer. You want this money? Yep. How about this woman and these drugs? Sure do. But after a while...I don't know." He rubbed his face again. "It's no fun anymore. And you know why? It's because I feel like someone is watching me all the time.

"It's like getting ready to smoke a joint by yourself in the basement. Got your fuckin Frampton on, lights down, lava lamp on, black light on, and then your mom comes in and wants to watch you do it. So, at first you think 'fuck it' and take a big hit. But you know she's watching you, maybe shaking her head a little bit. Maybe she's thinking, 'Of course he'd get stoned, just what I expected of him. That's what losers do, and of course he's a loser.' So now you don't want to get stoned so much. The fun has gone out of it. You feel, I don't know, like, predictable. You know, to whoever it is who may be watching you. You feel that way in this thing, Jilly? Like a lab rat?"

Jilly didn't respond, just turned again and looked out his window at the street. Neither man said anything for a while.

Eventually, Leonard finished his second drink and got up to go. "What are you going to do?" Jilly asked.

Leonard paused. "I think I'm going to do what's best for me. I think you should do the same. I feel like, I don't know, like that's what we're supposed to do. And maybe...maybe we aren't supposed to be predictable." As he said this, Leonard gave him a tired smile.

"Aza is bad mojo, Leonard," Jilly said. "You don't want to fuck with him. He'll squash you in about five seconds and never think twice about it."

"No doubt." Leonard replied. "Don't worry, I'm not doing anything crazy. I did my job just coming here to deliver my message. Putting my ass on the line. But I'll tell you what."

Jilly waited. But so did Leonard. He was going to deliver his exit line, but not until prompted.

"What?" Jilly finally said.

"I still say my second wife was meaner than Aza. And uglier," Leonard said and threw him a wink. "See ya in the funny papers."

With that, he threw the deadbolt and headed out into the morning sunshine. Jilly stared after him for a long time.

About an hour later, the bar still empty, his door again swung open. This time, it was a black-leather-coat-wearing Spatz Spasilovich who entered. He scanned the barroom, lifted his chin slightly to Jilly, and then turned quickly and opened the front door. He barked something in Russian, and after a few seconds, Alexi Volkov entered. He sat at the bar. Spatz lifted the heavy fur coat from his boss' shoulders and folded it over his arm, then took a few steps back to stand by the door.

"You have vodka?" the Wolf asked. "Good vodka?"

Jilly looked at him, then at Spatz, then back at Volkov. "Sorry, no pets. You'll have to leave your dog outside."

"My dog," Volkov said slowly. Jilly just looked at him. After a few seconds, Volkov half turned his head and said something in Russian to Spasilovich.

Spatz looked at Jilly for a long moment. Then he smiled broadly and said, his English thickly accented, "No pets. Verrry funny. You're a funny guy, hitman." As he said this, he came up to the bar to look Jilly in the eye. "Very funny," Spatz said again. Jilly returned his stare. Then Spasilovich turned to leave. As he exited, he paused at the Budweiser mirror depicting the bikini clad-models. He stared at it. Then he turned and smiled back at Jilly and Volkov. Then he drove his fist into the mirror, shattering it. He howled his version of a Wolf's call and then shouted, "No pets!" He laughed loudly as he pulled the door open and stepped out into the street.

As the door closed behind him, he leaned his back against it, still carrying his boss' fur coat. Jilly's was closed for the moment. "Does he have his shots?" Jilly asked Volkov.

"His shots?" Volkov repeated then said, "Yes, several each day. Usually vodka."

Jilly shook his head. Then, turning, he took down the bottle of Stolichnaya and poured a generous double shot in a highball glass before sliding it across to the Russian, leaving the bottle on the bar.

"Won't have one with me?" Volkov said. "Maybe you are biased against Russians. Racist." A smile played around the Wolf's mouth.

Jilly turned and grabbed the bottle of Jack Daniels and poured himself an equally generous shot of the bourbon. Volkov lifted his glass and tilted it slightly toward Jilly. "To good vodka, good food, and bad women." Jilly tilted his glass back, and they both drained their respective shots, Volkov slamming his glass on the bar and howling as he finished. "Not bad vodka. Not great, but not bad."

"What do you want, Alexi?" Jilly asked.

"I want nothing. I'm a simple peasant working hard to make a living, as you know. Now, your friend Brady, he is another story. He wants everything. Now he wants to meet with you."

"With me," Jilly repeated.

"Yes, with you," Volkov said. "At my place as a neutral site where he will feel safe that you will not kill him. Apparently, he is under the impression you'd like to do that." The Wolf smiled at Jilly.

Jilly waited, returning the stare. He did not smile.

"I told him, 'You have my friend Jilly all wrong. He is harmless as a pussy...cat.'" The Russian left just enough of a pause between the two syllables to get his point across, his smile widening.

"Why does he want to meet with me?" Jilly said, ignoring the insult.

"I have no idea," Volkov said. "Maybe he wants to be your friend—mend the fences, as you say. Maybe he wants to trade recipes for the apple pie. No fucking idea, my friend," Volkov finished, refilling his highball glass from the bottle on the bar. Jilly did not do the same. As Volkov drained his glass and again slammed it on the bar, Jilly gave the matter some thought.

Eventually, he said, "Okay, I'll meet him. Tell him I'm bringing the priest. And no weapons. I want your word on that, Wolf."

"Jilly, Jilly, Jilly," Volkov said. "You insult me as a gentleman, as a son of Mother Russia. Of course no guns. My guys will frisk everyone, including Pope Dave, huh? Scout's honor."

Jilly nodded as Volkov got up to leave. "Alexi," Jilly said. The Russian paused. "I want you to know if this goes sideways, your last Earthly vision will be Jimmy Hallendorf's smiling face as he blows your head off. That's a promise."

"Such vulgar words," Volkov said. "Yes, yes, we are all afraid of the old black man. Definitely. Dasvidaniya." The Wolf said the last over his shoulder as he opened the door and allowed his coat to again be draped over his shoulders.

Back in the car, Spatz said, "We will kill him, yes?"

"Maybe," Volkov said after a while.

"If we kill him, I will kill him." Spatz looked into the rearview mirror, but Volkov was looking out the window, lost in thought. "Maybe if we don't kill him, I will kill him anyway," Spatz said, but he did not check his mirror to see his boss' reaction to that statement.

Later that day, and in the dark bar over on Smallman Street, Jilly was again seated across from his old friend.

"I need a favor, Cheech," Jilly said.

"What can I do for you, amigo?"

Jilly told him what he needed, the older man told him he could get it.

"Back in the game, eh, big guy? I had a feeling," Chi Chi said, smiling. "I asked my statue of La Madre and she never lies to me." He took out and kissed a medallion he had around his neck, then tucked it away again.

"Just one last time," Jilly said.

"Yes, just one last time. Of course," Chi Chi said.

"What do I owe you?' Jilly asked.

"For what?" Cheech said, smiling again.

Jilly nodded. He knew this was a favor repaid and now no longer owed. He got up and left, sliding the bartender a fifty as he did so, the bartender appearing not to notice but noticing all the same.

Chapter Sixty

Jimmy Hallendorf drove them in one of the Don's armored Maybachs, a little smaller than a true limousine but the fanciest car Jilly and Father Bill had ever seen. The rear seats reclined and a footrest came out, just like a recliner chair.

"Sixty minutes," Jimmy said from the front seat, not turning, a very large man seated next to him who would not speak the entire trip. Mostly because he would not be spoken to.

"Sixty should do her. If we're not out by then, burn it down, because we're dead," Jilly said.

Father Bill grimaced but kept his gaze firmly out the side window. In a van and a large nondescript sedan behind them, Angelo Fanzi Jr. and ten more very armed men followed the Mercedes.

Jilly didn't make small talk. He never did when it was time to go to work. He figured you plan, plan, plan, and then you execute. If the planning is good, the execution is usually pretty straightforward. Of course, things could go wrong. In this one, he understood there was a much better chance of things going wrong given the cast of characters and what might be at stake.

They pulled up in front of the Wolf's building. Jilly got out, followed by Father Bill. Jilly turned back to the car as Jimmy rolled the driver's window down.

"On your own from here," Jimmy said, calm and cool as ever.

"If you can try and be here when we come out, that would be swell," Jilly said.

"Well, I have a few errands to run. Need a haircut. I'll see what I can do."

Jilly nodded. Jimmy nodded back, the window rolling up. Their backup vehicles were nearby, parked about two blocks away and communicating by two-way radio with Jimmy, but the reality was they were on their own once they entered the building. These men would just be here to even the score if things went badly; the Don had long ago tired of the Wolf and his antics.

Jilly turned and faced Father Bill, standing on the sidewalk. "You ready?" he asked the priest, who was once again in his Sunday best, complete with four-cornered hat.

"I guess." Father Bill said, but he looked very nervous.

"Good," Jilly said and turned toward the front door of the large, two-story stone building.

"Jilly," Father Bill said, and Jilly turned back. "You sure this is what you want to do?"

Jilly put his hands on his friend's shoulders and looked him in the eyes. "I am sure."

"Really sure?" Father Bill said.

"Absolutely certain," Jilly replied. He straightened his friend's hat, placing it firmly on his head.

"They're going to frisk us, aren't they?" Father Bill said.

"Thoroughly," Jilly replied. "You may want to throw up a little prayer that they don't search that fabulous hat, because if they do, this is going to be over real quick. Now let's go destroy the Antichrist."

As they entered Volkov's large and ornate living area, they were stopped by two very large and very serious-looking Russian men in ill-fitting suits. Both men lifted their arms as told and were subjected to a very thorough search.

"You know," Jilly said to Father Bill, "the quality of TJ Maxx men's suits has gone through the roof." The priest just looked at him, confused. Jilly sighed, a one-liner lost. They never touched the priest's silly-looking four-cornered hat with the pom-pom on top. Satisfied, the two men motioned them through a doorway.

Upon entering, they noticed the only other occupant of the large room was Leonard. Seated at the J.Lo bar, he had a highball glass and a bottle of vodka next to it. As they approached, he toasted them and said "L'chaim," then added, "Yinz." He downed the glass.

"We early?" Jilly said.

"Nope," said Leonard. I'm sure Our Gang will be along in a moment. "Skanky, Allfoulmouthed, and Buckteeth." Leonard collapsed into giggles, and Jilly realized Leonard was hammered.

"Can I get yinz a drink?" Leonard said. "You know, while we wait."

"I'm good." Jilly said, taking a seat on a stool for lack of anything else to do.

Leonard looked at Bill and said "Faddah? Some wine maybe?"

"Thank you, no," he said.

"Well, I could use one," Leonard said and refreshed his glass with a generous pour.

At this moment, several men entered the room. First the two Lennys, who scanned the room and then spoke into earpieces, stationing themselves at various vantage points. Then some of Brady's entourage. Then some Russian henchmen. Jilly knew they were henchmen because they had the classic henchman look—complete lack of even the smallest spark of intelligence in their dead eyes. Bad teeth. Bad suits. Bad childhoods.

Then Spatz entered, resplendent in a purple sharkskin suit that was only out of style by maybe forty years, paired with white loafers. He smiled and winked at the two men, then laughed for no apparent reason. He seated himself at the bar and took Leonard's bottle, drinking directly from it and making a show of tucking his suitcoat behind the Glock in his waistband. Jilly sighed and looked at Father Bill, who was still putting on a Nervous Clinic, continually adjusting his hat. So much for no guns. They both continued to wait.

When the Wolf entered the room, he was gregarious. "Gentlemen!" he said. "Welcome!" He smiled at the two waiting men. "Nothing to drink?" Volkov continued. Looking at Spasilovich, he said, "We are very poor hosts, not offering our friends a drink."

"We're here for a meeting, not a frat party," Jilly said. "Can we get on with it?"

"We can get on with it! *Yes!*" the Wolf shouted. Then, quieter, "But not yet. We await the Prince of Darkness!" He winked at Father Bill and smiled. As Volkov went to the bar and got himself a drink, Jilly noticed his girlfriend had appeared behind the bar. The Moushka was wearing the exact same sweatsuit as her man.

Jilly leaned over to Father Bill and said, "Do you remember that part in the second Austin Powers movie when Dr. Evil and Mini-Me do the jail rap video?" The priest turned and looked at him with a vacancy to rival the emptiest motor court hotel on Route 66.

"What?" he said.

Jilly smiled. "Never mind. Keep it light, brother. It's gonna be what it's gonna be. Just make sure you and that hat stay close."

Brady entered the room. He was talking on a cell phone. He finished the call by saying, "When I say and only when I say. Not before. You got that?" He waited, not looking at anyone. "YOU GOT THAT, OR DO YOU NOT?!" Then, after a pause, he said, quieter, "Good," and ended the call. The (possible) Antichrist then looked up at the assemblage as though just realizing they were in the room. His minions decided to take a knee and bow their heads.

Leonard did the same, although he was clearly unsteady and almost fell over. Volkov and his goons pretended not to notice and did not take a knee. Brady frowned at this lack of respect and then switched his attention to Jilly.

"Gang's all here," he said, smiling. "Including the failed priest." He walked over to Father Bill and stopped just a few feet in front of him.

Still smiling, he looked him in the eyes and said, "I am *sooo* glad you are here. It gives me great comfort in the Holy Host to know this is the very best they could do. A man who talked his high school girlfriend into aborting his first child, slept with an addict he was counseling in rehab, and lost his faith, oh, I don't know, like fifteen years ago? Best you can do for spiritual counsel, hitman?" Brady said, transferring his smiling gaze to Jilly.

Father Bill reeled. No other word for it. Everything Brady had said was true. He had no idea how he knew all that, but Father Bill had his suspicions. The truth was bad enough, but to hear it read aloud for the crowd was awful.

Brady headed to the bar and took the drink handed to him by Volkov. He turned and sat on a stool, his elbows resting behind him on the bar. Smiling.

Jilly looked at Father Bill. The priest looked like he had just seen a car wreck. Or Chilly Billy Cardille without his toupee. No help there. He smiled to himself.

Turning, he faced Brady across the room and said, "Manon says hi." Brady looked at him with suspicion. "Manon," Jilly repeated. "The Black Death. Biblical assassin. I believe you've been trying to pick her up like a cheap tart in a disco. You know, because everyone knows women dig fake Antichrists. She told you her name was Jeanne d'Arc, and you thought she was a hot French chick." Jilly smiled at Brady. "You crack her up, Casanova. She told me so."

Brady's smiling expression fell like a bad souffle.

"She hasn't killed you," Jilly continued, "because you aren't worth her time. After all, you don't send Nolan Ryan to strike out little leaguers."

With this, Jilly smiled his own smile. Brady's henchmen were looking at each other. Spatz said something to the Russian next to him, and they both laughed.

Brady did not care for the way this was going. "Look," he said, "Armageddon is here. The signs are all around us. Events are unfolding as foretold. I am ascending, and there is nothing your little God Squad can do about it."

Brady seemed to gather himself with these words. He looked smug again.

"Your ascension includes the fake saving of a woman's baby in Market Square?" Jilly said, smirking.

"Hey, hey, hey," Leonard said, wobbling to his feet. "I did a nice job setting that up. You don't know how hard it is to get potheads to do what you tell them."

Brady said, "Shut up, Leonard. Your pothead crew nearly ruined the whole act. I had to pretend that baby was actually in trouble by banging her around a bit to make it seem more real." Brady's henchmen laughed as if on cue.

"So, why did you ask me to come here?" Jilly said.

Brady took a sip of his drink, wiped his lips, and said, "Well,

I asked you here to show these good people"—he waved his hands at the freakshow cast around him—"that you and your silly friend are no danger to me."

Jilly turned and looked at Father Bill with an exaggerated show of concern. "We are apparently of no danger to Aza's shoeshine boy." The priest looked at Jilly. The room waited.

Collecting himself and looking down at his formal cassock as if seeing it for the first time, Father Bill said, "Damn. And I wore my best outfit."

Seeking to retake the room, Brady said, "You are here because you are working under the ridiculous concept that you can kill me. But you can't. I'm not some drug dealer or pimp you can eliminate to get paid. I am the Coming, the White Horseman. I have been foretold. I represent the beginning of the Epoch of Darkness. I will be President. Then Supreme Dictator. Eventually, the world will kneel for me. I will be an Earthly God. As has been foretold. You think you can stop this, paid killer of Insignificants and your silly little supporting cast?" Brady laughed. "Me?" he said, incredulous. "Kill *me?*"

He asked Volkov for a shot of vodka, drained it, and then turned to face Spatz. "Give me your gun," he said. Spasilovich looked at Volkov. Volkov nodded. Slowly, Spatz removed his Glock from his shoulder holster and handed it, butt first, to Brady. Brady examined the weapon. "Nice," he said.

He turned and walked across the room to Jilly. He stopped in front of him. Smiling, he said, "So, hitman, hit me." And, racking a round into the chamber of the pistol, he handed it to Jilly. "If you dare."

Jilly looked at the pistol. Then he looked at Father Bill. He breathed. This was a fairly easy call. They were offering him a gun. On one hand, he understood he could take the pistol, shoot Brady, and this whole thing would be over. If Brady truly had been intended to be the Antichrist, he felt pretty sure he'd have some kind of fabulous afterlife in a pretty garden with wood nymphs or something like that feeding him grapes. He'd be dead, of course. Once Volkov's boys opened up on him and the priest, then Jimmy's crew would show up and vaporize everyone else, and that's the curtain call. He could maybe get Anne off on a technicality given his status as the hitter who saved mankind and prevented the Apocalypse.

But on the other hand, he never liked anyone else dealing the play. Angelo Fanzi Sr. had taught him that. "Always better to be proactive than reactive." That lesson had stuck. Controlling the play gave you more options.

He looked at the gun in Brady's hands. Then he shoved his hands in his front pants pockets and tilted his head, staring at Brady.

"HA!" Brady cried. Turning to face Volkov and the rest of the crew, he exclaimed, "He cannot do it! As has been foretold! As I have said!" Turning, he took a few triumphant steps and then stopped in front of Volkov, smiling. "On to bigger and better things, my friend." Volkov looked at Brady. "I have a meeting," Brady suddenly said, handing the pistol back to Spasilovich.

Still smiling at Volkov, Brady clapped one hand on Spatz's shoulder and said, "Kill them both." With that, he started toward the door to the garage where his limousine was waiting, his bodyguards turning to follow him. Just before he exited the room, however, he stopped and turned. The entire room was watching him. "Oh," he said, as if remembering something, "Kill Leonard too. He's a traitor." And then he was gone. Leonard, processing this, whispered to nobody at all, "Fuck me."

When all of Brady's people had filed out, Spatz looked at the Wolf. Father Bill looked at Jilly. Volkov looked back at Spatz. Leonard considered urinating upon himself, but decided he was too tired and too drunk to make the effort.

Then the big Russian walked across the room to Jilly and Father Bill. He stopped directly in front of Jilly and stared at him, a hard look in his eyes. He was still holding the Glock, Jilly noticed. Habit made him be sure of where the guns in the room were at all times.

Spasilovich moved his face close to Jilly's. "How do you want it, barkeep?"

Father Bill's eyes widened. "Straight," Jilly said, cool as a cuke, his eyes never leaving the Russian's, both hands still in his pockets.

Spatz smiled. "He wants it straight, boss. You good with that?"

"Good with it," Volkov said, a flat expression on his face.

Leonard closed his eyes. In one fluid motion that could not

have taken more than three seconds, Spasilovich swung the Glock in an arc toward the ceiling and fired three shots in succession. The roar of the powerful handgun was deafening in the enclosed space. A snowfall of plaster dust cascaded down on the three men as if in some kind of surreal snow globe.

"MOUSHKA! THE MAN WANTS IT STRAIGHT. NO ICE. YOU HEARD HIM. POUR IT!" Spatz shouted. Leaning back into Jilly's face and placing his tattooed hand on the back of Jilly's neck, he said, "Maybe I will kill you another time, eh?"

Jilly did not respond but moved his eyes sideways to the arm encircling his neck. Spatz removed the arm, smiling a broad smile.

"VODKA!" Volkov shouted, moving to the bar. "Nobody dies today! A toast"—liquid was poured all around and the Wolf raised his shot glass high in the air—"to the *discount devil!*"

Father Bill closed his eyes and crossed himself, exhaling an enormous breath. Leonard closed his eyes, fainted, and fell off his stool.

Jimmy Hallendorf drove them to Kosmos Tomes. Nobody spoke. Seated in the basement vault, TK asked Father Bill for his hat which the priest gingerly removed from his head. Flipping it upside down, TK removed a very small, wired device from inside the crown of the hat, pulling a short cable connected to what appeared to be a small glass button on the front of the hat. The button was in fact a very sophisticated and very expensive lens and microphone attached to the recorder that was on the inside. The entire unit had a USB attachment that TK plugged into his Mac, and shortly all stared at his very large monitor. What they saw was crystal-clear HD footage of Dave Brady with similarly crystal-clear audio. At that moment, Dave was staring right at the camera, saying, "I had to bang that baby around a bit just to make it seem real." They continued listening and all began smiling as Mayor Brady said, "Eventually the world will kneel for me. I will be an Earthly God." Finally, the capper: footage of Brady clearly heard saying to Volkov, "Kill them both."

"Jackpot," Transcendental Kosmos said.

Jilly smiled, nodding his head. He had decided not to kill Brady, but he sure as hell intended to kill his career.

"Where'd you get that equipment? I've never seen anything like it," TK said. "That's the kind of stuff only the FBI or the military has."

"Friend of mine," Jilly said, thinking of Cheech.

The next day, a very pious-looking Catholic priest clad in full blacks with a brand-new collar arrived at the offices of the *Post-Gazette*. He had a very interesting story to tell, backed by video footage and to which he had been an eyewitness. He said he would like to speak to a reporter. He was quickly introduced to one.

EPILOGUE

Mayor Dave Brady's short-lived career ended quickly and with media fanfare. The once-darling quickly because a pariah. It is difficult to refute HD video and audio, far more difficult when presented by a humble local priest known for his work with disenfranchised kids. While his spokesman initially offered an explanation that this was all a misunderstanding, Dave was eventually forced to resign in the wake of the police investigation of the order, given to "Reputed Russian Crime Boss Alexi Volkov" to murder the aforementioned priest and two others.

The mother of the baby the Mayor had "saved" in Market Square sued, as did several other members of Mothers Mothering for Motherhood, for emotional stress. Two of Leonard's addled accomplices also found helpful attorneys and sued, hopping on the gravy train and claiming they had been helpful volunteers on what they thought was a charitable effort, only to be duped into cooperating with a monster. Dave's assets were seized, his insurance license permanently revoked. His prediction that he would become an "Earthly God" made him the laughingstock of social media and even warranted a joke on Jimmy Kimmel's late-night show.

For his part, Volkov took every interview he could get. He was no fool, after all. Staring earnestly into whatever camera was placed in front of him, he decried the "public opinion that honest, hardworking Eastern Bloc citizens should not have to endure this kind of ethnic racism." He became something of a local celebrity and threw out the first pitch at the Pirates' "Russian Night" themed ballgame.

Father Bill refused most interviews as he mostly hoped this would all die down, but also because he knew that had he ever tried to explain what had really happened, he'd have been labeled a religious nutjob and relegated to the world of those with fringe websites proclaiming the end of days or being able to interpret God's will through a really, really thorough examination of one's breakfast oatmeal. In his heart, he felt he had answered his life's calling and performed when events had demanded it. His faith had been tested, and he had Shown Up. He was at peace.

He was invited to the Vatican to meet with the Pope. He loved Rome and was blown away by the sheer spectacle of Vatican City. He was allowed thirty minutes alone with the Pope, whom he found a genuinely nice person. The Bishop of Rome, Supreme Pontiff of the Universal Church, and the Creator's voice on Earth asked him if he felt Dave Brady really had the potential to end mankind.

The priest thought about that for a few long seconds, and then, looking into this kind man's eyes who seemed to have the weight of the world upon him, he said, "You know, it's hard to say. He had his evil moments, but mostly he seemed like a jagoff to me." The Pope laughed loudly and genuinely and slapped him on the leg. In retrospect, Father Bill felt that really was the highlight of the whole thing.

Mostly Father William Wojtanowicz believed again, and it was a joy. He knew it was all real. He was the only living priest, or rabbi, or shaman, or pick your religious title, in the world who knew the Afterlife actually existed. It made him happy, and it made him exponentially committed to what he had already been (sort of) committed to.

Sister Mary Lee did not have the same concerns about being interviewed as her employer. She gave endless interviews on multiple media outlets. She praised Father Bill and portrayed him as a real-life Don Quixote. She made the *Today Show*. She was photographed with Michael Strahan, her personal favorite, and she was literally speechless when he talked to her.

Aza stared out at the city, his hands behind his back. His assistants were finishing packing his things, and he would be gone by morning. He would not miss this place. Truth be told, he was interested in very few places these days. He had seen it all, and few things surprised him anymore. He felt he was just waiting. For what, he wasn't sure. Would there ever be an Antichrist? He supposed probably, someday. He wasn't sure he cared anymore. He was tired. Very tired. Tired of playing the Creator's game, tired of being on this planet for so very long, and tired of poseurs like Brady.

Brady had been a mistake. He knew it, and worse, knew it was a mistake he would not have made even just a hundred years ago. He was losing his touch, and he wasn't sure what that meant for his own future. Lost in these thoughts, he did not notice the intruder approach him from behind until he heard the pistol being cocked behind his right ear. He stiffened, mostly out of reflex, then relaxed. He was not afraid of death as he really couldn't be killed. Unless...

"I could have cocked this pistol long before I approached and simply shot you from behind," Manon said. "The way you did to me. The way of a true coward."

Aza stiffened again, realizing now who it was, and he was very much exposed. This particular woman could actually "kill" him. And what happened to Aza after that would not be pretty or comfortable. The Rules were the Rules, and they could not be negotiated. Aza waited.

"You have been too long in this game, Azael. Perhaps you should retire," Manon said. "Now you are reduced to playing nursemaid to any fool who decides he's Lucifer's chosen one? Sad, really."

"How's Uriel?" Aza said, the hint of sarcasm evident in his voice. "You must respect him deeply to allow him to sell you out like a harlot to further his goals."

Manon's silence was validation Aza had scored a point with this salvo. "Any last words, Man in Red?" Manon asked.

"What can I offer you to spare me?" the fallen angel said.

Manon let him wait for a long time. "The one they call Leonard," Manon said finally.

"Leonard? The traitor?" Aza was certain he had not heard correctly.

"Yes. Leonard," Manon said. "I want him left alone. There is to be no retribution."

Aza considered this. "Done." he said.

"Done." Manon replied. "But we are not done, Dark Angel. Our destinies are intertwined, and I would beware of me, beware of me to the end as I will be coming for you. Like the dawn or the sea against the shore, I will come. You can be certain of that."

Aza relaxed. "Thank you for the warning, Black Death. But you know," he said, now turning. But she was gone.

When Manon returned to the Fairmont, Oliver greeted her, beaming. He started to hug her, then thought better of it and instead just said, "Thank you. I am indebted to you." He had heard the entire exchange with Aza as Manon had been wearing her transmitting device.

"Why you would want to save that parasite, I have no idea," Manon said.

"He is good. I can feel it in my bones," Oliver replied.

"Your bones are giving you bad advice," Manon said, not cracking a smile. Oliver smiled anyway. He was certain he had changed a life. The algorithm was never wrong, after all.

The meeting was held in the ornate conference room that sat between Jesus' and the Creator's offices. Uriel had been called back immediately following the release of the video of the showdown at the Wolf's lair and the resulting flameout of Dave Brady's ascension. Uriel was in a very good mood. He felt he had accomplished his mission. He felt like the victorious general he had been so many times in his glorious past. He winked at Jesus' secretary as she showed him into the conference room. She stared at him with no expression.

He sat down and arranged his robes to his satisfaction. He was the first in the room, but this was protocol and did not bother him. He sat comfortably, a man awaiting his proper praise and, he assumed, some type of reward. Eventually, the door from Jesus' office opened and a man stepped through whom Uriel did not recognize. He was wearing a blue pinstriped suit and red tie with a white shirt. He nodded at Uriel but did not speak, and seated himself in a chair at the conference room table across from and down a few seats from Uriel. Uri wondered who he was, but not too much. If the archangel didn't know him, then he wasn't important.

Jesus followed next, and behind him the Archangel Michael. Uriel frowned at this. He had expected Jesus and also the Creator. He had not expected Michael and didn't understand why he'd be here. After a few seconds of thought, Uriel decided it was a good thing. Let his rival witness his performance review and reward. It might be a good motivator for Michael.

Jesus also took a seat across from Uriel, but directly across. He gave Uriel a pained smile and said quietly, "Hey, buddy. How ya doing?"

"I am well, Lord, and thank you for asking," Uriel said. After waiting a few seconds, then looking down to the other end of the room where the door to the Creator's office met this joint conference room, Uriel said to Jesus, "Will He be joining us today?"

Jesus looked embarrassed, and his eyes moved to Michael's and then the man in the suit two seats down from him. His gaze finally returned to Uriel's as he said, "Uh, no. Not today." Uriel noticed Michael had not taken a seat at the table, but rather had seated himself at a chair behind and to the right of Uriel.

There were ten seconds of uncomfortable silence, and then Jesus cleared his throat and said, "Archangel Uriel, we wanted to talk to you about the matter of Dave Brady."

The formal reference to his title made Uri uneasy. "Yes, Lord," he said.

"As you know," Jesus continued, "Dave Brady was not the Antichrist." Jesus paused here and looked at Uriel directly.

"Well," Uriel said, "not anymore, no."

Jesus looked past Uriel and over his shoulder at Michael. Then, looking back at Uriel and taking a deep, audible breath, he said, "Not ever." Grimacing again as though giving a loved one bad news, he added, "Checked it with Dad."

Uriel sucked in his breath. He had not been prepared for this. He would have been ready to list all the evidence he felt verified his suspicions, rattle off all the events of the past month as backup, but when the Son of the Creator of Everything tells you that same Creator says Brady wasn't the Antichrist, then he just wasn't. Can't argue it. End of discussion.

His mind reeled. If Brady wasn't the Antichrist, then he was in trouble. He was trying to remember how many Rules violations he may have committed when Jesus waved his left hand further left toward the man in the suit and said, "Have you met Arnold Belvedere?"

Uriel dumbly moved his gaze to the man and just shook his head slightly.

The man nodded at the archangel and said, "Arnold Belvedere, Internal Affairs." He did not say "pleased to meet you," or offer his hand to Uriel.

Like any organization, the Creator's had internal auditors. As previously discussed, the Rules were many, and they were unwritten. And they were not to be violated.

"We received an anonymous tip"—Jesus paused, again looking past Uriel at Michael—"from a member of your own team that you had committed serious..." Again, Jesus paused, not meeting Uriel's eyes. "Violations of the Rules." he finished.

Uriel processed this, understanding almost immediately that it had been Manon. Oliver wouldn't have had the stones to betray him.

"Of course, given the serious nature of the allegations, we really had no choice but to involve IA," Jesus said, then, turning to his left, said, "Arnold?" The man in the suit was looking into a sort of iPad-like device in front of him and reading from notes.

"Our investigation into allegations of rules infractions has concluded that Archangel Uriel, during his time in Pittsburgh, committed no less than sixty-eight violations of the Rules of Existence, fifty-eight of these being Class C violations, nine Class B violations, and one Class A violation." Arnold Belvedere paused to look from his portable device to Uriel.

Uriel looked at him for a second, then to Jesus and said, "But I assure you—"

But Jesus raised his right hand, silencing him. "Please, Uriel. Let Mr. Belvedere finish."

Uriel switched his gaze back to the Internal Affairs investigator, no expression at all in his face, as though he had just been struck with a cast-iron frying pan in a cartoon.

"As you are aware, sir, Class C violations are generally handled with a note in one's performance record. Class B violations are more severe and, depending on the circumstances surrounding the infraction, can result in anything from a period of suspension, to demotion, and in extreme circumstances, permanent Loss of Privileges." The investigator paused here and looked at Jesus, who nodded for him to go on.

"As an archangel with an exemplary, I'd say even historical, service record, the Class C and Class B violations aren't the issue here. IA understands the circumstances of your mission and has allowed for the fact that you truly believed the nature of Existence may have been at risk."

These words made Uri feel slightly better, but he was still in a state of shock listening to this man.

The man continued, "The Class A infraction is a much more serious issue. As you are aware, Class A violations are extremely rare. We have no guidance on penalties for Class A violations—"

"Because the Creator decides the penalty," Uriel finished for him.

"Yes," Belvedere agreed. "Penalty for a Class A violation of the Rules of Existence is entirely the purview of our Creator."

"You offered absolution for the abortion Julian Tetanich's sister had performed upon her person as an enticement to convince Tetanich to murder Dave Brady. One, you are not permitted to offer absolution. Two, absolution is never to be offered in return for murder. Three, you interfered with Life. Four, you solicited a mortal sin. Five, and this is perhaps the most concerning to us, you offered absolution for a sin that had already been confessed to and absolved, according to the laws of the Creator."

Here the man in the suit paused and, looking directly into Uriel's eyes, finished quietly, "And you knew it had been absolved."

Jesus shook his head slowly, staring down at the table.

"But he was going to end mankind, I'm certain of it. He—" Uriel started, but Jesus was still shaking his head.

"Buddy…" he said, grimacing again. "Buddy, this is bad."

Later, after Uriel had been escorted out, Jesus and Michael

looked at each other. "Sad thing," Jesus said, looking mournful.

After a few seconds, Michael said, "Oh, I don't know. Maybe it will be good for him in the long run. They say what doesn't kill you makes you stronger."

Jesus considered this for a long moment, then, brightening, said, "You know what? They do say that, don't they? They do!" And he was suddenly smiling. Michael smiled back.

"Hey," Jesus said. "He wants to see you." He motioned his head toward the door to the Creator's office. Michael nodded. "Like stat, homie," Jesus said. "Move it, bro!" He smiled again.

Michael got up and headed down to the door and knocked. A voice said, "Come in, Michael."

The archangel stuck his head through the opening in the doorway and said, "Sir?"

The Creator turned from his desk to face him and said, "The thing with the bartender's friend, did you take care of that as we discussed? The cancer?"

Michael, a perplexed look on his face, said, "Cancer? Not sure I know what you're talking about, sir." then he smiled.

The Creator smiled back, giving him a thumbs up and returning his attention to his monitor. Michael pulled his head back into the conference room and quietly closed the door.

The day dawned bright and early in the afterlife, and Oliver was ready. He had arrived for work nearly fifteen minutes before he was required to—a personal record for him as he was anxious to make a good impression. When the door opened and his new master entered the room, Oliver took a knee and bowed his head.

Awaiting a barked command since he was used to that, or absolute indifference as he was used to that too, he was surprised when Gandhi knelt down beside him and, grasping Oliver's hand, said, "Always a good idea to begin the day with a prayer. I will join you."

When they were done, Oliver said, "Have you ever seen *The Pope of Greenwich Village*, Lord?"

After a moment of thought, and Oliver would eventually learn the Mahatma always took a moment to think before speaking, Gandhi said, "I have. But please do not call me 'Lord.' Up here, my friends call me Mohandas. I liked Eric Roberts in that film, but I think I enjoyed Bedbug Eddie the most." Oliver considered this and smiled to himself. Life was good.

A day later, Jilly entered his home at midnight. He had entrusted the closing of the bar to Mikey P., and he was tired. Jimmy Hallendorf had come into the bar for a drink and told him of the miraculous remission of Martin's cancer. Jilly had thought about that for a long time. He was sure that he had nothing to do with it. And then he was pretty sure he did. Good.

About an hour before he left, Leonard, who had arrived in jeans and a Twisted Sister/Ratt/Lita Ford concert T-shirt (Allentown, PA, 1984), had become heavily inebriated and told a thirty-something woman he "was pretty damn dark" and could satisfy her "fantasies." The woman told Leonard he looked pretty much Middle-Aged White Guy to her and slapped him. Jilly removed him from the bar but also did not ask him to pay his check. Leonard had earned the comp.

Anne was awake when Jilly returned home. He put his shoes away; he had started doing that without actually thinking about it. As he headed through the rear kitchen toward the stairs and his bedroom, he passed the living room. Anne, seated in a comfortable chair, looked up from her book but said nothing. Jilly just stopped in the doorway and looked at his sister.

"What?" Anne said.

Jilly, putting on his best thoughtful face, said, "You know, I think I know how it all works now."

Anne waited. After a beat of silence, she said, "How what works?"

"Religion," Jilly said. "Religion, God, the afterlife. All of it."

Anne processed this and then laughed out loud. Jilly just stared at her. "Julian, if you live another thirty years, and I hope you do as you are my favorite brother, you will still never, ever understand how religion works, or God, or the afterlife. You run your bar. Leave religion to me. I'm praying for you, and with some luck, you'll be fine."

Jilly grunted, then turned and headed up the stairs. He would have been lying if he said he did not have a small smile on his face. It was good that things were back to normal.

About thirty minutes north of Pittsburgh at a truck stop known to be one of the busiest in the country, Elvis Marburger the Swing Shift Manager surveyed his kingdom. Yes, he understood Swing Shift Manager was the third most important manager position of the three, given Day Shift was the Big Time and the Overnight Shift was the second most lucrative given the truck traffic during those hours. But he'd moved up steadily over the past four years from bathroom boy, whose sole responsibility was to make sure the showers, sinks, and especially the toilets were sparkling clean to a position of authority. Eventually, and he was as sure of this as he was that the Steelers had at least three more Lombardi Trophies coming in his lifetime, he would be General Manager. Or, at least, Daytime Assistant General Manager.

Tonight's crew was fairly solid. His two Cash Register Captains appeared to be fairly sober. The kid who re-stocked and handled truck driver requests had been in his employ for nearly six months now, which made him a veteran. The bathroom boy, though... That guy, he had to keep an eye on. He had hired the kid—although his working papers said he was twenty-three so maybe not so much of a kid—in a weak moment as his last bathroom boy had left for a Second French Fryer position at Burger King.

But he was unfocused and definitely didn't follow the Speed Pilot Truck Stop Ten Rules For Success. Elvis headed out back as he had not seen the new boy in almost half an hour. The night was clear, and he found him sitting on a milk crate by the dumpster, staring up at the sky. "Yoopi!" Elvis exclaimed. "You thinking those urinals gonna wash themselves, boy?"

The boy sighed deeply. Very deeply. Elvis thought maybe he was thinking of his long-lost mother. He figured this kid was Middle Eastern given the name, and while he didn't consider himself prejudiced, he followed CNN and knew that part of the world was always blowing each other up over all kinds of stuff.

"It's Uriel, Lord. But Uri is fine."

"Okay, okay," his manager said. "So, let's get to those 'Uri-nals' stat, okay? And you don't have to call me 'Lord.' My friends call me Elvis."

FINE